Also by Julia Brannan

HISTORICAL FICTION

The Jacobite Chronicles
Book One: Mask of Duplicity
Book Two: The Mask Revealed
Book Three: The Gathering Storm
Book Four: The Storm Breaks
Book Five: Pursuit of Princes
Book Six: Tides of Fortune

Jacobite Chronicles Stories
The Eccentric's Tale: Harriet (Summer 2019)

CONTEMPORARY FICTION

A Seventy-Five Percent Solution

The Whore's Tale: Sarah

A Jacobite Chronicles Story

Julia Brannan

Copyright© 2018 by Julia Brannan

Julia Brannan has asserted her right to be identified as the author of this work under the Copyright, Designs and Patents Act 1988

All rights reserved. No part of this publication may be reproduced, distributed, or transmitted in any form or by any means, including photocopying, recording, or other electronic or mechanical methods, without the prior written permission of the publisher, except in the case of brief quotations embodied in critical reviews and certain other non-commercial uses permitted by copyright law.

DISCLAIMER

This novel is a work of fiction, and except in the case of historical fact, any resemblance to actual persons, living or dead, is purely coincidental

Formatting by Polgarus Studio

Cover design by najlaqamberdesigns.com

ACKNOWLEDGEMENTS

First of all, as ever, I'd like to thank Jason Gardiner and Alyson Cairns, my soulmates and best friends, who put up with me on a day-to-day basis, and who understand my need for solitude, but are always there for me. They've both supported me through every stage of my writing, and, indeed, in all my other endeavours, both sensible and madcap!

Thanks to the long-suffering Mary Brady, friend and first critic, who reads the chapters as I write them, critiques them for me and reassures me that I can actually write stuff people will want to read, and to my beta readers Angela, Claire, Roma and Susan for their valued and honest opinions. I can't stress how important you are!

Thanks also go to Mandy Condon, who sends me useful articles, has already determined the cast list for the film of my books, and who has been a wonderful and supportive friend for over twenty years. Long may that continue!

I also need to thank some fellow authors. Firstly Kym Grosso who has been extremely supportive and has generously given me the benefit of her experience in the minefield of indie publishing. She's saved me a lot of time, money and tears, and I value her friendship and support enormously. Also to Helen Hollick, author not only of a host of excellent novels and willing imparter of useful advice, but also of the Discovering Diamonds blog, which helps to connect authors of quality historical fiction with new readers.

Also a thank you goes to the National Trust for Scotland, who are stocking my books at the gift shop in Culloden Visitor Centre and to the Clan Cameron Museum, which also stocks the Jacobite Chronicles. Both sites are well worth a visit, should you be in the area.

And thanks as always go to Jason at Polgarus Studio for doing an excellent job of formatting my books, to the talented and very patient Najla Qamber, who does all my covers, puts up with my lack of artistic ability, and still manages to somehow understand exactly what I want my covers to look like!

To all my wonderful readers, who not only buy my books, but take the time and effort to give me feedback, to review them on Amazon and Goodreads, and to recommend me to others, by word of mouth and on social media -- thank you so much. You keep me going on those dark days when I'd rather do anything than stare at a blank screen for hours while my brain turns to mush…you are amazing! Without all of you I would be nothing, and I appreciate you more than you know.

And finally, to Bob and Dee. You are wonderful people and I love you.

ABOUT THE AUTHOR

Julia has been a voracious reader since childhood, using books to escape the miseries of a turbulent adolescence. After leaving university with a degree in English Language and Literature, she spent her twenties trying to be a sensible and responsible person, even going so far as to work for the Civil Service for six years.

Then she gave up trying to conform, resigned her well-paid but boring job and resolved to spend the rest of her life living as she wanted to, not as others would like her to. She has since had a variety of jobs, including telesales, Post Office clerk, primary school teacher, and painter and gilder.

In her spare time she is still a voracious reader, and enjoys keeping fit, exploring the beautiful Welsh countryside around her home, and travelling the world. Life hasn't always been good, but it has rarely been boring.

A few years ago she decided that rather than just escape into other people's books, she would quite like to create some of her own and so combined her passion for history and literature to write the Jacobite Chronicles.

People seem to enjoy reading them as much as she enjoys writing them, so now, apart from a tiny amount of transcribing and editing work, she is a full-time writer. She has plunged into the contemporary genre too, but her first love will always be historical fiction.

PROLOGUE

Alliston, Cheshire, January 1731

It was dark in the cellar.

It was cold too, but Sarah didn't mind the cold so much; she was used to it. It was never warm anywhere in the house, except on the hottest summer days. There were too many places where draughts could get in; through ill-fitting windows, and under the door – the gap there was so big that the rain came in too, and sometimes in autumn leaves would drift under the door and blow around the room until she swept them out again.

No, in fact it was usually warmer in the cellar than in the rest of the house, and that was the problem. If there were no cracks to let draughts in, there were no cracks to let light in either. Which meant it was very dark, so dark that if she lifted her hand up to her face and wiggled it about, even if it was close enough to feel the movement of air against her skin, she still couldn't see it.

She sat shivering on the bottom step, her teeth chattering, and hugged herself, rubbing her hands up and down her arms to try to warm them, in the process disturbing some small creature that was living down there. She heard it skitter across the floor into a distant corner.

She hated coming down into the cellar, even when the door was open and she had a candle. She had to come down nearly every day though, especially in the winter, because the potatoes and carrots were kept down here nestled in crates of sawdust, apples were stored in boxes and onions were hung up along with bunches of mint and rosemary and strings of dried rosehips.

There were spiders down here, and the occasional field mouse like the one she had just heard. She wasn't scared of them though, as long as she could see where they were and make sure they weren't close enough to crawl on her. She couldn't see them now, so she pretended there were none there. Sometimes that worked. More often it didn't and she would utter a little shriek every time a strand of her hair brushed her bare skin, thinking it was a big spider crawling up her arm.

What she was really scared of was the monster that she thought might live here. She had never actually *seen* a monster in the cellar, but that didn't mean there wasn't one.

She had never actually seen God either, but she knew He was everywhere and could see every sinful thing she did. He could even see into her heart and know if she had a wicked thought. God was watching her all the time, and despairing. She didn't know what despairing meant, but it sounded like a sad word, maybe an angry one. God was very angry all the time, especially with her, because she was a Daughter of Eve.

Philip had told her that their mother's name had been Catherine, not Eve, but when she'd asked her father if that was true, he'd beaten her with his belt for insolence. She didn't know what insolence meant either, but she knew it hurt, a lot.

Philip had also told her, yesterday, when he had seen her standing on the top step building up the courage to go down and get some carrots, that there was only one monster in this house, and it certainly didn't live down in the cellar. She didn't dare ask her father if that was true, in case he beat her again. Father didn't like her to ask questions. It was not a daughter's place to question her father, but to obey him, as she would one day have to obey her husband, he had told her.

Philip was nine now, three years older than her. One day he would be a husband and his wife would obey him. She thought she wouldn't mind if Philip was her husband. It would be easy to obey him, because he was kind and didn't mind her asking him questions. He was clever too, could read and write and do numbers. He had taught her to count to twenty one day when Father was out. Soon he would be going to work for Mr Bradshaw, who owned the farm on the other side of the village, although he would still come home every night to sleep. Philip wasn't going to be a farmer when he grew up, but Father said a spell on the farm would teach him what hard work was.

Of course she knew she couldn't marry Philip; she might be only six, but she knew that you couldn't marry your brother, because that was a sin. Lots of things were sins. It was probably a sin for her to know that there were sixteen steps down to the cellar, too, because girls weren't supposed to learn letters and numbers.

Philip knew lots of things as well as how to count, so he was probably right about the monster. That thought had made her very happy when he'd told her, because she knew that she didn't need to be afraid any more when she was put in the cellar.

She sat there and thought about it for a minute, and then it occurred to her that Philip hadn't said there was no monster at all, just that it didn't live in the cellar. That meant it must live somewhere else in the house. It could be anywhere, even in her bedroom!

She had her own room, unlike most of the children in the village. She was very lucky, Father had told her, because he was a man of God, and therefore they lived in a house with enough space for both her and Philip to have their own rooms. Most of the houses in the village only had one room, and all the family lived and slept in it together, and sometimes even the animals too. She hadn't been in any of the village houses; she wasn't allowed to play with the village children, because they were all little heathens who would go to Hell.

Hell must be very big, because it seemed that everyone in the world except the people who came to Father's church on Sundays were going to Hell, and even some of them might too, if they didn't repent of all their wickedness. He reminded them of that every week, in case they forgot.

She had always felt lucky to have her own bedroom, but now she thought that maybe she would rather be like the other villagers. At least if there was a monster in their house, they would all be there in the room to fight it if it attacked one of them.

Never mind. At least she was safe for now, because she wouldn't be beaten for whatever it was she'd done wrong. Father never beat her *and* put her in the cellar. It was always one or the other. Until now she'd rather have been beaten, even though it hurt a lot and made walking and sitting painful for days afterwards, but now she knew there was no monster lurking in the darkness, waiting to tear her to pieces with long claws and sharp teeth, she'd rather be put down the cellar after all. But she wouldn't tell Father that, because if she did he might find another way to punish her.

It smelled nasty in the cellar, of earth and damp and old air. Last summer one of the village women had seen her pulling up weeds in the garden and had given her a bunch of fresh lavender and told her how to dry it so it would keep its smell, so that she'd be able to put it in her chest to make her clothes smell nice and keep moths away. She'd tied a piece of string round the stems and had stood on a box to hang it from the low beam in the cellar, thinking it might make the room smell good too, but when her father had seen it he'd thrown it on the fire, telling her perfume was for Jezebels.

He had put her in the cellar then, too, so that she could pray to God to be forgiven for the sin of vanity. At least then she had known what to pray for; but today she had no notion of what she'd done wrong. She'd been standing on the wooden bench scrubbing the kitchen table with a brush and some soap because Father always insisted the table was spotless before he would sit down to eat, when he had opened the door, bringing a cold breeze and a flurry of snow in with him, had gripped her by the arm and dragged her down to the cellar, telling her to use her time there wisely.

Thinking about monsters was not very wise, so she stopped doing that and sat and thought instead of what it might be that she'd done wrong. It couldn't be that she hadn't swept the floor properly, that the pottage was too hot or cold, or that there was too much wood or too little on the fire. He hadn't looked around the room at all, had just come straight in and put her in the cellar. So it must have been something she'd forgotten to do in the garden. She'd fed the chickens, and had swept the snow off the path as best she could. Had she left the gate open?

She closed her eyes and tried to think, but she couldn't remember. Maybe that was it. God would know, so she would just pray to be forgiven for whatever she'd done. She knew she would have to pray for a long time, because God hated sinners, and she was a sinner like her mother, who she remembered only as a soft voice and warmth, and who her father said was dead now and burning in Hell for eternity, but who had been called Catherine, or maybe Eve.

All women were sinners because Eve had eaten an apple and then had given it to Adam to eat as well. She wondered why her father wasn't a sinner too, because he ate apples all the time. Maybe it was because he was a minister of God, or maybe because he was a man. Perhaps it was all right for men to eat apples; although sometimes, when he was in a very good mood, he would cut a slice with his pocket knife and give it to her to eat. Maybe it was just that it was a sin for women to eat apples first, without a man telling them they could. Maybe her mother was burning in Hell because she had eaten an apple without asking Father for permission.

It was all very puzzling. Later she would ask Philip. He would probably know. But now she had to pray, very hard, because she had already wasted a lot of time sitting on the step, time that she should have been spending asking God for forgiveness.

Sarah knelt down on the earth floor, folded her hands and began to pray, hoping that God would understand what she was saying, because her teeth were chattering so hard that it was difficult to get the words out.

CHAPTER ONE

Alliston, Cheshire, June 1731

"Likewise, ye wives, be in subjection to your own husbands, that if any obey not the word, they also may without the word be won by the conversation of the wives; while they behold your chaste conversation coupled with fear. Whose adorning let it not be that outward adorning of plaiting the hair, and of wearing of gold, or of putting on of apparel…"

At this point Reverend Browne struck the wood of the pulpit with his fist, making the congregation jump and waking Sarah from the doze she was falling into. She must not sleep, she knew that, because later when they got home Father would question both her and her brother on his sermon and if she couldn't answer any of his questions, there would be trouble.

She glanced up to see, to her horror, her father staring straight at her, his face like thunder. She sat bolt upright, wincing as a bone, which had pierced the worn cloth of her miniature stays, dug into her armpit.

"In this way, ladies," he continued in a stentorian voice, "will you bring your straying menfolk back to the fold. For if they see that you, who are the weaker vessel, can stay upon the path of righteousness, then will they be shamed, knowing that it should be so much the easier for them to maintain God's path, who are made in the image of God Himself."

Now that Sarah was fully awake, her eyes focussing properly, she realised that Father wasn't staring at her, but at someone in the pew behind her. Vastly relieved, she surreptitiously stretched her legs out in front of her, wiggling her toes. She knew Father couldn't see the bottom half of her body from the pulpit; that was why if one of the siblings fell asleep, the other one would pat them on the leg, hard enough to rouse them, but not hard enough to make them startle and so attract Father's attention. It was an agreement they'd had since Sarah had turned four and had been deemed old enough to sit through the long Sunday services without fidgeting.

Nevertheless, the first week she had fidgeted incessantly, and when they had got home her father, furious, had told her that if she couldn't sit still in church, then she could stand until she learnt better. For three days she had been made to do everything standing, from the moment she got up until the moment she fell into bed, her legs burning and throbbing with pain.

She no longer fidgeted in church, or at least not so he could see her. It seemed a bit unfair, because even the adults started shuffling about and sighing after a few hours of Reverend Browne's sonorous monologues, but he didn't make *them* stand for three days. What he often did instead was to address a whole sermon directly to someone who had offended the previous week.

Sarah, now concentrating hard, listened to her father's next words. He had now abandoned St Peter in favour of Isaiah, and she knew exactly to whom he was referring as he intoned about the daughters of Zion, who had worn jewellery and fine linen and colourful clothes, until God had torn their clothing and made all their hair fall out, and had put a scab on their heads, too. Last week Ellen Reid had worn red stockings to church, and a silver bracelet on her wrist.

Sarah knew that because she had seen both the scarlet stockings and the bracelet and had wished with all her heart that she too could one day own such beautiful things, when she was an adult. But now, looking down at her unembellished arms and coarse brown linsey-woolsey dress, she was very glad to be Sarah Browne rather than Ellen Reid, who was surely burning with shame. She hoped that God wouldn't put a scab on Ellen's head, though, or make her hair fall out. She had such beautiful hair, like chestnuts in autumn, and she had smiled at Sarah once as they were coming into church. The people who came to Father's church didn't smile very often. She hoped Ellen would throw away the stockings and the bracelet so that she wouldn't burn in

Hell, which she was bound to do otherwise, if Father was right.

Of course Father was right! What was she thinking? He was an adult, and her father, and above all, a minister, called to preach God's word to try to save the wicked from eternal damnation. It was very hard work trying to bring souls to God, and there were a lot of wicked people in Alliston. She knew that because her father told her so, all the time.

She was one of them, but she had a better chance than the others to be saved, because her father was loving and kind enough to watch her all the time and correct her the moment she stepped from the path of righteousness, whereas the rest of the village had the whole week to get hopelessly lost in sin before being dragged back to the right way in the little chapel on Sunday by the stern-faced minister.

It was one of the reasons why she was not allowed to go into the village by herself; because the Devil walked amongst the people, and she was as yet too young to recognise him and resist his wiles. Whenever she was in the garden sweeping the path or weeding the little vegetable patch, and someone walked past along the dirt track, she would always look at them after they had passed, half-hoping and half-dreading to see a red tail peeping from under their frockcoats. But she never did. Of course Chapel Lane, where they lived, ended at the stream and there was no bridge over to the other side, so not many people walked down it, except to the service on Sunday. And she was sure that even the Devil wouldn't dare confront her father in God's house.

The other reason why she wasn't allowed to go into the village was because she had no spare time to go wandering about. There was too much to do at home. The house had to be swept every day, the fires lit, table and chairs scrubbed, the chickens fed and the henhouse cleaned out, water fetched from the stream, linen washed…there was far too much to do, and though Mrs Farrar took any clothes that needed to be mended, and some of the parishioners brought meals occasionally, most of the work fell to her, because she was a girl, and it was a girl's job to take care of the house.

After her mother had gone to Hell, a woman had come in three times a week to clean and cook. She had been a silent woman; so silent that Sarah, too shy at the age of four to speak directly to her, had never even learnt her name. In the two years she had come to the house she had never so much as said good morning to either Sarah or Philip, and it had become the custom for the children to go to their rooms when the woman was there. Sarah had thought she was dumb, like the man the people had brought to Jesus for Him to heal, who was possessed with a devil, although this silent woman didn't have a tail either, or if she did she kept it well hidden.

So it had come as some surprise when Sarah had woken up early one morning to hear raised voices downstairs, followed by the sound of a door slamming. She had jumped out of bed and run to the window, to see the no-longer-silent woman, her slender figure distorted by the thick greenish glass of the windowpane, standing on the path with her hands on her hips, her face red with rage.

"I've had enough!" she had shouted back at the house, presumably to her father. "Get someone else to slave for you, you bastard!" Then she had turned and marched down the path, through the gate and had disappeared up the road, never to be seen again.

Later that day her father had called her into his study and had told her, whilst she had stood staring modestly at the floor as she had been taught, that she was nearly six now, and it was high time she started repaying all his kindness to her in feeding and clothing her. No doubt she had watched Annie as she went about her tasks; she was old enough now to start doing them herself. At the least she could keep the house clean. Philip would help with some of the harder tasks until she was big enough to do them herself.

Later that evening as she had sat at the table putting salve on the blisters caused by the unaccustomed work of sweeping and dusting, she had watched Philip as he chopped up carrots and cabbage, and had asked him what a bastard was. The knife had slipped and he had narrowly avoided cutting his fingers.

"That's a very bad word. Where did you hear that?" he had asked in a whisper, glancing anxiously in the direction of the study, where their father was preparing his sermon for the next Sunday.

She had told him, and he had said she must forget that word, and on no account must she ever ask Father what it meant, because if she did he would be very, very angry. Philip's voice had been very earnest, his tone serious. But his green eyes had danced with laughter.

She still didn't know what a bastard was. But she did know that she was daydreaming instead of listening to what Father was saying, and that she had missed a lot -- the sun had moved along a whole window and a beam of yellow light was shining through the clear diamond-shaped leaded panes directly onto him, illuminating him as he stood at the pulpit in full flow.

He looks like an angel, she thought. Maybe like Gabriel, bringing God's message to His people. His face was pale, thin-lipped and severe, like she imagined an angel's would be. There were little dust motes dancing and glittering in the sunbeam. When the sun moved to the window behind Father, then the service would finish.

He had moved on from chastising poor Ellen now, and was reading from St Paul. Sarah knew St Paul well; he was one of her father's favourites. Hopefully she'd be able to answer his questions after all. And Philip was still awake – he reached across now, gripped her hand and squeezed it affectionately.

At least it was summer, so they would walk back in the sunshine, the two children strolling past the house and down to the stream, where they would sit on the bank and cool their feet in the water for a time while Father spoke to his parishioners outside the chapel. They were supposed to discuss the wise words they had just spent three hours trying to listen to, but they never did, unless one of them had gone to sleep, in which case the other would tell them what they'd missed. It was usually Sarah who dozed off because she was younger, so Philip would quickly tell her enough to hopefully answer Father's later questions, and then they would talk about butterflies, bees or fish, or whatever else they saw as they sat with their feet in the icy water. Sometimes they would splash each other, but only if it was hot enough for their clothes to dry before they went home. Otherwise Father would know they had been playing games, and on the Sabbath too. Sarah loved those precious times with her brother sitting hand-in-hand, the sun warm on their heads, chatting together.

She loved Philip. She loved her father too, of course. It was a child's duty to love and to obey her father, and she knew he loved her too, enough to labour night and day to save her from damnation. But it would be impossible *not* to love her brother; he was kind and he gave her the affection she craved. She was afraid of her father, but she could never be afraid of Philip. He would never hurt her, not even if she deserved it because she was wicked. Philip would love her whether she could be saved or not. Loving him was like breathing; she could not imagine living without it.

She was drifting again. It would be easier not to dream if there was something nice to look at, instead of plain whitewashed walls and clear glass windows. Once, when she was small, maybe four, she had tentatively suggested that God might like some flowers in His house. After all, she had said, God must love flowers because He had made so many of them.

For once her father had not chastised her, but had told her to sit down next to him. Then he had told her that there were no flowers in the church, nor any statues, decorated altar cloths or singing, because such ornamentation smacked of Papism, and we all knew where that would have led us had the blessed Prince of Orange not come to save us from Roman James and all his iniquities. And, he had added, people came to church to hear the word of God and to be saved, not to be distracted by unnecessary fripperies, which were a temptation to weak souls.

Sarah had had no idea what Papism was, or who Roman James was, but she had heard his disapproval of her behind his soft words, and had not asked for any further explanation. She thought now that it was a shame Ellen Reid had not been there when her father had talked to her; if she had then she would not now be sitting with her face flaming brighter than her scarlet stockings had been. No doubt she wanted the sermon to end even more than Sarah did.

Which was a comfort. She sat up again, resolving to listen harder.

* * *

Later in the week the spell of good weather broke, bringing thunder, lightning and torrential rain which battered against the house, driving under the ill-fitting doors and windows and through the roof, which was missing some slates. On days as bad as this the children didn't have to tend the garden, but Sarah had to place pots on the floor underneath the holes in the roof to catch the water, and had to remember to check them periodically and empty them out. Philip had to spend the time wisely, reading and practising his writing and sums on a slate his father had given to him. He wrote well now and no longer needed a slate, but paper was expensive so he only used it for lengthy tasks, such as translating passages from the Bible into Latin, a language he was struggling to learn, not only because it was difficult, but because it seemed to him to be pointless.

This particular afternoon he was painstakingly translating part of the epistle of Paul to the Colossians at the kitchen table, and was frowning, his tongue poking from the corner of his mouth as he concentrated. At the other end of the table Sarah was shelling peas into a bowl and looking out of the window from time to time; but there was no lessening of the rain. She sighed. Soon she would have to go out, feed the chickens and collect the eggs, rain or no.

Reverend Browne was in his study, writing his sermon for next Sunday, and would most likely be there until the candles needed to be lit. That didn't mean the children could relax though, because they never knew when he would suddenly emerge from the room to check up on them, and in any case when he *did* finally finish the sermon he would check that Sarah had done her chores and look over Philip's work, and if they hadn't completed their respective tasks to their father's satisfaction, they would have to go without supper and stay up all night until they were done.

Sarah finished the peas and got down from the stool she was sitting on, coming up behind her brother to see how he was doing. She looked over his shoulder, eyes wide with admiration at the neat lines of ornate lettering, which to her appeared as some fantastic mysterious pattern. Coming to the end of the chapter he was translating, Philip stopped and put his quill down, flexing his fingers to ease the cramp.

"It looks very lovely," she said, instinctively stretching out a finger to trace over the loops and curls of the writing.

"Don't touch it!" he cried. She jerked her hand back as though burnt. "It's just that the ink's still wet," he assured her, as if realising that she'd taken his words as a rebuke. "If you touch it now, you'll smudge it."

Relaxing, she turned her attention to the two books on the table; a Bible, open at the page he'd been translating, and a yellowed Latin grammar.

"That was Father's when he was a boy," Philip said of the latter. Both of them fell silent for a moment, trying to imagine the tall forbidding figure of authority as a child like them. It was too huge a stretch of the imagination for them, and after a few seconds they abandoned it. Sarah looked at the printed squiggles on the page, then at the neat loops and curls of her brother's handwriting.

"It doesn't look the same as that," she said doubtfully, not wanting to upset her brother, but curious as to why it looked so very different. "Is that because it's Latin?"

"No. Handwriting doesn't look the same as printed writing does," Philip said. "Here. I'll show you."

He took the slate, which he'd been using to conjugate verbs, and wiped it with a damp cloth. Then taking a piece of chalk he wrote the first line of the Bible verse he'd been translating at the top. Sarah watched, fascinated.

"'Paul, an apostle of Jesus Christ, by the will of God, and Timotheus our brother'" he read, running a finger of one hand under the words on the page as he read, at the same time pointing to the handwritten words on the slate with his other hand. "They're the same words, just a different way of writing them."

Sarah screwed up her face in puzzlement.

"How do you know what they say then, if they don't look the same?" she asked.

"Well, you learn to read them first," Philip said. He picked up the chalk and drew an 'a' on the slate as it was written in the Bible. "So you learn that that says 'a', and then when you know what all the letters sound like, and can read the words, then you learn what the letters look like to write, and they look a bit different, because when you write them you have to join them together so you don't make ink blots and you can write quickly. That's why you have loops and things, to join the letters together."

It made sense, in a way. Philip always knew how to explain things so they made sense.

"Did Father teach you that?" she asked.

Philip snorted.

"No, of course he didn't," he said. "When I asked he hit me

on the ear and told me that was just how it was and not to question him. No, it was Mr Stockdale who told me. Father took me to see him, to see if I could be apprenticed to him when I'm older. It was him who told Father I had to learn Latin first, and then he would see. Which is stupid."

"Why is Mr Stockdale stupid?" Sarah asked. James Stockdale was the notary, and thought to be very clever. He lived in a big house and knew all about the laws of the country, of which there were thousands. Everyone who needed advice went to him. Sarah had never spoken to him, but he had a kind face and when he laughed, which was often, his chins jiggled about. He was very fat. He didn't come to Father's church very often, but Father seemed not to mind. Maybe it was because Mr Stockdale was too clever to be fooled by the Devil.

"No, not Mr Stockdale," Philip said, "Latin. I like Mr Stockdale, but Latin is stupid. It's very, very old, and all the people who used to speak it are dead. So no one speaks it any more. And it's really, really hard to learn, too."

"Why do you have to learn it, if no one speaks it?" Sarah asked.

"Because it's the language of the courts, so if I'm to go into the law I'll have to learn it."

"Are you going to go into the law?" Sarah had an image in her head of a big impressive building, maybe as big as Mr Stockdale's house, called 'The Law', which Philip would have to go into every day. She hoped he would come home from it every evening.

Philip sighed, and cast another glance at the study.

"Well, I'd rather do that than go to work on a farm, and Mr Stockdale is nice. I think he'd be good to work for. But no, I don't want to go into the law and spend the rest of my life sitting in a dusty room with hundreds of books."

"What do you want to do, then?" Sarah asked.

There was a sudden sound from the room down the hall, as of a chair scraping across a floor. The two children sprang apart. By the time their father emerged from his study a minute later Philip was hard at work on the next chapter of Paul, and Sarah was halfway across the yard in the pouring rain carrying a bowl to collect the eggs in.

* * *

In August Father went on one of his regular trips to Chester, where, he said, he had important business to do with saving souls.

As always, once he'd disappeared down Chapel Lane and had turned the corner into the High Street, from where he would get the stage to Chester, Sarah and Philip set to work with a vengeance, intent on finishing the list of chores he had left for them as quickly as they could so that they could relax for a couple of hours before he returned.

Sometimes he didn't get back until they were in bed, which meant they had enough time to play some games. But they always made sure to go to bed when the town clock struck nine, whether Father was home or not, because if he found them up after that time, he would be very angry.

The last time Reverend Browne had been away, Philip had taught Sarah to play Three Men's Morris, drawing the board on his slate and using pebbles as counters, and Sarah was hoping that they would play again this time. She had enjoyed it, and had even won one game, to her delight.

They finished their chores at six o'clock, and with no sign of Father coming home, they sat at the kitchen table eating slices of bread spread with creamy butter from the neighbouring farm. One of the parishioners had made the loaf, Sarah not yet being strong enough to knead dough properly. Philip pulled the slate and the chalk over to him, and began to draw something.

"Are we going to play Three Men's Morris?" Sarah asked excitedly. Philip stopped what he was doing and looked up.

"We can if you want to," he said, "but I thought you might like to learn to write your name instead."

"Write my name?" Sarah echoed.

"Yes. And then if Father's still not home after that, I can show you what some of the letters sound like. Then next time he's away I can teach you some more, until you know them all. And then I'll teach you to read."

Sarah looked at her brother as though he had just suggested they conjure up the Devil, which had been the subject of last week's sermon, about the dangers of going to the old woman who lived at the edge of the village for herbal cures. She was surely a witch, Reverend Browne had said, and the parishioners were endangering their souls by visiting her instead of the apothecary.

Her potions only seemed to work better than the apothecary's because she was in league with the Devil.

"But…Father said that girls can't learn to read," she said doubtfully.

"Of course they can," Philip scoffed. "If boys can, why can't girls?"

She considered this for a minute.

"I don't know if I'm clever enough," she said.

"Mama could read. She—" Philip stopped abruptly, colour flooding his cheeks.

"She what?" Sarah asked with interest. They rarely spoke about their mother, not least because Sarah couldn't really remember her and Father had forbidden them to speak about her at all.

Philip sat with his head down, doodling absentmindedly on the slate. Then he came to a decision and looked across at his sister, his expression serious.

"Can you keep a secret?" he asked.

"What sort of a secret?" she replied. "Is it a bad secret?"

"No," Philip said. "It's a good secret. But if you tell Father, he'll think it's bad and he'll burn it." He scrubbed the doodles out with the back of his hand. "Let's play Three Men's Morris, then."

Sarah bit her lip.

"Is it to do with the Devil?" she asked in a frightened whisper.

To her surprise, Philip laughed.

"No," he said. "It's to do with Mama, and Father won't like it. Which is why you mustn't tell him, even that I've said anything to you." He started drawing the board on the slate.

It seemed unfair to have to say nothing, yet still not know what the secret was. And although Sarah couldn't remember what her mother had looked like, when she thought of her it always made her feel warm and happy.

"Tell me the secret," she said. "I won't tell anyone."

Philip looked at her, very intently, and she met his gaze unwaveringly. After a moment, he nodded.

"It's not a telling secret, it's a showing one," he said, abandoning the slate and standing up. He went to the mantelpiece and took down a candle, lighting it from the small fire that burnt in the grate. Father would want hot water for his nightcap when he got home. "Come on. It's in the cellar."

"In the cellar?" she said, immediately fearful. "Is it the monster?"

"No, silly. I told you, there's no monster in the cellar. No, it's a nice thing. Here." He gave her the candle he'd lit and lit another one, then opened the cellar door and made his way down the stairs, Sarah following hesitantly behind him. "If Father comes home while we're down here, we'll hear him walk across the floor and we can tell him we were seeing how much wood was left."

In the far corner of the cellar, tucked right against the wall and partly hidden by some rusting tools was an iron-banded wooden chest, covered in dust. Philip moved the tools and beckoned his sister over.

"Father must have forgotten about it," he said, "or he'd have got rid of it." He tilted the candle, letting the wax run onto the floor, then pressed the taper into it, before putting his fingers under the edge of the lid and lifting it, grunting with the effort. The chest opened with a groan of rusty iron.

Curiosity overcoming her fear that a monster might be hiding in it, Sarah stepped forward, gasping as the candle she was holding illuminated a bright blue shimmering material. Philip reached in, lifting the fabric out with reverence. Then he held it up, and Sarah's eyes widened in wonder as the folds of royal blue silk poured over his hands, pooling on the floor at their feet.

It was a dress, a beautiful dress, the bodice encrusted with tiny beads which glittered in the candlelight. It was the most exquisite thing that Sarah had seen in the whole of her seven years.

"Oh!" she breathed, rendered speechless.

"Isn't it lovely?" Philip said. "One day, when we're older, you can wear this, and I'll take you to a ball. We'll dance all night together, until the sun comes up."

She reached out a hand, touching the material reverently. Even in her wildest dreams she could never imagine owning something as beautiful as this, let alone wearing it.

"It was Mama's," Philip explained. "Everything in here was hers. Look." He placed the dress carefully on the floor and took Sarah's candle, putting it opposite his own. Then he reached into the chest and brought out a silver-backed hairbrush, speckled with age, but still containing hair from the long-dead woman in its bristles. A perfume bottle followed, and then a book.

"This was hers too," he said. "She wrote her name in the front. Look."

Sarah sat down heavily on the floor, her legs giving way beneath her as she inhaled the faint scent of orange blossom emanating from the bottle, and remembered.

"Yellow hair," she whispered. "She had yellow hair. And she used to sing to me, in bed." Her eyes filled with tears as she felt again the touch of her mother's lips soft on her forehead as she kissed her goodnight.

Philip looked up from the book and caught the glitter of tears in his sister's hazel eyes. He reached across and gripped her hand, squeezing it, but was too excited to give her any more comfort now.

"Look," he repeated. "Her name was Catherine Applewhite."

Sarah looked at the faded squiggles on the page.

"But wasn't she called Browne, like us?" she asked.

"Well, yes. But she wrote this before she got married to Father. When ladies get married, they take the name of their husband. But she's written the date too. *Catherine Applewhite, her book. September 10th 1715, age 10.* That was a long time before she married Father. But I wanted to show you this to show you that she could read, and write as well. And if she could, so can you."

"But…is that why Mama's in Hell, then? Because she could read and write?" Sarah asked.

"I don't believe Mama's in Hell at all," Philip replied fiercely. "I think she disobeyed Father, and so he *wants* her to be in Hell. But she was kind, and she loved us. She used to tell us stories at night, and play games with us when Father was out. I don't think God would send her to Hell just because Father wanted her to go there."

"I don't remember that," Sarah said. "Do you remember when she died?"

"Well, you were only very little then," Philip said. "But I was nearly as old as you are now. No, I remember that at the end she used to cry a lot, and spend a lot of time looking into the fire. And then one morning when I got up and asked where she was, Father said she was dead, and in Hell. And then he told me never to speak of her again, and when I did he hit me with his belt." He looked down for a minute, running a finger lightly over the writing on the front leaf of the book.

"It's a book of poetry," he said. "And some of them are

written by women. So lots of women must be able to write. Shall I read one?"

She nodded, and he leafed through the pages.

"Here's one by someone called Aphra Benn. 'A thousand martyrs I have made, all sacrific'd to my desire. A thousand beauties have betrayed, that languish in resistless fire. The untamed heart to hand I brought, and fixd the wild and wandring thought'." He looked across to where his sister sat, her eyes alight, but a little vertical crease above her eyebrows.

"What does it mean?" she asked.

"I don't know," Philip admitted. "But it sounds lovely, doesn't it? Mrs Benn must have been very clever to know all those words and make them into a poem. And then someone printed it, so that lots of other people could read it! They wouldn't do that if she was going to Hell, would they? They'd put her in gaol or burn her like they do witches. So if you want, I'll teach you to read and write, and then when I'm grown up I'll take you away with me, and we can live in a big house, and you can wear this dress and write poems too!"

It sounded wonderful.

"But will they let girls go into The Law?" she asked.

"I'm not going into the law," Philip declared. "When I'm sixteen I'm going to go for a soldier. And then I'll have a sword and a musket and a red coat. And I'll be very brave and kill lots of Frenchmen and King George will make me a general. And when I come home, you can write poems about me!"

"But won't Father be very angry?" Sarah asked.

"When I'm big I won't care if he is," Philip said. "And neither will you, because I'll look after you."

"I'd like that," she said.

"So do you want to learn to read and write after all?"

"Yes, please!"

Philip looked at the candle, saw how far it had burned down, and his belligerent expression faltered.

"We'd better put these away and go back upstairs," he said. "Father could be home any time."

Carefully they put the precious items back into the chest, and closed the lid.

"That's a wonderful secret," Sarah said as they made their way back up the stairs to the kitchen.

"It is. But you must never, never tell Father, no matter what. Because if you do, he'll punish us both, but worse than that, he'll burn all Mama's things, and then they'll be gone forever, and we'll have nothing left of Mama at all. You don't want that, do you?"

No, she didn't want that. She didn't want that at all.

"I won't tell him, I promise," she said. "And I want to learn to read and write."

But by the time they got upstairs and had put some more wood on the fire so it would not go out before Father got in, there was no time left to have a lesson, so they agreed to start next time he went away for the day. Then they went to bed.

After saying her prayers, Sarah lay in bed thinking about the wonderful secret in the cellar. She didn't think she would be scared at all now if she was locked down there in the dark. Because even though she wouldn't dare to go near the chest while Father was in the house in case he came down and caught her, and wouldn't be able to see the lovely things in it without a candle anyway, it would be like part of her mother was there with her.

She opened her hand, and kissed the soft, silky strands that she had pulled from the hairbrush before she'd put it back in the chest. Then, very carefully she tucked them inside the pillowcase before settling down and closing her eyes.

Her father would be very angry if he found out about the chest, she knew that. And he would be even angrier if he found out that Philip was going to teach her to read and write. It felt wrong not to tell him.

But it would feel even more wrong for all Mama's lovely things to be thrown away or burnt. And she really *did* want to learn how to read that book, more than she wanted anything except to grow up and wear that beautiful dress and dance with Philip in his lovely red soldier's coat.

And she had promised she wouldn't tell. And if you didn't keep your promises you went to Hell anyway. Father had told her that himself, and it was in the Bible too; if a man swear an oath to bind his soul with a bond; he shall not break his word.

That was what she'd done. And she would not break her word.

* * *

THE WHORE'S TALE: SARAH

Sarah's literacy lessons progressed somewhat erratically, because they could only hold them when Father was out of the house and likely to be so for some time. The chance of him catching them was too high otherwise.

Nevertheless, slowly over the next few months during their precious minutes of spare time she learnt to write her name, firstly in huge wobbly letters that took up the whole slate as she tried to master holding the chalk properly, and then later in smaller, neater letters.

"Now you can sign your name!" Philip announced proudly as the siblings sat together, admiring her latest effort. "That's the most important thing to learn to write."

"I can't sign my name on paper though, until I can use a pen," Sarah said, looking longingly at the holder full of quills and the sheets of pristine cream paper on the table.

"I know, but we can't use any paper because Father will count it and want to know what's happened if there's any missing," Philip said. "I'll teach you the other letters now though, and what they sound like, so you can start learning to read. Then you'll be able to read the poems for yourself. You don't need paper for that." He wrote some letters on the slate. "You already know some of them, the ones in your name," he said, "but there are more – twenty-six altogether."

Sarah looked doubtfully at the multitude of shapes on the slate.

"That's a lot," she said.

"It is, but it won't take you a long time, because you're clever," her brother assured her. He sounded out the letters one by one, and she repeated them after him a few times.

"Good!" he said. "Now you'll remember them better if you write them down as you say them. That's what Father made me do. Here, I'll write a letter, and then you copy it and say the sound it makes."

She did as he told her, her tongue poking out between her teeth, her face screwed up in concentration. When it started to go dark Philip lit a candle and they carried on, Sarah entranced with the increasingly neat shapes she was making, her brother entranced by his ability to teach what he knew to someone else.

"Reading is wonderful," he told her as she struggled to form the letter 'g'. "When you can read, you can find out about everything in the whole world. Mr Stockdale told me that."

The two children were sitting next to each other on the bench seat, their faces almost touching as they bent over the slate in concentration.

"No, not quite," Philip said. "You have to make the tail longer, like—"

Because they were so close, the blow when it came sent both children tumbling from the bench to the floor. Philip, who had taken the main force of it on the side of the head, was knocked temporarily senseless. Sarah, shocked rather than injured, looked up to see their father standing over them, immensely tall, his face almost purple with rage. How had he got into the house without them hearing him? He reached down, gripping the front of her dress and lifting her off her feet.

"So this is what you do, the moment I turn my back!" he roared, shaking her so violently that her head rocked backward and forward on her slender neck. "Get up, boy!" He kicked out at Philip, who was coming round now, blinking and looking blearily around. He let Sarah go suddenly, and she sprawled across the bench. "You, you should know better!" Reverend Browne shouted, now picking Philip up and slapping him smartly across the face. "You should set a good example for your sister! Not only is she younger than you, but a girl! You know she is not to learn to read and write, don't you? Don't you?" he roared, shaking his son like a rat.

"Y-yes, s-sir," Philip stammered, tears of pain and terror pouring down his cheeks.

"How long has this disobedience been going on? Answer me!"

"I-I, not long, Father. I…"

"Do you want your sister to go to the Devil, boy? Do you want to go to him too?"

"N-no, sir," Philip managed.

"And yet you, both of you betray my trust in you, break the Lord's Commandment to honour your father, the moment I am out of sight! By God, I will beat the Devil out of you, if it is the last thing I do!" He began to unbuckle his belt with one hand, whilst holding his terrified son firmly with the other. Still sprawled across the bench, Sarah looked up, saw the livid red mark across her brother's face, saw the dark stain spread across his crotch, saw his eyes widen in shame and fear, and could not keep silent.

"It was not his fault, Father!" she cried. "I wanted to learn to read! I made him teach me!" She had told a lie and now she would go to Hell, but she didn't care. Now Father would turn his rage on her, would put her in the cellar, and by the time he had done that his temper would have cooled a little, and he would not beat Philip so badly.

"Is this true, boy?" Reverend Browne asked. Philip's mouth opened and closed like a fish but no words came out.

"It is! I'm sorry, Father, please!" Sarah cried.

Still holding his son, Reverend Browne looked at his daughter. Her eyes were huge with fear and the tears stood in them, but she didn't look away. If she did he would know that she had lied to him, that Philip had offered to teach her, and things would be even worse.

"Well, then," he said after a moment, his gaze locked with hers. "This is not the first time you've disobeyed me, is it? What other mischief have you been up to while I've been away?"

Sarah swallowed hard.

"Nothing, Father. This is the first time," she said desperately. He had unbuckled his belt now, and was holding it in his fist.

"Nonsense! Do not try to keep things secret from me, you wicked child! I can see into your soul, see the blackness there. Would you dare lie to me?"

She felt rather than saw Philip tense as he waited for her to divulge the secret she had promised to keep. He wouldn't blame her if she did, she knew that. No one could resist Father when he was in a rage. And this was a cold rage, worse than anything she'd seen before. The end of his belt trailed on the floor at her feet, menacingly.

"I made a promise" she said, her voice shaking.

"Yes, you did, a promise to God," he answered.

For one horrified moment she thought he knew about the secret after all, and then she realised he meant she had made a promise not to lie. She thought, harder than she had ever thought before. He had told her never to lie, had told her he would know if she did, that God would know.

But she had never *promised* him she wouldn't, had never said the word that made it binding.

"I won't break my promise," she said.

"Well, I am glad to hear that, at least," her father replied. "But this disobedience cannot go unpunished."

With a sudden movement that made her squeal, he dropped Philip and slapped her hard across the face, toppling her off the bench onto the wooden floor.

"Undress yourself," he said curtly to his son, looking down at him with contempt as he lay on the floor, sobbing.

Then he leaned down, gripped Sarah's arm, and dragging her across the floor, opened the door to the cellar and pushed her inside. She grabbed the metal handrail just in time to stop herself falling down the stairs.

"You can stay down here until I decide what to do with you. Pray, and think on the promise you made," he said, before turning and closing the door. She heard the bolt shoot across, her father's heavy footsteps as he walked across the floor, and then the crack of leather on skin, followed by her brother's screams.

She sat on the top step for a time, her face throbbing, her hands over her ears, trying not to hear as the screams turned to moans, while the crack of the belt went on, and on, for longer than it ever had before. When she could bear it no more she felt her way carefully down the steps, holding the handrail, counting each step on the way down. Her father normally allowed her to go down the steps before he closed the door, so she wouldn't fall. He was very angry.

She had told a lie, no, two lies, and now not only her father but God was angry with her, and she had to pray for forgiveness, pray harder than she ever had before. Because she had done a lot of bad things in her life, she knew that, but this was the first time she had done a bad thing deliberately.

More than one bad thing. She had told her father that it was her idea to learn to write; and she had *not* told him about the chest, which was a secret she had kept from him. But if she had told him she would have broken her promise, which she would go to Hell for anyway.

She was going to Hell no matter what she did. But maybe if she prayed very, very hard, then God would not make her stay in Hell for all eternity, just for a time. And at least Mama was in Hell, so they would see each other again.

She sniffed, wiped her face and blew her nose on the skirt of her dress, then knelt down to pray.

She prayed for a very long time. Her father had gone to bed and the house had been silent for a long time before she stopped. In spite of the pain she was in, her eyes were closing, her mind drifting away from her prayers. She would sleep for a while, and then she would be able to pray much better, so that God would be sure to hear her.

She lay down on her side on the floor, and her eyes started to close.

Just before she slept, a realisation came to her, as often does in those moments between waking and sleeping.

She was not the only one who had lied. Her father had told a lie too. He had said he could see into her soul. He had always said that, that he could see every wicked thing she did or thought written on it, and until now she had always believed him. But he hadn't seen the truth about her mother's chest, hadn't known what her promise had been, that she was keeping a secret from him.

He couldn't see into her soul at all. God might be able to know what she was thinking, but her father didn't.

She smiled, and then her eyes closed, and she slept.

CHAPTER TWO

April 1732

Father and daughter sat side by side in the coach as it clattered down the dirt road. Outside the windows the fertile Cheshire countryside displayed its glories in the form of an endless array of fields, some dotted with fluffy sheep accompanied by tiny lambs, some with brown and white cows, while in others the cereal crops were pushing green shoots through the rich brown soil.

The seat was hard and the bouncing of the coach on the uneven track made Sarah's bones rattle and her teeth click. She had bitten her tongue because of it. It was very uncomfortable. What made her more uncomfortable was that her father hadn't spoken one word to her since he had told her to pack up her clothes, put on her Sunday dress and come with him. Her tentative question as to where they were going had been met with silence, and she hadn't dared to ask again.

As a result she had passed the first part of the journey in dread as she mused on where Father might be taking her. To prison? She had heard that prisons were terrible places, where people who had done wicked things were locked up in tiny rooms and then hung until they were dead. And after they'd been hung they went to Hell, which was even worse than prison.

She had done a wicked thing trying to learn to read, and another wicked thing by lying to her father. She knew he couldn't be taking her to Hell, because you had to die to go there. But he might be taking her to prison. She wanted to tell him that she would be very good from now on if he would only let her stay at home, but she didn't dare speak, and she knew he wouldn't pay any attention to her anyway.

Maybe being in prison would be like the cellar, except there was no monster in the cellar. There might be one in prison, though. Would being eaten by a monster be more painful than being hung?

After they had done the wicked thing, her father had kept her in the cellar for a very long time. She didn't know how long, because she couldn't see the sun to know if it was night or day. But she had had three long sleeps, and he had brought water down to her twice, but no food. She had spent a lot of time thinking about Mama, and a lot of time praying to be forgiven for thinking about Mama instead of praying.

When he had finally let her out of the cellar the sudden light of the kitchen had hurt her eyes, and she had blinked and squinted until they adjusted. On the table was a plate, and on the plate was some bread, a pat of butter and a piece of pale yellow cheese. On seeing it Sarah's empty stomach had contracted painfully and rumbled loudly. She had expected Father to chastise her for bad manners, but instead he had told her to sit down and eat, and afterwards to get some water from the stream to wash herself, then put on her good dress, because they were going on a journey.

She had wanted to say goodbye to Philip, and to see if he had recovered from his beating, but the house was empty and she hadn't had the courage to ask where he was. Maybe he had died, like their mother, and was in Hell? If he was, maybe it would be better to be hung or eaten by a monster so she could be there with them. She didn't think she could go on living without Philip anyway.

She looked out of the window, watching the fields melt into a green and gold haze as the tears filled her eyes before spilling over and running down her cheeks. She sniffed as quietly as possible so that her father wouldn't know she was crying and get angry again. Then she wiped away the tears with the back of her hand and kept swallowing hard until the lump in her throat went away and the tears stopped.

Some time later the coach stopped at a small village, where a red-faced woman got on, carrying a basket covered with a cloth. She sat down heavily opposite her two companions and smiled at them.

"Good morning to you," she said cheerily.

Her father tipped his hat to her, but didn't return the greeting. Sarah, not knowing whether to respond to the woman or not, pretended she hadn't heard her and stared with great concentration out of the window, blushing furiously.

"Are you going to Chester?" the woman asked.

Sarah looked at her father, and saw the nod of the head that constituted his only reply.

Chester! Where he went to do God's work! Was there a prison there? She had no idea.

Silence reigned in the coach for a time as the woman took the hint and occupied herself by looking at the passing scenery. It was a warm spring day, and the coach was very stuffy. Sarah's eyes grew heavy; she started to nod and would have fallen asleep had the woman not suddenly spoken again. She jerked awake and looked round to see the friendly woman holding out a linen cloth on which rested three cakes.

"Here, child, have a cake," she said. "I made them this morning, so they're fresh. Do you like almonds?"

Sarah had no idea whether she liked almonds or not, having never had them, but she knew she would like the cakes. They looked delicious, golden and fluffy. She could almost taste the moist sweetness on her tongue, and her mouth watered at the thought. Apart from the slice of bread and cheese, she had had nothing to eat for a long time. She looked nervously at her father, seeking permission. He glanced at the cloth with disgust, as though three cowpats were sitting on it.

"No thank you, madam," he replied curtly. Sarah sighed inwardly. She opened her mouth, resigned to refusing, when her father spoke again. "Would you like a cake, daughter?" he asked, his tone clearly indicating that he wished her to decline.

Lying was wicked. He would not wish her to lie. He could not be angry with her for telling the truth.

"Yes, please," she said, reaching out and taking one. She thanked the woman and ate it slowly, relishing every delicious mouthful. Then she resumed looking out of the window and by doing so managed to avoid meeting her father's disapproving eye for the rest of the journey.

They alighted at Chester, but Sarah had no time to do more than register that the street was very wide and full of tall buildings and people before her father hurried her down a side street and set off at a brisk walk, Sarah having to run to keep up with him.

They walked like this for a time, Reverend Browne stopping periodically to wait impatiently for her to catch up before marching off again, so by the time they came to a stop at the foot of a short flight of steps which led to a three storey brick-built house with lots of windows and a cherry-red door, she was gasping for breath. As they reached the bottom step the door opened and a woman came down to meet them.

Sarah looked up at her, open-mouthed. The woman had exactly the same face as her father! High forehead, long straight nose, hazel eyes, thin lips. Only her thick greying brown hair was different, worn high on her head with curls at the back, whereas her father's was tied with a black ribbon at the nape of his neck. And, of course, the woman wore a grey dress, whereas her father had breeches and a coat in black, the only colour he ever wore.

"Brother," the woman said unsmilingly by way of greeting. Her father nodded, then looked down at Sarah, who had almost recovered her breath now.

"Curtsey to your Aunt Patience, daughter," he said coldly.

Sarah blushed and sank immediately into a clumsy curtsey. When she rose and glanced up, her aunt was looking at her with distaste, her lips compressed into a straight line. She reached down and took hold of Sarah's chin, tilting it upward.

"Hmm," she commented. "Well, there's no doubt she's your child, and that's something. She has the Browne eyes and hair. But the rest is all her mother." She sniffed disapprovingly, running one finger lightly across her niece's mouth before letting her go. "Wanton," she observed. "I did warn you, brother, but would you listen to me? And now I have to make a silk purse out of a sow's ear. Well, I'll do my best. I can't promise more. What about the son?"

The reverend coloured.

"He's gone to work at Bradshaw's farm for a while," he said, to Sarah's utter relief. Philip wasn't dead after all! "He was due to go at Michaelmas, but I brought it forward. He'll have no time for mischief while he's there, Bradshaw will make sure of that. No need to make a silk purse – just teach the child to cook and sew a plain seam, that sort of thing. She's coming up eight soon, and it's high time she learnt such things. Once she can do that, she'll have no time to—"

"Percy, you've arrived at last!" came a jocular voice from the top of the steps. Three pairs of hazel eyes looked up at the owner of the voice, a stout man in early middle age, dressed in dark blue velvet. The man trotted down the steps to them, ignoring the two pairs of disdainful eyes, and addressing himself to the pair of wide, wondering ones. "You must be Sarah!" he exclaimed, engulfing her tiny hand in his large one and shaking it. "Delighted to make your acquaintance, niece. I'm your Uncle Arthur." He straightened up.

"Really, husband, I do wish you'd refrain from addressing my brother in such a disrespectful manner!" his wife said.

"My abject apologies sir," Arthur said unrepentantly. "But Perseverance is so long-winded. Although it is apt, I'll give you that. You do persevere in…well, then," he amended on catching his wife's thunderous expression, "I must be off. Customers won't wait, and that's a fact. Go on up, then, and make yourselves at home. I'll see you later, child," he said, ruffling Sarah's hair before striding off down the road in a flurry of swirling frockcoat and blazing red hair.

Patience sighed.

"Well, then, you'd best come in and we'll discuss the details. Is that all the clothes she has?" she asked, looking at the small bundle tucked under her brother's arm.

"She has two serviceable dresses and four changes of linen," Perseverance Browne said defensively. "She has no need of more to keep clean and modest."

"She will need a dress fit for church," Patience pointed out.

"She is wearing it, madam."

Aunt Patience looked at her niece's ill-fitting, badly woven dress in horror.

"Brother," she said. "It is possible for a child to dress modestly *and* be respectable. Why, the girl looks like a beggar! What are you thinking? No wonder your parishioners do not respect you as they should! I see we have no time to lose in teaching you to sew, child. Then we can buy some materials to make something fitting for the daughter of a minister to be seen in on the Sabbath."

"Patience, I will not have her getting ideas—"

"Of course not! What do you take me for? Let us go in," his sister interrupted, to Sarah's astonishment. No one interrupted her father, least of all a woman, a Daughter of Eve! Now he would be furious, and would chastise her soundly. Maybe he would beat her.

Aunt Patience marched up the stairs without waiting for her brother's reply. He looked up, watching as her dove-grey silk skirts disappeared into the house. He suddenly looked very tired.

"Go on then, child," he said wearily, poking Sarah hard in the back. "Don't keep your aunt waiting."

They sat on uncomfortable chairs in a freezing cold room which Aunt Patience called the drawing room. While the siblings discussed Sarah's future and what she was to learn, the object of their conversation tried not to shiver and looked around the room with interest. The walls had all been densely painted with twigs and leaves running right up to the ceiling. On the twigs sat a great many birds. It could have been beautiful, had the birds, foliage and background been rendered in bright colours. What a pity that the artist had only had brown paint. Maybe it was called a drawing room because of all the dull brown pictures drawn on the walls.

The floor was brown as well, and there was a brown rug in front of the cold firegrate, in which a large bunch of dried flowers had been placed by way of decoration. On top of the mantelpiece were lots of little dogs, lined up all the way along it. They were brown too, or brown and white. Aunt Patience must like dogs a lot. In the corner was a dark wood table, and that was covered with little dog ornaments too. The whole effect was one of being underground, or in a cave, perhaps. Sarah wondered whether, if she lay on the floor it would smell of soil, like the cellar. She hoped Aunt Patience had a dog. Maybe she would be able to make friends with it.

It wasn't until her father stood up to leave that Sarah realised she had been drifting again. And she also realised two other things: he was going home and leaving her here with this stony-faced stranger who clearly didn't like her; and she had no idea what she was going to have to do, because she had been dreaming instead of listening. Again.

* * *

She soon found out what she had to do. When there were adults in the room she had to be silent and only speak when directly addressed. Her father had been far too lenient with her and her brother, allowing them time to think up mischief, but now that would come to an end.

"Your father tells me that you are competent at cleaning a house, and washing light linens," Aunt Patience said doubtfully, "and that you can make a pottage, but that is all you can do in the way of cooking."

Sarah sat quietly.

"Well, girl, speak up!" her aunt barked, making Sarah jump. She hadn't been asked a question! She looked up at her aunt, confused. What was she supposed to say? "For Heaven's sake!" Aunt Patience continued. "Is that all you can do?"

"Yes, Aunt Patience," Sarah replied. "Oh, I feed the chickens and collect the eggs, and I help Philip with the vegetable garden too."

"Philip. Sarah. This is what comes of naming children thoughtlessly," her aunt remarked. "Had you been given good Christian names like your father and I, you would have had a virtue to live up to. Your mother named you, didn't she?"

"Er…I don't know," Sarah said. She had never thought about who had named her, or whether it was appropriate or not.

"Hmm. Well, it's too late now. We have to work with what we have. You are here to learn the skills you will need for the life that you were born to. You will learn plain sewing and plain cooking, modest and seemly behaviour and obedience. But I will start by making sure that you do know how to clean a house. I'm sure my brother has made allowances for your age, but you are nearly eight now, and it is time to take on responsibility. You have a lifetime of duty ahead of you. You will start tomorrow. I will show you to your room, which you will keep in perfect order at all times. There you can sit and think about the proper way for a child to behave."

Once in her room, which was a tiny chamber at the very top of the house, the only furniture a narrow bed under a window and a chest of drawers, Sarah put her clothes away and knelt on her bed to look out of the window. The glass was clear and thin, not thick and greenish with bubbles in like the windows at home, and she could see through it perfectly. On the other side of the street was a row of houses which looked just like her aunt's house, except the doors were all painted different colours; green, blue, brown. Looking down the street to the left she could see trees in the far distance, and wondered if there was a stream at the end of the street like there was at home. It looked a long way to walk to fetch water every day. To her right she could see houses stretching into the distance and a church spire rising into the sky, pointing to Heaven. She looked down to the street, and in a few minutes saw more people pass by, either walking or riding in carts or on horses, than she had ever seen in her life before.

She was supposed to be thinking about the proper way for a child to behave. Maybe her aunt would ask questions later, like her father did about the Sunday service.

She pulled herself reluctantly away from the window and sat on the bed. Instead of a scratchy blanket there was a lovely soft pink eiderdown on it. She stroked it, smiling. Her aunt's dress had been made of the same sort of shiny material, and when she had walked upstairs it had swayed and rustled. She had silver buckles on her shoes, and little heels. Sarah hoped that when she had learnt to sew, she would get to make a shiny dress to go to church in, and would have shoes with silver buckles.

What was the proper way for a child to behave? She knew more about the way a child should *not* behave. That was easy to remember, because she had been punished for it. Children, or girls at any rate, should not learn to read or write, should not run, shout, leave the gate open, break an egg, spill water when carrying it into the house, burn the pottage, let the fire go out, fidget in church, tell lies, think wicked thoughts, speak about their mothers.

There. Maybe Aunt Patience would be satisfied if Sarah told her that.

In the distance she heard the church clock strike seven. Her stomach growled, reminding her that she was very hungry. But she would surely have missed supper by now, and would have to wait until breakfast before she could eat again. She took off her dress and stockings, carefully unlaced her stays, folded them and put them on the top of the drawers, then knelt down in her shift to pray. She prayed that Mr Bradshaw would not make Philip work too hard, that God would let her mother out of Hell, and that she would learn the proper way for a child to behave so that her father would love her. And that she would be able to go home soon, because she was already missing Philip, and knew he would be missing her too.

* * *

"Really, I have no idea what I was thinking of when I agreed to take the brat," Patience said to her husband a few days later. "Perseverance had no business to be telling me she was competent in household tasks, when she has no idea how to polish brasses, use a copper, or even a duster! She broke one of my porcelain dogs yesterday as well! Swept it right off the mantelpiece! I'm beginning to wonder if she's an idiot."

"She seems perfectly fine to me," Arthur commented, stretching his legs out to the living room fire and holding his glass up to admire the ruby glow of its contents. "She's shy, that's all. I don't think Percy…verance has much in the way of brass to polish or ornaments to dust in his house, and the poor child has no doubt had to wash the clothes in the river! She's probably never seen a copper in her life. You only have to look at her hands to know she works hard, poor child. She's homesick, I think, and afraid of you. That's why she's clumsy when you're there."

"Afraid of me?! Why, I've been nothing but kindness! I've given the child my full attention for a week!"

A silence followed in which Arthur looked at his wife until she coloured slightly. She sat down in the chair opposite him on the other side of the fire. "Well, I can't leave her alone to get up to mischief. I promised Perseverance I would keep a constant eye on her."

"My dear, I know you mean well," Arthur said, "but really, the child needs time to adapt. You can tell just by looking at her that she's never seen a china ornament before, or anything decorative. She probably had no idea it was so light and delicate. You know what your brother is like. He won't even have a painting on the wall! I doubt he's taught her anything at all except to sit still and pray for hours on end – what chores she can do she's learnt by herself. She's brought herself up since she was three, poor thing. You must make allowances."

"Hmm. Well, I suppose you have a point," Patience admitted reluctantly. "Maybe I am expecting too much. But you can't blame my brother. His life's work is to bring souls to God, not to bring up children and run a house. It's hardly his fault that his wicked wife abdicated her responsibilities. And the child *is* half hers – she is bound to have inherited some of her ways. She certainly has her wanton looks."

"Let's hope that Sarah does like her mother then, when she's old enough, and seeks love and happiness elsewhere," Arthur said. "God knows she'll find precious little of that living with your brother."

"Husband!" Patience cried.

"Wife!" her husband responded.

"It is a daughter's duty to care for her ailing parents in their sunset years," Patience said primly. "He seeks only to fit her for her future, a future of piety and usefulness. No woman can wish for more."

"Nonsense. He seeks only to fit her for a life of drudgery and slavery, purely to suit his own purposes, which is exactly what he tried to do with Kate. He had no right to marry a chit of fifteen. If she did anything wicked, then he drove her to it."

"I was fifteen when you married me!" Patience retorted.

"Indeed you were. But I was sixteen. And with wisdom, I think both of us would admit we should have waited a little longer. We made our first years very hard by our impatience. But there is a big difference between two very young people falling in love and choosing to make a life together, and a man of nearly forty marrying a child, thinking he can bully her into accepting a life of loveless misery. Now he seeks to do the same to his daughter, and has enlisted you to help him do it. He thinks of no one but himself."

"That is unfair!" Patience protested, ever protective of her brother. "It is quite the opposite. He thinks only of the souls he seeks to save."

"Well, we will have to agree to disagree, as we do in all matters concerning your brother," Arthur said, draining his glass and standing. "I'm for bed. I have a long day tomorrow." He bent to kiss his wife on the cheek, then walked to the door. "Give the child some time to breathe, Patience. You're driving her too hard. She will respond far better to kindness than harsh discipline."

"It is having 'time to breathe' that has brought her here!"

Patience retorted. "Instead of using the free time Perseverance kindly allowed her to think on her sins and be grateful to him, she used it to disobey him! The Devil makes work for idle hands, as she has proved. She must be constantly occupied usefully, or she will go to the bad as her mother did. She has her mother's sly look about her."

"She is clever, not sly, my dear," Arthur said. "You would do better to let her learn to read, and to have some fun now and then. I doubt she has ever laughed in her life!"

"You have never liked my brother. He is a good man, and seeks to bring his children to salvation, as he does his parishioners. But you will not see that."

"No, it's not that I *will* not – I *can* not. And God knows I have tried to like him, for your sake. But he drove his wife to desperation and now seeks to spoil his daughter's life, and employs you to help him do so, and for that I neither like nor respect him. Listen to me. Show her some kindness, for if you do she will love you for it, and will open like a blossom."

* * *

She should be grateful. She would have known that even if her aunt hadn't told her so a hundred times a day. She should be grateful, and she should be happy. Sarah tried very hard to be both, but a month had gone by and she was neither. Instead she was miserable and homesick, and she missed her brother terribly.

There was a lot to be grateful for. The food here was much better and more varied than it was at home, mainly because she had not cooked it, although she was now starting to learn. And there was a lot more of it, too. She had eaten things she had never even heard of before, like rice pudding, creamy and sweet, pigeon pie with onions and thyme, beef pasty with a hot thick aromatic gravy that made her mouth water just to think of it. And she was learning how to make puff pastry now, so that when she went home she could make her own pies and pasties.

She had hoped that Mrs Lindy who did all the cooking would teach her, because she had a nice smiling face; but instead Aunt Patience had said she would do it, and had rapped Sarah's knuckles with a wooden spoon when she hadn't rolled the pastry out evenly, and had rapped them again when she hadn't stuck enough butter on it before rolling it up. Mrs Lindy had huffed in the corner as she kneaded the bread dough, but she had not raised any objections to the way her employer was conducting the lesson.

The house was nice and warm too, even her bedroom was warm, and her mattress was smooth, not lumpy like the one at home. And she loved the eiderdown, had wondered whether Aunt Patience would let her take it with her when she returned home.

But she didn't think that was likely. No matter how hard she tried to do the endless tasks she was set well, it wasn't good enough. She hadn't broken any more ornaments since that heart-stopping moment not long after she'd arrived, when she'd fumbled with the feather duster and had knocked one of the little dogs off the mantelpiece. She had watched in horror as it had fallen, missing the soft rug and shattering into a thousand pieces on the tiled floor.

She had waited for Aunt Patience to beat her, or to throw her down the cellar and leave her there. True, she had smacked her sharply round the head, making her ears ring, and hadn't allowed her anywhere near the drawing room since. But every day since then she had reminded her of how clumsy she was, and how she would come to nothing like her mother, until Sarah thought she would rather have been beaten with a belt or left to pray in the cellar for a day as her father would have done. At least once the punishment was over, he didn't mention the reason for it again.

Sarah thought it would be nice to be down in the cellar, just to have some time alone to think. Instead her aunt was there all the time, standing over her as she tried to lay the fire or sweep the floor, making her so nervous that she fumbled and made a mess of even the tasks she already knew how to do. She was never left alone for more than a few minutes at a time, and was constantly given chores to do, kept busy from the moment she got up until the moment she fell into bed, too tired even to pray, let alone think.

Even in church on Sunday her aunt sat next to her, so she daren't stretch her legs or lean back against the pew. And, like her father, her aunt questioned her closely on the content of the sermon when she got home, so she daren't let her mind wander.

Her uncle didn't go to church with them. She wondered if he

went to a different church, and wished she could go with him. She was sure that the church he went to would be warm and bright, not dull and cold like the one her aunt took her to.

She liked her Uncle Arthur, although she rarely saw him. He reminded her of the sun coming out from behind a cloud; he would sweep through the room in a flurry of velvet coat on his way somewhere, always smiling, always with a jolly word for her, sweeping her up into a quick embrace before popping her back to the ground and disappearing, after which the day would be grey and miserable again.

And then one day he swept into the dining room just as they were finishing breakfast, grabbed a buttered roll from a plate, folded a slice of ham into it and ate it standing up. Sarah was sitting stiffly at the table, drinking her first cup of tea. If she had been able to relax, she probably would have enjoyed it, because the steam rising from it smelt lovely, and it was very sweet. But the tiny cup was so fragile and she had to hold it just so, so she was terrified of breaking it, with the result that she hardly tasted the tea at all, just wanting the ordeal to be over.

"So then, niece," he began indistinctly through a mouthful of bread and ham.

"Arthur, please! You set a bad example, standing, and speaking with your mouth full!" his wife cried.

Arthur remained standing, but he did wait until he'd finished his mouthful before speaking again.

"So then, niece," he repeated when he had, "how would you like to spend today with me?"

"Impossible," his wife replied. "Today she is going to unpick the disgraceful stitches from yesterday and attempt once more to hem a handkerchief. And after that—"

"Oh, I'm sure we won't die for lack of a handkerchief. Not in one day, at any rate," Arthur interrupted. "You can teach her tomorrow instead. What do you say, Sarah?" he asked. Sarah looked up at him nervously, caught the twinkle in his merry blue eyes and smiled, in spite of the fact that her aunt would no doubt disapprove. The cup tilted, pouring some of its contents onto the pristine white tablecloth.

"Oh, for goodness sake!" Aunt Patience cried.

Sarah looked at the pale brown stain spreading across the cloth in utter horror. Too late she righted the cup and placed it in the saucer. She looked up at her uncle again, her eyes full of tears.

"Well, then, that's decided," he said, as though she'd spoken. "Put your boots on, child. It's a fair walk for someone of your age."

"Don't be ridiculous!" his wife said. "Look at what she's done!"

"It was an accident," Arthur said, "and my fault for distracting her. I'm sure it will wash out. Maybe tomorrow you can show the child how to remove a tea stain from damask. Although I doubt she'll need to know. Percy would never allow such a sinful beverage as tea to cross his threshold, I'm sure. Off you go, then, niece. I don't want to be late."

After Sarah had run off to get her boots, Patience sniffed disapprovingly.

"Really, this is quite absurd, Arthur," she said. "You will give her ideas."

"Oh, I do hope so."

"You will regret it. You have no idea how clumsy the child is. She will be under your feet all day. Don't say I didn't warn you!"

"I shan't," Arthur said. "I think it will do the girl good to get some fresh air, see something different, meet new people. I'll bring her home with me this evening."

"You mean to keep her with you *all day?!*" his wife cried.

"Of course. What do you think I intend? To put her out on the street to beg? Sell her to the gypsies?"

"No, of course not, but—"

"I assure you, she will be quite safe with me, my dear. Ah, there you are, child. Come on then! There's not a moment to lose!"

He turned, and as was his custom, swept from the room, Sarah following in his wake.

Patience looked darkly at the stain which marred her pristine cloth.

"That child will be the death of me," she remarked to herself. She lifted the pot and poured herself another cup of the sinful beverage.

CHAPTER THREE

Once out of the house Arthur trotted down the steps, then strode off down the street, Sarah running behind him as she had behind her father a month before. He kept this energetic pace up until he'd rounded the corner, then he stopped and waited for Sarah to catch up.

To her surprise, once she had, instead of striding off again he leaned down to talk to her.

"Now then," he said, "have you ever been to Chester before?"

"No, Uncle," Sarah replied.

"Excellent!" her uncle said. "Then I can be the first to show you the wonders of this beautiful city. Of course," he continued, smiling down at her, "I must go to my place of business. I have an appointment with a client. But that is not for…" he removed a fob watch from his pocket and looked at it, "…half an hour, so we can take our time and you can see more than just a blur. I'm sure that's all you saw when your father brought you here, eh? Now," he continued without waiting for an answer, "when I am in work I'll be very busy and won't be able to keep an eye on you, so you must be good. But I'm sure you know how to be good, don't you? You've had plenty of practice at that."

Sarah wasn't so sure. Her father wouldn't say she knew how to be good, and neither would Aunt Patience. She opened her mouth to answer the question but before she could, Uncle Arthur was talking again. "The girls who work for me are kind enough, and I'm sure they won't mind if you ask them questions. They know you're coming with me today and are looking forward to meeting you. And then later we can take the air a little, and I'll show you how lovely Chester is. What do you say to that?"

This time he waited long enough for her to answer.

"Thank you, Uncle Arthur. That would be wonderful," she said. Uncle and niece looked at each other. He beamed down at her. She smiled tentatively up at him. He held out his hand to her, and after a moment she understood what he wanted and placed her tiny, work-reddened hand in his large square one. Very gently he closed his fingers around hers.

"Let's make a start," he said, turning round and pointing back down the street. "This is Bridge Street, and it's called that because down there at the end of the street there's a bridge across the river. The river is called the Dee, and big ships sail up and down her. Perhaps there will be a big ship in port later, and we can see her. Would you like that?"

Sarah was looking back up the road. In the far distance she could see an archway over the street, which must be the bridge.

"Yes please, Uncle," she said. "I think I can see the bridge, but it looks as though it's going over the street, not a river."

He looked up the road, squinting to see better.

"Ah!" he said as realisation dawned. "No, that's not the bridge. That's the gate. The bridge and the river are on the other side. There's a wall that goes all the way round the city. In fact, later, if I have time, we'll take a walk along the wall. It's the best way to see the place anyway. It's very wide," he added, seeing Sarah's doubtful expression. "In the past it was used to keep enemies out, but now it's a very pleasant promenade for ladies and gentlemen like us. You'll see."

They set off down Bridge Street at a pace suitable for an eight-year-old, Uncle Arthur pointing out buildings of interest as they walked.

"This is a very old city, and many of the buildings are hundreds of years old," he said. "But those houses," he pointed to three enormous black and white buildings above an arched walkway, "are modern. What do you think of them?"

Sarah, unused to having her opinion asked about anything, took a moment to realise he was speaking to her. When she did, she looked at them closely, considering, and thereby missing the smile on the face of her companion as he observed her serious expression.

"I like them," she said at last. "I like the twisted black bits and the big windows. It must be nice and light inside. And I think you'd be able to see a long way if you were in the rooms at the top."

"I think you're right," Uncle Arthur agreed. "Those twisted black bits are called barley sugar pilasters, because they look like barley sugar sweets. Have you tasted barley sugar?"

"No," Sarah replied.

"Really? Oh, that will never do. We must remedy that! In France it's called *sucre d'orge,* and it was first made by Benedictine nuns, as a medicine. I don't know if it cures any ills, but it tastes very nice. You will see."

They carried on in this pleasant dilatory way, turning right at the end of the street and arriving at Arthur Young's premises a few minutes later.

"Here we are!" he said, stopping at some steps leading up to a walkway. "These are called the Rows, and I think there is nothing like them in the whole of England, indeed in Europe! The cellar of the shop is at street level. That's where I store all my materials. But the rest is up these stairs." They walked up the steps together, emerging onto the first floor. Set back were the shops, and in front of them a walkway, which ran the length of the street and which was roofed by the floors of the houses above, which overlapped the walkway, therefore ensuring that no matter the weather, shoppers would not get wet whilst moving from one shop to another.

"Of course, although it's very convenient for shoppers it does darken the inside of the shop a little, in spite of the windows at the back of the room where the ladies work, so we have a lot of lamps burning, because people like to see what they're buying, and I need to see to ensure my clients' wigs fit perfectly," he continued. "But it's all very cosy." He opened the door, causing a little bell hung over it to ring merrily, and walked in, Sarah following behind him.

"Do you like it?" Sarah's uncle asked after giving her a moment to look round, seeming really to care what she thought of his premises.

"Oh, yes!" Sarah exclaimed. "It's the most beautiful room I've ever seen!"

Her first impression on entering the room was that she'd

walked into a palace. Although it was clearly a shop, it was very luxurious. Along the back wall was a long counter behind which were seated three women, all busily working, various tools, lengths of hair of all colours and partly finished wigs spread out along the surface of the counter. Each of them had an oil lamp next to her. Another wall had shelves full of wigs, each displayed on a wooden head shape. A number of comfortable chairs were ranged around tea tables, and in one corner, which could be curtained off, was a barber's chair. A great chandelier ablaze with candles hung from the ceiling, and patterned rugs decorated the floor.

"Well, I'm gratified to hear you say so," Uncle Arthur said. He clapped his hands and the three women looked up in unison. "Ladies, may I introduce Miss Sarah Browne, my niece, who will spend the day here. I'm sure you'll make her very welcome." The three women smiled and said hello, before bending back to their work. "I'll show you around a little, and then I must get on, you know. But you can sit in one of these chairs and have some refreshments, and if you have any questions, you must ask them. No need to wait until you're spoken to; you are not in your aunt's house now. This is my world, and my rules apply."

Still holding her hand, he led her round the shop, explaining that some of the head shapes belonged to regular customers, and the shape was exactly the same as their head, so the wig would be sure to fit, whilst others were just used to display wigs that people could come in and purchase without having it made especially for them.

"Of course those are cheaper," Arthur explained, "because there's not as much work in them. We can make some adjustments for size, but the wealthiest gentlemen have their wigs made to order. We also make hairpieces for ladies, who don't in general wear wigs, you know."

Sarah didn't know anything about wigs, had never really thought about them. Her father wore his own hair tied back, as did most of the men in her village. And the ladies covered their hair with caps, so there would be no point in wearing a wig, she supposed.

"Mr Stockdale wears a wig. I thought he had lovely white hair, but then he took it off one day when it was very warm and said a bad word about how hot and itchy it was. He had no hair at all underneath," she offered suddenly, then blushed at her own temerity. She looked apprehensively at her uncle, but when she saw that rather than being angry, he was smiling at her, she continued. "Is that why people wear wigs, because they have no hair of their own?"

"Bless you, no, child," her uncle said. "It's the fashion. It's like wearing very good clothes – it tells everyone how rich you are, and therefore how powerful you are. A good, well-made wig is very costly. Anyone of fashion will know whether your wig is made of human hair or horsehair, and if it's been made to fit you or not. A lot of gentlemen shave their heads so the wig will fit well and not be so hot, while others tuck their own hair underneath it."

Sarah looked with interest at her uncle's head of thick wavy copper hair, interspersed with threads of silver.

"No," he said, catching her gaze. "I don't wear a wig, and ginger is not a fashionable colour anyway. This is all my own hair. Can you keep a secret?"

"Is it a bad secret?" she asked, frowning. "Is it to do with the Devil?"

To her surprise her uncle roared with laughter, making the women look up again.

"No, niece, this secret is not a bad one, but I'd rather you didn't tell my customers, that's all." Without waiting for her to confirm whether she could keep it or not, he sat down in a nearby chair so he was at eye level with her. "I hate wigs," he said softly. "Your Mr Stockdale is right. They're hot and itchy, and I have no idea why anyone who has hair of their own would want to wear one. Ridiculous things, like much of fashion." He winked at her, and she giggled.

"Why do you have a wig shop then, if you don't like them?" she asked, her curiosity making her bold.

"Because when I was a boy, just a bit older than you, my father apprenticed me to a wig maker, or rather a perruquier, which is the proper word. I didn't have any choice in the matter. I didn't want to do it, but I found that I was good at it, and I could make an excellent living. I'm good at talking to the customers too, and I like that part. In fact that's as important as making a good wig.

Having a wig fitted is a tedious business, but if you can have a little spirited conversation, a cup of coffee and a delicious pastry while it's being done, then the time will go quickly and you'll want to come back again.

"And speaking of delicious pastries, you sit here and observe, and I'll arrange for some tea and a pastry to be served to you. Because I must get on now."

She sat there and observed as her uncle bustled round the shop and the women worked with great concentration, and in time a pot of tea, a bowl of sugar lumps, a delicate cup and saucer and a matching plate with a raisin and cinnamon pastry was brought by a young serving girl who actually bobbed a curtsey to her before placing the tray on the table in front of her.

Someone had curtseyed to her, Sarah Browne! Feeling very important, she carefully poured the tea then put three lumps of sugar into her cup before stirring it, as she had seen Aunt Patience do. Then she lifted the cup, and pretending she was a great lady, sipped at it. It was delicious, much nicer when there was no one leaning over her waiting for her to make a mistake. The pastry was delicious too, the pastry soft and flaky, each raisin a little explosion of sweetness on her tongue. This was heaven.

One day, she thought, *I will be a great lady. I will wear shiny dresses in beautiful colours, and a big hat with flowers and a feather in it like the lady I saw walking down the street earlier. I will have a big light in my house like this one that makes rainbows, and I will drink tea and eat pastries and people will curtsey to me.*

She sat straight-backed in the chair as she imagined a great lady would until she had finished her tea and pastry, and then she relaxed back, looking eagerly around at what was going on, and in doing so became a child again.

From the corner Arthur Young watched as his little niece both poured and drank the tea with a steady hand, without spilling a drop, as she ate the pastry without dropping a crumb. Her ecstasy was written all over her face, and he was vindicated. She was not clumsy, nor was she an idiot. She was just a very pretty, very neglected little girl, eager to learn and desperate for love, exactly like her mother had been. He smiled sadly to himself. She would receive neither learning nor love from her father. He hoped she would one day find the courage to reject the life that had been planned for her.

Then the next customer came in, and temporarily he forgot about his niece.

Having nothing else to do, Sarah watched as her uncle made his client welcome, listened as he made conversation. She couldn't understand the subject they conversed about, but she saw the young man, who sported a prodigious amount of lace at wrist and throat, relax and smile, nodding approvingly as his new wig was fitted and a mirror produced to show him how fine he looked. She saw that her uncle gave all his attention to the person sitting in front of him, as he had given all his attention to her when he'd shown her round the shop. It had made her feel warm and special, and as she watched the client's satisfied face, she realised he too felt warm and special.

Later another client came in, a stocky red-faced elderly man, and although her uncle talked quite differently to this one, was much more bluff and hearty, he still gave the man his total attention.

That was the gift her uncle had. He could make you feel as though you were the only person in the world, and it seemed to come completely naturally to him. He genuinely cared about his customers, not just because they paid him money, but because he enjoyed making people happy.

She continued to watch the goings on in the shop, the people coming in and out, the serving girl bustling to and fro with trays of refreshments, and the women bent over their work, but still finding time to laugh and joke with each other when there were no customers in the room, and she realised that not only were they all happy, but she was happy too, for the first time since she had come to stay in Chester.

In fact, the only other time she felt that lovely warm bubbly feeling that she was feeling now was when she was alone with Philip down by the stream on Sundays, sitting with him and knowing that whatever she said, he wouldn't laugh at her or mock her. He might tease her, but he would never ridicule her.

Uncle Arthur would never laugh at me or mock me either, she thought. *He's kind, like Philip.* She had expected when she arrived to be put to work cleaning or washing, but as the morning passed and she was asked to do nothing at all, she realised something else; her uncle had brought her to work with him purely because he wanted her company, wanted her to be happy. It was a wonderful, wonderful feeling. Her heart swelled with joy, until she felt she would burst.

And in that moment Sarah fell completely in love with her Uncle Arthur.

In the early afternoon the shop was closed for an hour to allow everyone time to have lunch and a break from work. After he'd locked the door, Uncle Arthur came across to his niece.

"Most of the shops stay open all day," he said, "but I like to go out, and I find my workers do better if they can eat their luncheon without interruption. What do you say we go for a walk, stretch the legs?" he suggested. She agreed and followed him to the door, which he held open for her as though she was important.

Once in the street he turned to the left and walked down to a gate he said was called the Eastgate, where they climbed up some steps and emerged on to the top of the wall. Sarah was hugely relieved. She had expected them to have to balance on the top, and had been terrified at the thought of falling off. But there was a paved walkway set into it, wide enough for two people to walk abreast easily, whilst most of the battlements were low enough that she could see over the top of them, and she observed with interest as her uncle gave her a running commentary on the sights.

"Now this is the cathedral of Chester," he said, pointing to a somewhat neglected-looking red sandstone building to their left. "It was very fine when it was built, but after King Henry dissolved the monasteries it wasn't cared for, and then it was damaged again by the Parliamentary forces. A shame, in my view, but there you are. Times change. Maybe one day someone will care for it again. Ah! Now, this is interesting," he continued as they reached the north-eastern corner, at which was a tower with steps from the wall leading up to it. "This is called the Phoenix Tower, because a tradesman's guild whose emblem was a phoenix used to meet here some years ago– a phoenix is a magical bird," he added, seeing Sarah's puzzled look. "But local people call it King Charles's Tower, because he's said to have stood here in 1645 and watched his army being defeated by Cromwell's. Poor man, what a terrible thing to have to watch. Chester declared for the king, you know." He looked down at his little niece and realised that she had no idea what he was talking about. "Do you know about the king?" he asked gently. "You can tell me if you don't, you know. I won't be angry."

"I know that Christ is the king," she said. "But I don't know who Charles and Henry are, or why they say they're kings, when Christ is the only king and will rule for all eternity."

"Ah. Perc…your father taught you that," Arthur said.

"Yes."

He thought for a minute. It would not do to undermine the child's father. Although…

"Well, I suppose Christ is the king of Heaven, but there are kings here on earth too. Each country has a king or sometimes a queen, and they rule their country. The king in our country now is called George. Nowadays they usually rule with the help of a parcel of rogues called the government, but in the past they ruled by themselves. King Henry, who threw all the monks out of their abbeys, was a very nasty king. And King Charles, who stood here, didn't like his government because they wouldn't do what he wanted. And some people agreed with the king, and some with the government, and then they all had a big fight, lots of big fights about it, and one of the fights was here."

"And he lost," Sarah said. "Like Lucifer, who was cast down from Heaven."

"He did. He won some, but he lost more, and in the end he was captured and had his head cut off. So we didn't have a king at all for a while."

She looked up at the tower, and then over the wall. It was so green and peaceful down there in the fields that she couldn't imagine lots of men all hitting each other because they'd had an argument.

"Why was the king on the tower? Why didn't he go down and fight as well, if it was his argument?" she asked.

"Some kings lead their army in battle," Uncle Arthur replied, "but a lot don't, because it's a terrible thing when they're killed. Kings are very important people."

"But they cut his head off, so he can't have been *that* important," Sarah pointed out.

Arthur let out a huge whoop of laughter.

"Child," he said, bending down to her, his eyes sparkling, "don't ever let anyone tell you you're stupid. You're a very clever girl, and one day will be a very clever woman. And a beautiful one, too."

"When I grow up I want to make wigs, and make people happy like you do," she said on impulse.

"You do, do you?" Uncle Arthur replied. He straightened up again, and looked at his watch. "We must get back. If you want to be a perruquier like me when you grow up, then perhaps you should sit with one of the ladies this afternoon. Maria is very kind. And you can watch what she does, so you know what you will have to do. Because if you want to own your own shop like I do, you have to start by learning the basic things first."

Back at the shop he found a stool, and with the aid of a few cushions ensured that Sarah could see what was going on. Then he bustled off to shave the head of a new customer and take measurements so that a wooden head could be made to the man's exact specifications. Meanwhile Maria showed Sarah how to make the rows of hair that would later be sewn into the base. On the table in front of her was a frame with two vertical poles about eighteen inches apart. Between them were stretched three silk threads, and Sarah watched with fascination as Maria deftly weaved strands of hair through the threads, before pushing them along to the left side of the threads then taking another few strands of hair and repeating the process. As she worked automatically, she chatted to the little girl, telling her about the different kinds of hair used.

"We mainly use human hair," she said, "but sometimes horsehair too, because it's long-lasting, and being a little more coarse, it curls well. Some peruke makers use goats' hair too, but Mr Young won't have it in his shop."

"Why not?" Sarah asked, mesmerised by the flashing fingers, and astounded that the woman could talk whilst performing such a complicated task.

"Goats' hair is very soft to touch, but it's also short, too short to curl properly. But the reason we don't use it is because it becomes brittle and yellow very quickly, and then it looks like what it is – a very cheap wig. This establishment has a very good reputation. Only the very best wigs are made here. Mr Young tells me that you would like to be a wig maker when you grow up," she added, smiling. She had warm brown eyes and skin so soft-looking that Sarah wanted to reach up and touch it. She thought it would feel like rose petals.

"It looks very hard," she said doubtfully. "I don't know if I could do that. Aunt Patience says I'm very clumsy. I broke one of her china dogs."

Maria gave a most unladylike snort, and seemed about to say something, but then changed her mind.

"It's just practice, sweet," she said. "Like everything. It's hard at first, and you'll be very slow, but over time you learn to work quickly, and then you don't really have to think about it any more. If you ask your uncle he might let you try making a row of hair, maybe next week. Would you like that?"

"Oh yes!" Sarah cried. "I would, very much. I don't think it would be so bad if you were watching me instead of—" She stopped quickly, and blushed, aware that she had been about to say a wicked thing about her aunt, who was only trying to help her learn to do her duty, whatever that was. "I don't know if I will be able to come again," she said instead, somewhat sadly. "I have a lot to learn. I have to learn to cook, and to sew, and to clean a house properly. It's very hard to remember everything."

"But surely your aunt and uncle have servants to do that sort of thing?" Maria asked.

"Yes, they do. But when I go back home to Father then I will have to do everything myself, because we are alone – well, Philip is there, he's my brother, but he's working for Mr Bradshaw now. And Father works very hard saving the village from the Devil, and I have to keep the house clean for him. So Aunt Patience is teaching me what I must do. It's very kind of her," Sarah finished.

Maria's eyebrows lifted.

"Kind," she repeated with a tone of deep scepticism. "Well, you must ask your uncle. He certainly *is* kind."

The tall stout man with the fiery red hair and the undernourished child with the warm brown hair walked home together hand-in-hand, the child chatting away excitedly, relating everything Maria had taught her, the man listening with a smile on his face and thinking what a change one single day of kindness had wrought in this otherwise silent, cowed little girl. What a shame she had to go back to her bastard of a father. He continued to listen with half an ear to the happy voice at his elbow, whilst ruminating on possibilities. When they got to the turning into the street where they lived, he stopped.

"I was going to ask you if you've had a good day, but I think I know you have. Now, I have a question for you." He took both Sarah's hands in his and looked down at her. "What do you say to coming to work with me every Friday? And then you can learn more about making wigs. It will help you to decide if you really would like to be a wig maker one day."

"Oh, I would love that!" Sarah said. "But I don't know if Aunt Patience will let me."

"I'm sure she will. I'll talk to her. And I'll tell her that you will be working very hard all day for me. So it might be better if you don't tell her about our walk along the wall. Or about the raisin pastry and tea, for that matter."

Sarah looked up at him with troubled hazel eyes.

"But what if she asks me what I did? I can't tell her a lie, or I'll go to Hell when I die."

Arthur sighed inwardly.

"You don't have to lie. If she asks you what you did, you can tell her that you watched me fit wigs and shave a man's head, and that you sat with one of my workers and watched how to make rows of hair," he suggested. "Because you did do all those things."

Her little brow crinkled.

"But isn't that a lie, if I don't tell her about the walk?" she asked.

"Not at all. That's omission," he said.

The brow crinkled more.

"If your aunt asked you what you did today and you told her that you'd married a handsome prince and had tea with the queen, that would be a lie, because you didn't do any of those things," he explained. Sarah giggled. "But you *did* watch me, and Maria. So you've told the truth. If you miss something out, then that's not a lie. That's omission. It's not the same thing at all, and you can't go to Hell for it."

Sarah considered this gravely for a few moments.

"But what if she asks me if I went for a walk with you?" she asked.

"Trust me, she won't. I'm sure of that," he said. "But if she does, then you must say yes, so that you're telling the truth. Otherwise say nothing, and that's not lying."

Aunt Patience did not ask her if she'd been for a walk. Nor did she ask her what she'd had to eat, so when she said that she hoped Sarah had been kept busy and had had no time to be wicked, she said what her uncle had told her to say, and no more. When Uncle Arthur said that she was going to go to work with him every week, Aunt Patience had been very angry, but when she'd opened her mouth to object, Uncle Arthur had held his hand up and said they would discuss it later.

Lying in bed, for once wide awake, partly through excitement at the novelty of the day, and partly because she had just watched other people, rather than having to work very hard while being watched herself and criticised all day, she wondered if her aunt and uncle were discussing it right now in the room two floors down.

She hoped that she would be able to go to the shop again. Maybe when Philip was a soldier and she lived in a great house, she could wear Mother's beautiful dress and make wigs for rich people. That would be wonderful. And it would be fun to learn from Uncle Arthur and Maria. They were very kind.

She had learnt a lot today. About kings, magical birds, and people having fights, very big fights.

But the most important thing she had learnt was that telling the truth didn't mean telling *everything*. It just meant that what you *did* tell had to be truthful. But missing out things wasn't a lie. It was omi… omish… she must ask Uncle Arthur the word again.

So if her and Philip were in the cellar looking at the lovely things in Mother's trunk and they heard Father come home and ran upstairs, if he asked them what they were doing in the cellar, she could tell him they were checking to see how many potatoes were left or were getting some more wood. And to make that true they just had to actually look at the potatoes or pick up some wood before they looked in the trunk. And then it wouldn't be a lie at all if she didn't tell him about the trunk. And because he didn't know about it, he would never ask, 'were you looking in Mother's trunk?' so she would never have to tell him.

She turned over and pulled the lovely pink eiderdown up over her shoulders.

Omission. That was the word.

She smiled and closed her eyes.

* * *

It seemed that Uncle Arthur and Aunt Patience had discussed it, and that he had won, because the next Friday, and every Friday after that, Sarah went to work with her uncle and spent the whole day in his shop.

She learnt how to weave the hair between the silk threads, at first very badly; most of the hair she'd woven fell out as soon as she pushed it along the row. But Maria was patient, and showed her again, and again, and told her to do it very slowly until she got it right, and after a few weeks she managed to do a whole row of hair by herself. It took her as long to do that as it did for Maria to do about thirty rows, but she was very pleased, and even more pleased when her uncle, after examining it, said it was good enough to be sewn into a wig.

She learnt that the bases for the wigs were made of cotton, silk or linen, and were fitted to the wooden heads, then were wetted, so that when they dried they would shrink to the exact size of the head shape. She learnt about the different colours of hair, which ones were suitable for day wear and which for evening, that if instead of sewing a row of hair onto the wig base, you folded it over itself then sewed it in place, it became a hairpiece, which could be added to a lady's real hair to make it look very thick and beautiful.

The hairpieces could also be soaked in pomade, which was made of sheep's fat, spices and white wine, and which made the hair thick and sticky. Then it could be rolled up and secured to the base with a pin to make the curls at the side of the wig that were so fashionable at the moment.

She learnt how to brush and plait the long hair of the wig at the back, to tie a ribbon beautifully, and about the different colours of scented powder that were puffed all over the finished item when the wearer came to try it for the final time.

She also found out that the ladies could style not only wigs but real hair too, and that Uncle Arthur had no objection to them visiting ladies' houses in the evenings to dress their hair and make some more money; as long as they mentioned his establishment in the process and were not too tired to work efficiently the next day.

And on one beautiful, memorable day, Anna, one of the other women, who had lovely hair the colour of ripe wheat, and who always wore it high off her forehead and curled, sat Sarah down in front of a mirror and styled her hair in the same way, explaining everything she was doing as Sarah watched her reflection, rapt.

"You have beautiful thick hair, child," Anna said as she worked. "When you grow up you will be the envy of all your friends."

"Oh, I don't have any friends," Sarah said matter-of-factly.

"You will have, when you grow up. And you will have lots of admirers too," Anna stated.

Once she was finished Uncle Arthur came to look, and declared that she was the most beautiful little girl in the world. He bowed deeply to her, and asked for the pleasure of my lady's company at lunch, and she blushed prettily and said yes, she would be delighted, although they always spent lunchtime together. It was one of the highlights of her day, walking with her uncle, her small hand engulfed in his large warm one, feeling safe, relaxed and happy as he showed her the sights of his beloved city and expounded on its history.

He treated her as though she was beautiful, and precious, and clever, and she loved him completely, would have died for him gladly. Her time spent with him made the endless days of drudgery in between bearable.

No matter how hard she tried, her aunt was never satisfied with her work. Even when Mrs Lindy said that the pasty Sarah had just made was as good as anything she herself could make, Aunt Patience had sniffed and said no, the pastry was a little heavy.

When she managed to clean the whole drawing room from top to bottom without breaking anything, Aunt Patience had run a finger along every surface and looked at it for signs of dirt. When she had found none, she had commented that the rug was out of place and the fire badly laid in the grate.

From Saturday until Thursday she was ugly, stupid, clumsy and lazy and could not be left alone for a minute lest she fall into wickedness. She could not even pray alone, and when she had performed one of her tasks badly, which happened several times a day, she was rapped soundly on the head or the arm and made to do it again, and was never given a moment to think about what she'd done wrong. It was exhausting, and she missed her brother all the time and even missed her father sometimes.

But on Fridays she was transformed, and became beautiful, clever, nimble-fingered and hard-working, and just on that one day a week she did, as her uncle had predicted, blossom like a flower. And the happiness of that day carried her through the rest of the week.

One day in early October, when Sarah had been in Chester for six months and the leaves were turning the colour of Arthur Young's hair, uncle and niece went for their usual lunchtime walk. But instead of taking her along the wall and telling her the history of some building, or talking about the ships in the port and the cargoes they were carrying, he told her that they were going to do a very daring thing indeed, and that this was most definitely an 'omission' adventure, after which he took her to a coffee shop in the Exchange Building.

Sarah was the only child and the only female in the shop, but the serving man, having been briefed in advance, treated her as though she was a most honoured guest, and showed her and her uncle to a table in a quiet corner. Her uncle ordered coffee for himself and chocolate for her, and while they waited for it to arrive, Sarah looked eagerly around.

In another corner of the room a group of men were sitting around a table which was littered with periodicals, hotly debating some issue. As they were all talking over one another she had no idea what they were saying, but it looked very serious. She turned to her uncle, a little worried.

"Are they going to have a big fight, like the government and King Charles?" she asked.

Her uncle laughed loudly enough that some of the men

stopped debating briefly and looked across.

"No, child," he said. "They're not fighting, they're debating. That's what many men come to coffee houses for. They read the newspapers, and then they debate the great issues of the day, and sometimes the small issues. It's a place where you can learn a great deal. But we are here to have coffee and chocolate, and to talk a little. It's daring because ladies do not frequent coffee houses as a rule."

"Is that because ladies don't learn to read, and so they can't debate the great issues of the day?" she asked.

"Not at all. It's because men sometimes want to get away from the ladies and talk together. Just as ladies want to get away from men sometimes, which is why they have tea parties together. They usually do it at home, though, because the home is the domain of women, and most of them, unless they're poor, don't go out to work, at least not once they're married."

"Aunt Patience had a tea party in the drawing room once," Sarah volunteered.

"Did she? And were you allowed to stay in the room?"

"Yes, but I had to sit in the corner and be silent. It was very boring. They talked about how ugly some other lady who wasn't there was, and that she was no better than she should be. And then one of the ladies, who was very fat with a red nose, started saying that Mr Parr liked a woman who was no better than she should be too, and him married. Then Aunt Patience remembered I was there and sent me to my room to pray, so I didn't hear any more. The woman must have been *very* ugly if she looked worse than the lady with the red nose," Sarah commented.

Uncle Arthur started laughing again, spluttered a lot, went very red, and looked for a time as though he was going to explode.

"Are you ill, Uncle?" Sarah asked, her face a mask of worry.

With some effort, he brought himself under control.

"I am perfectly fine, my dear. You are all the tonic I need. But ladies *do* learn to read, and to write too, and many of them talk about very important issues indeed, far more important issues than who likes ugly women. Did your father tell you that ladies don't learn to read?"

"No. He told me that girls *can't* learn to read. But that was a lie, because Mama could read, and so could Aphra Behn. She wrote poetry." She stopped suddenly and blushed beetroot red. Uncle Arthur seemed about to ask her a question, but then changed his mind.

"She did indeed. And she wrote plays as well. And she was a spy for King Charles too," he said.

"A spy? For the man on the tower?" she asked. "What's a spy?"

"Not for the man on the tower, no. For his son, who was also called Charles. The Dutch were our enemies, and the king wanted to know what they were planning to do, and so Aphra went to Antwerp, which is a Dutch town and pretended to be a friend of the Dutch. And she listened and learnt a great deal, because men will talk in front of women without realising that they are clever enough to know what's going on. And then she came back to England and told the king what they said. And that is what a spy does, listens and learns what the enemy are doing."

"I think she must have been very clever to do all that," Sarah observed.

"She was. And so are you. I wish now that I had taught you to read and write while you were here. But I didn't have the time at the shop, and if I taught you at home I think Aunt Patience would tell your father when he comes for you and he would be angry."

"He would be very angry," she said. "He was very angry when Philip taught me my letters."

"The man is a tyrant," Uncle Arthur said without thinking.

"What's a tyrant?" she asked.

Instead of explaining, her uncle leaned forward, his face earnest.

"Sarah, my dear, I have something I want to say to you. I brought you here because there is no possibility of anyone listening to us as there is in the shop or at home. I think your father will come for you soon – he said he would come when the leaves change, and before he does I want to give you some advice, and I want you to make me a promise. So you must listen and remember."

She nodded, her eyes wide, her face very serious.

"If you have an opportunity to learn to read and write without your father knowing, you must take it. Because if you can read, then you can learn anything you want, not only what other people tell you, and you will learn to think for yourself. I think it's very important that you learn to think for yourself, because you are an intelligent child. I should not tell you to disobey your father, for you must do as he tells you while you are a child, but in this alone I feel you *should* disobey him, if you can. But this is not the promise I want you to make. It is just advice."

She nodded again.

"You have learnt a great deal about hair while you've been with me, and I think you enjoy it."

"Oh I do, very much!" she said.

"Anna tells me you have a talent for dressing hair, that you can see which styles will make a lady look beautiful and which will not. That is a rare thing. When I told you that you can come to work for me if you wish, that was not a joke. When you are a little older, you will realise that many adults tell children all kinds of stories, tell them that they are very good at something when they are not, to make them happy. Your father is not such an adult, and nor is your aunt. But you may come to think that I have told you such stories, just to make you happy, because I am a kind man.

"So I will tell you the truth now. You are a clever child, and a pretty one, and if you wish to come to work for me when you are a little older, I would be delighted. I think of you as the daughter I have not had, and I will always be your friend. If you are ever in need of a friend, I will be here for you. And the promise I want you to make is that you will come to me if you are in need, however many years from now that may be, and I will help you. Will you promise me that?"

She looked at him, and her eyes filled with tears.

"I don't have any friends," she said. "Except Philip of course."

"Well, now you have another friend," her uncle said.

"Are you an omission friend?" she asked.

His mouth smiled, but his eyes were serious.

"Yes, I'm an omission friend. And it's an omission promise too. Will you make it, and remember it?"

She nodded.

"Yes, I will. Can I be your friend, too? So if you need to you can come to me? Although I don't know if Father would let you in. I don't think he likes you very much."

"Of course you can. We are friends to each other. And that makes me very happy."

"It makes me very happy too," she said solemnly.

She lay in bed that night, the only time she had to herself to think, and thought about what her uncle had said, repeating it to herself until she was sure she would remember it forever. It *did* make her very happy to have a friend. A friend was someone you could say anything to, anything at all, someone who loved you and wanted you to be happy, and would help you if they could. Even if you were a Daughter of Eve and were going to Hell.

Philip was her friend, and Uncle Arthur was her friend. She was very lucky to have two friends.

Happiness was a very warm feeling that spread all over your body and made your heart feel all funny, but in a nice way. She wanted to remember that forever too, because she knew that when her father came for her she wouldn't feel happy again until Philip went for a soldier and took her with him.

Maybe he could go to Chester for a soldier, and they could live in a nice house, and she could wear her mother's dress and work for Uncle Arthur. And at night she wouldn't have to go home to Aunt Patience, but could go to her own house. Maybe Uncle Arthur could come and live with her and Philip.

Oh, that would be the most wonderful thing in the world!

She threw back the lovely pink eiderdown and climbed out of bed, then knelt down at the side of it and folded her hands. Then she prayed, harder than she had ever prayed in her life, for God to make that wish come true.

Four days later, while her Uncle Arthur was at work and Aunt Patience was scolding her because her stitches were still not neat enough, because she was a careless and stupid child, her father came for her.

"You have grown," he said accusingly by way of greeting.

While Sarah was trying to think of an appropriate response, Aunt Patience told her father that she had done her best with the child and could do no more, that she was now a passable cook, and could darn and sew well enough for his needs, though she'd never make a seamstress, and that she supposed she was quiet enough in church.

"Have you forgotten your catechism, child?" her father asked, clearly displeased with her already.

"What do you take me for, brother?" Aunt Patience retorted before Sarah could speak. "I have lectured her daily in the word of the Lord. If she has forgotten her catechism, it is no doing of mine, I assure you!"

"What is the misery of that state whereinto man fell?" her father asked her sternly.

"All mankind by their fall lost communion with God, are under his wrath and curse, and so made liable to all the miseries in this life, to death itself, and to the pains of Hell forever," Sarah replied automatically.

"Hmm. Remember that, child," he said. "I will question you more closely on your catechism on the journey home." He eyed her unembellished dark blue silk dress with distaste. "Why is she wearing her Sabbath dress on a weekday?" he asked his sister.

"My husband is a reputable businessman with standing in the community, and I would not have my acquaintance believe my niece to be a pauper, as she appeared when she arrived," Patience stated. "Her dress is perfectly modest and respectable, as befits the daughter of a minister of God. Her Sabbath dress is equally sober, the only decoration being a lace frill around the sleeve."

"A *lace frill?!*" her brother responded, aghast. "Since when were fripperies appropriate for the children of men of God? I hope you have not given her ideas, Patience."

"Only the ones you asked me to give her. And if this is all the thanks I get for months of continual toil, then it's a poor reward indeed. Go and pack your clothes, child."

Sarah packed her clothes, stroked the beautiful pink eiderdown sadly, and then carried the bag downstairs. It was somewhat heavier than it had been when she arrived, containing as it did four dresses, a cloak and two pairs of shoes.

Her father was still standing in the hall where he had been when she'd gone upstairs, but the expressions of both siblings had softened somewhat, in as far as they were no longer scowling at each other, so Sarah supposed Aunt Patience had received her reward for the months of toil.

"Come then, daughter," her father said, "if we are quick we can make the eleven o'clock coach. I will see you next month, sister."

He took her bag from her and set off down the steps. Sarah ran after him, as she had on her arrival, only realising that she had forgotten to say goodbye to her aunt when they were already halfway down the street. In truth she didn't really care about that, but...

"Father," she said breathlessly when he stopped, waiting to cross the road. "Can we go to Uncle Arthur's shop? It is only a little way along the road there. I would very much like to say goodbye to him."

He looked down at her.

"Don't be ridiculous. I will not set foot in any establishment that encourages vanity and pride. While you were packing your bag your aunt told me that your uncle has been taking you to his place of business each week. I am most displeased. I know your aunt has a duty to obey her husband – even such a husband as that. I did warn—" He stopped abruptly, as if suddenly remembering who he was speaking to. "Anyway," he continued after a moment, "I am most unhappy that he has tried to corrupt you, who are so weak-willed anyway. You will forget everything you learnt at that shop and any silly ideas he put into your head, and we will speak no more of it. Do you understand?"

Sarah cast her eyes down at the street.

"Yes, Father," she said meekly.

"Good. I am sure he will be glad to see the back of you. Now hurry. The coach is there. We must be quick if we are to get a seat."

He gripped her elbow and hustled her across the street, and ten minutes later they clattered across the stone bridge over the River Dee, leaving Chester and Sarah's new friend behind. She sat as she had when they had clattered over the bridge in the opposite direction six months before, looking out of the window, and once again the fields melted into a green and gold haze as tears filled her eyes.

She had changed a little outwardly, had grown a little, put on some weight due to the good food, and her clothes were nicer now. Her father could see that. Philip would see that too.

But she had changed inwardly as well, not just because she had learnt to cook and sew, wash clothes properly and clean without breaking things, although they were useful things to know. She had changed because she now had a new friend, who would not be glad to see the back of her, and she was not going to forget him just because her father wanted her to. She had made her uncle a promise, and would keep it if she was in need.

She had changed because she now knew that omission was not lying. That was a very important thing to know.

And above all, she had changed because she now had a dream of her own, which was not Philip's dream, although it included him, as his included her. It would be lovely to see Philip again, who would have missed her, as she had missed him. The next time they were alone, she would tell him about her dream, and he would be pleased for her, because he was her friend.

She had two friends, all of her own. And one of them thought she was pretty, and clever. She would not forget that, either.

CHAPTER FOUR

Summer 1734

Sarah's father didn't mention her birthday, and in fact she would have forgotten it herself if Philip hadn't brought her a present of a handful of strawberries from the farm he was working at. But a few days later the reverend came into the kitchen as she was struggling to carry the heavy pot of hot water from the fire to the wooden half barrel in the corner of the room which she used for washing. A batch of lye balls sat next to it, which she had made a few days previously from nettle ashes and urine, and on the other side a pile of wet clothes which had been soaking overnight in stale urine to bleach them and which it would take her most of the day to wash.

Reverend Browne made no move to help her carry the heavy pot, but waited until she had emptied it into the barrel, wrinkling his nose at the ammoniac smell of the pile of wet linen. Once she had finished she turned to him, eyes cast down respectfully as she'd been taught.

"It has come to my notice that you turned ten this week, daughter," he said.

Sarah glanced up briefly, surprised that he'd remembered, then returned her gaze to the floor.

"Yes, Father," she replied. Was he about to wish her a happy birthday? It would be the first time, if he was.

"I think you are now old enough to take on a new duty. It is an important duty, because as my daughter you will be representing me, and through me the church. Do you feel ready for that?"

She wanted to refuse it, whatever it was; she already worked from dawn till dusk, every day except Sunday. But of course she knew she could not say no.

"If you feel I am ready, Father, I will do my best," she said instead. What could it be? Philip had recently been given the task of reading from the Bible before Father's long sermons, a task he hated, because no matter how much he practised and how well he read, it was not satisfactory. But she couldn't read, and a sinful Daughter of Eve was not fit to touch the Bible anyway.

She stood and waited for her father to tell her what this new duty was, and wondered how she would find time for it.

"Several of my parishioners are in great need of charity," he said. "Although their souls are nourished by attending the service on Sunday, corporeally they are in want. Farmer Bradshaw, being a man who is strong in the Lord, has kindly agreed to provide extra provisions for you to make bread, which you will then take to those in need. You will set aside a morning each week for this task, let us say Wednesday. And you will ask after their health and converse in a caring and dignified manner as befits the daughter of a minister. Do you believe you can behave in such a way?"

Sarah was thunderstruck. Since she had returned from Chester nearly two years ago, she had only been allowed out of the house to fetch water, go to church, or to meet Philip at Mr Bradshaw's farm on days when she needed to help him carry the provisions that constituted Philip's pay for the fourteen hours a day of labour he gave.

"Yes, Father," she replied meekly.

"Well, then. You will start next Wednesday, and we shall see how you get on." He turned and left the room, leaving her fizzing with excitement. Whole days went by without her uttering a word to anyone. It would be wonderful to be able to walk about the village, to talk to someone other than her father, who only spoke to her to criticise or to catechize her, or her brother, who was usually too tired on coming home nowadays to do more than grunt goodnight and go to bed.

It would mean more work; not only would she have to catch up on the tasks she normally did on Wednesdays, but she would also have to find time to bake more bread. And although she was busy all the time except for when she was in the cellar for some misdemeanour, she was so very, very bored with her life. Even though the people she would be visiting would be the sour-faced members of the Sunday congregation, it would be a change. At least she would get to walk through the village on the way there and back. Maybe she would meet some other children her age. Maybe she would make another friend!

* * *

She loved it.

Not the part she had expected to love. The walk through the village was pleasant enough, except on very wet days when her thin cloak did nothing to keep out the elements; but the meeting with the other children part had not been pleasant at all.

She had expected them not to know who she was, and to be as interested in knowing about her as she was in knowing about them. But to her surprise when they had seen her on the first Wednesday making her way along the high street towards the market cross, a heavy basket of food on her arm, they had known exactly who she was. They seemed, for some inexplicable reason, not to like her, which she thought very odd, as she had never spoken to them before.

They had followed her, jeering at her and calling her names as she walked to the market cross and turned right. They had trailed after her until she reached the cottage of the first parishioner she was to visit, after which they had melted away.

She had four women to visit, and had been given their names and directions to their houses by her father. The first two, both elderly widows, Mrs Pearson and Mrs Fenner, took the offered bread, said thank you, and then went in and closed their doors without engaging her in conversation or asking her if she wanted to come in.

Sarah was a bit taken aback by this. Before she'd arrived at their doors she hadn't known who the women were – their names meant nothing to her, although she recognised the whole of her father's congregation by sight. But when Mrs Pearson had opened the door to Sarah's knock, she had recognised the woman immediately as being one of the more friendly-looking of the worshippers. At least she usually hung around outside the little chapel after the service to chat with her fellow parishioners. Sarah had smiled and bobbed a little curtsey, as it was fitting to do to elders, and had held out the bread, saying that she wished her good day and that her father had sent her with some food.

Staring at the firmly closed door, Sarah stood for a moment, bewildered, and then turned away, tucking the cloth round the remaining loaves in her basket. As she walked to the second house she ran through what had happened, trying to work out what she had done to offend the woman, but could think of nothing.

At the second house she had knocked more quietly, and had wished Mrs Fenner a good morning before offering the bread rather than *as* she had offered it. Mrs Fenner seemed even more reluctant to accept the food than her neighbour had been, and had stood muttering at it for a few seconds as though expecting the loaf to respond, before saying, "Thank 'ee, I'm sure," in a contemptuous tone and going in.

Sarah sighed as she carried on up the lane, pursued by the little gang of jeering children, who had magically materialised behind her as she turned onto the track leading up to Mrs Grimes' house on the outskirts of the village. This was going to be even worse than she'd thought. Not only was she not getting to speak to anyone, but she was being insulted by the children she'd hoped to befriend, and would have to spend the rest of the day trying to catch up with her chores.

The gang of children dematerialised again as she arrived outside a somewhat ramshackle cottage, whose door was already open. Having nowhere to knock, Sarah shouted a tentative "Hallo," and then waited for Mrs Grimes, whoever she was, to appear. A few seconds passed and then a voice called, "Come in, then!"

Sarah obeyed, taking a few seconds to adjust to the gloom inside the little cottage, after which she could discern the shape of a woman bundled in clothes sitting by the empty hearth.

"Hello, Mrs Grimes," she said, bobbing a curtsey. "My father sent me to ask if—"

"Wants to know why I wasn't in chapel last week, does he?" Mrs Grimes interrupted.

Did he? He hadn't said anything about that.

"I don't know," Sarah answered truthfully. "He told me to bring you some bread. I baked it this morning, so it's very fresh."

THE WHORE'S TALE: SARAH

She dipped in the basket and held out the loaf.

Instead of looking at the offered food, Mrs Grimes observed Sarah.

"You baked it?" she said. "You don't look strong enough to knead dough. You're a tiny slip of a thing."

"I'm stronger than I look, Mrs Grimes," Sarah said. "I've butter too, and some apples."

"Make the butter as well, did you?" she asked.

"No," Sarah replied. "I don't know how to make butter. Farmer Bradshaw made that."

"Or his wife, more likely," Mrs Grimes said. "Here, get a knife and cut us both a slice, and I'll tell you what I think."

Sarah did as instructed, although she hesitated over cutting herself a piece.

"I brought it for you," she said. "I've had some this morning."

"Hmm, not bad," Mrs Grimes said through a mouthful of food. "Don't be silly, girl. You need feeding up. There's nothing of you. And sit down."

Sarah sat down gingerly on the edge of the chair and observed her host from the corner of her eye. She had wispy grey hair, lots of wrinkles all over her face, not just round the eyes and on the forehead, and a big wart on the side of her nose. Sarah remembered her and Philip once discussing whether she was a witch, and Philip saying that if she was she would have burned to a crisp when Father looked at her.

Sarah turned her attention to the room. Although small and sparsely furnished, the cottage had clearly been looked after at one time, and there had been some attempts to make it homely. The stone walls had been whitewashed, crocheted lace runners decorated the shelves which held the tableware, and a picture of a very grand-looking man in a lot of heavy robes was hung over the fireplace. But everything was covered in dust, the paint was peeling off the wall in places, and the front door listed on its hinges. It was cold, too.

"Do you know who that is?" Mrs Grimes asked on seeing Sarah's gaze settle on the picture.

"No," Sarah said. The old lady was a widow, which meant her husband was dead. "Is he your husband?" she asked.

Mrs Grimes laughed so much, and went so red, that Sarah was

worried she was going to have an apoplexy and die. Her father would be very angry if she killed one of his parishioners. She watched in alarm until the woman's laughter died down and her face faded from beetroot to scarlet.

"Bless you, child, no," she said. "If he was I wouldn't be living here, accepting bread from your father, that's for certain. No, that's the king. My son brought me that picture the last time he visited me."

Sarah personally thought her son would have done better to bring her some wood for the fire, or to have painted the walls, but it didn't do to insult your host's family.

"King George," she said instead.

"That's right. You have heard of him, then," Mrs Grimes said.

"My uncle told me about him, and about King Henry and King Charles too," Sarah commented. "But I've never seen him. He looks very grand."

"Hmm, well. He brightens up the room, anyway."

"Would you like me to clean the room a little for you, and light a fire?" Sarah asked, then blushed, realising that it sounded like a criticism of the old lady's housekeeping skills. "Oh, I didn't mean—"

"No, I know what you meant. Yes, that would be very kind, if you have the time. My legs aren't as strong as they used to be, and I get these dizzy spells. That's why I wasn't at church on Sunday. Tell your father that."

Sarah set to work, relieved to have something to do. She didn't really know how to make conversation, she realised, had no idea what to talk to the old lady about, now she'd finally been invited into a house. But she knew how to make a house tidy, and Mrs Grimes would probably appreciate that more than making stilted conversation with a little girl.

While she worked Mrs Grimes chatted away, telling her about her life. She'd been married young, she said, to a stonemason, and they'd moved into this cottage.

"Over fifty years I've lived here," she told her, "and six children I birthed in that bed upstairs, and only one left to me."

"What happened to the others?" Sarah asked. She'd brushed all the cobwebs and dust down from the corners and surfaces and was now sweeping them into a pile by the doorway.

"They died," Mrs Grimes said flatly. "Not one of them reached five, except Robert. But he's a fine young man, and he's done well for himself. He sells haberdashery in Liverpool. His father was a handsome man and my Robert takes after him."

Sarah listened with half an ear as Mrs Grimes talked about her son, of whom she was clearly very proud. Sarah wondered why her son left her to live in a rundown cottage if he was doing well for himself, but thought it would be rude to ask. So instead she said nothing, and let the old lady ramble on.

"Would you like me to light a fire for you before I go?" Sarah asked after she'd finished dusting and sweeping.

Mrs Grimes looked around the room, which looked much brighter now Sarah had washed the two little windows and had cleaned as best she could. Her rheumy grey eyes filled with tears.

"Bless you, child, Sarah is it? You have a very kind heart," she said. "Yes, I would like that."

As Sarah walked to the final house, in peace this time as the gang of children had clearly got bored of waiting for her and had found something else to do, she realised that she was not the only person who didn't speak to anyone else for days. Mrs Grimes was far worse off than she was, being very old *and* lonely. At least she had Philip, even if she did only see him for a few minutes a day during the week. At least they still had their precious hour after Sunday service together. And her father, of course. She had him, too.

* * *

They sat by the stream, their feet dabbling in the water, their boots and stockings next to them on the grassy bank. It was very hot.

"What's a sorner?" Sarah asked suddenly.

Philip, who had been lying back on the sloping bank, his hands behind his head, looking up at the cloudless blue sky, sat up.

"Where did you hear that?" he asked.

She told him about the small gang of children who'd trailed after her to the first three houses she'd visited last Wednesday, laughing at her and calling her names.

"I knew most of the words, but I don't know what a sorner is," she said. "I didn't want to ask Father in case it was a bad word and he got angry with me. Anyway, they didn't say *I* was a sorner. They said Father was."

Philip didn't question why their father should get angry with her rather than with the boy who'd insulted him. It was just the way of things, and they both accepted it.

"A sorner is someone who lives off other people," he replied. "Like a beggar, except you can be rich."

She was none the wiser.

"How can you be a beggar, if you're rich?" she asked.

"Mr Bradshaw says that the king is a sorner, because he gets the money he lives on from farmers like him who have to pay taxes and duty on goods, so he can live in a palace. The boy who said that, was he ugly, with hair that stuck out all over the place like straw?"

"Yes!" Sarah said. "How do you know?"

"Because Mr Bradshaw's wife is a Scotchwoman, and sorner is a Scotch word. That's probably why you didn't know it. That'll be Simon Bradshaw who said that. I'll have a word with him tomorrow."

"No, don't do that," Sarah said. "I don't want you to get in trouble with Mr Bradshaw. It doesn't bother me. Names can't hurt me, and they didn't do anything else to me."

Philip looked somewhat relieved at this, and lay back again.

"I won't if you don't want me to," he said.

"But Father's not a sorner, is he?" Sarah said. "He works very hard saving the village from the Devil."

Philip raised one eyebrow.

"Maybe. But you don't get paid for being a dissenting minister like Father is. Mr Bradshaw says he gets his money from his brother, and that if he didn't, he wouldn't be able to survive. That's why he goes to Chester every month, to visit our uncle."

"Mr Bradshaw told you that?"

"Well, no, he didn't know I could hear, but I was outside weeding the herb patch when he was talking to Mrs Bradshaw, and the window was open."

"But Uncle Arthur doesn't like Father," Sarah said. "I don't think he'd give him money."

"Not Uncle Arthur. He isn't Father's brother. Uncle John."

"Uncle John? Aunt Patience never mentioned him. I didn't know we had an Uncle John."

"Neither did I. I thought Father just had a sister. But if Uncle

John is as miserable as Aunt Patience, I don't want to know him."

In spite of herself, Sarah giggled.

"I wonder why he's called John?" she said. "Aunt Patience didn't think much of our names. She thought we should be called after virtues. I would think he'd be called Tolerance Browne or something like that, not John."

"Or Angry Browne," Philip suggested. "If he's like Father. Father's always angry about something."

"Anger isn't a virtue," Sarah pointed out.

"Father seems to think it is."

"Sorner Browne," Sarah mused.

"No, that would be Father's name. Or Heartless Browne."

Sarah's mouth opened in shock and she looked around as though expecting their father to be hiding behind a tree, listening. It didn't seem right to talk about Father like that. It was sinful.

"Mrs Grimes was very lonely," Sarah said, by way of changing the subject. "She's only got one son, but he lives a long way away. She was nice. So was Mrs Peterson. When I got there I expected her to be very old like the others, but she wasn't *that* old. She is a widow, though, but her husband was a miner and he died when a big rock fell on him underground. She's got lots of children. It was very noisy in her house."

It had been, very noisy and very messy. And Mrs Peterson had looked very tired and pale. But she had been happy to get the bread, and had asked Sarah if she'd like a cup of small ale. She had seemed lonely too, in spite of all her children, but Sarah had spent so much time at Mrs Grimes' cleaning that she couldn't stay for long, or she wouldn't have been able to cook her father's meal and have it ready on time for when he came out of his study at four o'clock.

She looked up at the sky, reading the time from the sun's position.

"We need to go back. Father will be angry otherwise," she said.

"I might not be working for Bradshaw for much longer," Philip announced as they dried their feet with their stockings before putting them on.

"Really? But you can't go for a soldier at twelve, can you?"

"Nearly thirteen," Philip pointed out with some pride. "No, of course not. Mr Stanhope said I can start with him after my birthday next month."

"Do you want to?"

"Yes. It'll be better than working on the farm. I get all the horrible jobs, and it's really hard work. All I seem to do is work and sleep. When I get home I'm too tired to do anything. And when it's raining I'm wet all day, and cold. At least with Mr Stanhope I'll be dry. And I think he's kinder than Mr Bradshaw."

"You'll still have to work very long hours though," Sarah said. "And will Mr Bradshaw still send provisions for us?"

"I don't think so," Philip said. "But I'm sure the Lord will provide, as Father always says. Or if he doesn't, Uncle John probably will."

* * *

The new routine slotted into her week, and by cutting back on doing things Father didn't notice anyway, like cleaning the windows every two weeks instead of one, and the inside of the cupboards less frequently, she managed to pull back the time without too much trouble. After the third week of Mrs Pearson and Mrs Fenner accepting the bread and then just going in, Sarah had realised that it wasn't not liking her that made them rude; it was embarrassment at having to accept charity. After that she had felt better, and had tried to make it as non-humiliating as possible for them, by having a friendly attitude with no condescension in it. At church on Sunday she didn't acknowledge any of the charity cases, so no one would wonder why she was being friendly to them. She didn't know whether any of them realised what she was doing until Eleanor brought it up one day.

Eleanor was the woman with the six children, who had asked Sarah specifically to call her by her first name, as no one had ever used it since her husband died. Sarah said Eleanor was a lovely name and that it was a shame no one used it.

"When I was a girl everyone called me Nelly," Eleanor said as she half-heartedly swept the floor while Sarah made up the fire. "I thought that was my name until I got married and the minister called me Eleanor. I didn't know who he was talking to!"

"Was it Father who married you?" Sarah asked.

"No. I was Anglican. We got married in a lovely church, with stained glass windows and flowers. James didn't like it, but I told him it was my wedding and that I would obey him from then on and go to his church, but for that day I wanted my way. I got it, too," she said. "It was a lovely day. Worth fighting for. I haven't had many lovely days since then, so I'm glad I have that to remember."

"They have flowers in churches?" Sarah said.

"In Anglican churches, yes. Of course, you won't have been to one! The church at the other end of the village is opening up again. Did you know that?" Eleanor asked.

"No," Sarah said. She didn't even know there *was* another church in the village, open or shut! Could you have more than one church in a village? Were there enough people to fill two churches?

"Oh. I thought that was maybe why you were bringing me bread, hoping to keep me coming to your church instead of going to the other one. It's kind of you not to single me out on Sunday. Everyone would talk if you did."

"I'm bringing you bread because my father told me to," Sarah said. "He didn't tell me why he wanted me to bring it. But I like coming to see you. Will you go to the other church?"

"I don't know yet," Eleanor said. "I go to your church because it reminds me of when James was alive, and I'd feel as though I was betraying him if I stopped, somehow. But I miss the flowers and the singing. I always used to feel uplifted when I'd been to church as a child, instead of—"

She stopped abruptly and blushed scarlet, and Sarah realised Eleanor had been about to say that her church was boring or miserable, and that she felt ungrateful, because the boring miserable minister was providing food for her. Was that why her father had sent her to visit these women? She could hardly ask him.

"Don't feel bad. It's not my church," Sarah pointed out, "it's my father's. You have lovely hair. Would you like me to make it beautiful for you?"

She had spoken on impulse, to take Eleanor's mind off her *faux pas* and to make her happy. But half an hour later, the two of them on Eleanor's bed, Sarah kneeling behind the older woman trying to dress her hair as elaborately as she could with no tools other than a brush, a comb, two red ribbons and a good imagination, Sarah realised that not only was Eleanor relaxed and happy, but she was too.

This is what I want to do, she thought, as she plaited the woman's thick blonde hair in a crown around her head, weaving the scarlet ribbon through it as she went. She had never seen this style before. It was not fashionable and none of the women at Uncle Arthur's wig shop had taught it to her, although they had taught her to plait and weave ribbons. But she just knew that Eleanor's heavy hair would look beautiful on top of her head like a crown. And it would be practical too, would keep it out of her way as she tended her children.

When she had finished, she felt accomplished, and nodded as she tucked the odd stray hair into place. What a pity Eleanor couldn't see it.

"It feels strange," Eleanor said. "What does it look like?"

"It looks like a golden crown, and the ribbon looks like rubies," Sarah said. "You look like a princess, and it makes your neck look long too."

"Oh!" Eleanor said, her eyes sparkling. "It sounds wonderful!"

"Next week I'll do it again, if you want," Sarah said. "And I'll bring a mirror with me, so you can see it." There was a mirror in her mother's chest, Sarah remembered. It would be nice for Eleanor to see how lovely she looked. It would cheer her, and that was worth more than a loaf of bread. Although her father wouldn't see it that way if he found out.

"Don't tell Father that I dressed your hair," Sarah blurted out.

"Oh, no. He wouldn't approve, I'm sure. I won't say anything," Eleanor promised her.

It was strange having a secret with someone you weren't sure you could trust. She had never had that before. She could tell Philip anything, she knew that, and he would never tell Father. She could trust him completely, with anything at all. She could trust Uncle Arthur too. He was her friend.

But she wasn't sure about Eleanor, so instead of feeling happy and relaxed like she did when she'd shared a secret with Philip, she felt anxious. If Father found out, he'd be very angry. He had told her to forget everything she'd learnt at Uncle Arthur's shop, and she'd agreed to. But she hadn't *promised* to. And she could say that she thought he'd want her to do whatever she could to make life better for the women she was visiting.

He had told her that she would be representing him and the

church. He would hardly encourage a woman to be vain of her appearance, no matter how happy it made her.

Oh God.

She went down to the stream. Philip wasn't there and it wasn't the normal place, but it was on the way to Mrs Grimes, and Sarah thought that a few minutes listening to the river would calm her down a little, and then she could concentrate on the old lady without thinking about her own problems. She sat for a few minutes with her feet in the stream, listening to the cheerful burble of the water as it passed over the rocks. It was a lovely rhythmic sound, and it soothed her.

She'd been there for no more than five minutes when something thumped her in the back, making her gasp with pain and shocking her out of her reverie. She turned round. Just behind her was a smooth round stone, presumably the one that had hit her in the back, and a few steps away was the crowd of pasty-faced, taunting children who had followed her around for the last weeks.

She had actually grown accustomed to their taunts now and hardly noticed them at all as she walked to the various houses. She assumed that if she ignored them, sooner or later they'd find something else to do. She had no idea why they didn't like her, but she found, to her surprise, that she didn't really care. This was the first time, though, that they had physically attacked her.

They stood behind her in a little group, laughing and egging each other on to do something else. The leader of the group was the straw-haired boy that Philip had said was his employer's son. He was the tallest of them, taller than Sarah by nearly a head, and he always led them.

When she had been in Chester, so long ago now that it felt almost like a dream, her and Uncle Arthur had gone outside the walls of the town one day to see the big ships as he'd promised they would. On the way back to Eastgate they had walked along St John's Lane outside the walls and had been followed by a pack of wild starving dogs. They had kept their distance but had barked at them and Sarah had been afraid, wanting to run away. Her uncle had told her that that was the last thing you should ever do with a pack of dogs, because if you did, their hunting instinct would rise, and they would chase you and kill you if they could when they caught you.

"The best thing you can do with dogs like this is to ignore them," he said to her, "unless they get too close, close enough to really threaten you. Then you should stand up to them, make yourself look as large as you can and attack the biggest one, the one who is the leader. Hit him with your stick if you have one, or throw something at him if you haven't. Never run away and let them see you're afraid. A lot of people are like those dogs," he'd told her. "Watch."

On saying that he'd lifted his stick and had suddenly run at the dogs. They'd hesitated for a moment, then they'd scattered. Uncle Arthur had come back to her, somewhat breathless but laughing. "If they feel they have to be in a group to attack you, then as individuals they are afraid of you. Always remember that," he'd said to her.

She remembered it now, and stood up. She didn't have a stick, but she did have the stone that one of them had hit her with. She took aim and threw, and it sailed neatly over the head of the Bradshaw boy, who laughed at her, causing all the others to laugh, too.

With no stick and nothing to throw, she ran at the group, the rage rising in her at them attacking her for no reason damping down the fear she'd normally have felt. Unlike the dogs though, the children didn't run away, so when she got close to the straw-haired boy she drew back her fist and threw it forward, hitting him straight on the chin with all her strength and forward motion. The shock of the blow ran up her arm, numbing it for now, although she knew it would hurt later when the feeling came back.

Simon Bradshaw went down on the ground as though poleaxed, and for one impossibly long moment all the children, Sarah included, stared at his still figure spread out on the grass. And then Sarah raised her head and looked at them all.

"Leave me alone," she said authoritatively, and they stared at her now for a moment, before pulling back and slinking away, leaving her with her prone victim. She looked down at him. Was he dead? Surely not. You couldn't kill someone by hitting them on the chin, could you? If she had killed the Bradshaw boy then she would be hung. If you murdered someone you were hung, and then after you were hung you went to Hell.

She didn't care about going to Hell. She had always known she was going there, because she was a Daughter of Eve and her father told her regularly that he didn't believe she was one of the elect, even if she was his daughter. And he should know, being a minister. But she did care about being hung. It sounded like a horrible way to die.

She bent down to the Bradshaw boy and as soon as she did she could see his chest moving up and down and knew he was breathing, so he couldn't be dead. So she got up, went back to the river and put her shoes on, then carried on to Mrs Grimes, because she didn't know how to wake him up, but when he did wake up on his own he'd probably be alright anyway, and it would be better if she wasn't there because if she was he'd probably hit her back.

On the way home after the visit to Mrs Grimes, it occurred to Sarah that she'd now done two things in one day that were hardly representative of the way a minister or his daughter should behave. Encouraging woman's vanity, which St Peter had said not to do and which was *exactly* what she'd done to Eleanor, and now brawling with another child in front of half the children of the village. Hardly the actions a minister would be proud to hear about his daughter performing.

Oh, well. There was nothing she could do about it now. Father would almost certainly hear about her hitting Simon Bradshaw; but at least she'd had a good reason for doing it, if Father would give her the chance to explain once he found out. She just hoped Philip wouldn't lose his job because of it.

She waited.

Over the next week, every time her father came into the room unexpectedly with a disapproving expression on his face her heart sank, expecting that he was going to punish her for hitting Simon Bradshaw and tell her she was not fit to visit his parishioners. She wasn't really bothered about the punishment, or about her father's disapproval, as both of those things were so constant and out of her control that they were just an unpleasant part of her life that she accepted. But she didn't want to be stopped from visiting the parishioners. She enjoyed it, and it broke up an otherwise hard and boring week.

On Sunday she asked Philip if Mr or Mrs Bradshaw had said anything about her hitting Simon. The news came completely out of the blue to him, so she knew Simon hadn't said anything. Philip had told her that Simon was a bully, and the admiration in his eyes when she told him what she'd done made her heart swell with pride. He said he would give anything to have been there and seen it for himself, but then she pointed out that if he had he would have been the one hitting Simon Bradshaw on the chin, not her. And he agreed, but said that he was amazed she'd had the courage to just go and hit him like that.

By the next Wednesday she'd realised that for some reason none of the children had told their parents what had happened by the river. No doubt they were waiting to get her on her way to the women. With that thought in mind, she took a stick with her, and underneath the warm loaves of bread she placed some stones, in case she needed to defend herself.

But to her surprise the children were nowhere to be seen. It was the first week that she'd been able to travel to all four of the ladies without being insulted, and it was lovely! Maybe Uncle Arthur was right. Maybe as individuals they *were* afraid of her, and that was why they hadn't told their parents that she'd hit Simon. She should have hit him on the first week! If she had she wouldn't have had to listen to all their nasty insults for weeks on end as she had done.

When she got to Eleanor's, the woman asked if she'd do her hair for her again, as it had stayed up for two days out of the way, and when it had finally fallen down and she'd brushed it out it had been lovely and wavy, and she'd felt like a princess in a fairy story.

Sarah said she'd never heard a fairy story, so while they sat on the bed and Sarah plaited Eleanor's hair, Eleanor told her the story of Cendrillon, a girl who was badly treated by her stepsisters, but who went to a ball with the aid of magic and met a handsome prince who fell in love with her, and later found her through a shoe that she'd lost, and then they got married and lived happily ever after.

"I suppose it would be nice to be married if you had lots of money," Sarah said, looking around Eleanor's shabby cottage and thinking how awful it must be to try to look after all those children. She found it hard enough cleaning for her father and brother. "But I don't think I want to get married to someone poor."

THE WHORE'S TALE: SARAH

"You'll change your mind when you're older and fall in love," Eleanor said. "And anyway, what would you do if you didn't get married? You'd have to stay with your father for the rest of your life."

"I want to make wigs and dress hair, and look after myself," Sarah said without thinking.

"You are a funny child," Eleanor said. "Don't you want to fall in love and have children?"

"Not really, no," Sarah replied. "Are you glad you got married and had children?"

"Of course I am," Eleanor said. "What else could I do anyway? It's what women do. Men go to work, and women have children and stay at home and look after the house and the babies."

Sarah just stopped herself from saying that Eleanor didn't seem very happy, realising that would be rude. She'd never thought about what women did before. It was true, though, all the women she visited had got married and looked after their husbands and children. None of them seemed very happy, though.

But the women in her uncle's shop hadn't. They were working. And they laughed, and seemed happy. She wished now that she'd asked them if they were married with children, or if they were single and had their own houses to live in. Maybe if you lived in a big town like Chester you could do what you wanted, even if you were a woman. Anyway, she was going to live with her brother and make wigs while he went off and fought in battles and things. But she couldn't tell Eleanor that, because it was a secret.

"Do you know any more fairy stories?" she asked instead.

* * *

After a week of constantly watching her father, she now relaxed, and so she was completely unprepared for the sudden smack round the head which sent her flying from the stool she was sitting on peeling potatoes in the kitchen.

"'Whose adorning let it not be that outward adorning of plaiting the hair,'" her father quoted down to her as she lay on the floor surrounded by potatoes. "Go into the cellar and pray, and think about whether you have behaved in the way suitable for a minister's daughter when going about God's work."

She sat on the bottom step in the cellar, in the dark which

didn't bother her any more because she no longer believed in monsters, and knew who the monster Philip had referred to was, and he certainly wasn't in the cellar because he had just shut her down here. She did not think about whether she'd behaved in the way suitable for a minister's daughter. She didn't need to think about that, because she knew she hadn't. So instead she thought about why the children hadn't told their parents about her hitting Simon Bradshaw, even though they didn't like her, were her enemies, and had no reason to protect her from her father. Whereas Eleanor Peterson, who was a woman grown, not her enemy, and had known she would get into trouble if her father knew, had still told him that Sarah had plaited her hair for her.

People were strange. You did kind things for them and they got you into trouble. You did nasty things to them and they protected you. Family were sometimes nice to you, like Philip and Uncle Arthur, and sometimes nasty to you, like Father and Aunt Patience.

When she came out of the cellar after two days, she told her father the truth, that she realised she had not behaved in a fitting way for a minister's daughter, and that she would not encourage vanity or any other sins in any of his parishioners if she was allowed to continue visiting them. She had realised those things before she'd been sent down the cellar, although that part was omission.

It was also omission that she had realised that people were, in general, no matter how kind they seemed to be, not to be trusted, because they behaved in strange ways for no good reason that she could fathom out. She could trust Philip, and Uncle Arthur, and herself, but no one else.

To her surprise, she was allowed to continue visiting, although Eleanor was taken off her list and was replaced by an old woman who had almost no hair and who seemed hardly aware that Sarah was in the room at all when she was there. She would sit and mutter to herself, and pick at the blanket over her knee as though it was covered with bugs, although it wasn't. Sarah cleaned and chatted brightly to the old lady, receiving no replies to her conversation. And she missed Eleanor and her fairy stories, but most of all she missed her heavy, thick hair, the feel of it as it ran through her fingers, and as she plaited it into a beautiful golden crown.

CHAPTER FIVE

Alliston, Spring, 1735

The man stood, as was usual for him on the first Wednesday of the month, on the steps of the market cross. Surrounding him, as was also usual, was a crowd of children, including the children who had the previous year taunted Sarah, and a few adults.

Sarah didn't know who the man was, had only seen him three or four times before, but she knew that he told interesting stories, stories that made the other children laugh. Stories that made them come out to listen to him, and made them stay when they did, even if it started raining, as it was now about to do.

Sarah was not like the other children of the village. She knew that now, but she didn't understand why. She had two arms and two legs like every other child, and she certainly wanted to be like them, wanted to fit in and have them as her friends. She had secretly hoped that when she stood up to the big boy Simon, they would respect her and like her, and if they had she would have befriended them, regardless of the nasty things they'd said about her and her father. But they hadn't. The taunting had stopped but now they just ignored her, kept away even. The adults she met treated her respectfully but there was no warmth in their eyes when they saw her, and no welcome in their voices when they spoke to her.

Except for Mrs Grimes. She was the only person of the four she visited who laughed and joked with her. Eleanor had, of course, but Sarah didn't visit Eleanor any more. When Eleanor had seen her in the street a few weeks after her father had found out about the hairdressing, she had asked why she didn't visit any more, and Sarah had told her.

"I didn't tell your father!" Eleanor had protested.

"No, but you must have told someone else who did, because there's no other way he could have known that I dressed your hair," Sarah had pointed out.

Eleanor had blushed then, and Sarah knew she had told one of the gossips. She didn't blame her, not any more. No doubt someone had seen her hairstyle and complimented her on it, and without thinking she had said the minister's daughter had done it for her. She could tell by Eleanor's expression that there had been no malicious intent in her breaking of the confidence, so every week she baked an extra loaf and gave it to the young woman. If her father found out and chastised her for that, she would say that Eleanor was no less needy than she had been before Sarah was forbidden to see her, and it wasn't her fault that Sarah had not behaved appropriately.

She stood now, a little back from the crowd surrounding the man on the market cross, and listened to his story. He was telling the children about something someone had told a man called Nicodemus. The person had told Nicodemus that God so loved the world that He gave His only begotten son, that whoever believed in Him should not perish, but would have everlasting life. That He sent His son into the world not to condemn people, but so that the world might be saved.

"For you must remember that God loves *all* of us," the storyteller said. "He doesn't care if we're rich or poor. He cares only about what we do, and if we do bad things, then He is sad, and He hopes that we might change and turn to Him. And if we do, He is our father in Heaven, and like our father on earth He will always forgive us, and give us another chance, if He knows that we are sincere in our wish to give up sinfulness. He loves us so much that He sent His only son down to us, to show us how to be close to Him, in the hope that we will all turn to Him."

Sarah wondered who had told Nicodemus that whoever believed in God would have everlasting life. Because if it was someone who knew what they were talking about, then maybe they would have said something about Daughters of Eve, and why God didn't want them to be elect and to go to Him, why He didn't love them, if He loved the rest of the world so much. She decided to wait and see if she could catch the man on his own. Because it was probably a stupid question, and she didn't want everyone to laugh at her when she asked it. She didn't think the man would laugh, because he had a very kind face. He wasn't handsome at all; he had a bulbous nose and heavy eyebrows, but he had kind eyes with lots of crows' feet around them because he laughed a lot. His face was warm, lived-in.

Colin Baxter saw the child from the corner of his eye, standing to the side and away from the others who were listening to him. He'd seen her a few times now, only on Wednesdays and always alone. Although she was dressed cleanly, and her clothes, though old and mended, were neither dirty nor ragged, she had a beaten, hunted look about her that he'd seen before and that he hated seeing in children, because he knew what it generally meant.

Normally she listened for a few minutes then went on her way, but today she waited.

"And," he continued, addressing his words if not his looks or actions to her, "Jesus loved children especially. So you are all very lucky, you are closer to God than I am, because you have not lived in this sinful world for as long, and have had less time to become corrupted by it! If you remember that, then you can make a good start to be saved now! Jesus once said to His disciples, 'Suffer the little children to come unto me, and forbid them not; for of such is the Kingdom of Heaven,' and 'except ye be converted, and become as little children, ye shall not enter into the Kingdom of Heaven'. So you see, you must set a good example for us adults to follow."

She was still there. He started winding down his story, hoping the others would leave, because it seemed clear now that she was hoping to get him alone. It suddenly seemed very important to him to talk to this little outcast, without drawing attention to her. Finally everyone moved on, but she still kept her distance, hesitant. He had the feeling that if he looked at her she would bolt, like a wild animal. So he waited for a few minutes, and then he sat on the step with his back against the cross and looked up the street away from her.

"Did you wish to ask me something, child?" he said softly to the empty air. He felt rather than saw her move closer.

"Who was it who told Nicodemus that God loved *everyone*?" she asked softly, her voice coming from just behind him. Still he didn't look back.

"Why, child, it was Jesus Christ himself who told Nicodemus that," Colin said. "You know who Jesus Christ is?" He had never seen her in church, had never seen her anywhere except on Wednesdays near the market cross.

"Yes," she said, and seemed about to say more, then hesitated. "So Jesus said that everyone can be saved if we believe in Him. Everyone?"

"Yes, everyone, of course. God made all of us. Why would He not want all of us to be saved?"

Silence.

"Even Daughters of Eve? Are we not all reprobate?"

Ah. She was a daughter of one of the dissenters, then. He needed to be careful here.

"Well, it is not what Christ teaches us in the Bible, and that is all that I can know from. Because the Bible is the word of God."

"Last time I saw you, you told the children about the parable of the sower, and about where the seed fell, and that it made a difference to how well we can listen to God's word," the child said. "And Jesus also talked about the tares that grew among the wheat, and that they were all allowed to grow together, but when they were harvested, the tares were burnt and the wheat kept. Is that not Jesus telling us that the Daughters of Eve are the tares?"

Colin Baxter sighed.

"It is not what I hear Jesus telling us, no," he said. "And I can only speak of what I believe. He states only that the tares were planted by the enemy; but He does not specify who the tares are. It is not for me to say who are the tares, that is for God to say. But if you listen to the word of God and understand it, then you are not a tare."

He had never been good at being careful. There came a silence behind him that went on for so long that he thought she'd walked quietly away without him hearing her, so that when she spoke again and her voice was right behind him, he jumped.

"Does Jesus really not say who the tares are?" she asked.

"He says that the tares are the children of the wicked one, and that the son of man shall send forth His angels and they shall gather out of His kingdom all things that offend, and them which do iniquity."

"But the Daughters of Eve have offended, haven't they?"

"Are your parents dissenters, child?" he asked directly.

"I don't know what my mother was," the girl answered. "She's dead. My father is…I don't know if he is."

"But your father taught you about the Daughters of Eve?"

"Yes."

"Then I cannot speak against your father," Colin said. "I can only say what my understanding of God's word is."

"And in your understanding the tares are not the Daughters of Eve?"

"In my understanding, no. Eve offended God, but so did Adam. They were both punished for their transgression, and we are still being punished, all of us, for that, because we are tempted by sin, and we must grow old and die. But if we resist sin, then we can all be saved, through the intercession of Jesus Christ, who died that we might all be saved. That is my understanding. If your father is a dissenter, then he may have a different understanding."

"Thank you," she said, very softly. Now she was going to go. She was curious to know about Jesus. She was desperate to be saved. He must let her go, or he would have an angry father on his doorstep.

It was his job to save people.

"Have you ever rung a church bell?" he asked suddenly.

"No," she said. He took a chance now, and turned round. She had moved away, was leaving, but now stopped. Over her arm she had a basket covered with a cloth.

"My daughter normally rings the bell at church for me, to tell my parishioners who have no clock that it is time for my service on Sundays. But she has hurt her back, so now I have to do it myself. I wondered if you would perhaps like to come and ring the bell one Sunday for me. Then you could, if you want, come to the church and hear more about Jesus."

He saw her face light up when he talked about her ringing the bell for him, and the momentary smile transformed her features, made her beautiful, radiant. And then he saw the deadness creep back into her face, and his heart twisted. He loved children, and this one was very wounded.

"I am going home to lunch now," he suggested. "If you're not busy, you're very welcome to have lunch with my family. Then you could meet my daughter, Angela. I think she would like to meet another child. She cannot run about because of her back, and she is a little lonely. I think you are about the same age. She is nine."

"I'm eleven," the child said, slightly defensively. "Well, I will be, next month."

"And Angela is almost ten. So you are not so far apart in age," he said. "You can decide. If you're busy now, then you can come any time you wish. The invitation is open."

Instead of answering him the child looked up High Street ahead of them, then turned and looked along Church Street, peering into the distance.

"Where do you live?" she asked.

"I live at the end of the street along there," he said, pointing. "In the house next to the church."

"Let's go now, then," she answered urgently.

* * *

Before they went into the house he took her to the belfry, to show her the single bell that he used to tell the parishioners who either had no clock or who could not read the time by the sun, that it was time for the service.

"If you decide to help me, then you will have to pull this rope," he said, pointing to the thickly padded length that hung in the room, "and that will make the bell ring. We can't do it now, because everyone will think there's something wrong if they hear the bell at a strange time. But you have to hold the woolly part of the rope with both hands as high up as you can, then you pull down. Once you hear the bell ring, you let the rope go back up again, but keep hold of it. It's quite heavy to pull but Angela manages it, so I'm sure you can."

Sarah moved over to it and looked straight up to where the rope disappeared through a hole in the ceiling, a long way up.

"You can't see the bell from here," he said. "But if you want I'll take you up to see it. There are some stairs through that door. There's a nice view across the countryside too."

"I don't think I'm big enough to reach," Sarah said doubtfully, looking up at the rope.

"No, Angela's a little taller than you, but she stands on a box," Colin said. "If you want to do it, then I will come and help you the first time. It's easier to show you than tell you how to do it, and you can see if you like it."

"No one will see me ring the bell," she said, almost to herself.

"No. Did you want them to see you?" he asked.

"No!" she cried immediately. "When would I have to be here?"

"On Sunday, at about a quarter to ten. Do you have a clock to tell the time?"

Her face fell immediately.

"Oh, I can't," she said, with genuine regret. "I have to…do something else at that time. I'm so sorry."

Colin cursed himself. Of course, if she was a dissenter's child, she'd be in the chapel at that time, would have already been there for hours, poor thing. She looked terribly disappointed, and he felt guilty for not thinking it through before he asked her.

"Well, come into the house and meet Angela anyway," he said. "She's very bored, having to lie still for much of the day. I'm sure she'll be very happy to see you."

The girl did not seem convinced that Angela would like her at all. Dear God, what sort of life did she have, to be so unsure of herself at such a young age? He thought of his own daughter, confident, sure of her parents' love and her place in the world, and his heart ached for this lonely child.

"Can I see inside the church, just for a moment?" she asked unexpectedly.

"Of course you can! Everyone is welcome, any time," he said. He took her out of the belfry, locking the door so that no drunks from the nearby inn could get in and decide to wake the village up in the middle of the night, then he led her into the church. It was a relatively small, plain church, smaller than the last one he'd had, but then it had been his choice to move to the countryside, away from the town and the foul air that clogged his wife Helen's lungs. But it was pleasant enough, painted white with a lovely stained glass window. He had not been here long enough yet to make it his own, but he would. They all liked the village, and thought they would be happy here. They were already settling in, and the parishioners were in the main friendly, simple country folk.

To his surprise the child stopped at the top of the aisle, completely entranced.

"Oh! It's beautiful!" she murmured, gazing at the window with wonder. The sun was shining through it at the moment, painting the stone floor beneath the window with patches of watery gold, amethyst, ruby and emerald, and the colours of the glass itself were glowing jewel bright.

Of course, he thought, *if she's a dissenter's child, she may never have seen stained glass from the inside before.* For a moment he saw the window through her eyes, and became entranced himself. How had he managed to forget so quickly how surprised he had himself been at the quality of the window the first time he'd seen it? He had not expected it in such a small, unimportant church as this was. He was suddenly very happy that the first stained glass this child had ever seen was such a fine piece.

"It represents the ascension of Christ into Heaven," Colin explained. "The man in the centre is Jesus, with the angels next to Him, and the people on the ground looking up are the disciples, who carried on His work on earth, spreading the Good News to all the people. It's very old. A lot of these kinds of windows were broken by Cromwell's men, but I think this one was missed because it was just in a small church in an out-of-the-way village."

"Cromwell fought the king on the tower," she said somewhat cryptically. Then, before he could ask what she meant, she asked a question. "So is that what Jesus looks like?"

"No one really knows what Jesus looked like as a man," Colin Baxter said. "So artists show Him as *they* think He would have looked."

"What do you think He looked like?" she asked, looking away from the window for the first time since she'd seen it.

"I don't know," Colin replied truthfully. "But I think whatever He looked like, He would have had a very kind face. Because He loved everyone when He was a man, and still does now He's in Heaven."

"You have a kind face," the child said, matter-of-factly.

"Thank you," he answered, accepting the compliment.

"You have flowers too. Eleanor was right," she continued.

"Yes. My wife arranges them and puts them there. Angela helps her do that, too. But she can still help with that, just not with the bell. Shall we go and meet them now?"

The house was warm and cosy. Colin and his wife Helen did not always see eye to eye, but she was a good housekeeper and a wonderful mother, if somewhat overprotective. Which was understandable in view of the circumstances. Five miscarriages before Angela was born and three more afterwards meant that their precious daughter was everything to them.

The precious daughter was on a chaise longue in the living room, currently in a sitting position, propped up with cushions. A cheery fire burned in the grate and as Colin walked in, with Sarah behind him, Angela's eyes lit up.

"Papa!" she said. "I've been learning a new embroidery stitch! Look!" He moved further into the room, and then his daughter saw Sarah. "Oh!" she cried.

"I have brought someone to see you," he said. "I told her that you cannot ring the bell for me, and brought her to see if perhaps she would like to help me until you are well again."

"Hello!" Angela said immediately. "Would you like to ring the bell? It's fun to do, and it's not too difficult once you've done it a few times."

"I would like to," Sarah replied, somewhat shyly, "but I can't. I have to be somewhere else at that time on Sunday."

"Oh, that's a shame."

"I thought you might like to meet her anyway," Colin said. "We hadn't lived here for long before Angela hurt her back, so she hasn't made friends with the village children yet." The smile that lit up Sarah's face was worth the small lie. He had thought she would feel more at home if she believed Angela to be lonely too. In fact Angela had already made a few friends, but if this child was a dissenter's daughter, she was unlikely to know them. "I'll leave you to get to know each other and will see what your mama is doing."

"She's making lunch," Angela informed him, but he left anyway, closing the door quietly behind him. Angela looked at Sarah with interest. She looked very uncomfortable in the room.

"Do you like sewing?" Angela asked. "I'm practising my stem

stitch, trying to make it completely even, so that I can do better floral designs. Mama says the flowers are good, but the stems look untidy." She held up the piece of cloth in its round frame and Sarah scrutinised it, taking in the beautiful bright colours of the flowers, and the dark green silk of the stems Angela was stitching.

"I hate sewing," Sarah replied, "but I might like it if I did pictures like that. It's very pretty."

"What sort of sewing do you do?"

"Normal sewing. Repairing clothes or darning stockings. My aunt taught me, but she didn't show me how to make pictures with stitches."

"It's called embroidery, if you make pictures," Angela said. "Mama said it was a good opportunity for me to improve my stitching, because it's boring for me to sit here all day, and I've read all my books more than twice now. She thought it might pass the time, but now you're here I can pass the time with you instead!" She pointed to the end of the cream chaise longue. "Why don't you sit down? Do you have to leave?"

Sarah looked at the pale cream silk of the cushioned seat doubtfully. Everything in the room was pale, either cream or pale pink. It was a beautiful room.

"I don't want to get it dirty," she said.

"You're not dirty. Sit down," Angela replied.

Sarah sat down on the edge of the seat. She put the basket down at her feet and looked around. Angela allowed her to look. The strange girl was very pretty, but very sad, too. You could see that in her face.

"I go out on Wednesday and visit some people for my father," Sarah said after a moment. "I used to visit a lady called Eleanor and she told me a fairy story, about a poor girl who went to a big party in a palace and met a handsome prince. She had a coach and horses and a beautiful dress, all through a fairy godmother. I think the room at the palace might have looked like this. It's so pretty!"

Angela smiled.

"I don't know that story," she said. "I've read *Arabian Nights' Entertainments,* or some of it, because Mama said I'm too young to read some of the stories, but I don't think that story is in it. What's it called?"

"I can't remember," Sarah said. "But she has to get home

before midnight, because at midnight the magic stops and then her gown and her coach and everything will all turn back to nothing, but she's having such a wonderful time dancing with the prince that she almost forgets and ends by running away just before midnight. She loses her slipper, and the prince finds it. He hunts all over the land for the person who the slipper fits, and when he finds who it is, he marries her, even though she's very poor."

Angela frowned. "Why doesn't the slipper turn to nothing at midnight, if everything else does?" she asked.

"I don't know," Sarah said. "I never thought of that. I did wonder why the slipper wouldn't fit lots of ladies and not just her, though. It seems a stupid way of looking for someone."

"It does. I'd look for what their face was like. I'm sure if I fell in love with someone I'd know what their face looked like and would be able to remember it!"

There came a gentle knock on the door and then a slightly harassed-looking woman with the same wheat-blonde hair as her daughter walked in.

"Mama!" Angela said. "This is my new friend…oh! I don't know your name!"

"Sarah," Sarah said shyly, standing up politely.

"Well, daughter, what will Sarah think of your manners, if you haven't even asked her her name?" Helen Baxter said, smiling until she saw the new child's face suddenly grow pale.

"It was my fault, Mrs Baxter," she said immediately. "I should have introduced myself to her. It wasn't her fault at all."

"Mama is just teasing me," Angela said. "You don't need to worry. Are you staying for lunch?"

Before the worried-looking child could speak, Helen jumped in.

"I do hope you are. My husband said he had invited you, and I've set a place for you at the table."

So she was staying. After lunch, though, which she stated that she had really enjoyed, although the Baxters would have known that anyway because she ate every morsel set in front of her, she said she had to go and visit the old ladies and give them the loaves of bread she'd baked for them, which were in the basket in the pretty room.

"I visit every week, and they expect me," she said.

"That's very kind of you," Colin Baxter commented.

"Oh, no, it's my father who's kind. He tells me who to go and visit," Sarah said.

"Even so, it's kind of you to go so willingly. I'm sure your father is proud of you, to give you such an important task to do," he replied.

"Will you come back next week, and bring us a loaf of bread?" Angela asked.

"Angela!" her mother said. "These loaves are for people in need. We cannot take bread from them!"

"Oh, I didn't mean…I just wanted you to have a reason to come back and see me," Angela said, flustered. "I thought we could read that book I told you about, and maybe talk about some of the stories."

"Sarah doesn't need any other reason than that she is welcome to come back here. Any time you want to," Colin offered.

"Say you'll come back," Angela begged. "We can be friends!"

Sarah blushed scarlet, then smiled broadly.

"I'll come back," she promised.

* * *

She couldn't wait to tell Philip about her adventure today, about the kind man who had told her about Jesus, and his lovely family and house. And the church! But in the end she didn't tell him any of that, because when she finally arrived home, a little late, worried that her father would be angry, Philip was waiting for her at the door, flustered.

"Where have you been?" he asked as she walked through the gate.

"Why are you home so early?" she answered his question with one of her own.

"I'm not working for Mr Bradshaw any more," Philip answered. "Mr Stockdale came to see Father today, told him I can start working for him next week. Father came by the farm on his way to Chester, told me I could come home, that I had to make sure you stayed home when you got back, and that he wouldn't be back until tomorrow. Mr Bradshaw wasn't very happy, but Father told him that he's had enough slave labour from me, that he didn't expect to receive such poor quality foodstuff in return and he expects to see him in church on Sunday. I think he'll probably write a sermon about him."

"The apples have been full of bad bits for a while now. I had to cut them all away. And the last flour you brought had weevils in. I didn't know Father was going to Chester today," Sarah said, putting her empty basket down on the kitchen table. "He doesn't usually go on Wednesdays."

"I don't know why he went. He didn't tell me. But that's not why I was waiting for you. Tom brought a parcel for you!"

Sarah looked at her brother as though he'd gone insane. No part of the sentence he'd just uttered made any sense to her. Her face must have shown her utter confusion, because Philip laughed at her expression.

"Tom works at the post. He came this afternoon, said that he'd had a parcel for you for two days, but had instructions not to deliver it here until Father was in Chester. He said he was keeping it till Friday, because that's when Father usually goes, but when he saw him get in the stage today he thought he'd bring it. I put it in your room in case Father came back for some reason and saw it. It's under your bed."

Sarah went upstairs, got the parcel, and bringing it back down set it on the table as though it was an ornament. Then she sat down and looked at it. It was quite big and heavy, and was wrapped very well, with paper and string. Philip sat down on the other side of the table and looked at it too.

"Aren't you going to open it?" he asked after a while.

"I never had a parcel before," she said. "Are you sure it's for me?"

"It's got your name on the top, look."

She looked, and recognised the letters Philip had taught her so long ago. S for snake…

"Who's it from?" she asked.

"I don't know. But it came from Chester, so it must be from Aunt Patience or Uncle Arthur. Or Uncle John, maybe!"

"Uncle Arthur!" Sarah said. "He's the only person I know who would send me a present!"

"I'd send you a present!" Philip replied.

"You don't need to though, because we live together, and

always will. You can give me presents," Sarah said logically. "I wonder what's in it?"

"Why don't you open it and find out?"

But she didn't. Instead she bustled about in the kitchen for a while, enjoying the anticipation of opening something that someone had taken time, thought and trouble to get together, pack, and send to her. To think that someone cared enough about her to do all that, just to make her happy!

Eventually she opened it, excruciatingly slowly, for Philip at any rate. When the string had been unknotted and rolled up for future reuse, and the paper folded, a box sat on the table.

"Please don't leave it there for another hour before opening it!" Philip begged.

Inside the box were half a dozen oranges, a big bag of raisins, a small bag of brown powder, a bag of white crystals, a wooden head shape, and a silk bag full of hair. And a letter, which had a word on the front which started with the snake letter.

"Oh!" Sarah said on seeing the head shape. "He remembers!"

Philip didn't ask what he remembered. He picked up the letter.

"Do you want me to read this?" he asked.

She nodded, and he broke the seal.

"It's got your name on the front," he said, carefully unfolding it. "'My dearest niece Sarah,' it starts. 'I hope you like the fruit, sugar and spice I sent you. If you remember how to make that puff pastry that your aunt taught, you have the ingredients to make the cinnamon and raisin pastry.'" He looked up. "Is that what the brown powder is? Cinnamon?"

"Yes," Sarah said. "Smell it. It smells wonderful. It tastes wonderful too. I'll make the pastry that he gave me when I was at his shop, if I can."

He stuck his nose in the bag and inhaled.

"Mmmmm," he commented, then looked back at the letter. "'I have written the receipt for you. I am sure Philip will read it for you, and that you will both enjoy the pastries, and will maybe think of me. The oranges are for both of you to enjoy, too. They are from a country called Portugal and came on a big ship, like the ones I showed to you. I hope you remember the offer I made, which I would like you to take up, when you can. I am sending you something to help you remember what you learnt from Maria, and to allow you to practice when you have the time to do so. I think of you every day and hope to see you again soon.'" He looked up. "He's talking about you working with him, isn't he?"

Sarah, listening to the letter whilst carefully taking the pieces of hair out of their cloth bag, nodded, then looked across at Philip when he didn't continue reading. To her surprise, his eyes were full of tears.

"What's wrong?" she asked.

"Are you going to leave me, and go and live with Uncle Arthur?" he said.

"No, of course not!" she answered immediately. "I told you, when you go for a soldier, I'll go and live in Chester with you, and while you're away soldiering I can make wigs and dress hair, and then when you come home we'll be together!"

"So you won't go until I become a soldier then, even if you can?"

"No."

"But you're very unhappy here, and you could leave sooner, I think."

Sarah stopped arranging the hairpieces and the wig that was in the bag and leaned across the table.

"You're very unhappy, too," she said. "And you're older than me, and a boy too. When you're sixteen and you go for a soldier, will you leave me here?"

"No, I'm going to take you with me!" he said immediately. "But soon I'll be bigger than Father, and then I'll stop him if he hits you, and we'll leave together. When I'm sixteen."

"Have an orange," she said, handing one to him. He swallowed back his tears, and smiled weakly, then took the offered fruit. "I'll have to hide the head and the hair, because if Father sees them he'll throw them away, and I want to practice. I can do it when he's away."

"Where will you hide them?" Philip asked.

"In Mother's trunk," she said. "I think I'll have to tell Father about the raisins and cinnamon though, because he'll smell them in the house if I bake the pastries here. I can tell him that Uncle Arthur sent them and ask him to thank him for me. And then Uncle will know I got his parcel."

"Or I could write a letter for you, and we could send it to his shop so Aunt Patience won't know."

Sarah smiled. It might be evil or wrong, but it was nice having secrets. It was nice having friends, too. That evening Philip wrote a letter to their uncle, and Sarah carefully signed the bottom with her name. She showed him all the pieces of hair that her uncle had sent to her, the ribbons and clips, and the jar of pomade, and told him how they worked. And he read the recipe out to her, so she knew how to make the pastries.

The following Tuesday she made cinnamon and raisin pastries, using some, but not all of the ingredients her uncle had sent to her. When her father, who had been in a terrible mood since he'd returned from his unexpected trip the previous week, came out of his study attracted by the strong smell of the baking, she told him that she was making a pastry for him to cheer him, because she hated to see him so sad.

She didn't tell him that she and Philip had hidden the oranges to share. She didn't tell him about the wooden head and the hair, or the letter. And she didn't tell him that she'd made enough pastries not only for him, but also for the old ladies she visited, her new friend Angela and her kind parents, and that the reason she'd waited until Tuesday night to make them was not to cheer him, but so they would be nice and fresh on Wednesday morning.

It was nice having secrets. She didn't think the Jesus Mr Baxter had told her about would mind her having these sorts of secrets that made other people happy as well as her. He seemed to be a much nicer Jesus than the one her father knew. He probably liked flowers too, and that was why Mr Baxter's church had flowers in it.

Maybe Mr Baxter's Jesus would like her as well, and would forgive her for being a Daughter of Eve. Then she wouldn't have to go to Hell after all when she died!

CHAPTER SIX

"No," Colin Baxter said. "Absolutely not."

His wife stood in the kitchen facing him, her arms white with flour, the pastry she was making temporarily forgotten.

"Colin, you know I wouldn't ask this without good reason. I like the child too. But we are settling here. It's a lovely village, my health is better, Angela is happy, and you are doing very good work at the church, bringing people back to God, giving them an alternative to that man. It's important work you're doing. Will you risk all of it just to make one child happy?"

"I think you're being over-protective of me," Colin said. "What can he do to me? After all, I'm not actively trying to reduce his congregation. I'm merely teaching God's word in the Anglican way, and people are choosing for themselves who to follow. And although I think his views are extreme, I have never said as much outside of this house. I'm more concerned about how he will punish Sarah if he finds out that she visits us, now you've told me she's his daughter. I must make her aware of that, and then let her decide if she is happy to take the risk. But I think she must know that already. She's a clever child. I think that's why she and Angela have become so close so quickly, because they are of like intelligence."

"You really didn't know, or even suspect?"

"No. I thought she was a dissenter's child, because of her talk about the reprobate and Daughters of Eve, but I had no idea she was Reverend Browne's daughter!"

"You would have invited her here anyway though, wouldn't you?" his wife retorted accusingly.

Colin thought about this for a moment.

"I might have done, yes. Because she was so wounded, so desperate for kindness. And you must have seen how different she is now. Just a few hours a week with Angela and look at the improvement! I cannot reject her now, Helen. It will undo all the good we've done. And Angela would miss her dreadfully."

Helen could not argue with this. The difference in Sarah in the four weeks she'd been calling was astounding. Her confidence had grown, she chatted and laughed easily, smiled all the time. She had arrived as a cowed and broken child, and was already becoming a happy, confident girl. Helen was very proud of the wonderful effect her beautiful daughter's friendship had had on Sarah.

Even so…

"Colin, I found something else out today. Do you know why Reverend Browne is allowed to preach here? Where he gets the money from to do it?"

"No. What concern is that of mine? I assume his parishioners donate the funds he lives from."

Helen sighed.

"It *is* our concern. His brother is Sir John Browne."

"What?! Are you sure?"

"Yes. You might not be worried about crossing Perseverance Browne, but you do *not* want to cross the man who owns most of the village, including the house we're sitting in right now!"

Colin sat down at the kitchen table and wiped his hand across his face.

"I can't believe that that badly dressed child is Sir John's niece! The man's rich! And he's not a dissenter, is he?"

"It seems not. He goes to the Anglican church in Chester where he lives, at any rate. But what he has done is to provide for his brother by giving him a chapel here where he can preach to his heart's content. He owns the chapel and the house that the family lives in, but has nothing more to do with them than that. He lives in Chester."

"This doesn't make sense," Colin said. "The man owns this village, has given his brother the ministry, pays for him to blast all the parishioners with Hell and damnation every Sunday for hours, but is an Anglican? He made no objection to me coming here, yet he must have known I'd be in direct competition with his brother!"

"I don't know about all that. I do know that it's generally believed that Sarah is being sent out to visit the poor because Sir John told Reverend Browne that he needs to show more compassion to his congregation if he wishes to keep them. I also know that his congregation is dwindling as more of them come here, and that the reverend has been to his brother to complain about you, recently."

"Really?" Colin looked at his wife with admiration. "How do you find all this information out?"

"I talk to the ladies of the village, as minister's wives are supposed to do," Helen said. "And they tell me all the gossip. Most of it is extremely tedious, but some of it is not. It seems that while you were inviting his daughter to ring the church bell last month, he was haring off to Chester to complain that you were stealing his worshippers. And he came back with a face like thunder, and gave a raging sermon on Sunday about the faithlessness and ungratefulness of family, which half the congregation took as an attack on those who've deserted his chapel for our church, and the other half took as being an attack on his brother, who had refused to throw you out."

"Well, then, if he refused to throw me out—" Colin began.

"I think he may feel differently, or be persuaded to, if he believes that you're attempting to convert his actual niece to Anglicanism!"

"But you said he goes to the Anglican church himself! And I am *not* attempting to convert Sarah to anything!"

"He may well go to the Anglican church because it suits his ambition rather than his faith," Helen said. "But he must have some consideration for his brother, if he's paying for him to preach here. He will certainly have consideration if he thinks you're directly interfering with his family's religious beliefs! He is powerful enough to have us thrown out of here, Colin, and to blacken your name in ways that would make our lives difficult, possibly stop you getting another church. You *must* take this seriously."

Colin sat with his head buried in his hands for a few minutes while his wife carried on making the pastry, giving him time to digest the information and come to a decision.

"I cannot do it," he said finally. "I cannot reject that poor child, who I believe has not known a moment's happiness with that father of hers. She is ten years old and firmly believes that she is damned to everlasting Hell, no matter what she does, just because she is female! Can you imagine the torment of that? I will not try to convert her, I swear it, but I will not banish her from my house either. I can't."

Helen came round the table and took her husband's hand in her own, covering it with flour in the process.

"Colin, you are a good man, and part of me loves you for feeling that way. But you are doing wonderful work here. Every week you bring more unhappy souls away from that damaged and bitter man who hates everyone, to the goodness and kindness of Jesus. Will you risk all that? And my happiness? Angela's happiness? Because we are happy living here and don't want to leave."

"But Helen, did not Jesus tell us about redemption in the parable of the young son who was lost, but then came home and his father rejoiced, and said he was dead and is alive again? He did not turn away his younger son because the older one was jealous. This child Sarah was dead to Jesus, because her father has shut her away from His love, and now she is alive again. If Sir John calls me to explain myself, then I will. But I cannot forsake her and remain the man I am."

"No," Helen said. "No, you cannot. I see that now. I should not have asked you to."

* * *

The next week when Sarah went to the house, Helen Baxter was waiting for her at the door, as she often did if Angela should not be disturbed.

"Is Angela asleep?" Sarah asked. She had her basket over her arm as usual, but normally it was empty, because she came to the house after she'd visited the poor women and had given away her bread. But today there was something in there, covered with a cloth. Sarah saw that Helen had seen it, and smiled. She was relaxed, happy, sure of her welcome.

"It's only bread," she said. "I have some raisins and cinnamon left though. I'll try to make more of the pastries next week, if I have time. I just wanted to bring something for you, because you're so good to me. I don't think my bread is as nice as yours, though. You don't have to eat it."

Helen sighed. Sarah was not making this easy.

"Come in, child," she said. "I need to talk to you."

Sarah looked up and caught the woman's expression.

"Is Angela ill?" she asked, instantly worried.

"No, she's sleeping, but she's not ill. Come in."

Sarah obeyed, sat down at the kitchen table when asked, but was clearly worried, sensing that something was wrong. Helen sent up a silent prayer that she would manage this conversation well, then looked at the child. Colin was right; the change in her was incredible. Hopefully that would stay, had made its mark on her for life.

"Why didn't you tell us that you are Reverend Browne's daughter?" Helen asked directly. Sarah's face paled so rapidly that for a moment Helen thought she would faint. The child swallowed hard, and looked down at the table for a minute. She started to speak, stopped, swallowed once more, then tried again.

"I-I didn't think it would matter," she murmured, still looking at the table. "Mr Baxter, he told me…" Her voice trailed off for a moment, then suddenly she stood and looked straight at Helen, her eyes bright with unshed tears. "I'm sorry," she said. "I understand. I'll go now." She turned and was at the door before Helen realised that she was just leaving, had assumed the rejection she hadn't actually worded yet and had completely accepted it, as simply as that.

"Wait!" she cried, and Sarah turned back.

"Oh," she said, looking at the table, where her basket was sitting. "Yes. Thank you." She moved back to the basket, lifted the cloth as though to take out the loaf, then hesitated. "Do you want it? I made it for you, but I understand if you don't want to take it."

"Sarah, let me explain," Helen said, thoroughly unsettled. She had anticipated many possible reactions from the child, but not this instant and complete acceptance of rejection. She wanted to explain to the child, *needed* to explain to her why these visits could not continue.

"No. I understand. I should have expected this," Sarah said firmly. Impulsively she reached out, touched the older woman's arm. "You don't have to explain." She lifted the loaf out and placed it on the table. "You don't have to eat it, but if you want to, you can," she said. "Will you tell Mr Baxter and Angela that I'm sorry? And goodbye? And…and thank you."

She smiled once, and then she left, quickly, quietly and without any fuss.

Helen sat at the kitchen table after the child had gone, and stared at the loaf for a long time. Then she closed her eyes, and saw again Sarah's smile as she had said goodbye and had thanked her.

It was the saddest and the bravest smile she had ever seen, and, in view of what happened later, it would haunt her periodically for the rest of her life.

* * *

Sarah sat by the river, in the spot where the gang of children had challenged her, where she had hit Simon Bradshaw. They kept away from her now, which she supposed was a good thing, but at least when they'd followed her and insulted her she had been a part of them, in a strange way. Now she knew that she would never be a part of anyone. Except Philip, of course.

She knew why Mrs Baxter had rejected her, why she mustn't go to their house any more. It was because now they knew who she was, they knew that she was a Daughter of Eve, and damned, and they didn't want someone who was full of sin and going to Hell to be friends with their daughter, who was so lovely that she was named after angels, and would certainly go to Heaven. Of course they didn't want that. Nobody did. Sarah understood it.

But it still hurt. It hurt more than anything else had ever hurt, much more than when her father hit her or put her in the cellar, more than when she had been slapped and insulted by Aunt Penelope. Because Angela had completely accepted her, had loved her, had really been her friend for that reason only. Not because she was family, like Philip or Uncle Arthur, but just because she loved Sarah for who she was. No one had ever loved Sarah just for herself.

But she could not love a Daughter of Eve. No one could love such a corrupt thing. The gang of children had seen that in her and had thrown stones, and now rejected her. Her father saw it, which was why he hated her. Angela had not seen it, but her mother had, probably because she was older and knew how to see darkness. And she wanted to protect her daughter from evil. She hadn't allowed Mrs Baxter to explain, because she couldn't have borne to hear the words, to see the look of distaste that she would surely have had, had she had to tell her why she was unsuitable to be friends with Angela.

She understood. And she would keep away.

But it hurt inside, in her chest. It hurt so badly that she thought her heart would stop, and she would die. And right then she wanted to, because she thought even Hell could not feel as bad as this.

* * *

When Helen told Colin what she had done and how Sarah had reacted to it, the Baxters had the first serious argument of their seventeen-year marriage. They reconciled after a time, because Colin was not a man to hold resentment for long, and because Helen was, on one level, sorry that she hadn't listened to him, although she had in her way been trying to protect him, and Angela. She had not had bad intentions.

And he could not make amends. At first he thought that the next time he saw Sarah at the market cross he would find a way to make her stay, so that he could explain to her that Helen had made a mistake, that Angela had cried for days when she knew her new friend would not come back again, even though neither Helen nor Colin had told their daughter exactly what had happened. Instead they had explained that Sarah was the other minister's daughter, and that if he found out she was visiting the house he would be very angry with her, and none of them wanted that.

That of course was true, though not the whole truth, and that was what Colin wanted to explain to Sarah when he saw her.

But he did not see her. If she was still visiting the old people on Wednesdays then she had found another way to go to them. After a few weeks he realised that she must be avoiding him deliberately, and if she was doing that, it was because she had taken the rejection badly.

He could hardly go to visit her. If her father found out, that would cause her endless trouble. Nor could he talk to any of the villagers to try to get a message to her, because gossip was the lifeblood of the community, and Reverend Browne would surely learn of it.

He could do nothing, except hope that he would run into her. Surely he would? This was a small place, with only a few hundred people in total. She could not avoid him forever! On Wednesdays, after the stories he still told, he took to walking the streets around the village, hoping to see her, praying that he would see her.

But he never did.

* * *

December 1737

She was bleeding. And she couldn't understand why, or how she could have cut herself there, where she made urine, and why the place didn't hurt. Even small cuts that hardly bled hurt you, but this one didn't, and yet there was a lot of blood and it went on for days. It was true that she had strange cramping aches in her stomach at the same time, but she thought that was something she'd eaten that had maybe not agreed with her. Certainly she had had stomach aches before, but had not bled like this!

She must be really ill. Maybe she would die because of it. Maybe that would be a good thing. She had no particular love of life. It was lonely, hard work, and mainly boring. Philip would miss her if she died, but he was growing up, was sixteen, and had other friends now, friends of his own gender and age. He had not become a soldier yet though, and didn't talk about it any more, which surprised her, because he had been so enthusiastic when he was younger.

Then the bleeding stopped, and so did the cramping pains and she forgot all about them after a couple of days, and life went back to normal. In the mornings she would get up early, light the fire, feed the chickens, make the breakfast for her father and brother. Then they would get up and eat it, after which Philip would dress in the suit he wore for his job at Mr Stockdale's, and Reverend Browne would either go out if he was going to Chester, or go into his study if he wasn't, and do whatever needed to be done to save souls. Sarah would clean the house and prepare everything for the later meal, then either do the gardening, washing, clean the chapel or visit her old ladies, only one of whom spoke more than a few words to her, and whose rambling stories she had now heard so many times that she was bored to distraction by them.

On Sunday she spent four hours in church listening to Father, and then one precious hour by the river with Philip. That hour had become the only light in her week, the only thing that really kept her going from day to day. The unhappiness and loneliness were like a leaden lump in her body, deadening everything. Flowers no longer made her smile, food tasted bland; everything was bland, colourless.

The following month the cramps and the bleeding came again, and she knew that whatever it was it must be serious, and she had to tell the only person she *could* tell things to. She wore her black dress rather than the grey so if the blood came through her petticoat to the dress it wouldn't be visible, and that evening she sat up after she would normally have been in bed, and waited for Philip to come home from his long working day. She occupied her time by darning the heels of his stockings as carefully as she could by the light of a candle, because now he was in the law he had to look as respectable as possible, but because he wasn't earning any money they could not afford new stockings for him.

Father had gone to bed without asking her why she was staying up, without speaking to her at all, which was a relief, because she didn't have an omission lie to tell him. Philip came home about an hour later and jumped when he saw her sitting at the kitchen table. He blushed violently and looked extremely guilty, and normally she would have noticed that, would have seen that his hair was extremely untidy, and that rather than wearing his shoes he held them in his hands.

"Is there something wrong?" he asked immediately.

She blushed as violently as her brother, if not for the same reason.

"I need to ask you something, but…" Her voice trailed away. "There isn't anyone else I can ask," she added after a moment's silence.

He put his shoes down, ran his hand over his hair and came to sit down at the table opposite her. She stuck the needle in the stocking she'd been darning and put it down.

"What is it?" he asked. "You can tell me anything, you know that."

She nodded.

"I'm bleeding," she said. "And I don't know why. I haven't cut myself, and it doesn't hurt. And I'm frightened. I wanted to talk to someone about it."

Philip frowned, and looked very worried.

"Don't worry," he said. "We can get a doctor to see you, I'm sure, if we have to. Where are you bleeding? Can you show me?"

The blush, which had started to fade, returned with a vengeance.

"No," she said. "I can't show you. It's…a place I can't show people, any people. It's a bad place. But I've got stomach ache too," she added quickly.

"How long have you been bleeding for?" he asked.

"Just today. This time, but it happened last month as well, for a few days, and then it stopped, and I forgot about it then, thought it had gone away. But it hasn't," she ended, her eyes filling with tears, which shimmered in the candlelight.

"Where's Father?" Philip asked suddenly. "Is he in his study?"

"No," Sarah said. "He went to bed earlier. But I can't tell him!"

"Get your cloak, we'll talk in the garden," Philip said cryptically, standing up. "Don't worry, it's all right. But I don't want Father to hear what I'm going to tell you."

Once outside, with the icy wind blowing straight through their thin clothes, they stood huddled together and shivering, while Philip told her that the bleeding would happen every month, and it meant that she was a woman now. This happened to all girls when they became women.

"And soon you'll start to change shape too, and look like a woman instead of a girl," Philip added, his face as scarlet explaining as hers was listening, although neither of them could see that in the dark.

"How do you know all this?" she asked, impressed. "Do you learn it in the law office?"

Philip laughed out loud, and then put his hand over his mouth so Father wouldn't hear if he was still awake. "Er…no. We don't learn that sort of thing there!"

"How do you know, then? Are you just making it up to make me feel better?" Sarah asked.

Philip sighed, hesitated a moment, then came to a decision.

"No, I'm not making it up," he said, leading her down to the end of the garden, where there was no danger of anyone hearing what they were saying at all. "I've met this girl, called Mary. You won't know her because she doesn't come to our chapel, and she lives a bit away from the village, but she came here to the fair in September, and I met her there."

"You went to the fair?!" Sarah said, astounded.

"Yes. Mr Stockdale gave us the afternoon free to go, and so I did. I thought if Father found out I could tell him that I needed to be part of the office when they did things, so as to prosper."

"But you're going to be a soldier!" Sarah said. "You don't need to prosper in the law to do that, do you?"

Philip breathed in hard.

"No," he said, "but we're not talking about me being a soldier. We're talking about you being a woman. So this girl, Mary, she…she likes boys, and she goes with a lot of them. She's very pretty."

"Goes with them? Where does she go?"

God, she was so innocent. He had a sudden urge not to tell her anything, to keep her innocent, protect her from the world. But he couldn't. If he didn't tell her, no one would. And she needed to know.

"She gives herself to them. Lets them swive her," he said. He saw her eyes widen in the moonlight, and her mouth dropped open.

"Like Mary Madgalene?" Sarah asked, horrified.

"No," he said. "Father says Mary Magdalene was a whore. But it doesn't say that in the Bible, because I've read it. A lot of what Father says in church isn't in the Bible. It's in his head. But my Mary is not a whore. She's sweet-natured, and very pretty, and she's just…generous," he ended a little lamely. He had never wanted anything in his life as much as he wanted to sleep with Mary. He fancied himself in love with her, even while he knew that her love of sexual pleasure put her beyond him as a partner. Everyone knew she had slept with half the boys of the village. One of the things he loved most about her was that she really didn't care what people thought about her, and that made her free to do whatever she wanted. He wished he could be like that.

"Anyway," he said, dragging his mind back to the present and his shivering sister who he was trying to console, "a few weeks ago she let me kiss her, and then she said she couldn't do any more because she had her courses, and I didn't know what they were, so she explained them to me. Which was good, because now I know to tell you. It's normal. It'll happen every month now. And soon you'll need to make some new clothes."

"What, because of the blood?" she said. "No, I can wash my dress. But I'll have to make something to soak it up, if it's going to happen every month. Does it happen to men, too?"

"No," Philip said. "It's part of the curse of Eve, I think. But that's not why you'll need new clothes. You'll change shape, grow…things up here, like the ladies have," he said, pointing to his chest, "so your dress will be too small. Mary said she can have babies too. But I don't know if that's because of the blood, or because she's a lot older than you. And she's not married, so I don't see how she can."

"Babies!" Sarah said. "What, just have a baby? I don't think Father will like that!"

"No, you can only have a baby if you get married," Philip said. "Then when you and your husband live in the same house, it makes you have babies. It doesn't make them until then, I don't think. I don't think Mary knows about that properly. She didn't tell me about it, anyway."

This was all very confusing. And embarrassing.

"I…can't believe it," Sarah said, after a minute. "I don't *feel* like a woman. But I don't know what a woman feels like, really. I just feel like I did before, but with a stomach ache. I thought being a woman would be special. But this is horrible! Thank you for telling me, though. At least I'm not going to die of it!"

They were freezing, so they turned and walked back down the garden path together, and into the house. Then they sat as close to the fire as they could get for a while to warm themselves before they went to bed. They sat silently, Sarah trying to take in that she was a woman now, and Philip dreaming about Mary.

"Sarah," Philip said after a while. She looked up, saw a question on his face and knew him well enough to know what it was without him uttering it.

"Of course I won't tell," she said. And with that, another promise was made between them, and a secret kept.

* * *

Philip was right. After a few months, although Sarah didn't grow upwards enough to need a new dress, she grew outwards, and her shape slowly changed, became more curvy. She waited for as long as she could, dreading having to ask her father for the material to make more clothes because she knew he would ask her why, and she thought he would think that her becoming a woman was a sinful thing to do, even though she couldn't help it.

To her surprise though, when she told him that her dress was too tight for her now, and that she would need the material to make a new one, he just glanced at her, nodded, and a few days later came home with two new lengths of material, in dark blue and black. She cut up the top part of her old dress to make a pattern for the new one, and made it a bit bigger at the top, then sewed the old skirt back on to the new top. By doing this she managed to make an extra dress with the material he'd brought for her, and although it was obviously home-made, because her Aunt Patience had not taught her enough about sewing to enable her to make something as complicated as a dress, the dresses covered her and didn't look too bad, and that was all she needed, because she had no friends and nowhere to go where she needed to look good.

Mrs Grimes was the only one of the old ladies who noticed her when she visited, but she had become very strange lately, sometimes calling Sarah Catherine, which had been her mother's name, and often not recognising her at all. Sarah thought she could turn up there in her shift and Mrs Grimes wouldn't blink. So a badly-fitting dress didn't matter at all.

She cut up some pieces of the material and made herself clouts and a kind of little belt that she could tie on to hold the clouts in place to absorb the blood. And in a few months she got used to the physical changes.

What worried her more was that she felt more weepy sometimes, and more angry too, and sometimes she couldn't hide it and the emotions bubbled up through her lips into words, or actions like banging her fist on the table or crashing about the house.

Then she would sit in the cellar, nursing whatever part of her body her father had hit as he dragged her to the door in the kitchen, and would sometimes feel such hatred for him that it frightened her. If she had a tinder box in her pocket she would light a candle once she heard her father's steps mounting the stairs and not coming back down. She knew then that it was night, and she would go to her mother's chest, take out the wooden head shape and practice styling the wig her uncle had sent to her.

It was looking very worn by now, because she spent a lot of time in the cellar since her courses had started, but styling, or even just combing the hair comforted her, reminded her that one day she would be able to go to her uncle's shop to work, and that she would be able to prove to him that she was serious in her wish to be a wig maker. He would not have sent her the wig if he hadn't wanted her to join him. But she couldn't go yet, not until Philip became a soldier and took her away with him.

She had never felt emotions this strongly before she started to change shape. Everything was different, not just her body. The slightest thing, things that she wouldn't have noticed at all before, could make her cry; a nasty look, someone laughing as she passed on the way to visit the old ladies, even though they probably weren't laughing at her. She, who had learnt emotional control as a survival technique, was now at the mercy of her feelings, and it was horrible.

The greatest, most constant feeling she had was misery, but now, instead of accepting it as she had for so long, she raged against it, or sometimes sank under it so badly that even getting out of bed in the morning was an enormous effort. Philip was sixteen; why didn't he go for a soldier and take her away from here so she could start living? No one would know she was a Daughter of Eve in Chester! When she asked him he avoided answering her. Did he not want to be a soldier any more? Or did he not want to take her with him any more, but didn't know how to tell her? It was agony. She would lie awake some nights, crying into her pillow, not knowing why she was crying but unable to stop.

She *hated* being a woman.

Apart from putting her down the cellar a lot more, the only other change her father made was to change the day she visited his parishioners to Saturday afternoon, when Philip was not working and so could accompany her, 'to make sure she did not fall into temptation and sin,' he said. He did not elaborate as to why Sarah was more likely to fall into sin now than she had been for the last few years.

But both of them knew better than to question Father, so every Saturday when Philip arrived home, Sarah would be waiting with her basket of provisions and they would walk to the various houses together, he waiting outside while she went in and gave out the bread and did any small tasks in the cottages.

In honesty Sarah enjoyed this change, because it meant that while they were walking together they could talk, and often they would go down to the river together and spend a little time there, which meant that Sarah had that to look forward to on Saturday *and* Sunday now. Also, when Philip was with her, people would say hello to him as they passed and exchange a few words with him, and sometimes they would greet her too and ask her how she was, which made her feel, even if only slightly, as though she belonged in the village. Which was a new feeling for her and a pleasant one, even though she knew that it wasn't real – if Philip wasn't there, they would stop speaking to her.

He still wouldn't talk to her about becoming a soldier though. But he did talk about Mary, a lot. Maybe when he went for a soldier he would want to take Mary instead of his sister. Even the thought of him doing that made Sarah feel physically ill, so she avoided the subject altogether. Because if he did want that and he told her so, rejected her as everyone else had, then she would not be able to bear it, and would die of grief.

CHAPTER SEVEN

Late Summer 1738

Since April Sarah and Philip had a new routine, one which suited Philip, but which made Sarah a little sad.

Since December, every week on Saturday afternoon he had accompanied her to the ladies she visited and had waited outside their houses. But for the last few weeks, when she went to Mrs Grimes, who was the last person on her list and with whom she stayed for the longest time, Philip would escort her to the cottage and then would disappear to meet with Mary, with whom he was completely infatuated and had been for some time. It was the perfect opportunity for the couple to meet, because Mrs Grimes fortuitously lived near the end of the lane that Mary lived on, and as there were only fields between the two houses, the chance of anyone seeing them and reporting back to Reverend Browne was extremely unlikely.

Mrs Grimes' memory continued to fail, and other villagers had started to call in during the week, just to keep an eye on her. But no one sat and listened to her stories like Sarah did, and she could tell by the way the old lady's face lit up when she arrived that she might not remember her name or why she was there any more, but she certainly remembered that this was the visitor who would sit and listen with interest while she chatted, and would even comment and ask questions from time to time.

Sarah did not *actually* sit and listen with interest, because she had already heard all the stories of Mrs Grimes' early life many, many times. But living with the father she had, she knew how to feign interest. For as long as she could remember she had had four hours of practice at that every Sunday in church. So she let her mind drift, returning every so often to listen to which part of her life the old lady was happily chatting about and to give a sign of encouragement or a comment. The rest of the time she was far away from the dingy cottage in her mind.

It was harder now to imagine a wonderful future for herself sitting in a cosy house in Chester wearing her mother's beautiful dress and making wigs while she waited for Philip to come home in his lovely red soldier's uniform. It was pretty clear to her that Philip no longer wanted to be a soldier, but instead was settling to life in the village working for Mr Stockdale. He was seventeen now, taller than their father and broader too, but he still didn't dare to openly defy him. Instead he sneaked around behind his back, meeting his friends on the days when the reverend was in Chester, and Mary on Saturday afternoons.

Maybe he would marry Mary. He had told Sarah that he wouldn't, that Mary wasn't a marrying kind of girl, that he wouldn't leave her alone with Father, but she could tell that as he grew older, had a life outside the house at work, and started to make new friends, he was drifting away from her. One day he *would* marry, if not Mary then some other girl, and he would set up a home of his own. Then she would be left to look after her father until he died, which unmarried daughters were expected to do, and by which time she would be old herself, too old to learn to make wigs.

She realised now that all those years ago in Chester, when her aunt had told her she was going to train her for the life she'd been born to, what she'd meant was that she'd been born to look after her father for the rest of his life.

Maybe one day she would be sitting in a little house like this one, boring some poor young girl like herself half to death with stories about her completely uninteresting life. She wouldn't even be able to talk about falling in love, marrying, having a son she adored like Mrs Grimes could. All she'd be able to talk about would be being a dried-up old spinster who had done nothing, nothing at all with her life except look after a father who hated her, and live in a village where no one wanted to be friendly with her because she was an evil Daughter of Eve. And after all that, she would then die and go to Hell.

She could not think like that. She would go mad if she thought about her unbearable future. Sarah shook her head, and with a great effort dragged her mind back to the present, to what Mrs Grimes was saying.

"And so then he went to Liverpool, which is near the sea, you know, and he has a shop there, which sells haberdashery," the old lady was saying. Robert, her son, then.

"I've seen some of the ships," Sarah said suddenly, interrupting. "The big ships that sail across the sea from Ireland and the Colonies and come into Liverpool. I saw them when I was at Chester. They come up the River Dee, although my uncle told me that there are a lot of problems with the river silting up, and that the town is trying to do something about it, because they're losing trade."

"I saw the ships too, when I was a girl, younger than you," Mrs Grimes said, smiling. "In Bristol. I was born in Bristol, I was. My mother had ten of us, you know."

Yes, Sarah did know, so she let Mrs Grimes carry on, but got up and did some cleaning to try to stop her mind returning to sadness. Philip would not come back until about four o'clock, so she had time to tidy the house, and then make some food for the old lady's evening meal.

The siblings still went down to the river after he came back for her, but it was not the same now, even though they still trusted each other and still had secrets from their father, which kept them close. But Philip was no longer interested in the details of Sarah's dull life, instead wanting to talk about Mary. In fact, Mary was *all* he wanted to talk about, all the time. Sarah supposed that was because he couldn't talk about her with anyone else.

Mary was a 'bad' girl, apparently. Sarah expected that was because she was a Daughter of Eve *and* didn't go to church, not even to the Baxters' church. She had told Philip that her family were Roman Catholics, and that was why they lived right on the edge of the village, because people kept away from them. Roman Catholics were even more evil than Anglicans, it seemed, and if Father found out that his son was courting a Papist, which was another word for Roman Catholic, he would be angrier than he'd ever been in his life.

Sarah wondered what the Roman Catholic Jesus was like, and

she asked Philip one warm August day when they were sitting with their feet in the stream.

"I don't know," Philip said. "Jesus is the same. There's only one of Him. He's the Son of God to everyone. What do you mean?"

"When Mr Baxter spoke about Him, he made Jesus sound kind and gentle. But Father makes Him sound angry and cruel. I just wondered what the Roman Catholics make Him sound like."

"Mary doesn't talk about her religion," Philip said. "And I don't want to. I get enough of that at home. I'd have thought you would have had too."

It was different for Philip of course, because he wasn't a Daughter of Eve, so wasn't automatically condemned to Hell regardless of what he did. Sarah thought that Mr Baxter's Jesus might let her into Heaven after all, if He judged her when she died instead of her father's Jesus. But if Mary was a Daughter of Eve too, and bad, then maybe the Roman Catholic Jesus was angry and cruel like Father's. Poor Mary.

She had never met Mary, had never even seen her, but she knew that Mary was the most beautiful girl in the world, with long black hair, eyes as blue as a summer sky, the most perfect little nose, and lips like a rosebud.

Philip was very much in love and Sarah was pleased for him, because it was lovely to see him so happy. She just prayed that he wouldn't marry Mary and leave her alone with Father, even though she knew that was a selfish prayer.

* * *

September 1738

At the little gate of Mrs Grimes' garden Philip said goodbye and continued up the lane to Mary's house, whistling, his step jaunty. He had told Sarah that he was going to try to arrange for her to meet Mary, because he wanted the two people he loved to know each other and he was sure they would become good friends.

Sarah wanted to meet her brother's girlfriend, but wasn't as sure as he was that they would be friends. Most people didn't like her very much, so she didn't see why Mary would just because Philip wanted her to. But she had said yes, if they could arrange it without any danger of Father finding out, because it made him happy, and his happiness was contagious, lightening the atmosphere whenever he was at home. Philip was so different that Sarah was amazed Father didn't suspect something. But then he would never expect his children to disobey him so profoundly. And that was his weakness, Sarah had realised. As long as you appeared superficially to be obedient, he didn't look beneath the surface. He probably thought Philip was just happy with his work.

When she got close to Mrs Grimes' house she noticed a horse tied to the fence at the side. It was a chestnut-coloured horse, beautiful and very large. Sarah was a bit afraid of horses. Even though they had lovely gentle brown eyes, they were big and moved unexpectedly, and quickly. Most of the horses in the village were working horses though, smaller, rugged and black, but this was a completely different kind of animal. She had not seen it before.

Because of that, rather than just knocking once and then walking into the house as she normally did, she knocked briskly on the door and then waited for a minute. She was just wondering whether to knock again when the door suddenly opened, to reveal a man.

For a moment the two of them looked at each other, and then he spoke.

"Hello!" he said in a friendly local accent. "Are you Sarah?"

"Yes," Sarah replied, surprised that this complete stranger knew who she was.

"Come in," he said, standing to one side of the doorway so she could pass. "Mother's told me all about you. But she didn't tell me she was expecting you today!"

Robert. It had to be. Mrs Grimes only had one surviving child. Sarah wondered what she had told him about her, but whatever it was it couldn't be that she was evil, a Daughter of Eve, because surely he wouldn't have greeted her in such a friendly way if he knew that?

"You must be Robert, then," Sarah said, stepping past him into the living room. He must have been here for a little while. The fire was lit, there was food on the table, a delicious-looking pork pie with a big piece cut out of it, and sitting in the chair by the fire was Mrs Grimes, looking happier than she had for a long time. Sarah turned back to him and smiled. "Your mother's told me all about you, too!"

"Oh, God," he said, smiling. "Sit down. Would you like a piece of pie?" As he was already picking up the knife to cut it, she just nodded and sat down on the opposite side of the fire to the old lady. "Mother," he said as he was cutting a decent slice of pie, "you didn't tell me how beautiful Sarah was!"

Sarah blushed scarlet as he turned to her with the plate.

"I'm sorry," he said immediately, seeing her confusion. "I didn't mean to embarrass you, but I'm only speaking the truth. Mother said you're a very kind girl who comes here every week and who brings her food, and chats with her. But surely all the boys must tell you you're lovely?" He handed her a plate with a slice of pie on, and she looked down at it, not knowing how to respond to such a question.

"I don't really know any boys," she said finally, "except my brother and Simon Bradshaw."

"Ah. Is Simon Bradshaw your lover then? For I think you must have one."

"No," she said. "He's the farmer's son. I knocked him out. He doesn't speak to me now, and I'm glad of it."

Why had she said that? Now he would think she was some sort of brawling madwoman! She felt her face burning and knew she must look like a tomato. She wasn't pretty normally, couldn't understand why this sophisticated man thought she was, but now, beetroot-red, she must look a sight. She felt the embarrassment and incipient tears rise, form a lump in her throat. She couldn't eat. The food would get stuck at the lump. Now he was laughing. Why was he making fun of her? She hadn't done anything to him!

Coming to a decision she stood up suddenly and put the plate down on the table, then turned to Mrs Grimes.

"I'll leave you to enjoy your son's company," she said, her voice trembling slightly. "I'll see you next week." She turned to leave, but as she reached the door he leapt for it, putting his hand flat on the wood to stop her opening it.

"I'm sorry," he said, and sounded it. "I think we've made a bad start. I didn't mean to upset you, but I only spoke the truth. You *are* lovely, and if no one's told you that before, then they must all be blind. Please, let's start again. Sit down. I promise not to compliment you if you don't want me to."

She stood, undecided.

"I think it might be better if you have time with your mother," she said after a moment. "She talks about you all the time. I don't want to be in the way."

"You're not in the way, not at all. Is she, Mother?"

"No, not at all," said Mrs Grimes automatically.

"There you are," he said. "Please, don't leave now. I'll never forgive myself if you do."

Sarah looked up at him. His brown eyes were pleading, not mocking. He seemed genuine. If she left now she would have to wait outside for Philip anyway. And she didn't want to upset Robert if he wasn't really making fun of her. She went and sat back down and he gave her the plate.

"Mother told me that you're the minister's daughter, and that you look after her. I wanted to say thank you to you. I worry about her living here alone."

Why don't you take her to live with you in Liverpool then? Sarah wanted to say, but that would be rude, and she didn't want to be rude to Mrs Grimes' beloved son. He must have his reasons.

"I'm not the only person who calls in to see her now," Sarah said. "I can only come once a week, unfortunately."

"Mother said you came on Wednesday. That's why I was surprised to see you."

"I used to come on Wednesdays, but Father changed the day last year. Your mother gets a little mixed up at times."

Robert smiled. His teeth were white and very regular, even though he was quite old. When had Mrs Grimes said she'd had him? Sarah couldn't remember right now, but she could remember that she'd said he was handsome like his father, and he certainly was that. He wore his own hair, which was long, dark brown and wavy, tied back with a brown ribbon which was the exact shade of his velvet suit. The edges of the coat were covered with embroidery, flowers in shades of orange and yellow, the stems and leaves in beige. He seemed foreign, exotic in this little stone cottage, and yet his mother had told her he had been born here.

"Stem stitch," Sarah said to herself, then blushed again.

Robert followed her line of gaze and picked up the edge of his frockcoat to look at the embroidery, as though he'd only just noticed it was there.

"Do you do a lot of embroidery?" he asked, smiling.

"No, I can only do serviceable sewing," Sarah said, "but I have…I had a friend once, who was trying to master her stem stitch and she talked to me about it, that's all. Your coat is beautiful."

It was. She had never seen anything like it in the village, only in Chester. Her Uncle Arthur would love it. He had worn lovely clothing like this, but Sarah hadn't felt tongue-tied and awkward with her uncle and didn't know why she was with this man, who was paying her the same steady attention as her uncle had, as though she was important, as though she had interesting and valuable things to say.

She didn't have anything either interesting or valuable to relate. She hadn't known that as a child with her uncle, but she did know it now as a young woman with this handsome, exotic stranger.

"I…I really do have to go," she said, even though it was a lie. She could go and walk up the lane past the curve and wait for Philip there, out of sight of this cottage.

This time Robert nodded.

"Very well, then," he said, making no move to impede her this time as she stood. "Will I see you again?"

"I don't think so," Sarah said. "I've never been to Liverpool."

To her surprise, he laughed.

"No, I meant here," he said. "If I come back to visit Mother, will you be here?"

"Only if you come on Saturday afternoons," she said.

"Well, then, I shall come on Saturday afternoons," he replied, smiling.

Sarah sat on a tree stump just round the bend of the lane, waiting for Philip and thinking about Robert. What a strange man he was! She would never have expected Mrs Grimes to have had such a son. He seemed glamorous, sophisticated, with his lovely horse, his beautiful clothes, his warm brown eyes and hair, and his smooth, sallow skin. He didn't look anything like his mother. He didn't belong in the village at all, and she couldn't imagine that he ever would have. Maybe that was why he'd left and gone to live in a big town like Liverpool, where he would not be out of place.

He could not really have thought she was beautiful, in her dull, badly-fitting black dress, with her red chapped hands and mud-brown hair. He must be used to seeing all kinds of beautiful ladies in Liverpool. But it was very nice of him to say she was. He hadn't been mocking her, she realised. He was just being kind, very kind, trying to make her happy.

When Philip came down the lane and wondered why she was waiting for him, she just told him that Mrs Grimes' son was visiting her, so she'd left them alone. She didn't tell him about the conversation they'd had, and just let Philip chat about his girl instead. Philip didn't ask anything about the old lady's son. He wasn't really interested in anything any more, except Mary.

* * *

To her surprise, Robert was there again the next week when she called. His horse wasn't in sight this time, so Sarah had knocked once as normal and then walked straight in, and was covered in confusion when she saw Robert sitting opposite his mother. He stood politely when she walked in. Stood, for her, as though she was a lady!

"Miss Browne," he said, bowing slightly. "Or may I have the privilege of calling you by your first name?"

Again, she blushed scarlet and was immediately angry with herself. What would the man think of her, if every time he saw her she was as red as a tomato?

"You called me Sarah last week," she said, willing her colour to return to normal. "It would seem silly to be formal now."

He smiled, showing his beautiful teeth.

"Excellent!" he said. "Then you must of course call me Robert. I've brought you a little present. I hope you don't think me presumptuous, but when I saw it, I had to bring it for you." Before she could say anything, he dipped in his pocket and brought something out in his hand, reaching across and dropping it into hers.

It was a length of silk ribbon, in a lovely shade of green.

"Oh, that's very kind of you!" Sarah said, smiling.

"When I saw it, I thought it was the same colour as your eyes, because they looked green last week in the sunlight through the window," he said. "But today they look quite different, more brown."

"Do they?" she asked, genuinely puzzled, and realising for the first time that she had never thought about the colour of her eyes before. She could see well with them, and that was all she ever thought about them.

"You are remarkable!" Robert said. "Your eyes are hazel, I can see that now. You should wear green like the ribbon, though, because that would bring out the beautiful green shade in your eyes and the red highlights in your hair."

Sarah looked down at the dark blue woollen dress she was currently wearing.

"I don't choose my clothes," she said. "Father brings the material home when I have need, and I make a new one for myself." Her mother's dress, the one in the trunk was bright blue. Sarah wondered if her mother had had bright blue eyes, like the dress that she had loved enough to store in the trunk. Perhaps the dress had brought out the shade of her eyes and that was why she'd loved it.

"Maybe I should bring you a length of material, then, the shade of the ribbon," Robert said. "Then you could make yourself a dress with it. Would you like that?"

"No!" Sarah said immediately, then saw his face fall, and felt unaccountably upset that she'd hurt him. "I'm sorry," she said. "I would like it very much, but my father would not, and he would be very angry. But thank you for the offer. You're very kind."

"My son has always been very kind," Mrs Grimes said, reminding them both that she was in the room.

"No, Mother," he said. "I'm not being very kind now, ignoring you. There's no excuse for that. Not even a beautiful girl should make me ignore you." He bustled about, getting his mother a glass of wine and a cake, which he had obviously brought this week, then doing the same for Sarah. He had said she was beautiful again, but not in a direct way, so she didn't blush but did feel very special. What a lovely, kind man he was!

"Here," he said after she had a cake in one hand and a glass of pale wine in the other. "Let me put the ribbon in your hair, and get rid of that piece of string you're using now."

Before she could reply he moved behind her and deftly removed the tatty piece of twine she'd tied her hair back with this morning. He gathered her hair together in his hands, his fingers brushing her neck for a moment as he did so, and she shivered instinctively, although his fingers were warm.

Still holding her hair in one hand, he bent over her to pick up the ribbon, which she had placed on the arm of the chair when he'd handed her the food. His breath was warm on the side of her face as he did so, and he was so close that she could smell his cologne. Orange blossom. She closed her eyes for a moment, locking this memory in her mind forever, instinctively knowing that it was special, but telling herself that was only because he wore the same scent as her mother had so long ago.

"Your hair is so thick and heavy," he said softly, intimately to her as he tied the ribbon. "It's glorious. Every woman I know would envy you this." She shivered again, deliciously, as he very gently stroked the back of her neck with one long, strong finger.

Sarah glanced nervously at the old lady sitting opposite, but she was chewing on her cake, oblivious to what her son was doing. She would not have seen him stroke her neck anyway, from where she was. Even if she had, she would forget it in a minute, would not tell other visitors.

Sarah relaxed as much as she could, when every nerve in her body was alight with a pleasure she had never known before.

Later at home, the ribbon out of her hair and hidden in a little slit in her mattress, she thought about the afternoon, what he had done, and how she had felt. What was wrong with her? When she had been in Chester, Maria had brushed her hair for her and tied it, told her it was beautiful, but she hadn't felt every fibre in her body sizzle like it had today!

It must be part of being a woman, she thought. *Like crying about nothing, and losing my temper. Like that.*

Crying about nothing and losing her temper was not wonderful, though. But his hands against her neck, his warm breath on her cheek, *had* been wonderful. She wondered if he would be at his mother's again next Saturday, and prayed that he would be.

Robert Grimes didn't come to his mother's every Saturday, but he came as often as he could. He never told Sarah that she was beautiful any more, but he chatted with her, telling her about Liverpool, about his shop and the lovely things he sold and funny stories about some of his customers, and soon she began to relax with him.

Every time he came he brought her small presents; sweets, tiny exquisitely iced cakes, more ribbons for her hair, in different colours. Once he had brought her some earrings, tiny leaves made of silver, and she had been hugely disappointed that she couldn't wear them, even if only when she was with him, because her ears were not pierced.

He had dismissed her apology, had told her that it was thoughtless of him to bring her presents that she could not wear, that he should have noticed her ears were not pierced. He took the earrings away, and the next week brought her a packet much bulkier than would be needed for earrings.

He did not give her this gift while his mother was sitting there, but asked her to walk in the garden with him for a few minutes, as he had something to say to her. She agreed, but took him into the garden at the back of the house, where no one would see them even if they walked down the lane at the front. The garden had once been cared for, with the remains of a little herb bed, a wooden seat and a scented spindly rose bush, but was now overgrown with weeds.

He led her down the garden as though they were taking a constitutional around a great home, and sat her on the seat. She looked around.

"I should tidy this," she said. "It would be hard work, but worth it, I think. I could do it when you're here to keep her company. Then you could plant vegetables for your mother to eat, and maybe she could sit outside in the nice weather. It must be terribly boring to sit indoors all day. The fresh air would be good for her, would lift her spirits."

She looked up at him standing next to her, waiting for his reaction to her suggestion, but to her surprise he looked upset.

"What's the matter?" she asked.

"Do you dislike my company so much that you'd rather be digging in the garden than talking to me?" he asked.

"What? No, of course not! I just…I'm sorry," she said. "I didn't mean it that way. I thought it would be good for your mother, and would make you happy too, because you love her enough to come all this way to see her so often. And I like working in the garden. It's hard, but it's peaceful too. I like to make things look pretty."

"You make everywhere you are look pretty," he said.

He sat down next to her suddenly, and took her hand in his. It was the first time he had touched her since he had tied the ribbon in her hair the second time he'd seen her.

"Sarah, have you not realised yet that I come here every Saturday that I can to see you?" he asked gently. "I want to see Mother too, of course," he added hastily, "but it would be more convenient to come on other days than Saturday, with my work. But I want to see you. I *need* to see you. Do you not feel the same way for me?"

His hand was large and warm, his nails square and short. On his index finger he wore a gold ring with a motif of a tiny lion on the front in a square setting. She noticed all of this, and that the touch of his hand on hers made her feel safe, happy. She thought about her reply, and he didn't rush her, let her take the time she needed.

"I really hope that you'll be here when I come," she said finally, "and if you're not, then I'm unhappy. And you holding my hand now feels warm and wonderful, and makes me tingle inside. Is that what you mean?"

He smiled.

"Yes," he said, "that's what I mean, except that for me just looking at you makes me tingle inside. Let me give you your present, and show you why." He took the package out of his pocket and gave it to her.

She couldn't put it on a table and look at it for a time like she had the last parcel she'd received, so she opened it straight away, because his expression told her he was eager for her to do so. In the parcel was a tortoiseshell comb, a mother-of-pearl-backed hairbrush and a matching hand mirror. She had never seen anything so beautiful. It was far more beautiful than her mother's hairbrush in the trunk.

"You brought this for me?" she said, stunned.

"Yes," Robert replied. "You have the most beautiful hair. It's only right that you have beautiful things to look after it with. But

I said I want to show you why, or one reason why, I need to see you. Look in the mirror."

She picked up the mirror and looked into it. Looking back at her was a serious young woman with an oval face in which were large greeny-brown eyes, a small nose, and a full wide mouth. She had freckles on her nose and a bit of dead leaf in her hair near the ear, which she wanted to reach up and remove, but couldn't because she had the mirror in one hand, and Robert, once she had opened the present, had grasped her other hand again.

"That's me," she said softly. "That's what I look like."

"Yes," he said. "Do you not know what you look like? Have you no mirror at home?"

"No," she replied. "Women are full of vanity, and mirrors only encourage that and lead them to sinfulness. I looked in a mirror a long time ago, when I was at my uncle's shop, but I was a little girl then." There was a mirror in her mother's chest too, but it was too dark in the cellar for her to see her reflection, and how she looked had never seemed important to her before. "I've seen myself in the village pond," she added, "but the water wasn't still, so I couldn't really see what I looked like. So these are hazel eyes?"

Robert smiled, completely entranced by the simplicity, the complete lack of vanity of this lovely young woman.

"Yes," he said. "You see, now they look more green, because we are in the sunlight. But in other lights they look light brown. You are beautiful. Can you see that, now you know what you look like, what I see every time I look at you?"

She frowned, and watched the forehead of the little image in the mirror wrinkle slightly.

"I don't know," she said with honesty. "It's nice to see what I look like, but the mirror doesn't make me feel beautiful. I…you…" She stopped talking, and felt her face grow hot, and turned the mirror over because she didn't want to see herself going bright red. "Thank you," she said. "It's a wonderful present. I'll use it every day, and think of you when I do!"

She looked up at him and smiled, and on impulse he bent his head the few inches to hers and kissed her lips, which were soft and warm from the sun. She did not kiss him back, because she didn't know how to, but she did not pull away either. His free arm moved around her waist, drawing her closer to him, and he let go of her hand, lifting his behind her head, pulling her cap loose and tangling his fingers in the soft glory of her hair.

Then he kissed her nose, her eyelids, her forehead, in between murmuring endearments she didn't understand, and she laughed aloud from the sheer joy of this handsome, sophisticated man finding her beautiful, of him wanting to be with her, of him caring enough for her to want to make her happy by buying her thoughtful presents, and of him wanting to kiss her, to care for her. She wanted this amazing feeling never, never to end. Desperately she wanted that, more than she had ever wanted anything in her life. Shyly she put her arm around his back, felt the solid strength of him, felt safe, protected, and loved.

When she got home her father was in his study, probably putting the final touches to his sermon for tomorrow. She had hidden the hair set in her basket, and once in the kitchen she put it on the table, then asked her brother if he would see if the hens had laid any eggs, then while he was in the garden checking, she took out the parcel and ran lightly upstairs, hiding it under her pillow before running back down again and making a start on the evening meal.

That night she lay in bed, wide awake in spite of her normal bodily fatigue, and thought about the day, reliving the wonder, the glory of Robert's kiss, how it had made her feel protected, desired, special. She had never felt like that with anyone before, not with her brother, not with Uncle Arthur, not with Angela, even though they had all cared about her in their way.

It suddenly occurred to her that this was how Mary must be making Philip feel, because she too wanted to whistle as she walked along and smile all the time, as he did. Philip had told her he was in love with Mary, that if he could he would spend all of his time with her, and right now, if Sarah could, she would spend all of her time with Robert, and he must feel the same way or he wouldn't come all the way from Liverpool, which was a long way, nearly every Saturday, to see her! True, he came to see his mother too, but he had told her that he came on that inconvenient day to see *her*. Every week.

This was love, then, it must be. It was wonderful! Even though she wouldn't see Robert for another long week, everything looked brighter, everything was happier, all her jobs, normally so tedious, were suddenly lighter, easier. The sun was brighter, the rain was softer.

She hadn't told Philip today, even though part of her had wanted to. Lying in bed now, wide awake, she realised that she couldn't tell him. Because as much as she trusted him and knew that he would not tell Father, he was incapable of hiding his own love. The change in him was blatant and now Sarah knew how he must be feeling, she understood why. On one level she wanted to tell him that she understood exactly how he felt because she now felt the same, wanted to share the details with him, share the wonder of being in love with someone who would be happy for her, as she was happy for him.

But she couldn't. Because somehow she had to carry on behaving exactly as she had when her life had felt gloomy and hopeless. If Father hadn't noticed the change in Philip, or had and assumed it was because he was happy in his work with Mr Stockdale, he would not be the same if she was to start smiling all the time and whistling or singing as she went about her work. Philip was different. He was male, probably elect, was going to Heaven when he died. Although Father was hard on him, he was proud of him too, trusted him, would not mind if he was happy, although would not like the reason why if he found out.

But she was female, weak, stupid, had no value except as a housekeeper for him. She was full of sin, reprobate, was going to Hell and should be miserable about it. If she started showing happiness Father would see it immediately and would suspect that she was up to something, and would stop it. And if he did, she did not think she would be able to bear that.

She had to keep this completely to herself, shut the wonder and new beauty of her life off, hide it like she was hiding the little presents during the week, and only let it out on Saturdays with Robert. And the only way she could be sure of doing that was to tell no one at all. This was the biggest omission thing she had ever had, and the most important. Nothing, not even the thought of making wigs with Uncle Arthur had made her feel as wonderful, as beautiful, as happy as Robert Grimes did, and she was going to keep that for as long as possible, hopefully forever.

CHAPTER EIGHT

Both Philip and Sarah continued their secret relationships. Sarah had warned Philip that appearing too happy might make Father suspicious, so he now attempted to keep his joy hidden at home; but on Saturdays and Sundays down by the river he still talked about Mary a lot of the time, and when he wasn't talking about her, he spoke about his job and how well Mr Stockdale said he was doing.

"It's not as boring as I thought it would be," Philip told Sarah. They were sitting by the stream, but as it was now November there was no chance of them splashing their feet in the freezing water. Instead they were sitting on a big stone at the edge, shivering but willing to accept the cold to have the freedom of talking openly. Catching Sarah's doubtful look, he continued. "It's true that there's a lot of reading and memorising the law, but it's worth it because you can actually help people, people who are really in trouble through no fault of their own. Last week Mr Stanhope stopped an old lady's son from throwing her out of her own home and leaving her destitute!"

"Who would throw their own mother out?" Sarah asked, shocked. *Robert would never do that,* she almost added, but just stopped herself in time. She had still not told Philip about her and Robert, and as the weeks went on it was easier not to say anything. She told herself that if she told him now he would want to know why she'd kept it secret for so long, so it was easier just to keep it to herself.

"You'd be surprised how horrible people can be to each other," Philip said. Both of them went silent for a moment.

"No, I wouldn't," Sarah replied quietly. "People are not very nice to each other, are they?"

"No," Philip agreed. "Unless you find the right person. Some of them are nice. You have to look until you find that person who will always love you and care for you, and then make sure to keep them."

"Do you think Mary's that person?" Sarah asked.

To her surprise, instead of saying "Yes!" emphatically and immediately, Philip looked pensively into the stream and thought about it before he answered.

"I think so," he said finally. "She's very sweet, and when I'm with her I think she's the right person for me to live with forever. But I know she's had a lot of other lovers, and she's so friendly with everyone. I try to tell myself that she's just a friendly person, but part of me is jealous of that."

"So you don't trust her?" Sarah asked.

"Of course I do!" he protested immediately.

"It doesn't sound as if you do. It sounds as if you wonder whether she's got another lover as well as you. Have you asked her?"

"Well, no. How do you ask someone that?"

"I don't know. But if you love her and you're thinking of marrying her, then don't you think you should be able to ask her anything, and trust her to tell you the truth?"

"You make it sound so easy," Philip said. "But being in love with someone is strange. It makes you…it makes you different, your emotions, so you don't always know if you're being sensible in what you're thinking or not. And it makes you afraid too."

"Afraid?" Sarah said. "Why afraid?"

"Because you worry that if you say or do the wrong thing, you'll lose them. And that feels like the worst thing that could happen in the whole world. It's hard to explain."

No, it wasn't. She knew how he felt, although it was a bit different for her with Robert. Every time she saw him she knew he must love her, because he was making such a long journey to see her. True, he came to see his mother as well, but he had never come to see her *every* week before he'd met Sarah. Even Mrs Grimes herself had commented on that. But the old lady was very pleased to see him, so probably wouldn't have questioned him too much even if she'd been in full command of her faculties.

The couple had settled into a pattern now. They would sit in the cottage with the old lady and eat whatever delicacy Robert had brought with him from Liverpool, and maybe drink a glass of wine. They would let the old lady chat to them while they ate and drank, even though sometimes she made Robert blush with the stories she told about the mischief he got up to as a child.

Sarah loved the way Robert blushed. His ears would go pink at first, and then the colour would deepen slowly from his neck up to his forehead. It was adorable. He had lovely ears, small for a man. She had never thought about ears being lovely before.

She had never thought about lots of things before she had met him.

After the food they would go and sit outside on their little wooden seat, unless it was raining heavily. As it got colder he had at first taken his coat off and put it round her shoulders to keep her warm, and while she loved feeling the intimacy of the residual warmth of his body in the coat as he carefully placed it round her, and loved his tenderness and care for her comfort, she hated to see him shivering in his shirt sleeves while she was warm, and had said so. So one week he had brought a heavy woollen cloak for her, a full-length one which was big enough to wrap round both of them if they sat close together.

They sat close together.

While they sat they held hands, and they talked. He talked about Liverpool, what an interesting town it was, a town where it was possible to become rich, but which was dangerous too.

"Because it's by the sea," he explained, "there are a lot of privateers, and they and the crews of the slave ships can be very violent men indeed. So there's a deal of crime there."

"Why do you live there, then, if it's full of violent men? You could live here, where it's peaceful."

He slid his arm around her shoulders and pulled her closer to him, and kissed her on the forehead.

"Because it's exciting too," he said. "And it may be dangerous, but it's never boring, as Alliston is. There are lots of products and people, from all over the world. And when the sailors come in, many of them have money and want to spend it. They buy new suits of clothes from me, and then they go into the taverns to have a good time. You can talk to people who have been to places on the other side of the world, and who will tell you about the amazing sights to be seen there, things no one in a village like this would ever dream of.

"And then there are the people who are very rich from the shipping trade, and they too have money and want to spend it. And they spend it buying clothes made from the most expensive materials, because then everyone who looks at them will know immediately that they're rich and powerful. It's a wild place, but an exciting place to live."

"I would like to visit it one day," she said wistfully. "I've been to Chester, which was very beautiful and had some ships, but Liverpool sounds even more interesting, with all the fancy houses you told me about. I should like to see those very much."

"Maybe one day you will," he said vaguely.

She wanted to ask him to take his mother there, and her too, and that she would happily look after his mother and his house for him, if he would only take her away from her father. But she never quite got the courage to ask, partly because she knew that it would hurt her to leave Philip, and partly because she was aware that it probably wouldn't be acceptable for a single woman to live in a bachelor's house, even if she was his mother's carer. But mainly she didn't ask because Robert never spoke about his private life at all, nor did he give her an opening to ask the question.

He spoke about his shop and the different things he sold, and he spoke about the ships, the sailors, the products that came off the ships, about the wide thoroughfares of the town and the beautiful buildings, about the Irish immigrants who spoke a strange language, and about the slaves whose skins were as black as tar. But he never talked about his own house, and when she tried to mention it he would change the subject, comment that she looked cold, or produce a little present for her from his pocket.

Only later, when she was away from his disturbing enigmatic presence that made her senses reel and her mind unable to think of anything but his nearness, did she realise that he'd avoided answering her question. When she was close to him it made her brain dim but her body sparkle like the bubbles in the champagne that he'd brought one week to celebrate his mother's birthday.

Sarah had laughed as the bubbles went up her nose, but had only had one small glass because it made her feel silly and reckless, and she could not be silly and reckless when she went home or her father would suspect something. Robert had asked her later if she didn't like champagne, and she had told him that she loved it. But then she had told him why she couldn't drink any more of it, and he had nodded and said he understood, and that if her father was so strict it was probably better if she didn't tell anyone that they were meeting, and if they didn't go anywhere where they might be seen.

And so the little bench in the back garden had become their special place. She had thought he might be angry that she was keeping the truth from her father, from everyone, that he might think she was ashamed of knowing him. But he hadn't been angry or upset at all. Really, he was so kind and understanding!

"I'm really sorry that I won't be able to come and see you at Christmastime," Robert said. They were out in the garden on their customary seat, snuggled together under the warm shawl, their breath misting in the frosty air as they spoke. "I really wanted to spend it with you…and Mother, of course. But I'll just be too busy."

"I've never celebrated Christmas," Sarah said, "so I don't mind. I wouldn't know what to do."

He looked at her, clearly shocked.

"You've never celebrated Christmas? Why ever not?"

"Father says it's a Popish heathen festival, that it's just an excuse to drink and eat too much, and sin, and in the name of Christ, which makes it even worse."

Robert sighed.

"I think your father confuses having fun and loving people for sinning," he said. "Why would God allow us to be able to invent music and dancing, if He didn't want us to enjoy ourselves? Why, Christ Himself even went to a wedding and celebrated!"

"Did He?" Sarah asked, surprised. "Did He dance and sing?"

"I can't remember," Robert admitted. "But I do know that during the party they ran out of wine, so Christ turned water into wine so they could carry on having a good time. I don't think He'd have done that if He was worried about them getting drunk."

"I didn't know that," Sarah said. "Is it in the Bible?"

"Yes, I'm sure it is. I'll find out for you. But I think you should celebrate Christmas, at least once. It's a lovely time. People put greenery in the house, so it smells and looks wonderful, and they have big fires so the house is warm and welcoming. Rich people have huge banquets and balls, but when I was a child, even we used to eat mutton or goose and plum pudding and drink hot spiced wine, and then we'd all sing songs and tell stories, and play games. And we'd give each other little gifts. It's all very warm and friendly."

"It sounds wonderful," Sarah said wistfully.

"It is. And it cheers up the winter too. But most of the people in Alliston keep Christmas, even if your father doesn't. You must at least have seen the celebrations."

She hadn't talked a lot about her family circumstances to date, following Robert's lead of not doing so. She was silent for a minute.

"I don't go out and do things with the people in the village," she said finally. "I've always had to stay at home, and I've looked after Father and Philip for as long as I can remember. This is the only time I go out, to visit your mother and three other ladies, and I have to go straight home afterwards. So I don't really know what the village people do." She couldn't tell him that Philip even had to accompany her so she didn't do anything sinful, because if she did he'd want to know where Philip was now, and she couldn't tell him because it was a secret.

She looked up at Robert's handsome face and saw the pity in it, and hated it.

"But it's alright," she added cheerfully. "I like being on my own, and I don't know how to make plum pudding anyway. I don't even know what it is! And I don't know any songs, so it's maybe better that we don't celebrate it." She smiled up at him, but he still looked unhappy, and thoughtful.

"Let's celebrate Christmas!" he said suddenly, clasping her hands.

"What, now?" Sarah said.

"No, in December, or in January. Yes, January would be better. As I said, I'm too busy to be able to come at Christmas itself, but I can still show you what it's like! We'll have our own little party, just the three of us. What do you think?"

"But I don't know how…"

"You don't need to know anything. I'll arrange it all. All you have to do is come. And we'll do it on a Saturday when you call here anyway. It might be a little rushed, because we only have a few hours, but we can wear our very best clothes, have greenery, wine and good food, and I'll teach you a Christmas song or two. Mother will love it, I'm sure! What do you say?"

Sarah was silent for a moment, wondering how to tell him that the dress she was wearing, plain as it was, was the best one she owned, and he mistook her silence for reluctance.

"I'm sorry," he said. "I should not be trying to make you disobey your father, or go against your religious principles. Think no more of it."

"No!" Sarah cried, seeing how disappointed he looked. She could not bear for him to be disappointed, and Christmas sounded beautiful. "They're not *my* religious principles. It sounds wonderful. Yes, let's do it!"

January the thirteenth. That was the magical date they had arranged. It was a Saturday, and it was the first Saturday Robert could come to Alliston after the start of the Christmas season. He couldn't come on the sixth because that was Twelfth Night, and people had balls on that night. He hadn't told Sarah, but she supposed that as an important businessman he would have lots of friends, and be expected to go to their parties. Also of course, all the people, ladies and gentlemen would want beautiful clothes for their balls, and Robert was a haberdasher so no doubt Christmas would be an extremely busy time for him. That must be why he would not be able to come to Alliston for the whole of December.

She missed him terribly, far more even than she expected to. Six weeks without seeing him seemed like a lifetime. Every day dragged, and the Saturdays with Mrs Grimes just reminded her of how dull and gloomy the cottage was without Robert, and how dull Mrs Grimes was. In fact Sarah now realised that her whole life was dull and gloomy, and always had been.

She told herself that she only felt that way because it was winter, with horrible weather and long dark nights in which she could do nothing, not even mend clothes, because her father refused to waste any candles that were not needed in his study to write his important sermons. She would sit as close to the meagre fire as possible, staring into the flames and thinking of the only thing that brought any light into her life.

Robert.

She no longer dreamed of wearing her mother's beautiful dress in Chester, making wigs for her Uncle Arthur and looking after their house while her brother went soldiering. Philip was not going for a soldier anyway. Sarah had realised that, even if Philip hadn't.

It didn't matter, because it was clear that Robert cared very much for her. So much that he was going to make Christmas in January, just for her! Soon, surely, he would take her to Liverpool. Then she could wear the dress anyway, and look after Mrs Grimes during the day, and then in the evening Robert would come home and they would have every evening together. Maybe she would make wigs anyway. After all, people who wanted beautiful clothes would want beautiful wigs too! They would get married, and then they would live happily forever. And there would be no scandal about them living in the same house if they were married.

She knew it was a dream, but just as the dream about Chester had seemed possible at one time, the dream about Liverpool seemed possible now. More possible, because it made sense, and because Robert already had a business and a house. He was not young and changeable like Philip was. And even if it was only a dream, it was lovely to think about, and brightened up the dark and lonely winter nights.

The dress. Of course! Robert had told her that people wore their most beautiful clothes at Christmas, and she had been worried about that. But there was her mother's dress! It was incredibly beautiful. If it actually fitted her, she would wear it for Robert on January the thirteenth. Oh, it had to fit her!

She resisted the urge to run down to the cellar immediately and try it on to find out. Father was in the house, and Philip was out but might come home at any moment. There was plenty of time until January. And she was good at waiting.

She waited, until her father had gone on one of his trips to Chester and Philip was at work and would not be home for several hours, and then she went down the stairs to the cellar, and brought her mother's dress upstairs. She had never seen it by anything other than dim candlelight, but now as she laid it out on the kitchen table she realised just how lovely it would have been when new. Even in the weak winter daylight she could see that the silk of the bodice was worn, and some of the lovely beads were missing. But it was still incredibly beautiful, the silk a shimmering royal blue, and the lace at the sleeves, although yellowed and torn in a couple of places, was very delicate and would froth beautifully over the forearms. The stomacher was of cream silk, but embroidered with blue flowers the exact shade of the gown.

She knew that the first thing she should do was to try the dress on to see if it fit her. But she also knew that if it didn't the fluttery excitement in her chest would become a lump of sadness, so, just as she had with the parcel from Uncle Arthur, she stretched the anticipation out by carefully repairing the torn lace as best she could. Then she took everything upstairs to her room, took the ribbons that Robert had bought her from the slit in her mattress, and the brush and mirror from the space under the loose bedroom floorboard where she had hidden them and the other little trinkets he'd bought for her, and spent some time sitting on the bed in her shift and stays, styling her hair.

There was no point in doing a style that would take hours, because she knew that on the day she would have to dress as normal and then change at Mrs Grimes' house, and needed to be able to do it quickly. But she did manage to sweep it high on the top, with the aid of a little pad that Uncle Arthur had sent her, and she swept the sides up too, securing them with clips and allowing the rest of her hair to cascade in waves down her back. Then she carefully dressed herself, finding to her utter delight that apart from being a little large around the bosom, which meant that the bodice almost closed at the front, the dress fitted beautifully. It would be a shame that the embroidered stomacher would therefore be almost hidden by the bodice, but she was not skilled enough to alter the dress.

It felt strange. The skirt was very full and heavy and a little long on her, as it was designed to be worn with panniers which Sarah didn't own, and the sleeves were slightly tight, the lace scratchy where it was sewn into them at the elbows. But even though she couldn't really see properly how she looked with only the tiny hand mirror, she *felt* beautiful, truly an adult. Robert had only ever seen her in her plain cotton or woollen dress, her hair scrunched up under a cap. At least at Christmas he would see that she could be more than a dull village girl, that she might be fit to grace a town house.

While she had been dressing it had gone dark, so she went downstairs and recklessly purloined six candles from her father's study to light her bedroom. They reflected the shimmering beads on the dress beautifully. She twirled around, feeling the skirts swirl out around her legs and then settle, and she laughed with the pure joy of feeling, just for a moment, beautiful.

There came a knock on the door and she froze. Oh God, no. Surely her father could not be home already! What time was it? And then Philip's voice came from the corridor, asking her if he could come in, and the relief was so huge that without thinking she said yes.

He opened the door and walked in, and then he saw her and stopped. His eyes widened and his mouth fell open, and for a long moment he just stared at her.

"My God!" he said finally.

Sarah licked her lips nervously, all her confidence draining away instantly.

"Do I look horrible?" she asked tremulously. He would tell her the truth. He always told her the truth. It would be better to know, before she made a fool of herself in front of Robert.

"Horrible? God, no. You look beautiful! I...I never imagined you could look so lovely!" Philip said. He sat down suddenly on the edge of the bed. "You're really a woman now," he added. "I never realised it until this minute."

Sarah wanted to shout with delight, but instead she beamed, and sat down next to him, her eyes sparkling.

"Do I really look beautiful?" she said. "You're not just being kind to me?"

"No, of course not," he replied. "You just took my breath away, that's all. But why are you wearing it? And what did you do to your hair? It makes you look more grown up even than the dress does!"

"I need to take it off," she said. "I didn't realise the time. If

Father comes home and sees me, he'll be very angry. I just wanted to try it on, see if it did fit me now my body has changed shape, that's all. I…I need to tell you something," she added. She had known that she would have to tell him something, and now, when she felt beautiful and confident, was the right time. She started taking the pins out of her hair. "Mrs Grimes' son is coming to see her on the second Saturday of January, to celebrate Christmas with her, because he'll be too busy to visit before that, and she wants me to go and join in. And I would really love to. There'll be plum pudding and greenery, and I thought…I'd like to look nice. She told me all about the Christmasses she used to celebrate in Bristol when she was a young woman, and it sounds lovely." The only lie she'd told so far was that it wasn't Mrs Grimes but her son who wanted her to go. That was a tiny lie. Surely she wouldn't go to Hell for that?

"Well you can, if it's a Saturday," Philip said. "That's when you go to visit her anyway, isn't it?"

"Yes, but I thought I'd tell the other ladies that I can't see them, and then I can just visit Mrs Grimes and have more time with her. I wanted to tell you because it'll give you more time with Mary too, if you want," she added.

Philip smiled, and she saw the change in his expression and knew that he would agree to anything if it would give him more time with Mary.

"I'll need your help," she said, "because I can't wear the dress to go, and it's too big to hide in my basket, so I wondered if you could maybe take it to work one day and hide it there, then bring it on the day. I really want to wear it. I've wanted to wear it for years. I can change at Mrs Grimes' cottage."

"Father will be very angry if he finds out you're celebrating Christmas, even if you don't wear the dress," Philip said.

"I know. But you're not going to tell him, and if he finds out another way I really don't care. My life is so boring, and at least this will be something different and interesting. I'll take my chance on him finding out. But I don't see why he would. Mrs Grimes isn't likely to ever come to church again, and Father never goes to visit any of his parishioners."

"That's true. The others might mention that you didn't go to them though."

"If they do, then they do. I just want to do something interesting for once. And I'm not afraid of being in the cellar any more. Do you remember, years ago, when you told me there was only one monster in this house and it wasn't in the cellar?"

"No," Philip said. "Did I really say that?"

"Yes. After that I felt happier in the cellar because there was no monster, but worried that it might be in my bedroom under the bed. But now I know who the monster is, and where he is, and when he's not there I'm going to enjoy myself, because if I don't I'm going to grow old and die without having had any fun at all. I'm more frightened of that than I am of the monster, now," she said. She put the hairpins in their little box and closed the lid. Then she looked at her brother and smiled at him. "It took me a long time to put this dress on, so now you're here you can help me get it off and hidden, before the monster comes home."

Philip laughed, and they both stood up and set to work liberating her from the garment.

"You really are a woman now," he commented after everything was safely hidden, the candles were back in the reverend's study and they were both sitting by the fire in the kitchen.

"Does the dress really change me that much?" Sarah asked.

"Yes, it does, but it wasn't just the dress, it was what you said when you were wearing it. Did you mean that, about not being afraid of Father?"

"I didn't say I wasn't afraid of him," she pointed out. "I said that I'm more frightened of never having any fun. It's different for you. You're a man. You'll get your own house, get married and be away from him, and everyone will accept that. But I'm expected to stay and look after him for the rest of his life. So if I have to do that I'm going to take whatever fun I can get, because I'll be old by the time he dies."

"You can come with me, when I get my own house," Philip said, and for the first time she heard how uncertain, how half-hearted he sounded about that. Had he always sounded like that, or had wearing the dress made her older, wiser somehow? Impulsively she leaned across the space between them and gripped his hand.

"Philip, I know you're not going for a soldier now, and we're not going to live in Chester together," she said. "It was a lovely dream, but we were children then. You're going to get married, if not to Mary, to another girl, and she will not want your sister living with her. And that's natural. I will still love you. I will always love you."

He squeezed her hand.

"I won't let him ruin your life, or beat you any more," Philip said. "I told you that when I was a man I would protect you, and I will. You know that, don't you?"

"Of course I do," she said.

And she believed it, utterly.

* * *

The siblings arrived at Mrs Grimes' cottage two hours earlier than they normally would. Sarah was fizzing with excitement, and able to show it now, after weeks of having to be very careful not to rouse her father's suspicions. Over her arm she carried a basket, which contained her hairdressing equipment and some pastries she'd made with the last of the raisins and cinnamon her uncle had sent to her. Philip had the dress in a bag, carefully folded, which he now handed to her. Then unexpectedly he reached out and gave her a quick, fierce hug and kissed her cheek.

"You look lovely right now, even without the dress," he said, making Sarah blush. "Have a wonderful time. I'll come back for you at five o'clock." Both of them had decided that was the latest they could stay out without arousing their father's suspicions that they were up to something.

Seven hours, Sarah thought. Seven hours celebrating Christmas with Robert. She closed her eyes, took a deep breath, and knocked on the cottage door, as she always did before opening it and walking in.

"Wait!" Robert cried from within. He came to the door and opened it. "Close your eyes," he said, smiling. "Don't open them until I tell you to."

She did as she was told, and he took her hand and led her into the cottage, steering her into the living room of the little building. Even without opening her eyes she knew the fire was burning merrily and had been for some time, because the room was lovely and warm. It also smelt amazing, of pine, roasting meat and spices.

THE WHORE'S TALE: SARAH

"Now you can open them," he said.

She opened her eyes and gasped with surprise. The room was transformed. The kitchen table had been brought into the room and covered with a white tablecloth. It was set for three people, with silver cutlery and wine glasses. In her chair by the fire Mrs Grimes sat, wearing a blue flower-sprigged dress that Sarah had never seen before, her wispy hair combed and covered by a new lacy cap.

In the centre of the table was a candelabra with three beeswax candles burning in it, and other candles were dotted about the room. And there was greenery everywhere; around the frame of King George's picture, around the doorframes, and looped along the beams of the room, which ran along the ceiling. Laurel, pine, ivy and holly, all garlanded and tied in place with red silk ribbons. It was like fairyland. Sarah had never seen anything so beautiful. She stood looking at his work, entranced, not just by the beauty of the decorations, but by the fact that it must have taken him hours, and he had done all of this for her. Nobody in her whole life had ever taken this much time and effort to make her happy.

"Do you like it?" he asked. She looked up at him. He was still holding her hand, and his brown eyes were dancing with happiness.

To her horror her eyes filled with tears, and she watched his face blur for a moment, then as the tears ran down her cheeks she saw that his expression had changed, was now distressed.

"I'm sorry," she said, brushing the tears away and smiling weakly at him. "It's beautiful. It's the most beautiful room in the world. I didn't mean to cry. It's just that..." her voice trailed away.

"It's just that..." he prompted.

"I can't believe you've done all this for me," she murmured, feeling embarrassed.

"You deserve it," he said, smiling again. "As long as you like it, then I'm happy."

"Oh, I do!" she said. "I never expected this. Thank you!"

He bent down impulsively and kissed her quickly on the lips, and her heart melted. Then she remembered that they were not alone. She glanced at Mrs Grimes, but the old lady was looking into the fire, oblivious.

"Here," Robert said, "I wasn't expecting you quite this early, but I don't want you to do any work today. The food is cooking, and if you sit down I'll get you a glass of spiced wine. Let me take your basket and parcel."

"No!" Sarah said, remembering. "I came early because I thought I might arrive before you, and I have a little surprise, but I need to be alone, just for a short time. Mrs Grimes, can I go upstairs for a few minutes?"

The old lady turned from the fire at her name, and smiled.

"Of course you can, child," she said. "Isn't it lovely? It was always like this when I was young at Christmas. Didn't take no notice of that damned Puritan idiot. Ran him out of town we did, once we knew the king was back to stay and we could have fun again. That was a good day, that was."

"Er…perhaps you might go up?" Robert said, aware that Sarah's father seemed to be a minister not unlike the one his mother had helped to run out of town.

She went upstairs to Mrs Grimes' little bedroom, which was colder than the room below but still warmed by the chimney breast from the fire in the living room. She looked around. To her delight there was a dressing table in the corner, with a mirror! She went over to it, put her basket down and sat on the little stool, looking at her reflection.

She was a woman. She had a waist, and breasts, and her face had lost its childish roundness and was now oval, her cheekbones high and firm. She didn't think she was beautiful; her mouth was too wide and full, but she was, most definitely, fifteen years old and a woman grown. And downstairs was a handsome older man who thought she was beautiful, and who had spent hours decorating the cottage just to please her. She smiled at herself, and then she took out her brush and clips and began transforming herself.

When she returned downstairs, holding her skirts up so that she wouldn't trip over them and spoil the whole surprise by falling down the stairs, he was sitting in the chair opposite his mother chatting to her, but when Sarah walked in he looked up, and the expression on his face mirrored Philip's when he had seen her in the dress, and she knew she had done well. Robert stood and walked over to her, the embroidered skirt of his burgundy silk frockcoat flaring out as he did. And then he bowed expertly to her, as though she were the queen, and he took her hand, raising it to his lips and kissing it.

"You," he said softly and earnestly, "are the most beautiful young lady I have ever seen. Mother, look at her. Is she not glorious?"

Mrs Grimes looked at her.

"You look like your mother, child," she said, having one of her now rare lucid moments. "She was beautiful too, like you, but she had fair hair and blue eyes. Lovely she was, but delicate. Didn't belong here. Never belonged with that, poor thing. Should have gone long before she did."

Sarah stood, struck dumb. In all the months she had been coming here, Mrs Grimes had never mentioned her mother. Sarah had no idea she'd ever known her.

"What was she like?" she asked. "I don't remember her really. She died when I was three," she explained to Robert.

"Died," Mrs Grimes repeated. "My husband died, you know that? Handsome man, looked just like Robert," she said, smiling up at her son. "Look good together, you do. Better than…than… what's her name again? Never liked her."

Robert blushed furiously, let go of Sarah's hand and rushed over to his mother.

"Sarah's asking about her mother, Mama," he said, "wants to know if you remember what she was like."

"What? What who was like?" Mrs Grimes said. "Warm in here it is. I haven't been this warm in ages. Lovely." She smiled up at Robert. "Good boy, you are."

The moment was gone, but Sarah tried not to feel disappointed. If Mrs Grimes had never liked her mother, maybe it was better not to know what she thought Catherine Browne was like. She forced the thought aside, and smiled. Nothing could spoil today, nothing. She pulled out one of the chairs round the table and sat down, loving the feel of the heavy silk skirts on her legs, and accepting a glass of the warm wine. She sipped it, enjoying the spicy smell and the warm fruity taste of it.

"I want you to open your present," he said, "before dinner's ready. I know you can't stay too long." He bent down to the side of the chair, and brought out a small parcel, beautifully wrapped in pink chiffon, with a cream silk ribbon tied in an elaborate bow. "Here," he said. "I hope you like it."

Shyly she took it off him. He had brought her small presents before, but never anything beautifully wrapped. She stared at it in wonder. He produced a similarly wrapped larger present for his mother which he handed across, then looked back at Sarah.

"You're not going to cry again, are you?" he asked, only half in jest. Sarah looked at him.

"No! But…I haven't brought you a present," she said. "I would have, but I don't have money of my own, and—"

"Seeing you happy, and being able to spend today with you is all the present I want," Robert said. "Go on, open it."

Inside was a silver heart-shaped locket on a chain.

"Oh, it's beautiful!" she cried. He stood up, and taking it from her walked behind her to put it round her neck. As he did he stroked her neck again, as he had months ago when he had put the ribbon in her hair, but this time he bent and very gently kissed her ear.

"There's a small lock on the side," he whispered. "If you open it later, there's a little something inside it, which means a part of me will always be with you, if you want."

The whole day she was happy, so happy she thought she might die of it. She did help him to finish the dinner, in spite of his declaration that he didn't want her to do anything today, because it was so obvious to her that he had no idea how to cook food. In the kitchen he had a piece of paper, and he admitted when she asked that his housekeeper had written out all the instructions on how to prepare the food, which the cook had already made, so that he wouldn't ruin it. Touched beyond words that he'd gone to so much effort for her, Sarah insisted on helping him to finish and put it out, in lovely silver dishes that he'd brought from home especially. He rewarded her for her assistance with a long passionate kiss, the intensity of which he'd never given before and which left both of them flushed, Sarah's legs weak and wobbly, and almost resulted in the meal being burnt.

The two of them returned to the living room carrying dishes of food, and covered their heightened emotions by bustling around making sure everything was perfect. Robert helped his mother to the table and served the food to her, painstakingly cutting it into tiny pieces that she could eat herself without having to chew, as she had no teeth, before sitting down opposite Sarah and smiling at her, his brown eyes burning with a passion that made Sarah blush again. She concentrated on her meal to recover her poise, but in spite of her efforts was intensely aware of everything about him, every move he made, every word he spoke, and her body burned with a fire that had nothing to do with the temperature of the room.

He was the most handsome man in the world, elegant but masculine, sophisticated. The hand holding his wine glass was square and strong, the fingers long. His features were regular, his nose long and straight, his eyes smiling and deep warm brown. He wore his own hair, unpowdered, tied back with a burgundy ribbon that matched his exquisite outfit, but small strands had escaped to curl adorably over his forehead.

As she tried not to look at him, terrified that if she did she would just melt, be unable to eat, unable to do anything but worship him openly, disgracing herself in front of his mother, she felt his toe brush her foot, and then slide softly and smoothly up the front of her leg to the knee and back down again.

Then she did look at him, her eyes wide, and he smiled, amused by her reaction. She knew she should be shocked, that her father would be horrified if he knew she was sitting here in her mother's beautiful dress, allowing a man to stroke her legs, his eyes full of passion.

To hell with her father. To hell with everything except this perfect, perfect day, when she was beautiful, and for the first time in her life knew the glory and the power of her femininity, that could make a man do all this just because he wanted her.

After dinner, as promised, he sang a Christmas song, his voice a deep baritone, while Sarah and Mrs Grimes sat by the fire.

> "Hark how all the welkin rings,
> Glory to the King of Kings
> Peace on earth and mercy mild,
> God and sinners reconciled."

"I never heard that song before," Mrs Grimes said when he'd finished and Sarah had applauded.

"It's a new festive song, Mama," Robert said. "It was only published this year."

"Oh, it's wonderful!" Sarah cried. "And you have a perfect voice for singing it."

"Always had a lovely voice, my son," his mother replied. "Was known for it. Used to sing at all the festivals, he did."

"I still do, Mama, when I have the time," Robert replied. "Do you want me to teach it to you?" he asked Sarah.

"No, I can't sing," Sarah said, although in fact she had no idea whether she could or not. With a sudden shock, she realised that she had never sung a song, knew no songs at all. Singing, dancing, anything to do with music was a sin, invented by the Devil to lead people to Hell.

"I'm sure you can," Robert said. "Here, have another glass of wine. That will give you the confidence to try, and then I'll teach you."

"What time is it?" Sarah asked. She glanced out of the window, noting that it was dull outside, but not dark yet, although it probably would be soon. Where had the time gone? Her wonderful day was almost over! Her heart sank. In the meantime Robert had taken out his pocket watch and glanced at it.

"It's a quarter before four," he said. "You have an hour yet. Plenty of time to drink a glass of wine and learn a song."

"No," she said, standing. "I can't drink now. If I do, Father will know when I get home. I must change my dress now, too. Five is the very latest I can leave."

He made no more objections, allowed her to leave the living room and go up to the bedroom.

She went in, moved over to the dressing table and sat down. The room was lovely and warm now, but her day was almost over, and then her life would be miserable again. It was too much to bear. Unbidden a tear spilled over her lashes and ran down her cheek, followed by another. *I cannot be sad yet,* she told herself, *the day is not over.*

She brushed away the tears, sniffed, and then reached up to unpin her hair. In the mirror she saw the door open behind her and then Robert was there, his form wavering slightly in the uneven silvering of the mirror.

"Don't be sad," he said softly. "It's been a delightful day, and we will have more, I promise." He bent and lifted her hair, kissing the back of her neck and making her shiver deliciously. "You are so very beautiful," he murmured. She reached up to take the pins out of her hair, but he captured her hand in his, stopping her. "Let me do it for you," he said.

"What about your mother?" Sarah asked. She would know he had come upstairs, would wonder why.

"She's fallen asleep in the chair," he said. "She'll sleep for hours unless I wake her. Come, let me do this. It would make me very happy."

She sat still while he carefully took the pins from her hair, laying them on the dressing table. Then he picked up the brush he'd given to her and brushed her hair, slowly and languorously. She closed her eyes, wanting to savour the pure sensual pleasure of it, and when he stopped she opened them, seeing first her own dreamy smile and then his eyes, alight as he looked at her hair, a sheet of wavy mahogany silk down her back.

"Your hair is exquisite," he said, and then he buried his face in it, wrapping his arms around her waist and lifting her from the stool she was sitting on. She stood, and he turned her gently, then his lips were on hers, and they were not gentle; they were hard and passionate, and she responded to him, instinctively parting her lips to allow him to invade her mouth with his tongue.

Her legs buckled, but she didn't fall, because his arm was round her waist as he held her easily, his mouth plundering hers, one hand tangled in her hair. Then he pulled away and she almost did fall, her bones all turned to jelly.

"Can I…can I help you to undress?" he asked. "I would give anything, anything at all to see you in all your glory."

Unable to speak she nodded shyly, and he reached across, began taking out the pins which held her stomacher to the bodice, after which he took off the bodice and attached outer skirt. Then he moved behind her and unlaced the lower skirt, and then the petticoat beneath it, allowing them to fall to the ground at her feet. He continued undressing her, feathering kisses across her shoulders and arms, every move slow and smooth, although, innocent as she was, she sensed how hard he was fighting the impulse to disrobe her quickly – she had felt exactly the same when opening the present he had given to her earlier, and before that, the present from her uncle.

Her stays fastened at the front and she lifted her hands to the laces, suddenly shy. No man had ever seen her in anything less than stays and shift, and in fact the only man who ever had seen her even in those garments was her brother, and he didn't really count as a man. But she was fervently, urgently aware that Robert was very much a man, and if she didn't stop him now, he would soon see her as naked as the day she was born.

"My darling girl, you have no reason to fear me," he said. "I will do nothing that you don't want me to do. But I would like more than anything in the world to see all of you. Will you allow me that, and only that?"

His voice was soft, gentle and reassuring, although his eyes were ablaze. After all he had done today to make her happy, and the lovely present he had bought her, letting him see her naked was the least she could do, if it would please him so much. She nodded again, and removed her hands, allowing him to unlace the stays and then remove them. She thought he would lift her shift over her head then, but to her surprise he did not.

Instead he knelt, and running his fingers featherlight up her leg, he untied the ribbon above her knee that secured her stocking, then rolled the woollen stocking down her leg. After repeating the action with her other leg he looked at the ribbon in his fingers.

"Is this one of the ribbons I bought for you?" he asked, his voice husky.

"Yes," she said. "I can't wear them in my hair in case Father sees them, but I wanted to have something of yours against…" *my skin* "…with me all the time," she said.

He looked up at her and smiled a smile of infinite tenderness, and then he stood. Quickly he shrugged off his coat and waistcoat, then taking her in his arms he kissed her again, his tongue plundering her mouth as before, but now that there was only the thin material of her shift and his shirt separating their torsos, she could feel the heat of his chest against hers, the hardness of the muscles in his arms as he held her, and the tension vibrating through his body.

She had no idea why he was tense. For her part, she felt like her whole body was liquid. If he let her go she would pour across the floor. Every inch of her that was in contact with him was on fire, and her heart was hammering in her chest. Never, never in her life had she felt like this, and never, never did she want the feeling to stop.

Very carefully he moved her backwards, his mouth still on hers, his orange blossom scent all around them, and then he lowered her to the bed, lifting her shift as he did, so that once she was sitting he could remove it without her having to stand.

She could not have stood at that moment, could not have done anything, even if her life depended on it. He threw the shift to one side and then stepped back to look at her, and she mewed a little at the sudden loss of contact with him.

"Let me just look at you, just for a moment," he said. "You are the most exquisite creature I have ever seen." He knelt down in front of her as though in worship, and took her hands in his. "Don't be shy," he said softly, seeing her blush. "You have nothing to be ashamed of. You are perfection." He kissed her hands, then let her go and quickly removed his shirt, pulling it over his head, revealing his chest.

She had seen a male chest before, of course; her brother's, when he was outside washing himself. But there was no comparison between Philip's smooth boyish chest and the taut muscled chest of the man kneeling at her feet now, this worldly, intelligent, successful businessman, who was kneeling in worship of her perfect body, her woman's body, the present she had allowed him to unwrap, and with which he was so very, very pleased.

Suddenly, impulsively, she launched herself at him, desperate to feel his skin against hers, not caring about anything else, not the time, not her father's wrath, nothing. He toppled backwards, and then he laughed, and lifting her he stood, laying her on the bed, and then joining her, drawing her into him, and kissing her nose, her cheeks, her mouth, before feathering gentle kisses down her neck, along her collarbone, then lower, until he reached her breasts.

Very tenderly he ran the tip of his tongue around her rose-pink areola, and she jerked as an electric tingling coursed through her, pooling low down in the secret part of her, the part that no one had ever seen or touched, but which he now was trailing down to, his lips gentle on her skin, but creating a trail of fire down her body.

Her legs opened like a flower to receive him, and she felt his breath hot between her thighs. He parted her skin gently with his fingers, and then his tongue caressed her most intimate parts, causing her to moan and arch up from the bed, every last remnant of her senses scattering, leaving her aware only of the exquisite physical torture of his mouth on her body, and desperately needing more. She would die if he let her go now.

He moved back up her body, his hands stroking up her sides, and then he was kissing her mouth again, his hair, which had come loose, falling over his face onto hers. He moved his legs between hers, and vaguely she realised that he was naked, but could not remember him removing his breeches.

She wrapped her arms around him, rejoicing in the feel of the powerful muscles of his back tensing and rippling as he supported his upper body on his elbows, although his hips were against hers, and something hard and unyielding was pressing against the place where his tongue had been a few moments ago, and she moaned and arched again, her upper body lifting, her lower body pinioned to the bed by his.

The hard, unyielding thing between her legs suddenly pushed into her, and there was an intense burning pain which made her cry out. He stopped moving.

"Shh, sweetheart," he murmured, "It's normal. Wait, just a moment, and the pain will go, and then it will be even better than before."

The pain was, in fact, already ebbing, and she felt the fullness of him inside her, joining their bodies in a way she had never thought possible. But he was lying to her, surely. Nothing could be better than the way he had made her feel up to now.

But then, after waiting for her body to accommodate to his, he began moving inside her, slowly at first and then with increasing speed, and she instinctively lifted her legs, wrapping them around his buttocks and pulling him deeper into her, and he was right, it *was* better than before. Never in her life had she imagined pleasure like this, a pleasure so intense that it was almost unbearable. Her whole body was sparkling, in a way it never had before, and she knew that this and only this, was what happiness was.

And then her orgasm hit her, and she shattered into a million ecstatic fragments, aware of nothing except the violent ecstasy that caused her to buck against him, making him moan as he lost himself in his own climax.

Afterwards he turned a little so as not to crush her, and they lay facing each other, still joined, in a tangle of arms and legs. They lay in silence as their breathing slowed, then he slipped out of her.

"Are you alright?" he asked. "Did I hurt you?"

"No," she said. "Well, yes, but it doesn't matter. Is that what married people do?"

"It's what people do when they love each other," he replied. "But yes, married people do it too, whether they love each other or not, because it's expected of them. But it's better when they love each other."

"It was the most wonderful feeling in the world. Do we love each other then?" she asked softly.

"I think maybe we do," he said, and kissed her.

CHAPTER NINE

After their Christmas celebration Robert came to his mother's every week, and made no secret of the fact that his primary reason for coming was to see Sarah, although he did of course love his mother. For her part, Mrs Grimes' mind was deteriorating rapidly now, and a lot of the time she sat silently, or spoke gibberish. She was incontinent and could no longer feed herself, even when other villagers brought meals round for her.

Robert paid for one of the village women, Ellie, a widow who needed the money, to come round every day except Saturday afternoons, when he said he or Sarah would be there. Ellie helped to get his mother out of bed, lit a fire, and made sure she was eating properly. As he paid well for Ellie's services and she was very grateful, when Sarah arrived on Saturdays the house was cleaner than it had been for years, Mrs Grimes was washed and fed, the fire was lit, and Sarah really had little to do other than spend time with Robert.

She had been worried that his mother would talk to Ellie about what went on on Saturdays, but then she realised that even if Mrs Grimes became coherent enough to remember and mention it, Ellie would just think she was wandering and would probably take no notice, and so she relaxed.

Every week they made love, spending most of their time in his mother's bedroom together. He told her that he wanted to bed her, not here but in a beautiful room, with rose petals sprinkled on the bed, silk bedding and velvet curtains, and that one day he would. She told him that making love in a pigsty would still be heaven, as long as he was with her. But secretly she felt ecstatic, because his words told her that he intended their relationship to be long-term and one day would take her to his house, where presumably the silk bedding and velvet curtains were.

She had no doubt that he loved her, because he told her he did, every week when they were in bed, sated from lust and lying tangled in each other's limbs, enjoying being together. One day he would take her to live with him, would ask her to marry him. She just had to be patient, she knew that, and one thing she was an expert at was being patient.

She knew that men didn't like women to be too eager, because her and Philip had talked about it one day by the river.

"She's just pushing me all the time to set a date to marry her," Philip had moaned after a particularly trying tryst with Mary.

"But isn't that nice?" Sarah had asked. "It shows how much she loves you. She wouldn't want to marry you if she didn't, would she?"

Philip looked at her askance.

"Do you really think women only want to get married if they love the man? Or the other way round, for that matter?"

"Of course! Why else would anyone want to spend the rest of their life with someone?" Sarah asked.

"You are so innocent, sister," he said, and she bristled, but when she looked at him his eyes were soft and she realised he was not insulting her, just stating a fact. She *was* innocent in the ways of the world, although not as innocent as he thought she was. But of course she couldn't tell him that. "People marry for all sorts of reasons," he explained. "For financial reasons if they're rich, to get titles, land and money, and if they're like us, to get away from their families so they don't have to do what their parents tell them any more."

"Is that why Mary wants to marry you? To get away from her family?"

"Partly at least, yes. I think so," Philip said. "But also because I'll be earning a good wage once my apprenticeship's over, and I think she wants to capture me before any other girls come along."

"Don't you think she loves you then?" Sarah had asked, puzzled.

"I don't know. I *did* think that, but now, every time we meet she spends most of the time pestering me about marriage, and I'm not enjoying being with her as much because of it. I do love her, but I'm not ready to settle down and have a family yet. I'm only seventeen! I wish she'd just enjoy being with me for now, and let things progress naturally."

Sarah remembered that conversation when she was with Robert, when she wanted to ask him why, instead of paying Ellie to look after Mrs Grimes and travelling all the way from Liverpool every week to see her, he didn't just move her and his mother to his house and solve the problem. She remembered it when she wanted to ask him why he never talked about his private life. But she didn't want him to think she was pestering him for commitment. If he didn't enjoy being with her any more he might stop coming to see her.

And if he did that she would die. She could not imagine a life without him in it now, had not realised how desperately unhappy she had been, until he had brought happiness into her life. Now she had known that, she could not imagine living without it. And she would do anything, anything at all to keep him.

So she let him lead the pace of their relationship, and if he was happy seeing her for a few hours once a week, then she was too. She loved being with him, always had, but now that they made love every time they met, she was addicted to him. She had had no physical affection from her father, and only vaguely remembered her mother holding her and kissing her tenderly, and she loved and craved not only the intense climaxes she enjoyed with Robert, but the affectionate kisses and touches too. It was glorious to be so cherished.

At night in bed at home she would close her eyes and relive their passionate embraces, the feel of him moving inside her, the adoring expression on his face when they were together. It was wonderful. He was wonderful.

She was in love, completely and utterly. There was no other man for her and never would be. How could anyone ever be as delightful, as handsome, as intelligent, as considerate and caring as Robert Grimes? It wasn't possible.

The hardest part of the relationship, apart from living six days of every week without him, was not letting her happiness show to her father, not making him suspicious. The only way she could do that was to compartmentalise her life. She had done it in a different way as a child in the cellar, when she had closed her eyes and disappeared into a fantasy world to make her sadness and fear go away. Now she did the opposite, pushing her wonderful time with Robert away and enveloping herself in the misery of her normal life, only taking out the Saturday memories when she was alone.

It worked, and because of that, she did not tell Philip about Robert. Because she knew that if she told one person, especially a person who lived in the same house as her, who was the only one she *could* tell, the only one she could trust, that all her emotions would fizz up and overflow, and she would not be able to bottle them up again. And she *had* to keep them bottled up, because if he found out, her father would stop her going to Mrs Grimes', and she could not let that happen.

* * *

In March she got some sort of a stomach problem, not a bad one, but enough to make her feel sick every day for weeks, which made it difficult for her to cook her father's breakfast eggs, because the smell of them cooking made her throw up. She was really tired too, even more so than usual. Luckily the sickness didn't last all day, just for an hour or so, although she would get dyspepsia at all hours, and would have to go outside to spit out mouthfuls of hot water periodically. But the tiredness was pervasive, and when she was sitting mending clothes she would often find herself nodding off, sometimes waking to find a couple of hours had passed and the fire had burnt low.

It was just the winter, she thought. She always felt under the weather at the end of the winter. It was normal. Everyone looked forward to the lighter nights and the sun being warm and strong on your face, instead of watery and cold.

And she was right, because in May, when the green leaves hazed the trees and everything burst to life the intermittent sickness disappeared completely, as did the tiredness. She loved May, when the morning was loud with birdsong and everything was green and full of life, but this year she loved it even more, because she had Robert, and so for the first time ever she was part of the sheer exuberance of being young and alive, and happy.

Now the weather was warmer they spent more time outside, and in early May, when the blossom was heavy on the apple tree in the garden, Robert brought a blanket outside and they made love slowly and affectionately in the garden, with the spring sunshine kissing their bare skin and the soft white-pink petals raining down on them like confetti in the breeze, and she had laughed aloud for pure joy. Afterwards he held her, told her that she was the most beautiful woman in the world, and she had known that no matter what the future held for her she would never forget this magical day, with her hair sprinkled with petals, the scent of the crushed grass in her nose, and the feel of his warm hard body on hers.

In June he had to go away to London for a few weeks, to buy material and products to sell in his shop. He went every year, he told her, but would bring her a present back, a lovely present that she would like, to make up for his absence. And every Saturday he would look up at the moon in the evening and would think of her, and if she did the same, then they would be together. She had promised him that she would, and he had kissed her passionately before she had left the cottage, and had told her that he would miss her terribly.

He was away for four Saturdays in the end, and every night Sarah would take out the locket he had given her for Christmas, the one with a lock of his hair in it, and would kiss it and then put it under her pillow, hoping it would help her to dream of him. On Saturdays she would be sure to stay up until it was dark, and then she would go out into the garden and look up at the moon, and send up a silent prayer to God to bring him back to her safe, and to let her have him forever, even if only on Saturdays.

She was a little concerned, because she seemed to be gaining weight. At first her breasts had grown a bit, and had been tender for a while, but she thought that was just part of becoming a woman – after all, her mother's dress had fitted her well except at the bust, so perhaps now if she wore it it would fit her perfectly, which would be wonderful. But then her stomach started getting bigger too, and she had to lace her stays more loosely, and tie her skirts more loosely round her waist.

It was all very odd, because she wasn't eating any more than normal, couldn't even if she wanted to, because her father kept a close eye on the amount of provisions used, not wanting to waste money unnecessarily. Gluttony was, after all, a deadly sin. Reverend Browne ate sparingly and made sure his children did too, although Philip confided to Sarah that he ate a lot at work, and he sometimes brought something home for her, a cold pie or a sweet pastry, especially on days when the reverend was away. Surely those small treats would not cause her to put on so much weight?

She wouldn't have minded putting on weight if it wasn't for Robert. He loved her body, always told her how utterly perfect she was just as she was. But would he still love her if she got fat? Even though he was some twenty years older than her, his body was so strong and muscular, his stomach flat; he might not want to make love to her any more if she was repulsive to him. He might find someone else, another woman with a perfect body!

It did not bear thinking about.

She stopped eating the treats that Philip brought home for her, and only ate when she was so hungry she felt dizzy, but she didn't get any thinner. In fact her stomach seemed to be growing bigger. It was distinctly rounded now, where it had always been flat before.

Because of this, on the first Saturday of July when he had promised he would be back, she didn't feel as overjoyed at the prospect of seeing him as she should have been. He, however, was delighted to see her and made no secret of it, picking her up in his arms as soon as he saw her and swinging her round, making her laugh in spite of her anxiety.

"Oh, I have missed you so much!" he said, kissing her all over her face. "Tell me you've missed me too."

"Of course I have, terribly," she replied. "I kissed my locket every night and stayed up late on Saturdays to look at the moon, but it wasn't the same as being in your arms!"

He smiled and put her down.

"Now," he said, "it's a beautiful day, so let's sit outside and I'll tell you about London while you open the present I bought for you."

They sat outside on their bench and he gave her a beautifully wrapped small box. He knew by now that she liked to take her time opening presents, enjoying the anticipation, so while she did he told her about how busy London was, how many people there were all living in such a small space, how grand the buildings were, that you could buy anything you could ever desire, but also how smelly it was.

"They don't tell you that part," he said, wrinkling his nose at the memory. "They only tell you about all the rich people and their grand houses and carriages, the huge churches and monuments. And it is very exciting – it's where everything happens first, and where all the important influential people live, including the king."

Sarah had just untied the ribbon on the top of the little box, but stopped now and looked at Robert.

"Is that the king in the picture over the fire?" she asked.

"Yes, it is," he affirmed, smiling, "although that picture was painted when he had only just become the king, so he's a bit older now. Twelve years older."

"Did you see the king?" Sarah asked.

"No. I was there on business, so most of my time was spent buying things for the best price I could. And buying that for you. Are you going to open it?"

She opened it. Inside the box was a black velvet cushion, and on the cushion was a bracelet of gold and gemstones. She lifted it out.

"Oh, it's beautiful!" she cried.

He took it from her and placed it round her wrist, fastening it.

"As soon as I saw it, I knew I had to have it for you," he said. "Do you like the stones?"

"Yes!" she replied, looking at them with curiosity. They were very unusual, different shades of green, with specks of amber and brown in them. "What kind of stones are they?"

"They're jasper," he said. "Jasper comes in lots of different colours, but those reminded me of the colour of your eyes, and that's why I had to buy it for you, so every time you look at it you'll know how beautiful your eyes are, even if you haven't got a mirror."

She looked up at him, her eyes wide with wonder, and he bent his head to hers and kissed her with a warmth and passion that she had missed so very much in the last weeks. As was usual now, their kiss soon inflamed them both into wanting more, and after a few minutes of embraces during which the temperature of the day appeared to rise considerably, Robert broke away briefly to run inside and fetch a blanket to lay on the grass under the apple tree, which was no longer covered with blossom but with glossy leaves and the first signs of fruit.

Although he was quick, by the time he came back out Sarah's ardour had dampened, and she looked distinctly worried. He laid the blanket on the ground, then came over to the bench and seeing her expression his forehead creased with puzzlement.

"What's the matter, sweetheart?" he asked. "Don't you want to make love? It's a beautiful day, and I've dreamed of this for weeks!"

She looked up at him nervously.

"I do," she said hesitantly. "It's just that…" Her voice trailed off, and she avoided his worried gaze by looking down at the bracelet, fiddling with it until she felt his finger under her chin lifting her face to his. He sat down next to her.

"What is it?" he asked. "You know you can tell me anything, don't you? What's worrying you?"

She remained silent for a moment, plucking up her courage, and kindly he allowed her the time she needed. After a minute she took a deep breath, and then spoke.

"I've…while you've been away, I've got a bit fatter," she said. "And you told me that I had a perfect body, but now it's changed, and I was afraid."

"What were you afraid of?" he asked.

"That you might think I'm ugly now, and not want me any more," she said, so softly he could hardly hear it.

"Sarah, you could never be ugly to me," he said. "And I don't care if you have put on a little weight. If you've been eating well, that's a good thing!"

"No, I haven't been eating any more than normal!" Sarah exclaimed. "Well, except for the little pies and cakes Philip brings me sometimes. But once I saw I was getting fatter I stopped eating them. It hasn't made any difference though."

Robert nodded.

"That must be it, then. But really, I don't care, unless you grow so huge that I can't lift you up any more, like this," he said, lifting her smoothly off the bench and laughing. "Really, you're silly to worry. You're every bit as beautiful to me now as you were the first day I saw you. More beautiful in fact, because now I know you, and you're mine!" He laid her down on the blanket, then sat down next to her. "You don't feel any heavier, anyway," he added.

"I look fatter though."

"Let's find out then," he answered, smiling and undoing the neckerchief she wore and taking it off, before unbuttoning the bodice of her dress, bending to kiss her bare skin as it was exposed. "Well," he said, "your bosom has grown, that's certain. That's just what happens when you become a woman though. Nothing to worry about. They're beautiful!" he said, softly stroking the creamy globes of her breasts that swelled above the stays.

"You really don't mind?" she said bashfully.

"God, no," he said fervently. "You are so young, I expected you to grow a little here in time. It's normal, sweetheart." He untied her stays and her skirt, and then slipped off his own coat, waistcoat and shirt. Then he smiled at her as she sat watching him, dressed only in her shift now. He took off his breeches and rolled down his stockings.

"You are so handsome," she said.

He turned and smiled.

"And you are beautiful. Take your shift off, for Heaven's sake! I don't care if you've put on a little weight."

He was so sure that her confidence blossomed. She had been worrying needlessly, she realised that now. Decided, she took off the shift in one sudden move and sat there naked in front of him.

He hid it well, but she was watching him intently, saw his eyes widen in shock and his expression change before he could school it into normality, and her heart plummeted. She drew her knees up to hide her stomach and her eyes filled with tears.

"I knew you'd mind when you saw me," she said brokenly. "But I promise I won't eat any more of the treats Philip brings! I'll get thin again, I will!"

With infinite tenderness he took her in his arms, cradling her against him.

"It's all right, darling," he said. "I don't mind, really I don't.

You must eat the treats if you want to. It's kind of your brother to think of you."

"Philip and I look after each other," she said into his neck. He lifted his hand and stroked her hair gently.

"That's good," Robert said. "It makes me feel happier to know someone is there for you when I'm not, when I can't be."

"I'm sorry," she said, her voice trembling with sadness.

"Sarah," he asked. "How long is it since you had your monthly course?"

That was such an unexpected question that she lifted her head from his neck and looked at him. "I don't know," she said. "I haven't had them for a while, a few months. But I haven't been as clumsy or as bad-tempered as I was when I started bleeding either. I expect that's all stopped now because I'm a woman. I'm really glad, because I hated that bit!"

He smiled, but sadly, and she knew that he really was upset about the weight she'd put on. But he didn't ask her any more strange questions. What he did instead was make love to her, not with fire and passion as he normally did and as she'd expected him to after weeks of absence, but slowly, with great tenderness and taking infinite care to make sure she climaxed. Afterwards they lay together as was their custom, and he held her close to him, stroking her and kissing her hair.

"You are beautiful, Sarah," he said earnestly to her. "Don't let anyone ever make you think you're not. I'm sorry."

"It's alright," she said. "As long as you still want me, that's all that matters."

"I still want you," he told her. "I will always want you, as long as I live."

She smiled, happy again, and they lay together for a while longer, enjoying the sun on their bare skin and the feel of each other's bodies. And then the sun went behind a cloud and the air cooled, and they realised that they had been outside for far longer than normal, so they got dressed and went back inside after which Sarah collected her things and prepared to leave. She kissed Mrs Grimes goodbye, but the old lady was far away, not even aware she was there.

"I worry about her," Sarah said.

Robert looked at his mother.

"I know," he said. "Ellie does a very good job of looking after her, but I think Mama needs someone with her all the time now, really. I'll have to make other arrangements."

Almost she blurted it out, that she would happily look after his mother, if he would only take them both to Liverpool, but then she remembered that she had promised herself not to pester him at all. He had just told her he would always want her, and she determined to do nothing to make him change his mind, as Mary was doing to Philip.

So she smiled and picked up her basket and said goodbye, but just as she was about to open the door he leapt for it, putting his hand flat on the wood to stop her opening it, as he had the very first time she'd met him and had tried to leave.

He took her in his arms and kissed her, then he took her head between his hands and looked her in the eyes, very intently.

"I love you," he said. "And I *am* sorry. I never meant to hurt you."

Sarah smiled.

"You haven't hurt me," she said. "You've made me happy. No one else has ever done that. I'll see you next week."

She opened the door and went out, walking up the path a little way to meet Philip, who was waiting for her in his usual place around the bend in the lane.

* * *

The following Saturday when Sarah arrived at Mrs Grimes' Robert wasn't there. Although he was usually already there when she arrived, once or twice in the past he'd been late, so she didn't worry unduly. She did a little tidying, although Ellie had not left her much to do and then she sat down opposite Mrs Grimes, who was staring into the hearth and picking at her clothes with her fingers, an action she would sometimes repeat for hours at a time. When Sarah had expressed concern about it, Robert had told her that when he was young his mother had taken in sewing to earn extra money, and would often sit in front of the fire, stitching.

"I think she's reliving the past in her mind," he had said.

So Sarah tried to make conversation, but Mrs Grimes was far away, didn't even seem aware that she had a visitor. After a while, Sarah went into the garden and pulled up some weeds that were growing over the path. Ellie did no work in the garden, which was rapidly becoming overgrown, and although her and Robert had done a great deal in the garden, none of what they did could be classed as tending it.

She smiled at the memories of sitting on the bench sharing their warmth, of lying under the tree making love. Where was he?

At four o'clock she left and met Philip as was their custom. She couldn't remember Robert saying he wasn't going to be here today. But then she couldn't remember him telling her he *was* going to be here either. Having said that, he always came on Saturday now, so didn't tell her unless he had some other arrangement which would stop him calling over. *Maybe he did, and I didn't remember,* she thought. She had been both excited and upset last week, had not been thinking right. That must be it.

But he wasn't there the following week either, or the one after that, and by then Sarah was worried that something had happened to him. Had he had an accident, or fallen ill? How would she ever know, if he had? She only knew that he lived in Liverpool and ran a haberdashery shop. She had no way of contacting him, and even if she'd had an address, couldn't read or write.

She tried to engage Mrs Grimes, to ask her if Robert had said anything to her about being away again, but only got a rambling story about a holiday in Wales for her pains, and knew the old lady was deep in memories of her childhood when she had lived in Bristol, which was close to Wales.

The next Saturday, after a week of agony in which she imagined all sorts of terrible calamities having befallen him, Sarah, on finding Robert was not there again, went to Ellie's house, hoping she would know something.

Ellie, always smiling and friendly, invited her into her tiny home.

"No," she said. "I haven't seen or heard from him in three weeks. He used to call in on the Saturday mornings to pay me on his way to his mother's, but he hasn't been. In truth, I was going to call up to your house to see if you knew anything, but, er…" Her voice trailed off and she blushed a little.

"But you didn't want to see my father?" Sarah suggested, making Ellie blush even more.

"He's just so…*fierce*," Ellie said. "Whenever I see him, he always looks at me as though I'm naked, makes me feel as though he's caught me doing something evil, even if I'm just walking down the street."

Sarah laughed, knowing the look exactly.

"Oh God, don't tell him I said that, please!" Ellie begged.

"I won't. I know exactly what you mean. It's nothing to do with you, though. He looks at everyone that way."

"I'm still going round to Constance's every day, getting her dressed and cleaning a little for her, making sure she breaks her fast," Ellie confirmed. "And then I take her something later, whatever we're going to eat. I'm sure Robert will turn up, though. He really loves his mother, coming over like that every week to see her, all the way from Liverpool. Maybe something has happened at home to stop him."

"Maybe. Has he said anything to give you an idea of what it might be? I'm just a bit worried that something bad has happened to him." Sarah did her best to sound casual, but Ellie glanced at her oddly, so she realised she must have sounded a bit fervent.

"No," Ellie said. "He doesn't talk about his private life in Liverpool. He just calls, asks how Constance is, pays me and says thank you."

On the next Saturday Sarah walked to the cottage so silently and morosely that even Philip, chatting away as usual about little happenings at work and, of course Mary, noticed.

"Is something wrong?" he asked. "You seem very unhappy. You always seem happy when you're going to Mrs Grimes. Have you had an argument with her?"

"No," she said, and then seized the excuse he'd inadvertently given to her for the mood she'd failed to hide. "It's just that she's getting worse. A lot of the time she doesn't even know I'm there, and when she does she thinks I'm someone else, or a stranger. I'm just worried about her."

"She is very old," Philip said. "She's close to eighty, I think."

"Seventy-five," Sarah replied. "I know. It just makes me sad."

"You always were kind-hearted," Philip said. "I'm sure she appreciates you going to see her. And you said someone else is going on other days, so I'm sure she's looked after."

Sarah forced a smile.

"You're right," she said. "I'm just being silly."

Even so, when she'd waved him off she stood by the gate for a moment, steeling herself to go in, instinctively feeling a sense of absence. He wasn't there, again. She didn't know how much longer she could bear this, not knowing what had happened to him, but knowing it must be something very bad that would stop him coming to see her every week.

She braced herself, walked up the path, knocked on the door once, then opened it and walked in. And stopped on the threshold. For the first time in the five years since she'd started visiting, Mrs Grimes was not sitting in her chair near the window, and the fire was not lit in the hearth. Sitting in the chair instead was Ellie, who stood as Sarah walked in.

"Hello!" she said cheerily.

"Hello," Sarah said warily. "Is something wrong?"

"No!" Ellie replied quickly. "It's good news, really. Well, not for me, because the money was really useful, but for Constance. Robert came to my house last Wednesday, told me that his mother was too old now to do anything for herself and that he was going to move her closer to him and make sure she was looked after all the time. He asked me to wait here today to tell you, and to say…are you all right? You've gone white!"

With an effort so enormous she later had no idea how she'd managed it, Sarah let go of the doorpost that she was holding onto with a death grip, took a few steps into the room and sat down in the other chair.

"Yes," she said, her voice seeming to come from a long way away. "I just felt a bit dizzy, that's all. It's very hot outside, and I walked quickly. That must be it."

Ellie sat down opposite and looked at Sarah with concern. Then she stood up again and went to the table, poured a cup of ale and handed it to her.

"Here," she said. "Drink that, it'll make you feel better if you've overheated. I brought it because I didn't know how long I'd have to wait for you."

Sarah drank it slowly, using that as an excuse to pull herself together. After a minute or so, she looked across at Ellie.

"I'm sorry," she apologised. "I feel a bit better now. What did

Robert ask you to say?"

"He asked me to say thank you for all you've done, and to tell you that he'll always be grateful to you, but that this is the best thing, the only thing he can really do. And he's right, of course," Ellie continued. "Constance needs someone with her all the time now, in her last days. He gave me a nice bonus though, which was very kind of him. He's a good man."

"Yes," Sarah said. There was a silence. "I'm really alright now," she added, sensing Ellie's concern but impatience to go. "You can go if you want. I'm going to miss coming here, so I'll just stay for a few minutes and think."

"Of course," Ellie replied, jumping up immediately. "I've just left the children on their own, and I never know what James and Luke will get up to. They're at that age where they're into everything. Robert said you were very close to his mother, and might be upset. I can stay if you want, though?"

"No. That's very kind of you, but I'd like to be alone, to…to remember," Sarah said. She wanted to grab Ellie, push her bodily out of the house, lock the door and then scream and cry, roar her grief and misery, smash everything in the cottage to tiny pieces.

But after Ellie left she just sat there for a time, completely numb, completely silent, paralysed with a grief she had never known before. Then she got up and walked out into the garden, and sat down on the bench. Their bench. At the moment the spindly rose bush was covered with pink roses, and their scent filled the warm summer air.

She sat for a long time staring blindly across the overgrown garden, until a petal fell from the rose bush and brushed her cheek softly before settling on her knee, reminding her of other petals falling like confetti on them as they lay on the ground, just over there. They would never do that again. He had left her, and he would never come back.

He was gone.

A pain came in her chest, a pain so terrible that she was sure she must die of it, prayed to die of it. Nothing could hurt this much and not kill her. But then the pain became a great lump which rose into her throat and choked her. She swallowed heavily and closed her eyes so tightly that they stung, but still the roar of pure grief came from her mouth, followed by the tears, scalding her eyes and pouring down her cheeks, and she gave into them, rocking backwards and forwards, moaning and sobbing with a desolation that was unbearable.

And yet she bore it, somehow, and eventually the sobs became hiccups and coughs, and then little gasps for breath, and then they stopped, leaving her feeling completely wrung out. She wiped her face with her skirt and continued to sit for a while, taking deep breaths and trying to regain control of herself. She had strange fluttering movements in her stomach, had had them for a while, but right now it felt as though the grief was alive and trying to get out.

That was just her being silly. She was not going to die of her misery, she realised that now, and this feeling was not going to get out and run away, so somehow she had to pull herself together, and learn to live with it. And learn to hide it.

How could he do it? How could he tell her she was beautiful, that her weight gain didn't bother him, that he would always want her as long as he lived, and then just leave her? Without explanation, without a goodbye? And then, to come all the way from Liverpool on Wednesday, deliberately on a day when he knew he wouldn't see her. Did he think her so hideous now that he couldn't even bear to look at her, had to leave a message with Ellie, a cold message, a message someone would leave to a mere servant who had given good service but was being released?

She stood suddenly, so suddenly that she went dizzy for a moment and had to hold onto the back of the seat until it cleared. She could not stay here any longer, could not bear to look at the place where she had been so happy, where she had known the only happiness she had ever known, and know now that it had all been a lie.

He did not love her. He *could* not love her and do this to her. She had to leave this place now, or she would go mad.

She left, walking straight through the kitchen and the living room, out of the front door and down the path, leaving all the doors wide open in her haste to get away. She would walk up the lane, away from the village, toward Mary's house, and would wait somewhere where Philip would see her as he came back. The walk would do her good, would clear her mind a little and give her the strength to somehow get through this, alone, and without telling anyone.

She walked, and once out of sight of the house tried to compartmentalise it, to push it away, distance herself from it. All her life she had done that when bad things had happened. It was the only tool she had, but it was a good one, and it worked.

It was not working now, though. Not yet. The pain was too intense.

It would get better in time though, like all the bad things that had happened. This was the worst thing by far, but it would fade in time, like the bruises from the beatings her father had given her. Like the fear of the monster in the cellar. She would grow older and she would have a miserable life with her father, but this pain would fade. It had to fade, at least enough for her to be able to put it in a little box and push it away, to get on with her life, and deal with it in tiny portions when she was alone, until it went away.

She had walked for a while along the dry and dusty winding track without being aware of her surroundings as anything other than a green haze with plants and trees in it, until suddenly her eyes were attracted by a flash of rich blue, and she focussed, to see Philip walking toward her down the path, arm in arm with a young woman who had to be Mary.

She resisted the urge to run away, because they had seen her. Philip lifted his arm in greeting, and Sarah raised hers in acknowledgement and then stopped, waiting for them to catch up to her. There was nothing she wanted less than to meet her brother's sweetheart for the first time now, but recognising she had no choice, she used the time to paint a smile on her face and hopefully school her expression into something normal.

"Is something wrong?" Philip asked as soon as they were close enough.

"No," Sarah replied. "I just wanted a walk, so I thought I'd come this way. I didn't expect to see you yet."

He nodded, and then smiled.

"Mary," he said, turning to her with such a warm expression on his face that it made Sarah's heart lurch, remembering when Robert had looked at her like that, "this is Sarah, my sister."

"I'm so pleased to meet you finally, Sarah," Mary said, smiling at her. Philip had not been exaggerating when he'd spoken of her beauty. The young woman was lovely, with dark brown hair, sparkling blue eyes and a peaches-and-cream complexion. She had an open, friendly face that made Sarah instinctively warm to her, sensing that here was a woman who spoke as she saw, who had no pretence about her.

Sarah returned the smile.

"Philip's told me a lot about you," she said. "It's very good to meet you, too."

"Are you sure you're well, Sarah?" Philip cut in. "You look terribly pale."

"Yes, I'm fine," Sarah said hurriedly. "I just got a bit breathless and dizzy walking up the slope there, that's all."

"Oh, that's normal at your time," Mary said incomprehensibly, looking Sarah over with an expert eye. "Ma always gets that way. About five, six months, are you? Why didn't you tell me?" she said to Philip. "Typical of a man, not to tell me such an important thing!" she added, looking back at Sarah.

Both siblings stared at her in puzzlement.

"Didn't tell you what?"

"About the baby," Mary replied. Her smile faltered as she took in their twin looks of shock and disbelief. "Dear God in Heaven, don't tell me you didn't know you're with child?"

There was a moment of profound stunned silence, and then Philip, by leaping forward with extreme agility, managed to catch his sister just before she hit the ground in a dead faint.

CHAPTER TEN

She was in bed, but for some unfathomable reason it was raining on her, even though there wasn't a hole in her bedroom roof. She could feel the splashes on her face but when she tried to lift her hand to brush them away, it was as heavy as lead. Her whole body was as heavy as lead. She moaned softly.

"Oh, thank God!" Philip's worried voice came from somewhere above. "She's coming round. Sarah, can you hear me?"

With a huge effort Sarah opened her eyes, to find she wasn't in bed at all but was lying in long grass near the river, with her brother and a woman leaning over her. Their faces rippled suddenly, as though she was looking at their reflections in a still pond and somebody had stirred the water. She closed her eyes again, listened to the river, felt someone rubbing her hand. Then she remembered what had caused her to faint and what had happened earlier, and she prayed to just be allowed to sink into oblivion again, but this time not wake up at all.

But her prayer wasn't answered, so after a few more moments she opened her eyes again, and this time their faces stayed in focus. Mary. The woman's name was Mary.

"I'm all right," Sarah mumbled indistinctly. She tried to will her limbs to obey her, so she could sit up. She suddenly felt terribly embarrassed, stupid. What was wrong with her?

Mary leaned closer to her.

"Just lie there for a minute, until you feel better," she said. "You fainted. It was my fault. I'm so sorry."

"No," Sarah said. "Not yours. I didn't know."

Philip put his arm under her shoulders and lifted her upper body off the ground, so that she was half-sitting, leaning against him. She fought the waves of dizziness and nausea, and after a minute or two started to regain control of herself. She looked up at Mary.

"Are you sure?" was all she said.

Mary and Philip both looked at Sarah's stomach, which, now she was half lying, showed a distinct bump, one not so obvious when she was standing or sitting with her skirts flowing past it rather than enhancing it as they were at the moment.

"Yes," Mary said simply. "My Ma's had fifteen not including me, and I'm the eldest girl, so I've helped her since I was old enough to walk. She's always with child. I know all the signs."

"What signs?" Sarah asked. "How did you know I am?"

"When Ma's with child, after a while the way she walks changes. She kind of waddles, and leans back when she's walking. I've never seen any woman who isn't with child walk like that. But you were, before you saw us and stopped. And you're thin, but your stomach isn't. You can't see that so much when you're standing, but when you stopped you put your hands on your back to rub it and grimaced, and I saw your stomach when you massaged it, because it pulled the material of your skirt back. Have you got back pain?"

"Yes," Sarah replied. "Oh God, what am I going to do?"

"Sarah," Philip said. "What happened? Did someone attack you? Was it Simon Bradshaw? I'll kill him if it was. Why didn't you tell me?"

Sarah winced under the bombardment of questions, then tried to think, rapidly. She couldn't lie outright to her brother, nor could she let an innocent man take the blame. She didn't want to talk about this now. Didn't want to talk about it ever. But she had to. And Philip was the only one she could trust with her secret. And hopefully Mary, but she had no choice in that anyway.

"No," she said. "No one attacked me. I've been seeing a man every week. I love him, and he told me he loved me too. He…he made me feel so good," she added brokenly. "I've never been so happy as I was with him. He made me feel beautiful."

"You are beautiful," Mary said forthrightly.

"Who is it? Is it one of the village boys? He'll have to marry you, Sarah."

"I don't know how I could be with child!" Sarah cried. "I thought that only happened when you were married!"

"No, of course not," Mary said. "What made you think that? It can happen any time if you lie with a man, married or not. There are things you can try to make it less likely to happen, but it often does anyway."

Philip blushed scarlet.

"Oh, Sarah," he said. "I'm so sorry. I told her that," he explained to his sweetheart. "I…I thought it was true at the time. Father never told us anything about sex. He seems to think it's an evil thing to do at all, whether you're married or not. I…I've learnt everything I know from you. But you know that."

"Stop blushing, Philip Browne," Mary said. "If you're not judging me for knowing more than most, then I'm not judging you for *not* knowing, either. No one knows anything unless they're told. Your father should have told you, both of you. This is his fault as much as anyone's. It's a parent's responsibility to tell his children the things they need to know about life. And if he thinks it's so evil to do, why did he do it? At least twice," she added dryly, looking at her two companions.

Sarah and Philip both stared at Mary with looks of utter astonishment. No one had ever said their father was at fault, was not a good parent, did evil things.

"What?" Mary said. "I'm sorry if you're upset, but it's true. Or true as I see it. Would you have done what you did with your sweetheart if you'd known you might catch a baby?"

Sarah opened her mouth, and then closed it again. Would she? No, she probably wouldn't have. She would have been too afraid of the consequences. And she wouldn't have known how amazing lying with him was, so it would have been easier to say no at that point.

"Does he have parents who don't tell him anything as well? Did he know he could get you with child?"

"Who is it, sister? We must speak with him," Philip said.

Sarah closed her eyes and swallowed hard, forcing the tears back.

"We can't," she said. "He's left me."

And then the tears came, and for a time neither Philip nor Mary spoke, and if they had she wouldn't have heard them anyway, so deep in her suffering was she.

* * *

The three of them walked to the end of the lane together and then Mary stopped, pointing out that it would do neither Sarah nor Philip any good if rumours were to get around that he was courting her, which they would if the three of them walked down the main street together.

"I'm not ashamed of you!" Philip had said fervently, and Mary had leaned forward, stroking his cheek.

"I know that," she said. "But I also know that your father will be angry if he finds out we're meeting each other. And I don't think you want him any angrier than he's going to be. I don't think this is the best time for him to find out about us."

"Maybe not," Philip agreed reluctantly. "But I'm going to marry you anyway, whether he likes it or not, so he'll have to know at some point."

Mary's face lit up at these words, and even through the fog of her grief Sarah realised that Philip had just, albeit clumsily, betrothed himself to his sweetheart. She smiled weakly.

"Congratulations," she said. "I think you'll be happy together. Father doesn't want anyone to be happy. You have to do as your heart says, Philip," she added, realising as she said it that doing as her heart had said was what had led her to this impossible and terrible place.

"Good luck, Sarah," Mary said, giving her a sudden hug. "Tell me if there's anything I can do to help you."

After she'd turned round and headed back up her lane, the siblings walked on together, unconsciously slowing as they neared their house.

"She's lovely," Sarah said. "I think you'll be happy if you marry her. She has kind eyes. And she loves you, that's really clear."

"I know. I think it needed something extreme to push me into saying that to her. But I'm glad I did, because now I realise that I really *do* want to be with her. But what are we going to do about you?" Philip said.

"I don't know. It's such a shock, I can't think properly. I need time to work out what to do."

So when they got home Philip immediately announced to their father that Sarah was sick, and that was why they had come home early. He was sitting in a chair by the fire, and looked up, surprised to see them back so soon.

"Good Lord, you look dreadful!" Reverend Browne said. "What ails you?"

She must look dreadful, if he was noticing it. She had often thought that she could die and he wouldn't notice unless he tripped over her corpse.

"It's my stomach," she told him. "I feel very sick and weak. I'm sure I will be well soon if I can just lie down for a time."

"Maybe you ate something that disagreed with you, Sarah," Philip said. "I'll help you up to your room."

"What will we do for our evening meal?" Reverend Browne said. "You will need to prepare it, before you go lying in bed in the middle of the day!"

"I don't think she is capable, Father," Philip said. "I will go to the inn and buy us a pie, just for tonight. I almost had to carry her home. She's very weak."

"Hmmm. It's most irregular," the reverend complained, his expression one of the utmost displeasure. Philip, recognising that she was about to offer to make a meal, ignored him and virtually dragged his sister up the stairs.

"He won't die for want of your cooking tonight," he whispered fiercely as they reached the bedroom door. "And neither will I. You've had a terrible shock. Lie down, sleep, and then think about what you're going to do. We can talk when Father is in Chester, and make a plan."

Her eyes instantly filled with tears.

"What would I do without you?" she said. "I think I'd die."

He smiled sadly.

"No you won't," he said. "We'll think of something."

She got undressed, got into bed and then lay there, thinking. Once Mary had left, Sarah had told Philip that Robert Grimes was the father of her child, and that he'd left her, and taken his mother away too now. So it was very clear to her that he didn't mean to come back at all.

"Did he know you were with child?" Philip had asked.

"Of course not! How could he, when even I didn't know until Mary told me?" Sarah had exclaimed.

But now, lying in bed, she thought about the last time they'd been together, and the look in his eyes when he'd seen her stomach. At the time she'd thought it was disgust because she had grown fat and ugly, but now she realised that it was most likely he had realised that she was pregnant, and his expression had been one of terror at the thought of having to take responsibility for her, which would mean getting married and raising a family. And he had been so terrified of that that he had left her to deal with it alone.

He did not love her. He had never loved her. You could not do what he had to someone you loved.

Even the thought of that brought tears flooding from her eyes, and she buried her face in the pillow so her father would not hear her sobbing downstairs and wonder at it. After a while the sobs subsided and she wiped her face on the sheet and then lay staring at the ceiling, forcing herself to face the facts.

Robert had found her attractive, had maybe liked her as a person. But he did not love her, not at all. If he did he could not have left her to face the consequences of their lovemaking alone. He was older than her, a lot older. Surely he knew that what they had done could lead to children? And he had not cared, had taken advantage of her youth, her ignorance and her trust. And then had abandoned her without another thought once he realised what he'd done.

She could not hide this forever, and her father would kill her when he found out. She had not known that this wonderful thing they had done was the thing that led to the ruin of unmarried women, to bastard children. If she had, she would never have done it. How could something that felt so wonderful be so catastrophic?

Because the Devil was in it. Unless you were married, and then God had blessed you and it was no longer a sin, unless you enjoyed it rather than just doing it to have babies.

She felt the despair rise up in her, and behind it hatred towards a man who could do such an evil thing to her, and she reached past the despair to the hate, pulling it to the front of her mind, and feeling the rage rise in her body, driving out the weakness, the tears and the despair. She needed the rage. She needed every tool at her disposal that would give her strength right now.

Strength to think of what she could do. And strength to behave as though nothing whatsoever had changed in front of her father, who absolutely must not find out.

She remembered what she had done to hide her happiness about her relationship with Robert from her father, how she had packaged up the Saturdays as though they were happening to someone else and had put them to the back of her mind, to be taken out and opened only when she was alone. That was what she had to do with the misery and despair she felt now. It would be harder, because now she knew that the weird flutterings in her belly were actually a child growing in there and moving about, she had a constant reminder with her.

But it was the only thing she could do right now if she was to carry on as normal. Her father was uninterested in her in general, unless she did something to attract his attention. She would use that to keep him in ignorance until she could work out what to do.

* * *

The following Friday Reverend Browne went to Chester, and Philip took the day off work, sending in a message that he had the same sickness that had incapacitated his sister the previous Saturday, and then the siblings sat together to plot what to do.

She had to talk to someone, and Philip was the only person in the world that she trusted, so she told him that she and Robert had been meeting each other for months, and that until yesterday she had thought that she loved him, and that he loved her.

"I feel so stupid now," she said sadly. "But I was so happy. He made me feel beautiful and loved, and I wanted that so much. I had no idea that what we were doing could lead to this." She ran her hand over her stomach, then impatiently brushed away a tear from her face. "Do you think I'm dirty or evil?" she asked.

"What?" Philip said. "No, of course I don't! How can I blame you for anything, when I'm doing the same thing with Mary?"

"Are you?" Sarah said, surprised. "Aren't you afraid she'll get like me and be ruined?"

"No," Philip said. "We have these things made of sheepskin, with a ribbon that you tie over…anyway," he continued, blushing furiously, "it stops the woman getting a baby. Mary told me that. But if she did get with my child, then I would marry her, of course. I could kill Robert Grimes for what he's done to you. I wouldn't dream of leaving Mary if she was having my baby. What a bastard he is! Sorry."

"Why are you sorry?"

"Well, you love him, don't you?"

Sarah shook her head fiercely.

"No," she said. "I thought I did, but…no. It was just a fairy tale, and I feel really stupid for believing it. I'll never believe anything a man tells me again. Except you, of course. I still have no idea what I'm going to do."

They sat together and they talked, and at the end of the day they had come up with a few ideas.

Firstly, Father never noticed anything about his children unless it was brought to his attention, so if she was careful, she could probably hide her pregnancy from him for a little bit longer. Mary had told him that babies grow in the stomach for nine months, and she thought Sarah's had been there for five or six.

"But in the last month, maybe two months, it becomes really obvious, so everyone will notice," he said. "So we have a month, maybe a little bit more, to think of what we can do. I think you'll have to leave Alliston, go somewhere else where no one knows you to have the baby, and then come back afterwards."

"How can I do that?" she said. "I don't have any money, and I don't know anyone outside the village."

"I have a little money," Philip said. "It's only a very little because I'm not earning yet, but Mr Stockdale is kind and sometimes gives me a few shillings if I've done very well. I've been keeping it. You can have that. It might keep you for a few weeks, until after the baby's born."

"You'd do that for me?"

"Of course I would. You're my sister. I'll be earning soon, but not soon enough, otherwise I'd give you more. Could you go to Uncle Arthur? He sent you that present, so he must like you."

"Yes, but he's Aunt Patience's husband. If I went there she'd tell Father in an instant. She wouldn't let me stay with her; she's as bad as Father, or almost. I don't know where I can go. And how could I come back? Father would never accept a baby in the house!"

"Maybe you could leave it somewhere?"

"No!" she cried instantly, shocking both of them. As if it had heard, the baby suddenly moved violently inside her, making her gasp. "I'm sorry," she said, "but…no, I can't." She laid her hand protectively over her swollen stomach, her instinctual reaction surprising her. Ever since she had found out she was having a baby, she'd thought of it as nothing more than a huge, insurmountable problem. But now, for the first time, the truth hit her.

Another human being was growing inside her, depending on her totally, a part of her. Its father did not want it, had abandoned it. She knew what being abandoned felt like, and she could not, would not do that to her child.

"I'm going to be a mother," she said, her voice full of wonder. Philip gaped at her.

"Yes," he said, "but Sarah, you can't keep it. How can you look after it, with no money and no way to get any? The money I can give you will only keep you for a few weeks at the most. You won't be able to look after it without a husband to provide for it."

Oh God. He was right. She scrubbed her hand across her face and her distress must have shown clearly on it, because Philip, never demonstrative, leaned across and took her in his arms.

"I'm so sorry," he said.

"No, you're right. I have to face up to the truth. But I don't want to. And I don't know anyone who would take the baby. If I can't look after it…it would have to be someone who would care about it. And where can I go to have it?"

"I'll find somewhere," Philip said. "I'll be careful. I'll think of an excuse for asking about places to stay. We'll find a way through this. We will," he said firmly, sounding a lot more sure than he felt.

By the end of the next week he'd found a lodging house in Manchester, which was far enough away for no one to know who she was. It was run by a woman too, and Sarah could say that she was a widow because then people would be more likely to help her.

"I'll give you all the money I've got, and that will pay for the coach fare, your lodgings and food for at least six weeks, if you're careful."

Sarah had thought about people who would care for the baby,

and had come up with the idea of leaving it on the Baxters' doorstep, or at the church. They were kind people and even though they had rejected her once they found out she was a Daughter of Eve, they had only done it because they loved their daughter Angela so much and had not wanted her to be corrupted. Surely they would love another baby, providing they didn't know it was hers? And then, although she would not be able to keep her baby for herself, at least she would be able to see it sometimes, to know it was being taken good care of.

It was the best plan she could come up with. Mr Baxter had told her that Jesus loved children especially, and he was a minister of God. Not a minister like her father was, but one who loved people and cared for them now on earth while they were alive, not just for what would happen to their souls after they died.

So. It was settled.

Philip went to Manchester himself on the next day their father was away, looked at the room, and arranged to rent it from the middle of September. Sarah visited Mary on the same day and found out everything she knew about childbirth, which was a good bit, because Mary had assisted her mother and the midwife at six of her siblings' births.

They had decided that Sarah would not tell her father she was leaving, and would just disappear. It would be horrible when she came back, and whatever excuse she gave, he would probably beat her and lock her in the cellar.

"I don't know what we'll do if he won't take you back though," Philip said worriedly.

"He'll take me back," Sarah replied. "He needs me to look after him. He's already decided that's my duty for the rest of his life. If he refused to take me back he'd have to find someone else to cook and clean for him, and he'd have to pay them. He won't do that."

She felt a bit better once the plan had been made. The grief about the loss of the man she had thought loved her was made bearable by her hatred of him, which she stoked whenever it died down. The loss of her dreams and his betrayal hurt terribly, but the hatred was like a salve, which stung when applied to the wound, but stopped it destroying her.

She did not think at all about giving up the baby once born, not once she'd decided. She was doing the very best she could for the child. And once it was outside her body and not part of her any more, she thought it would be easier to give it away to someone who would look after it.

* * *

Early September 1739.

Philip and Sarah sat by the stream after the church service, dabbling their feet in the cool water. They didn't play any games of splashing each other, didn't even think about it. Although only fifteen and seventeen they were adults now, and feeling the weight of adult responsibility heavy on their shoulders.

"We've agreed to wait until I'm earning a wage before we marry," Philip was saying. "I was going to tell Mr Stockdale, to see if he knew of any places we could rent, but I'm not sure that's a good idea."

"Why not? You said he's a kind man. I'm sure he'll help you if he can."

"Yes, but he might tell Father."

Sarah looked at the water for a minute.

"You'll have to tell Father anyway, you know. And there's no sin in marrying. Not like—" She stopped suddenly, placing her hand on her stomach, unconsciously protecting the increasingly active life inside her.

"You'll have to leave soon," Philip said. "Your body's changing quickly now. I can see it."

Sarah looked up at him, alarmed.

"Do you think that's just because you know anyway?" she asked. "Would you suspect if you didn't know?"

"I don't know," Philip answered. "I mean, I *do* know, so maybe I'm noticing things because of that. But even so, you can't wait much longer. I'll miss you when you're gone."

"I'll miss you too. But it won't be for long, not as long as when I went to Chester."

"No, but it's different. I'll be worried about you. Maybe I can come and see you."

"Oh, I'd like that!" she exclaimed. "I'll leave the next time Father goes to Chester. Why don't you tell Father while I'm here, about you marrying? Then at least I can support you."

"No. I think I'll wait until I'm earning and we're planning it properly. It's because it's Mary. She's a Papist. Father will be very angry."

"He will. But you're bigger than him now. You said you wouldn't be afraid of him any more when you grew bigger than him."

"I did, didn't I?" Philip laughed, but there was no humour in it.

They stood, dried their feet on their stockings, put their shoes on and walked home together, each absorbed in their own problem.

When they walked in the door the reverend was standing in the middle of the kitchen, clearly waiting for them.

"Undress yourself girl," he said, his face white with anger.

"What?" Philip and Sarah said together, shocked.

"I have heard a most wicked thing today, and I will know the truth, and now. Disrobe."

The adrenaline surged into Sarah's blood so rapidly that for a moment she felt giddy with it. Her breathing and heartrate quickened as she realised that somehow he knew, and her mind calmed, readying itself for what was to come.

"No," she replied simply. Her hand lifted towards her stomach automatically and Philip, seeing, grabbed her hand, arresting it.

"Why would you ask such a thing, Father?" he said.

"Shut your mouth, boy. Do as I tell you," their father said, looking at Sarah again. She shook her head, pulled her hand from her brother's grasp and started to back away.

And then her father was on her, grabbing her arm with one hand and placing the other roughly on her stomach, before pulling it away as though he'd been stung.

"My God!" he roared. "It's true! You filthy whore!" He brought his hand back, clenched his fist and hit her in the face, sending her crashing backwards against the door. She slid down it onto her hands and knees and stayed there, shaking her head to stop herself fainting, spraying drops of blood across the floor.

She saw him move back and lift his leg to kick her, and then he staggered backwards and she looked up through her hair and saw that Philip had seized his shoulder, pulling him off balance.

"No," he said. "No, you mustn't, Father. It's not—"

The reverend hit his son neatly in the stomach, cutting off the words and his breathing. Then he pushed him, knocking him to the floor.

"I sent you out with her to stop her from wickedness, and you have failed me," he said, looking down at his red-faced son who was gasping for breath. "Stay there. I will deal with you later."

He returned to Sarah, bent down, gripped a handful of her hair and twisted her face up to his.

"How long have you been whoring yourself round the village?" he shouted. "By God, you are Satan's get, nothing of mine! Do you know the father, or have you corrupted so many to your master that you do not know?"

"He didn't know," Sarah said somewhat indistinctly through her broken nose and swelling mouth.

"Of course he knew! No man can fuck you and not know he's doing it! Who have you whored with? I will have all their names!"

She had never, never heard her father use such terrible language. Vaguely, she wondered if she was losing her mind, because right now she was not afraid of him. All he could do was kill her, and it would solve her problem if he did. But her brother…

"Philip didn't know," she said. "Leave him alone. It's not his fault." She looked across the room. Philip was breathing now, clutching his stomach, the colour of his face changing from red to pink.

"Answer me," her father said.

She looked him straight in the face.

"No," she replied. She watched the look on his face change from rage to utter disbelief that she was defying him, and then back to rage again. And then he tightened his grip on her hair and smashed her head back into the door, and she saw stars.

He let go of her then and stood, and this time he did kick her, aiming for her stomach, and she twisted, fuelled by the instinctive maternal drive to protect her unborn baby. She curled up in a ball, her arms wrapped round her stomach, and felt his kicks and blows as dull thuds rather than pain. He was shouting at her too, but she didn't listen, knowing that nothing he said would be other than an insult, and she was not going to answer his question about the father, so it didn't matter what he was saying.

Eventually, after what seemed like a long time, he stopped. There was a moment of silence, and then her arm was gripped and she was hauled to her feet and dragged across the kitchen. As she passed Philip, she saw that he was still sitting, his hands over his face now, trying to block out what was happening.

And then she was in the cellar, in the dark. He had pushed her in, no doubt intending that she fall down the stairs, but as he'd let her go her knees had collapsed under her and she'd dropped onto the small top landing, so his hand in her back just caused the top half of her body to fall forward. She put her hands forward to save herself, hitting the second step and gasping as white-hot pain radiated up her arm. She stayed there for a moment, gathering her strength, and then she crawled down the stairs to the cellar floor and lay there.

He had never beaten her this badly before, had only ever hit her with a belt or the flat of his hand, never with his fist or feet. She had no idea how badly she was injured, but at least the baby was still alive. She could feel it moving inside her. Had it heard what had happened, and was distressed? Could babies hear before they were born?

"Shhh, little one," she said softly, lying on her side and stroking her stomach. "It's all right. You're safe in there." She had no idea if that was true or not. Normally once Father had put her in the cellar, the beating was over, and he would just leave her there for hours or days to think on her sin. But she had never committed such a huge sin before, and she had never openly defied him. What had possessed her not to tell him who the father was? She owed Robert no loyalty after what he'd done to her. But even so, she didn't want the whole village to know what a fool Robert had made of her. She did not want him to know, would not tell him.

Upstairs she could hear voices, but not what they were saying, and noises that she assumed were blows. Was Philip standing up to Father, as he had said he would once he was bigger than him? She hoped so, but she wished he'd done it before Father had beaten her.

She needed to think, to work out what to do once she was allowed out of the cellar, either by a victorious Philip, or by her father. She could still go to Manchester, maybe, to have the baby. But for now, she just wanted to sleep, and in sleeping escape. She would feel better then, more able to plan.

She lay on the dirt floor, the blood sticky on her face, stroked her stomach and whispered meaningless comforting words to the child within her, until sleep came.

CHAPTER ELEVEN

Mid-September 1739

Sarah stood at the front of the church building at the top of the steps where the altar would have been when it was a Papist church, before it had been removed at the reformation. Altars were for sacrifices, and communion was not a sacrificial event in her father's eyes, although it seemed that sacrificing his daughter for the sake of a sermon was acceptable.

The only person higher up than her in the church today was her father, who stood in the pulpit to which he had ascended via some wooden steps that curled round a pillar, giving him a commanding view of both his daughter and the congregation, which was now starting to enter the building for the long service.

As the parishioners entered they were conversing quietly together, as was their way, greeting people they may have not seen during the week; but once they saw Sarah standing before them they gasped, and then silently filed into their pews, staring at her. She stared back at them, keeping her face as expressionless as she could. If she had to undergo this, she would not give them the satisfaction of seeing her break down.

She had been left in the cellar for a full week, although she had lost all sense of time and so had not known that until her father had opened the door and taken her straight out of the house to the church building, still in the clothes she had worn to church eight days previously, which were now dirty and stained with a considerable amount of dried blood from her smashed nose and lips. Her face would be covered in blood too, she knew. She had

had no water to wash herself in the cellar. She had had no water to drink either, nor any food. Neither her father nor Philip had brought her anything at all, nor had they visited her.

She had eaten raw potatoes, carrots and apples from the boxes of stored vegetables, and raspberry and strawberry jam from the jars on the shelves, and when it had rained she'd licked the water from the wall as it ran down it, and had put an empty jam jar on the floor where there was a leak and had drank that water too, once it built up. She was lucky that it had rained considerably during the week, because looking at her father's implacable face as he had dragged her from the house, he would not have cared had she died of thirst.

Apart from that she had rested a lot, allowing her injuries to heal as best she could, stretching every so often so her body would not stiffen too much. Even so, she still could not straighten up fully due to the pain in her back, and her face was swollen and very painful. She had not felt like playing with the hairpieces her uncle had sent her, as there was no point. She would never sit in a nice house in a beautiful dress making wigs now. She had no idea what she would do, that was her father's decision, but any idea of a pleasant future had been a dream, a childish thing.

She was no longer a child. But she was soon to have one, and the growing love and protectiveness she felt for this little helpless being that was inside her surprised her.

In the cellar, in the dark, she had thought about that. She had reasoned that she should hate this baby. After all, it would be a constant reminder of her stupidity in believing anyone could love her, especially a sophisticated older man like Robert Grimes. It might look like him too, and be a strong visual reminder of him. By becoming implanted in her it had ruined her life, such as it was. Robert had left her because of it, and her father had found out because of it, was making her pay for her stupidity, for her sin, and would never let her forget it. She was ruined for life, would never marry anyone, for no one would take a single woman with a bastard child. And she could not now leave it with the Baxters in secret and pretend nothing had ever happened.

And yet she did not, could not hate this child. She was going to be a mother, and in spite of everything, that thought filled her with wonder and awe. She was creating life, and that life would be totally dependent on her, was already totally dependent on her. It was a miracle.

She had sat in the cellar, leaning against the wall, talking to it, telling it that everything would be alright, that she would look after it as best she could. It was for the baby that she had eaten and drank during the week; and it was for the baby that she was standing as straight as she could now, looking at the crowd of shocked parishioners blankly.

When her brother had brought her neither food nor drink secretly, she had worried that Father might have beaten him to death, or to a point of injury where he was incapable. But here he was, sitting in the front pew of the church, also looking at her, not with shock but with sympathy and some other emotion that she couldn't identify in his eyes.

His face was a mess too, even cleaned of blood. His mouth was swollen, and one eye was bruised blackly and almost closed. As he saw her observing him, he coloured and looked away. She reasoned that he had already been seated when her father brought her in through the private door of the church. Perhaps he had been unable to walk, had been carried into the church, and that was why he'd been unable to bring her any food or drink secretly.

She waited until he looked back at her and then she smiled, even though it made her swollen lips crack, to show him she was not broken, and that she understood why he had not defended her as he had promised he would when grown. Father was a bitter brutal man, and Philip was not. It was as simple as that. He was a good, trustworthy and gentle person, but he did not know how to summon the anger he would need to attack the reverend. It was not in his nature to be violent.

And then her father spoke, and as one every eye in the church turned away from her, to him.

"Today I bring before you an example of how subtle and insidious the ways of Satan are, and I will show you by this that no one is safe from wickedness, for it may enter into the house of the most faithful of men, even those dearest to God. And you must be constantly looking for it, and on guard against it, lest it overthrow you.

"We know well that woman, by her descent from Eve the

temptress, is most likely to fall to temptation, and that we men must govern our wives and daughters sternly, that they do not so fall, nor that they lead us to evil as did Delilah, Jezebel and many others whose examples are given to us in the Bible as a warning. You all know that I have endeavoured to raise my daughter in the ways of the Lord, have dealt with her strictly in order to preserve her from the serpent.

"And yet here, in spite of my unceasing effort to bring her to God, she stands before you, fallen, swelling with the bastard fruit of her most heinous sin of lust and fornication."

Sarah listened to the gasps of horror and looked at the sea of disapproving faces, although she noted that a few members of the congregation looked uncomfortable rather than condemning. When her father spoke again, she realised that he had noted that too.

"Now some of you may be feeling pity or even an understanding with her, those of you who were a little eager to enjoy the embraces of marriage before your weddings, with predictable results. And it is true that that is fornication, which is a great sin and which God is most displeased by.

"But you have gone on to marry, and in sanctifying your unions, so have you attempted to make amends for your weakness and your straying from the path of righteousness. Whereas this…this harlot…that I am ashamed to call daughter, has wilfully corrupted not ONE, but TWO men with her evil compact with the Devil!"

What was he talking about? Two men?

"She has deliberately and joyfully enticed a man with her sexual wiles. This man many of you know, for he attended this very church as a child, and this whore visited his ailing mother weekly, speaking to the fragile old lady sweetly to gain her trust, while spinning her web of lust and corruption around the son Robert until he fell into her arms, forgetting his wife and children and entering into most mortal sin, not only of fornication, but of adultery with her. An abomination!"

Sarah did not hear whatever vitriol her father spat from the pulpit next, so shocked, so doubly shocked was she. A wife, and children? Robert was married? He had lied to her from the moment he had met her, had never intended any more than a brief affair with her, had known there could be no more than that! And her father knew who the father of her child was, and she had told only one person, the person she loved and trusted, who she had always loved and trusted, who she would gladly have died for, have killed for, until this second.

She looked at him, sitting in the front pew, and he saw the expression on her face and blushed scarlet then looked down at his hands, which were clenched in his lap. She saw a tear fall onto the clenched hands, and she did not care.

Her brother had betrayed her. No matter how badly her father had beaten her, she would never, never have told him that Philip was courting Mary, because it was a secret and a trust. Robert had been her secret, and she had trusted Philip utterly with his name.

She had thought nothing could hurt worse than Robert leaving her, but she was wrong. This betrayal, by the one person she had loved and trusted her whole life, broke her heart. She actually felt the pain of it breaking, a burning deep in her chest. And she could not show it, would not show it in front of this group of heartless, uncaring people, who were looking at her as though she was filth, because she had trusted a man. Two men.

Two men. The second man she had apparently corrupted, her father's continuing sermon filtering through her stunned mind, was her brother, for sending him away, encouraging him to engage in fornication himself in order to be rid of him so that she could have the company of both him and Robert in her fall to Hell.

"It is too late for her, she has made it clear that she wishes nothing to do with the righteous ways of the Lord, although I will do my best at least to make sure she cannot corrupt any other innocents," Reverend Browne continued, to murmurs of approval from the congregation. "Now my struggle will be for the soul of the child she carries, which will be doubly cursed, having a whore for a mother and being a bastard, born of sin, and triply cursed if it be a girl child. I have tried and failed to bring my daughter to Christ; but I swear before you all now that I will double my efforts with regard to this fruit of her corruption and will do everything in my power to bring it to the glorious light of the Lord."

No.

Instinctively Sarah placed both hands protectively on her

swollen stomach, eliciting gasps of shock and titillation from those watching.

No.

Hatred roared through her veins, drowning out her father's voice, the gasps of the hypocrites in front of her, her brother's betrayal, drowning out everything except one thing, the only thing that mattered now that everything else had been taken from her.

Her baby.

She had lived with her father's 'efforts' to bring her to God for fifteen years, and they had been fifteen years of misery, of hunger, drudgery, beatings, of indifference and dislike. She had not known *one* moment of love from her father. She would not allow him to inflict even that on this child she carried, let alone double that. Her brother was not worth dying for or killing for, she knew that now.

But this innocent baby was. It was the only thing in her pointless miserable life that was worth anything.

She stood for another few moments, feeding off the rage that the hatred gave her, looking at the congregation with such utter contempt that some of them could not meet her eyes and looked down instead, as her worthless brother was still doing.

And then she straightened up, feeling the resulting back pain only as some vague background sensation, and she walked down the steps and along the aisle to the door. Through the blood roaring in her ears she heard her father command her to stop. But she was done with his commands, and with him. She lifted the latch, opened the door and stepped out of the dimness of the church into the light of a beautiful sun-filled day.

She did not close the door, unwilling to hesitate for even a moment in case she lost her courage. She left it open and walked down the path, through the gate and then turning left she walked along the main street of the village.

It was deserted, it being Sunday. Everyone was in church; if not her father's, then Baxter's, and so there was no one to try to stop her or to comment as she walked steadily through the village, turning onto the street where Mrs Grimes had lived, where her faithless lying bastard of a son had visited and had ruined her.

By the time she was passing the cottage a tiny portion of her sense had returned, and she realised that wherever she was going, and as yet she had no idea where that would be, only that it was not here, she would need some equipment, if not for her, for the baby.

The door was closed now, and when she tried the latch she discovered it was locked. She turned and walked round the back of the house, finding to her relief that the door there was unlocked. She pushed it open and walked in.

She took the heavy cloak that Robert had bought her, which was still hanging on the door, and laid it on the floor. And then she went into the kitchen pantry and took out the little food that was not spoilt, a pan, platter, spoon, a cup and a sharp knife. She took twine, a comb, some soap and the tinder box, and a blanket, and wrapped them in the cloak. Then she tied it, picked it up, realised that she could carry no more, especially with her back as it was, and left. In her hand she had a leather wine flask that she'd also taken which she filled at the stream, drinking her fill before she carried on.

She walked past Mary's house, determining that if she saw the girl she would tell her to leave Philip, for he was as worthless as every other man in the world, although she doubted the girl would listen, any more than she would have listened had someone told her what Robert was really like a few months ago.

But she did not see Mary and later was glad, because if she had the girl would probably have been sympathetic to her, which would have dissolved the hatred that was fuelling her to leave this place and everything in it forever.

She walked and walked, out of the village and along the track which led eventually to the forest at Delamere.

She had no money for a coach and could not walk a very long way, injured and pregnant as she was, so the forest was perfect, because it was only a few miles away, but she could hide there, be by herself, not in a black cellar where the monster who was and always had been her father might come and beat her, but in the light and the greenery, where she could think and heal.

She had never been there, but Philip had and had told her about it, that he had once spent a day there and had not seen one person all day. That was what she wanted, to go to a place where there were no people. Because people judged you and they hurt you and they betrayed you, and she wanted no more to do with them. People had nothing that she wanted right now, maybe not ever, and she wanted to be as far away from them as she could.

The only person she wanted was the one growing inside her, who when born would be fresh and innocent, who would know nothing of Sarah's past, and who therefore would respond to the love she would give it, and would learn to love her in return. They would live together in the forest, and would be happy.

She stopped once, but only for a short time so that her muscles and back wouldn't stiffen, and ate a few wild blackberries that she saw growing, and a stale and hard, but still edible biscuit from her food supply, and then carried on walking, reaching the forest in the early evening.

That first night she slept under a tree, covering herself with the cloak, and in the morning she drank some water, ate another biscuit and carried on, slower now because she was stiff, both from her injuries and from the unaccustomed amount of walking she'd done the previous day.

It was around noon when she found it, purely by accident. She had found a lot of brambles heavy with fruit and was picking and eating them, and also collecting as many as she could for later, and as a result had wandered off the thin track a little to a sunny spot where the blackberries were particularly big and juicy-looking.

It was, or rather had been, a cottage, but was now empty and falling into ruin. Sarah forgot the blackberries and examined the ruin critically. Part of the roof had fallen in, and ivy was growing all over the walls. The door was open, hanging from one hinge, but when she walked inside, looking at it critically, the floor was of packed dirt, there was a glassed window with rotting but serviceable shutters, and most importantly the roof was still intact over the main room, the one with the hearth and chimney, which also had a floor of cracked stone slabs, although weeds were growing in the soil between them. It would give her shelter and she could light a fire for warmth. She could probably fix the door, although it was unlikely anyone would disturb her – as well as being away from the tiny track she'd been following, the rioting brambles and ivy rendered it invisible unless you were very close to it.

Although she was tired and wanted nothing more than to sit

down and rest for a while, she decided to use the remaining hours of daylight practically. She had no candles, so would have plenty of time to rest when the sun went down. So she put her burden down on the flagged floor, looked up inside the fireplace and saw far above a little light, which told her nothing had blocked the chimney by nesting in it, then went outside again to look round, get some firewood and start making a home for herself.

A couple of hours later she'd collected a pile of small fallen branches for firewood, had picked more blackberries, gathered some hazelnuts, had found a small lake a couple of hundred yards away where she could wash and get water, and, the greatest find of all, an old cooking pot out in the tangle of what had once presumably been a vegetable plot and was now a riot of weeds, but through which the foliage of potatoes, carrots and onions could still be seen.

The cooking pot was a real find. She had looked at the one in Mrs Grimes' cottage, but it was far too heavy to carry. This pot was cracked, which was maybe why it had been left, although a smith could mend it, but the crack was high up enough that she could still boil water and cook food in it. There was a hooked chain in the fireplace too, a bit rusty but hopefully solid enough.

So, she had shelter, warmth, water and food. As the sun was going down she repaired back to her new home, swept the floor with a bunch of twigs tied together with string, and made a fire. She decided to eat the biscuits tonight, because they were hard and wouldn't last any longer, and so she warmed them by the fire to soften them a little and then spread jam from Mrs Grimes' larder on them.

She felt better now she'd made a home for herself. She felt safe here, far safer than at home. If Philip had spent a whole day on the visible tracks in the forest and had seen no one, then the chance of anyone finding her little home was minimal. And she had lived in a house with a monster for fifteen years; at least she was free of him now. Tomorrow she would try to fix the door hinge, and would collect some bracken and grasses to make a mattress of sorts so that she could sleep more comfortably.

She determined to live one day at a time, because if she thought too far ahead, for instance to the birth of the child, or to the winter, then she would falter in her determination. And really, apart from what she was doing now, she had only two choices; return to her father's and condemn both herself and her baby to a living hell, or find her way to town and become a beggar, because she would not be able to find work while pregnant or with a small baby.

No, better stay here and try to manage. Begging was illegal, and prison must be far worse than this little cottage, and she would never submit this child to her father's idea of parenthood.

She put some more wood on the fire, spread the blanket out near the hearth and lay down on it, folding the cloak up to use as a pillow for now, as although it was September the weather was warm. She was asleep within minutes.

She woke up once in the middle of the night. The fire had gone out and she was confused by the pitch darkness, and thought herself in the cellar again. But then she heard an owl hoot somewhere outside and the soothing shushing of the night breeze in the leaves of the trees, and remembered where she was.

Then her lips curved in a smile, and she slept again, heavily and without nightmares. It was a good sign.

* * *

Over the next few weeks she established a new pattern of life. The first few days she spent learning more about what was around her, repairing and cleaning the cottage as best she could, and making it as comfortable as possible.

Once that was done, her next priority was food, because she had to eat as well as possible, for her own and the baby's sake, and had no money to buy any provisions. She dug up the potatoes, carrots and onions from the weed-covered garden and stored them in a ramshackle cupboard in the cottage, that being the best place to keep them from vermin. She dried nettles and dandelion leaves, and discovered a farm a couple of miles away from which, by venturing out in the early evening, she managed to steal some more vegetables, apples and pears, and one glorious day a chicken which had somehow got free from the pen.

She kept it for a few days, trying to work out how to feed it, but as she had no corn and the chicken didn't lay, she wrung its neck and ate it. It was frustrating, because there were fish in the lake, but she had never learnt to catch them, nor had she learnt to

THE WHORE'S TALE: SARAH

trap animals – that had been Philip's job. Even so she managed to catch a few woodpigeons by scattering the dry biscuit crumbs outside then throwing her cloak over them to trap them.

She was managing for now and would think about what to do in the winter, when it came. Her baby would be born by then, and she would make a new plan of what to do. She kept herself busy, but became slower, more breathless and sometimes faint as time progressed and the baby grew larger. At least it was healthy and strong, or seemed so by the amount of kicking and moving it was doing as it filled its home and prepared to come into the world.

Being alone did not concern her at all. She had been alone for much of her life and enjoyed her own company, always had. She was not lonely, although at times she missed Philip, and then reminded herself that she was missing an illusion of a trustworthy loving sibling, as she missed the illusion of a loving trustworthy sweetheart in Robert, whereas the real Philip and Robert were not worth missing at all. She was better alone, and told herself that whenever weakness crept in.

And soon she would not be alone. She just had to get through the birth. For that, and that only she would have liked company, the company of a midwife, or perhaps of Mary, who had told her as much as she could about the practicalities of childbirth. It would be nice to put herself in the hands of someone who knew what they were doing. She was very afraid of going through that alone.

But she had no choice, so would have to. And if the worst happened and they both died, well, the baby would surely go to Heaven, being innocent? And for herself, she would not miss living much. Life had not been particularly wonderful so far.

She prepared for the birth as much as she could based on Mary's advice, and had warm water to wash the baby after birth, bracken spread out near the fire to absorb the blood, and cloths to wrap the baby in once it was born. At least she didn't have to worry about food for it, because Mary had told her that that was what breasts were for, that they produced milk to feed the baby, and that if you put the baby next to your nipple it would know what to do without being taught. Sarah had really not believed any of that until her breasts had started to leak a little, when she was really big.

Before it was born the baby would move down, so it would feel as though it might fall out by itself when she was walking around, but it wouldn't. Mary's mother had told Mary that. And then she had described the actual birthing process as best she could, which didn't sound very pleasant, but she didn't have any choice but to go through it, so she would have to accept it.

And if Mary's mother had had sixteen children, it couldn't be *that* bad, or else she'd have only had one and then would have stopped, Sarah reasoned.

Time went on, and September turned to October. Sarah had been back to the farm, using a stick and her knife to dig up late root vegetables, and stripping the hazel trees of nuts, to the chattering annoyance of the squirrel population. She felt as big as a house, and sometimes thought that she would be like this for the rest of her life, that this baby would never come out. She would just keep on growing and growing forever until she popped. Or maybe she would be like some Queen of England who Philip had told her about, a long time ago, who had thought she was pregnant with the next king, and who had gone to bed a month before the baby was due, because that was what rich women who didn't have to work did – they went to bed in a closed room with their women servants and didn't come out until the baby was born.

Except this baby wasn't born, and the queen…Mary, that was it! Just got bigger and bigger and then, all of a sudden, a long time after the baby should have come, her stomach just went down and there was no baby after all. It had all been air, maybe.

God, what would she do if there was no baby after all? Now she had accepted it, and everyone knew anyway so there was no need to hide it, she desperately wanted this child. No, that was rubbish. Air didn't kick like this did! She was just being silly.

It was hard not to have silly, scary thoughts though, when there was so much time to think, when the nights were drawing in and there was no sewing to do, and no candles to do it by, and she was alone.

And then one day in the middle of October – she knew that because she had made a scratch on the door for every day she'd been here, so although she didn't know the exact date, she knew it was within a few days of the fifteenth - she was outside collecting more firewood, with a good fire going in the hearth and a pot of potatoes and carrots boiling with some nettles and mint for flavour, when she felt water pouring down her legs. At first she thought it odd because she hadn't felt any urge to piss; but then she remembered what Mary had said, and for a moment froze in utter shock, as she realised that, after all this time, this was actually it.

She took the wood and went back inside, dropping it in the corner of the room. Mary had given her some blue cords, telling her that they would help to stop her getting a fever after childbirth, Sarah wasn't sure how they could do that, but reasoned that she needed all the help she could get, so wrapped them round her neck as she'd been advised to, then took off her wet petticoat, hanging it to dry, and got water, the knife and cloths ready before sitting down by the fire. She'd had dull cramping pains now and again today, and her back had been aching this morning, but she had put that down to the consequences of her father's attack on her. Although she was healed now, her back occasionally hurt.

But now the pains started coming more regularly, like the pains she had had each month when she became a woman and bled, but much stronger. She took off her dress, outer petticoat and stays and pulled up her shift so that she could see what was happening. Although her stays had been loosely tied, without them she could breathe more easily, and she tried to breathe with the pains, to ease them. It didn't work, but focussing on breathing at least helped to allay the sense of utter panic that she felt about the fact that her baby was coming, and she might be about to die alone and almost naked in a ruin in the woods, and if she did her body would probably not be found for years.

Then she laughed at the thought that she was worried about someone finding an indecently dressed skeleton. It wouldn't matter then. Only now mattered. If she died she died, but she was going to do her utmost to live and ensure her baby lived too.

She lay there, sipping water between the pains, breathing and watching her stomach grow hard and then soft. Mary had said that when she felt she needed to push she should, but she didn't feel at all like that. It just hurt, but she had enough time between the pains to eat some of the soup and put more wood on the fire.

And then more wood. And more. God, these pains were going on forever! They had started in mid-morning, and now it was afternoon. Was that normal, or did it mean that there was something wrong? She prayed that the baby would be born before it got dark, because it would be much harder if she had to do everything by firelight alone.

It was late afternoon when the pains changed, and she began getting the urge to push down, and to cry out too. She started by gasping with the pains, but then found herself first moaning, then screaming as they intensified, and she put her hands over her mouth to reduce the volume. She could not endure this amount of pain in silence, but she was afraid that someone in the woods would hear her and investigate. She did not want anyone to come upon her like this, not now when she was so vulnerable, and when every ounce of her needed to focus on what was happening in her body.

Between the contractions she gasped for breath, wiped the sweat from her face with her discarded petticoat, and laughed to herself at how foolish she'd been thinking she could have given birth in secret in her room without her father knowing. Then she waited with dread for the next surge of agony. By now she was lying on her side, because lying on her back was making her feel ill, and it was easier to reach down with her hand to feel herself when she was on her side.

It was growing dark in the room now as the sun set, but she no longer cared, because she had just given one great push and then had felt a rounded lump come out of her body, and stay out. Was that normal? She had no idea, but her body was working automatically now, and she just did what instinct told her to do.

And then there was a great pain, and a slithering rush, and her baby slid out onto the bracken, slippery and wet. Sarah waited a few seconds until her breath evened out, and then, with a huge effort she sat up, grabbed the first cloth to hand and started wiping the baby vigorously to dry it. Mary had told her she must do that, because inside her body it was warm, but outside it would feel terribly cold, and rubbing the newborn dry, hooking any slime out of its mouth with your finger and then wrapping yourself up with it and resting for a while was good.

She could see it only by firelight now, as evening had come, but she heard it give an angry mew of protest, and then she laid it gently in the crook of her arm, putting its mouth to her breast and pulling the cloak over both of them. She felt a sudden pinch on her nipple as the baby latched on and started to suck, and laughed then cried for the pure joy of having done it, and because both of them were alive. She would rest, just for a minute, because she had never felt so tired in her life. And then she would cut that cord she had to cut and wait for the bloody lump to come out.

She lay there, feeling the warmth and the little movements of this new life sucking at her breast, this life that she had created. She watched the firelight dance on the walls. And then her eyes closed and she dozed.

It was the new contractions that woke her, and Sarah jumped, feeling drugged and disoriented. And then the baby gave a little cry, and she remembered.

The cord! She should have cut it! She reached across, feeling for the knife with her fingers, and then sat up, uncovering and turning the baby because she remembered that she had to cut the cord about a hand's width from its navel. And after that, before she could pull it gently to help the bloody lump come out, it came out anyway, and she picked it up quickly with the bracken leaves and threw it in the fire, because Sarah did not want rats anywhere near this tiny life, and she was so tired now that she knew she was going to sleep heavily.

Then slowly and with considerable discomfort, she put more wood on the fire, moved to the mattress she'd made, settled herself and the baby down and pulled the warm cloak over them both, before falling asleep, completely content for the first time since Robert had left her.

CHAPTER TWELVE

The next morning Sarah woke late. The sun was up and birds were singing and the baby was suckling at her breast again, the sensation of which had woken her. She peeled back the cloak carefully and looked at the little head feeding, and felt an incredible sense of wonder and accomplishment.

How had this little being grown so big inside her – and without her knowing for most of the time? It was amazing! Now it was daylight, she looked at her baby. It had a little fuzz of soft dark hair on its head, a tiny snub nose and rose-petal lips suckling at her nipple. Its eyes were closed, so Sarah couldn't see if they were hazel like hers or brown like Robert's. But Mary had said something about eyes changing colour after a while, so maybe that didn't matter yet. Its ears were almost transparent, like tiny curled shells, and it was the most beautiful thing Sarah had ever seen.

The baby was lying across her body, so she could only see the left side of it, its tiny starfish hand splayed out across her breast, with the most minute perfect fingernails.

"You are beautiful," she murmured, entranced. Then it occurred to her that she still didn't know whether this perfect little creature was a son or daughter! Very gently so as not to disturb the feeding, she sat up and lifted one chubby little leg to look.

A girl. She had a little daughter!

Triply cursed, her father had said. In that moment Sarah was absolutely convinced that, no matter what happened from now on, however hard life was, she had done the right thing in walking out of the church, and away from that evil monster who called himself a man of God and her father.

"Hello, Lucy," she said. She loved the name Lucy, liked the

simplicity, and the fact that it didn't refer to anything, whether a flower, a person in the Bible or some virtue that she would be expected to live up to. Lucy was clean, fresh, new, like her daughter.

The baby stopped suckling, and Sarah remembered that Mary had told her you needed to wind babies by putting them at your shoulder and rubbing or patting their back so that they didn't get tummy ache, and then you could put them on your other breast to empty that one.

She lifted her daughter, holding her bottom in one hand and gently patting her, making soothing noises. She had never felt so happy in her life. Then she carefully turned Lucy over, to settle her on her right breast.

And that was when she saw her daughter's right leg for the first time, and she gasped, all her happiness draining away in a second. Because although her left leg was chubby but straight, with a perfect little foot and five tiny toes, the right leg was very short and inwardly curved, and her foot was twisted in on itself at an impossible angle. Was that normal? Would it straighten out after a while?

Sarah racked her memory, trying to remember if Mary had said anything about some parts of the body looking funny at first. She had told her so much in such a short time, it was hard to remember it all. She recalled that Mary had said the head was soft and might look a bit squashed at first, and you had to be careful to support it all the time, but she couldn't remember her saying anything about legs being strangely shaped.

Triply cursed. Four times cursed, her father would say if it wasn't a normal baby thing. A punishment on the child or a devil's mark because of the evil through which it was begotten.

No. Her father was a monster, and she would never have to listen to his judgements, which he claimed were God's judgements, again. And if God *had* done this to her baby to punish her mother, if He was that cruel, then she wanted no more to do with God. She was finished with all men. And God was male – everyone said 'He' when referring to Him.

Males were cruel, brutal, untrustworthy, even the ones who appeared not to be, like Philip and Robert. Like Mr Baxter, who had made her welcome and then told his wife to reject her, just so it would hurt even more.

She was glad her baby was a girl, twisted leg or not. She would rather have a daughter with a twisted leg than a perfect-looking son who would grow up to deceive and ruin women.

"I love you," she said earnestly to the infant suckling at her second breast lustily now. "I will always love you and protect you, as best I can. You will never know a day when you're not loved while I live, I swear it. I don't care if your leg is a bit twisted. You are perfect."

The next days were tiring, but were also the happiest days of her life, because this baby was hers, all hers, and they were alone, so no one could tell her what to do, or try to separate them. Finally she had someone to love, someone who would not lie to her, betray her, leave her. Someone who would truly love her.

It was a wonderful feeling.

She let Lucy feed whenever she wanted to, and tore up one of her petticoats to make clouts to wrap round her, and one for herself to catch the blood which she was still losing. Mary had said that after she'd had her baby, her monthly bleeding would start again, so maybe it was that. She was very sore, but then that was not surprising. She'd brought some marigold salve with her, and she smeared it on her nipples, which were also a bit sore and cracked, and on her daughter's bottom after cleaning her with water she'd warmed on the fire.

She kept the fire in the cottage burning day and night, and took care to eat as well as she could, but apart from that she spent all her time with her baby, holding her, talking to her, and humming to her, feeling sad because she didn't know any songs, because it would be nice to sing to Lucy. She tried to remember the song Robert had sung at Christmas, but she couldn't bring to mind the tune or words, and it made her unhappy to think of him at all. So she hummed tunelessly and told little Lucy all about her life, even the bad bits, because the baby didn't know any words yet so didn't know what she was saying. She seemed to like the sound of her mother's voice anyway, gazing up at her with hazy blue eyes which would one day change, and be hazel, or brown.

How amazing it would be, if Lucy had the same colour eyes as she did! Then one day Sarah could give her the bracelet Robert had bought, which she had with her because it had been in her pocket all the time. Sarah would tell Lucy that her eyes were beautiful, like jasper, but she would actually mean what she said. She would not tell her that Robert had bought it. She would never tell her anything about him. They did not need him; he no longer existed for them.

After Sarah had talked about her past, she told her daughter about the wonderful life they would have living in the cottage until she was older, and then they would move to…somewhere beautiful, and she would make wigs and dress ladies' hair, and they would both live in a lovely house, just the two of them, forever, and they would wear beautiful clothes, and Lucy's leg would grow and straighten, and if it didn't the luxurious silk skirts she wore would cover it anyway, so it wouldn't matter.

By telling the stories to her baby, Sarah managed to believe that they might come true, and it comforted her. In reality she was doing what had always helped her to survive; focussing on the wonder of being with her baby, and putting in a box the fact that she was living in a rundown cottage with no money, almost no belongings and only a few days' food to hand, with winter almost upon her and no idea how she was going to feed herself through it.

Take no thought for the morrow: for the morrow shall take thought for the things of itself. Had Jesus said that? It was in the Bible, anyway. One day at a time. She had enough food, water and wood for today. And she had her utterly wonderful baby, who made her heart contract with love every time she looked at her, washing away the past and filling the future with the promise of happiness.

When Lucy was a few days old, Sarah had fed and winded her daughter, and was sitting holding her on her lap, carefully supporting her wobbly head and back, telling her she loved her and making silly faces and raspberry sounds to her, watching the big eyes, still blue, looking at her in wonder. And then all of a sudden Lucy looked her straight in the eyes and smiled at her. It was a wobbly, somewhat lopsided smile, but Sarah had never in her life seen anything so entrancing.

She held her daughter to her, and cried tears of utter delight. *If I live to be a hundred, I will never forget this moment,* she thought. If it was possible to die of happiness she would have been in real danger at that moment.

* * *

The following morning Sarah woke up early, to find her tiny daughter lying in the crook of her arm, still, quiet and no longer breathing, although still warm.

Panicked and horror-stricken, she did everything, everything she could think of to try to make her live again. She rubbed Lucy with a cloth hard, as she had done to warm her and make her breathe after she was born. She prayed fervently to the God she had said she would have nothing more to do with. She held her close, stroked her, begged her to wake up, promised God desperately that she would do anything, anything at all, if her daughter would only awaken.

And then, when it became clear that nothing she could do was making any difference, *would* make any difference, she sat, cradling her baby to her breast, and wept as she had never wept before, great howls of anguish and desolation, until the body grew colder and stiff, and she knew, really knew, that Lucy had gone forever, and that she could not survive this agony. She would die too, surely she would? Because this was a pain beyond bearing.

But before she died, she would do the only thing she could now do for her child. She would give her a proper burial. With a huge effort she pulled herself together, fought to stop the crying, gasping and retching with grief until she had some measure of control. Then with infinite gentleness Sarah wrapped her daughter in one of her petticoats, gently smoothing her soft fuzz of hair and kissing the top of her head with tenderness and despair.

Then she went into the other room of the cottage, the one with the broken roof and the dirt floor, and using her knife and her hands she dug a grave deep enough that woodland animals would not dig her daughter up, so that she could rest in peace there. By the time she'd finished, her nails were smashed and her fingers bloody, but she didn't notice, didn't care.

She laid her daughter carefully into the hole, and then she felt in the pocket of her dress and took out the bracelet that she had intended to give Lucy when she was older, the one that Robert had said would remind her of the colour of her eyes, when he had told her she was beautiful and that he would always want her, for as long as he lived. On the last day she had ever seen him, before he'd left her. As her daughter had now left her, alone.

She would never know whether Lucy would have looked like

her or Robert, whether her eyes would have been the colour of the jasper bracelet or brown. How could she bear it, that she would never know that, never know any more of her precious, beloved daughter than this one tiny week with her? Would never have more than one smile, which would have to last her for the rest of her life?

Sarah closed her eyes tightly, forcing herself to keep going until her baby was safely buried and could rest in peace. She carefully placed the bracelet on top of the cloth-wrapped bundle, said as many prayers as she could remember, begged God to take her to Him, and then quickly and decisively, knowing that if she hesitated she would not be able to do it, she pushed the dirt back into the hole, patting down the soil before going out and collecting some pretty stones from near the lake and placing them on the grave, along with some red campion flowers that she found.

Afterwards she went outside and sat on the wet grass, heedless of the rain which soaked her through and chilled her to the bone. She sat for a long time, staring at the trees which were a riot of colour as the leaves turned to gold, red, orange and brown, a scene which just yesterday she had looked on with wonder, inhaling the unique scent of rainswept autumnal woodland, and laughing with sheer joy at the glory of nature. Life had been so wonderful yesterday.

But now she realised that all she had been looking at was incipient death. The leaves were dying, and soon the trees would be bare, the leaves brown and rotting underfoot. The scent she had thought so invigorating yesterday she now recognised as the smell of death. Death was everywhere. Autumn was the season of dying. Winter was the season of being dead.

So, then. She would lie here, and she would die like the leaves, and then when the winter came the snow would cover her, and she would stay here forever with her daughter.

She closed her eyes, prayed to God to grant her at least this wish, just this one thing, which was surely not much? And then she lay down and waited to die.

* * *

She lay there all night and part of the next day before she realised that she was not even going to be granted this wish. Her mind could not bear to live any more, could not cope with this much grief. But her body had other ideas, and so when she was thirsty her mouth opened to take in the rain that was pouring down on her. And part way through the next morning, when she had shivered half the night, her teeth were chattering hard enough to hurt, and without thinking about it she got up, went inside and lit a fire to warm herself. And then she took off her wet clothes, wrapped herself in her cloak and sat in front of the flames, enjoying the feeling of warmth on her soaking wet body and feeling guilty that she could enjoy anything, when her daughter was lying dead in the next room.

After sitting for a while staring at the flames, she realised that it was just as impossible to die of grief as it was to die of joy. If she really wanted to die then she would have to actively *do* something to kill herself. She would not die just by wishing to. But in spite of her grief and her hopelessness, she could not imagine hanging, stabbing or drowning herself.

She sat for a while longer, and then knew that she did not really want to die. She just did not want to live, which was not quite the same thing. She did not want to live right now because her daughter had died, and apart from the terrible grief, she felt that she had caused Lucy's death by taking her to this cottage instead of staying with her father, where at least the baby would have had a proper house to live in, clothes, and food.

But grief would pass. She knew that from remembering how she had felt when Robert had left her. It still hurt terribly, but not with the blinding intensity of the first few days. She didn't think she would ever recover completely from the grief of losing her daughter, but the intensity of the emotion would fade eventually and become bearable. And, she reasoned, she had not done the wrong thing in bringing her here. She had done the only thing she could. Because her father had beaten her badly, had starved her in the cellar for a week, had not even brought her water, although he had known she was having his grandchild.

He did not care about either her or the baby. If she had stayed until the end of the church service, he may well have put her back in the cellar until she starved to death. And she knew now that she could not have counted on Philip to rescue her. No. She had done the right thing, because at least they had had a week together, and Lucy really *had* known only love in that time, and had died curled warm and well-fed against her mother. That was better than the alternative would have been.

She had done the best she could for her child. And she was fifteen, too young to die; a crucial part of her knew that, and that dying would not bring her daughter back, nor would it reunite them, because Lucy was surely in Heaven, but she was destined for Hell. She would be there for eternity, so she might as well live while she could. And she was free of her father at least, because she would never, never go back there, no matter what happened.

She stayed in the cottage for a few days, whilst outside it rained almost incessantly. She alternated between sitting by the grave crying and then talking to her daughter, as she had for that precious week of her life, and sitting by the fire to get warm, crying and staring trancelike into the flames, thoughts going round and round in her head. When she was exhausted with all the crying and thinking she slept, and when she woke up she repeated the process until she was tired again.

And then one day she woke up and felt different. It was subtle, but it was there; at some crucial level she had decided to go on with her life. She still spent time talking to her daughter, but when sitting by the fire she started to plan for the future.

She could not stay in the cottage. She realised now that regardless of what she had told Lucy, even if her daughter had lived she could not have brought her up in a tumbledown cottage. Maybe if she had been there from the springtime she could have repaired the building, collected more food, made forays out to steal things, as she had stolen the hen. But as it was they could not have survived the winter – they would have starved to death. Now *she* would starve to death if she did not leave.

She sat, and thought of where she could go. Not to her father, not to Philip or the Baxters; not to Alliston at all. The whole village would know what had happened now, and would despise her. Or pity her, which would be just as bad in a different way. She would have to start again, but she had no money, only the one set of clothes, and no skills except the ability to do a little hairstyling, but not enough to earn money at it.

And it was then she thought of Uncle Arthur. In the parcel

he'd sent to her there had been a letter, which Philip had read. He had said he thought of her every day, and had told her to remember the offer he'd made to her. The offer to teach her to make wigs and dress hair. It had been over four years since he'd sent the parcel and she had heard nothing from him since then. But he had seemed genuine, and had always been kind to her.

Mr Baxter had been kind to her too, and so had Robert, and Philip, but they had still hurt her. However, she didn't exactly have a lot of options, so she might as well go to Chester and see if he had meant what he'd said. If not, maybe she could find other work there, as a servant. It was a sensible start.

Decided now, she took her clothes off, wrapped herself in the cloak and went down to the lake with her soap, washing her dress and one remaining petticoat as best she could. When they were dry she put them on, then went back to the lake and washed the cloak, and then herself, combing her wet tangled hair as best she could with her fingers.

And then at the end of October she dressed herself and sat down by the little grave to say goodbye to her daughter, telling her she would always miss her, would never forget her, and one day, if her father was wrong, maybe God would take pity on her and let them be together in Heaven when she died. After that she left quickly, because if she didn't she knew she might not be able to do it, even though it was silly to stay by Lucy's grave when Lucy herself was certainly in Heaven now, looking down on her and glad that her mother was going to carry on with her life.

* * *

She had no idea where Chester was, but when she got to the farm she'd stolen the chicken from a woman was outside in front of the farmhouse, hanging out washing as it was a fine day, and so Sarah asked her the way. The woman didn't seem shocked by Sarah's appearance, which was a good sign and probably meant that she didn't look too scruffy.

Chester was not as far away as she'd thought, less than a day's walk, which meant she arrived there late in the afternoon, while it was still light. She went straight to her uncle's shop, thinking she would rather meet him there. Maybe he would let her sleep there so she would not have to meet Aunt Patience at all. Then she could live at the shop, keep it clean, and have all the lamps lit and ready every morning before the others arrived to start work. For the first time since Lucy had died she felt a tiny pulse of hope.

But when she got to the shop it was shut, the windows shuttered. For a moment she wondered if it was Sunday, because she had no idea what day or date it was, but then she chastised herself for an idiot. If it was Sunday then none of the shops would be open, but they were. The clock had just struck three, so he would normally be there. Maybe he had closed early for some reason.

She stood outside and sighed, knowing there was only one way to find out. Then she set off along Eastgate Street and turned left into Bridge Street, stopping at the bottom of the steps which led up to the cherry-red door she remembered from…over seven years ago! So long. Would he remember that he had told her he was her friend, and that she must come to him if she was in need? Well, she was certainly in need.

She smoothed her hair, and before she could lose her courage, walked up the stairs and knocked firmly on the door. She stood there for a moment, looking down the street and realising that the reason everything looked smaller was because she was bigger, and then she heard the sound of the bolt being drawn back and her heart started hammering in her chest.

The door opened and her aunt stood there, looking exactly the same as she had all those years ago, even down to the dove-grey silk dress, except that her hair was now completely grey, and Sarah no longer had to look up at her. In fact she was taller now than the woman who had done her best to make Sarah as miserable here as she'd been at home.

Aunt Patience looked at her questioningly for a moment, and Sarah realised that although the older woman had hardly changed in seven years, of course she must have, dramatically. She was about to introduce herself when her aunt's expression of curiosity changed to one of utter disgust, and Sarah thought that maybe she hadn't changed that much after all, just grown taller.

"You!" Aunt Patience said, clearly shocked. "How dare you show your face here, you harlot! You think I will take you in?"

She knew then. Of course Father would have told her. They would probably have spent a whole day in that horrible brown parlour discussing how evil and ungrateful she was, and rejoicing in the fact that she would surely burn in Hell forever.

"I don't want you to take me in. I have come to see Uncle Arthur. Is he here?" Sarah said, amazed by how cool she sounded, when her heart was battering against her ribs and a trickle of cold sweat was running down her back.

Her aunt's face twisted into an expression that Sarah could not interpret. Disgust? Hatred? Indigestion?

"If you tell him I'm here, then I'm sure he'll want to speak to me," Sarah continued.

"I am sure he would *not* want to have anything to do with you at all, as no decent-living person would!" Patience said. "Begone, and now!"

"If he does not want to see me, then let him tell me himself. I will wait here, and will go nowhere until I see him," Sarah replied.

"You will have a long wait, then," Aunt Patience told her, and now Sarah recognised the expression and tone of her voice as triumphant. "He's dead. Died last spring. Didn't Perseverance tell you?"

Sarah felt all the colour drain from her face, and for a moment thought she would faint. She gripped the stair rail, saw the sparkles dancing at the side of her vision. And then she saw her aunt smile at the distress the news had caused, and pulled herself together. She was damned if she would give her aunt the satisfaction of falling at her feet. With a supreme effort she forced herself to stay upright.

"Thank you," she said. "I would offer my condolences, but you don't seem at all upset. I expect it was a relief for him to die, after all those years of living with you." She looked her aunt in the eye with the utmost contempt, then saw her mouth twist with sadness, with grief, and felt ashamed of herself.

She turned and walked down the steps, then blindly down the street, heard her aunt shout after her that she was a whore and would go to Hell, and just carried on, neither knowing nor caring where she was going, just knowing she had to get out of sight of her aunt's house before she broke down.

And then she was standing outside her uncle's shop again, at the foot of the steps which led up to it, remembering how proud he had been to show it to her. Her legs gave way and she sat down suddenly on the bottom step and cried, not caring that people looked at her strangely, that they gave her a wide berth, thinking she was a madwoman or drunk, or both.

She could not do this any more, take blow after blow and still keep going. It was impossible. To hell with it. She would walk back to the cottage, dig a grave next to Lucy's, lie down in it and cut her throat. Maybe she would be able to cover herself up with some of the dirt before she died, and then they would lie there, physically together forever, no matter where their souls were. She wiped her face with her cloak, took a few calming breaths, and then stood.

Then she saw the woman who was standing a few feet away watching her, a small woman with soft brown eyes and a puzzled expression on her face. She must want to go up the stairs, but was frightened in case this mad sobbing woman attacked her.

"It's alright," Sarah said, "I'm not mad. I just had some bad news. You can go up the stairs if you want."

"Sarah?" the woman said. "It is Sarah, isn't it?"

* * *

They sat in the tiny room that Maria called home, which had one chair, a small table positioned under the window to take advantage of the light, and a bed in it. The room was very cold when they got there, but Maria lit the fire and soon it was warm and almost cosy.

On the way back to her lodgings she had bought a pie from a street vendor, and now they sat on the bed eating it together.

"I couldn't believe it was you," Maria said. "I don't think I'd have recognised you if you hadn't been outside Mr Young's shop. That's what gave me the connection. Although you haven't really changed to look at – you're just much bigger, that's all."

"You haven't changed either. I'm sorry I didn't know you. I think it was the shock. I wasn't thinking properly."

On the way back to the house Sarah had told Maria that she'd just found out about her uncle's death and how.

"That bitch would have really enjoyed telling you too, I'm sure," Maria said. "He thought the world of you, did you know that? He used to tell us that you had something about you, that you'd be ideal, once you'd learnt the ropes, to take over from him when he got too old. I think he thought of you as the daughter he never had."

A tear trickled down Sarah's face, and she wiped it away with her hand.

"He sent me a parcel once," she said. "Just the once. It had a wig stand in it and hairpieces. And there was a letter too. I can't read, but my brother could, and he read it out loud to me. That's the reason I came here now. He told me he was my friend, and if I was ever in need I should come to him."

"He was a good man," Maria agreed. "Always kind to us. Made us work hard, but he paid well, and was very caring. I miss him every day."

"Were you going to the shop when you met me?" Sarah asked. "Who's running it now?"

"No one. It's closed."

"Oh! That's a shame. I'd have thought you could have taken it over," Sarah said. "After all, you and Anna could make the wigs and do hair. You'd just have to find someone who was good at talking to people. Or maybe one of you could do that, too. Although the male customers might want a man to fit their wigs for them, I suppose. What are you doing now?"

"I take in sewing, plain sewing," Maria said, pointing to the table, where a pile of neatly folded material lay.

"Does that pay well, then?" Sarah asked. It didn't seem as though it did. Even from her narrow experience of the world it was clear to her that Maria was poor. There was nothing in the room that was not essential, and Maria looked thin and pasty-faced, her eyes red-rimmed, no doubt from working long hours sewing. But then she knew nothing of how single independent women lived.

Maria laughed bitterly.

"No," she said. "I used to live in a lovely place just outside the walls. I had a bedroom and a living room, and it was beautiful. Warm too. But after Mr Young died I couldn't pay the rent any more, because your aunt came to the shop the day after the funeral – we all came back to work, thinking she'd probably carry the business on. But she told us to pack up and leave immediately. And she stood there watching us while we did it. Said she didn't want us taking anything that wasn't ours with us, and that it was time we got married, like proper women. Everything's still in there as far as I know, so we thought she'd reopen, but she never has. She wouldn't even pay us for the work we'd done before Mr Young died. I was lucky really, because my landlord understood why I couldn't pay the rent and had to leave, and said he wouldn't go to the law about the debt."

"That's not right," Sarah said. "Aunt Patience has got a lovely house. She could afford to pay you what you're owed. I don't know why she didn't keep the shop open though. It would make money for her too, surely?"

"Probably. But she always hated us. She used to think Mr Young was having affairs with us because we were single women." She saw Sarah's eyes widen and hastily added, "It was just her jealous mind. He never loved anyone but her. She was his childhood sweetheart, did you know that?"

Sarah shook her head.

"No, she never talked about him to me. She just watched me all the time and told me I was stupid and clumsy. She didn't like him paying attention to me, though. But she couldn't have been jealous of me. I was only seven!"

"She was jealous of anyone who took his attention away from her," Maria replied. "She said it was indecent of him to employ us, that he should have given men the jobs instead. He told her that women have got smaller fingers and pay more attention to detail, and he knew more than she did about the work that kept her in a comfortable house. She wasn't going to do anything to help us, once he'd gone. Not even if it would make her money."

Sarah could certainly imagine her aunt thinking like that. She couldn't imagine Aunt Patience being anyone's childhood sweetheart though, couldn't imagine her ever being young, even. She was one of those people who seemed to have been born an adult. Like her father. And yet they must have been babies once, innocent and sweet. Like Lucy.

"What are you going to do?" Maria asked, breaking into Sarah's thoughts. "You can stay here, if Mrs Young won't take you in."

Sarah heard the hesitation in Maria's voice as she made the offer, and realised that it had probably cost her a day's work to buy the pie she'd shared with her. She couldn't stay here and impose on this kind woman. She had no money to give her, no job to earn any. She couldn't even pay for her half of the pie.

"I'm going to Liverpool, to stay with a friend," Sarah said, surprising herself. Liverpool was the first name that had come to mind, although she had never thought of going there. But she didn't want Maria to worry about her. She would relax if she thought Sarah had friends to go to. She looked out of the window at the twilight, and made an impulsive decision.

"Let's go back to the shop," she said. "I want to see it again before I leave."

"There's no coach to Liverpool tonight," Maria said.

"I was going to walk. I haven't got any money for a coach," Sarah said.

"Oh! But it's a good way. You can't start tonight. It'll probably take you two days to walk there anyway. You can stay here tonight. I'll enjoy your company," she added quickly, obviously seeing the incipient refusal in Sarah's expression.

"All right," Sarah agreed, even more decided on what she was going to do, if it was possible. "But let's go to the shop now. Then I can make an early start for Liverpool in the morning."

By the time they got to the shop it was almost dark and had started raining, so the streets were almost deserted.

"Uncle Arthur told me he kept all the stock in the cellar downstairs," Sarah said. "That's on the ground floor?"

"Yes," Maria answered. "I used to hate going down there, because it was very dark and there were spiders there."

"Did you go in there from the shop?"

"Yes. There were stairs down to it."

"And was that the only way in?" Sarah asked.

"Well, there's a tiny door at the back, but it's very narrow and low. It's more like a window, because it's half way up the wall, but it has stone steps up to it from the inside. Mr Young always said it was hundreds of years old, maybe even as old as the Romans, and that there were ghosts down there. Terrified me more than the spiders, the thought of Roman ghosts walking through while I was down there!"

"Did you ever see a ghost?" Sarah asked.

"No. But after he said that, I never stayed down there long enough to!"

"Show me the door," Sarah said. "Uncle Arthur never showed it to me. Can you see it from the street?"

Maria took her through a tiny arch and down a dark alleyway at the back of the shop, stopping about half way down and pointing up at a small wood-covered square in the wall. Sarah felt around the edges of it, then smiled to herself, while Maria chatted on about the Romans and ghosts.

"There was a Roman camp here somewhere," she said, "and there was an altar to a heathen god, Jupiter something. That's what Mr Young told us, and he said that they lived here and so their ghosts are heard marching through the cellars sometimes! What are you doing?" Maria added, squinting in the darkness.

"He was probably joking with you," Sarah said, inserting her knife under the wet and rotten board of the shutter and wiggling it about. "There!" she added, feeling it pull away from the framework it was nailed to. Then she thought for a moment.

"Maria," she said, turning back to the other woman, who was just a vague shape in the gloom. "Why don't you go back home now, and I'll come and join you in a little while?"

"What are you doing?" Maria asked again, suspiciously.

"I'm fulfilling my father's prophecy about my future," Sarah replied cryptically. "Go. I promise I'll see you soon. Go on. I know where you live. I won't be long. I'm cold, and it'd be lovely to come back to a nice warm room. Go and build the fire."

She said the last as a command, in a voice her father or aunt might have used, and to her astonishment Maria, although a lot older than her, obeyed her. She waited until she couldn't hear the older woman's footsteps any more, and then she levered the remaining boards from the window, hoisted herself up and squeezed through, tearing her skirt and getting a splinter in her hand in the process. But she was in.

She had spent enough time in a dark cellar in her life not to be afraid any more. She felt carefully along one wall, and then around the corner, after which she ran into shelves. After some fumbling along she found what she was looking for, and using the small tinder-box in her pocket she managed to light a candle after a few minutes.

Then, as quickly as possible and refusing to allow sentimentality or grief for the death of her uncle slow her, she went through the shelves, taking things that she thought Maria might find useful to help her, and finding a few small items for herself. She also found some cloth wig-bags, and filled two of them up with her finds, along with some coins lying on one of the shelves near the steps up to the shop, which she put in her pocket.

She looked up the inside steps, but decided not to risk it. While it was highly unlikely that anyone would come down this tiny alleyway, if she went into the main shop with a candle, the light flickering through the gaps in the shutters would be instantly visible to anyone passing on the main street.

"Thank you, Uncle Arthur," she said. "I loved you, and I'm sorry for damaging your shop, but I think you'd understand."

Then she went back to the opening, up the steps, snuffed the candle, and in two minutes was walking casually down the street towards Maria's with her two bags, not rushing in case that would look suspicious.

When she got back the room was lovely and warm, and Maria was sitting by the window sewing by the light of one candle. She had left her door unlocked and looked up as Sarah entered, her eyes growing huge as she saw the bags, which Sarah put down on the floor before closing the door.

"Oh my God!" she cried. "What have you done? I thought…but I know your father's a minister, and you said you were living up to his prophecy for you, so I didn't think…did you break into the shop? Oh, tell me you didn't!"

By way of answer Sarah picked a couple of things out of the bag and handed one to Maria, before lighting another candle from the one burning.

"Here," she said. "I bought us a pie each. Let's enjoy them while they're hot. I think we both need food."

"Did you steal them?" Maria asked fearfully.

"No, I bought the pies," Sarah said. "But I took the other things from the cellar at the shop, yes. It wasn't stealing though. The only thief in my family is Aunt Patience," she continued, seeing Maria's puzzled expression, "and as a member of the family, I consider it my duty to make amends for her stealing your wages from you. So I brought some things from the shop for you, that you might be able to use to start up your own business. You were kind to me, are being kind to me, and I'm sure Uncle Arthur would want to pay you what you're due, and would be happy for me to do it on his behalf. Anyway, there's no use in arguing now. I'm not taking the things back!"

Maria laughed.

"Your uncle was right about you," she mumbled round a mouthful of meat and gravy.

"In what way?" Sarah asked, relieved that Maria wasn't going to pursue the subject of theft.

"He said that you had a lot of courage, and that one day you would learn that and would stand up for yourself, and for others. And that he looked forward to seeing that."

Both women fell silent for a moment.

"He won't see that," Maria said, "but he was worried about you, about the way you were treated. He didn't say much about it, but I know he didn't think much of your father. So he would be pleased to know you've got away from him, at least."

Sarah had been going to tell Maria about Lucy, but now she changed her mind. Maria clearly thought highly of her, and that was something Sarah wasn't used to. But it was a very good feeling and she didn't want to spoil it by telling Maria that she had been stupid, and was a whore in the eyes of her family.

"Yes, I have," she said instead, "and I'm never going back." She moved across to the bags and started taking items out. "I brought you lots of candles so you can see better when you're working," she said. "And some wigs, hairpieces, combs and so on. I don't see why you can't start your own wig-making shop, just a little one at first. After all, lots of men must start like that."

Maria came over and knelt on the floor next to Sarah, picking up the treasure that she was pulling out of the bags. She stroked the hair of one of the wigs thoughtfully for a moment.

"I can't start my own business, not making wigs," she said.

"Why not?"

"I don't have any money to do it. It's different for men. They can borrow money from other men, and from other people in business who want to invest for a share of the profit. But no one would lend money to a woman. It isn't legal to do it, so if she didn't pay a loan back, she couldn't be taken to court."

"But you said your landlord was kind because he didn't take you to the law about the rent you couldn't pay," Sarah said.

"No, he didn't. But rent isn't a loan, it's money you pay to have a roof over your head. So no one would think he was mad for giving me a room, when I was working. Everyone has to live somewhere. But to give a woman a loan to start her own shop…no one would do that. Women are not thought sensible enough to do that. Our job is to get married and have babies. That's all we can do."

"You don't believe that," Sarah said, aghast.

"It doesn't matter what I believe," Maria said. "What matters is what the people with money believe. The people with money are men, and that's what they believe. Men make the law too, so they make it according to what they believe. Women can work if they're single, but it isn't thought that they're clever, just unlucky because they can't find a man. And some women run their husband's business if he's away, or carry it on when he's dead. But they don't start up their own business."

Sarah sat and absorbed this. No. That couldn't be right! It wasn't fair. But of course it could be. She ought to know better than anyone how unfair life was. Even so…

"Uncle Arthur said that you and Anna used to go to houses and dress hair for women," Sarah said. "He said he didn't mind as long as you got your sleep and weren't tired at work."

"No, he didn't mind. He even used to give us pomade, and let us buy hairpieces at cost," Maria said. "I miss him so much."

"Well, then. You have hairpieces now, and combs and things. I didn't bring any pomade though, but if it's made of sheep's fat it would be too smelly by now anyway. But I brought some perfumed oils and ribbons, hair pins. Can't you still dress hair? You might make a bit more money so you don't have to do that horrible sewing."

Maria sat silently.

"If you don't want to do that, you can sell it all, and at least have a bit more money," Sarah said desperately, and then squealed as Maria lunged across and enfolded her in her arms, giving her a hug.

"You are a good woman, Sarah," she said emotionally. "Don't let anyone tell you you're not, ever. Especially not your horrible aunt."

* * *

THE WHORE'S TALE: SARAH

Sarah left the next morning, but not as early as she'd intended. Part of the reason was because, being extremely tired, both physically after her long walk the previous day and emotionally because of all the tumultuous events, she slept very late, and Maria did not wake her, telling her when she awoke that she had needed the sleep, and that she had decided to pay for her coach to Liverpool, so there was no need for a very early start.

When Sarah objected, Maria insisted, saying it was the least she could do and that she really wanted to. And then they breakfasted together at the tavern, and Maria stayed to wave her off as she left, wishing her luck and saying she would never forget her.

And so it was that Sarah, who had intended never to go anywhere near Robert Grimes again in her life ended up going to the city he lived in, armed only with the coins from the shop which Maria had insisted she keep, her tinder-box and knife, some hairpieces and clips, which Maria said might help her to set up dressing hair in Liverpool, and her most precious possession; the silver heart locket Robert had bought for her, the lock of hair inside no longer his. She had burnt that in the fire, and had replaced it with a tiny soft fuzz of dark hair, which she had carefully shaved from Lucy's head before she'd buried her.

She sat back on the seat of the coach and touched the locket, which was round her neck but hidden by her kerchief, and thought. Life was strange. She had told Robert that she would love to see Liverpool one day, but after he left her she'd thought it would not happen, in fact hadn't *wanted* it to happen. And yet here she was, on the way.

From what he'd told her it was a big place. She was unlikely to meet him, if he actually lived there at all. After all, he'd told her so many lies, and if he was married he'd surely have lied about where he lived too, in case she came after him. No, she was probably safer going there than any other town within a day's ride of Alliston.

What the hell, she thought. *It's as good as anywhere else to start a new life.*

She closed her eyes and pretended to be asleep, although she was not tired. Then she listened to the chatter of the other passengers, enjoying the friendly casual banter of strangers travelling together, absorbing it and learning, because she had not heard this kind of conversation before and was very aware that she knew almost nothing about the world, so sheltered had she been for most of her life, even from the normal life of a village, thanks to her father.

She knew that men, most men, were untrustworthy, brutal liars. She knew that people judged others without knowing the truth. She knew that women could not borrow money, and were expected to marry and have children.

She also knew that thanks to Robert she was ruined, and no man would ever want to marry her. Which she thought was good, because she hated men, and certainly had no intention of ever marrying one.

She needed to find a way to live independently, learn how to fit in with society, and to do that she had to learn, and quickly. So she listened intently to the conversation, noting that at first everyone sat in silence, until someone broke the ice by making a remark about the weather, which started the company chatting, firstly about the weather then about the state of the roads. One person talked about a previous journey which had been hard, after which everyone complained about the discomfort of travelling in coaches.

This surprised Sarah a little at first, as she reckoned it was much better than walking for two days and probably sleeping outside overnight, but then she realised that the people did not necessarily *actually* agree with each other, but were willing to do so because it was easier than to argue for the whole journey about such a neutral topic.

Such neutral topics comprised the bulk of the conversation for the journey, although towards the end of the trip two of the gentlemen got into a political debate, about which it seemed quite reasonable to express a violent opinion. It seemed that some man she'd never heard of, called Robert Walpole, was a rogue who richly deserved to be hung but sadly never would be, although she didn't find out either what crime he'd committed or why he was going to get away with it, because at that point the coach stopped.

They had arrived in Liverpool. And at the start of her new life, whatever that was going to be.

CHAPTER THIRTEEN

November 1739

Sarah had a somewhat interesting arrival into Liverpool, the coach stopping on the Wire Hall, after which she had to take the ferry over the River Mersey to Liverpool itself, which she found extremely exciting. She'd never been on a boat before, and although she had seen a few in Chester with her uncle as a child, they were big, nothing like this small sailing boat which took her across the wide river. It was very cold and the wind blowing off the sea numbed her cheeks, in spite of her pulling the hood of her cloak up over her face. She sat, looking across the water to the jumble of buildings on the other side, wondering if Robert really did live there with his wife and children, and then telling herself to stop thinking about him. She must forget him, as he had certainly forgotten her.

When they reached the other side and stopped they were still in shallow water. Sarah was preparing to kilt up her skirts and wade to shore when a group of men came to the side of the boat, wading knee-deep through the water and carrying all the passengers piggyback to shore at a run, leaving her to enter her new home town dry but somewhat shaken and wobbly-legged.

Sarah gripped the bag which contained her few possessions. The little money she had was in her pocket, along with her knife and tinder-box, and because she was travelling lightly she decided to walk about a little and get an idea of the layout of the town, and find a place to stay. If she saw a likely house or shop that might need a worker, she would call in and ask. She was very aware that she had only enough money to stay in an inn for one or maybe two nights, so obtaining some sort of employment was her greatest priority.

She walked along Water Street and then onto Dale Street where there were a number of inns, and she asked at each one the price of a room, choosing in the end the cheapest one. The landlady, a plump rosy-cheeked woman with a mass of frizzy brown hair was very friendly, asking her if she'd just arrived in the town, where she'd come from and what she was doing there, visiting friends maybe?

Sarah was wary, but as the woman showed her the tiny room, which she would share with two other ladies, she thought there was no harm in telling the landlady that she had come lately from the countryside and was looking for work, if she knew of anyone who needed an honest hard-working girl, maybe as a servant, or doing plain sewing. Her new acquaintance smiled and told her that she knew someone who might have an interesting proposition for her, and would make enquiries.

She also offered Sarah a bowl of hot onion soup and some bread, and when Sarah asked, frowning worriedly, how much that would cost, the woman told her that she could have it for free, as she remembered herself how overwhelming it was to arrive in a new place alone, and that a little food would set her up for the day.

The landlady was right. Once she'd eaten she did feel a lot more optimistic, not just because of a full stomach, but because the landlady was very friendly, seemed genuinely kind, and was clearly popular with the customers too, who laughed and joked with her as she travelled through the tavern delivering food and drink.

After the food Sarah went out again, without her bag this time, and walked around the city. She asked in a few shops, but no one wanted an assistant of any sort. She also went to some of the nicer houses, and after knocking at the front door of the first one and receiving a rude dismissal, she made a point of going round the back of the other houses to the servants' entrance, where she asked if they needed a maid of any sort. Most of the housekeepers or butlers said no, but the last one she went to looked her up and down, seemed markedly unimpressed with her appearance, then asked if she had a character.

As she had no idea what a 'character' was, she could hardly pretend she did, so she opted for honesty and asked what that was. The housekeeper told her, not without sympathy, that if she had worked somewhere else and given good service, she would receive a paper saying so when she left, which was called a 'character'. If she had never worked before, then she would usually be recommended by either a relative or another servant already working at the house.

"Without either of those things, you're not likely to be employed at a good house," the woman told her. "You'll understand that the master and mistress need to be sure the servants are discreet and trustworthy, as they will have access to everything in the house, and will no doubt hear some private conversations. Very few houses will take a chance on someone who is unknown and has no recommendations at all, especially here, where there are so many looking for work. I'm sorry."

Sarah walked back to the inn in the dark, feeling very dispirited. It seemed that obtaining work would be very difficult, and she was intensely aware that she did not have the luxury of time to look for it. She had enough money to stay at the tavern for two more nights and to eat frugally. And then she would have nothing at all, except the few hairpieces, the sale of which would not buy her much time.

That night she lay in bed awake, listening to the snores of her roommates and wondering what to do. Should she sell the hairpieces and buy some nicer clothes, then go hunting for work again? Or would that be pointless, if she had no 'character'? Or should she go back to Chester, sell the hairpieces and stay with Maria, see if she could get some sewing work as well?

No. She could not go back to Chester. There was too much chance of running into her father there, and she did not want him to see what she had come to. Also there was the strong likelihood that if he saw her he would force her to return home with him as he was legally entitled to do, and if he did no one would protect her from his anger or violence. Uncle Arthur might have helped her, but Aunt Patience certainly would not, and Philip had shown that he would not either.

She was still undecided as to what to do when sleep overtook her, and after a few hours' rest and with the sun shining as she made her way downstairs, she felt a little more optimistic, although she knew her situation was no better than it had been the night before. She went outside to the pump and washed her face and hands, before combing out her hair, smoothing it and deftly braiding it.

Just as she was finishing her ablutions, the landlady came out to her.

"Oh, I'm so glad you haven't gone out already!" the woman said. "I sent a message to the woman I mentioned yesterday, Mother Augustus, about work for you, and she is coming here today hoping to see you, at nine."

Sarah's heart lifted immediately, and she smiled radiantly.

"Oh, thank you!" she cried.

"You really are a most beautiful girl," her new friend commented. "You should smile more often."

Unaccustomed to compliments from relative strangers, Sarah blushed.

"What sort of work would she want me to do?" she asked.

The landlady looked away.

"She'll tell you about that when she sees you," she said evasively. "Now come in and have some breakfast, and then you can wait for her."

Mother Augustus arrived on time, just as the church clock was striking nine, by which time Sarah was almost prostrate with nerves, aware that she absolutely had to make a good impression as this might be her only chance of employment. Even so, when she saw the woman, she found it very hard to keep her face straight.

Mother Augustus, although seemingly elderly, wore an incredibly ornately decorated dress in a shade of pink so bright it hurt the eyes, and which contrasted horribly with her vivid orange hair, swept up into a very elaborate style which only served to emphasise the scrawniness of her neck and how long her face was. Balanced on the top of this confection was a ship in full sail, which bobbed about quite alarmingly as she walked up to Sarah, gripped her by the shoulders, and pulled her to standing.

"Hmm," she said, looking Sarah up and down with obvious

approval. "Very promising." She stroked Sarah's cheek with one knobbly finger and Sarah resisted the urge to step backwards. She dared not offend this woman, who could literally mean the difference between her living or starving to death. "What have you told her?" she barked, still looking at Sarah.

Sarah was trying to work out how to answer this nonsensical question when the landlady, who had silently re-entered the room behind her, spoke up.

"I haven't told her anything about the work," she said. "She's fresh from the countryside, only arrived in the city yesterday."

"Ah," replied Mother Augustus.

"I'm a very hard worker," Sarah leapt in, in case it was a disappointed 'ah'. "I can clean, wash, and can do plain sewing as well. And I have some experience in styling hair," she added desperately.

"You do?" Mother Augustus replied, smiling and revealing a mouth completely devoid of teeth. "Tell me then, child, what do you think of my hair? It was styled only this morning."

Oh God. What did she do? Tell the truth and possibly offend the woman, thereby losing any chance of employment, or tell a flattering lie and maybe fall into a trap, if the woman knew the style did nothing for her? She thought frantically, looking at Mother Augustus for a clue. The woman's eyes were shrewd, calculating. Intelligent then, in spite of her hideous dress sense. And she had the money to employ Sarah, so was presumably successful in whatever she did, or had married well.

"Your style is very intricate," Sarah said, thinking rapidly, "and I'm sure it is the height of fashion, although I have not had enough time here to observe the current styles. I would say though, that a slightly…softer style might flatter you more. Perhaps not quite so high at the top, and with a few graceful curls flowing down behind?"

Although it was not warm in the room the sweat was pouring down Sarah's back by the time she'd finished speaking, and Mother Augustus did not help – her bland expression gave no indication of her thoughts. There followed a short silence, during which time Sarah thought that at the worst she could walk back to the woodland cottage and dig a real grave for herself, as she appeared to have dug a verbal one just now.

And then Mother Augustus smiled again, this time with her eyes as well as her gums, and Sarah knew she'd passed some sort of test.

"Come, child," she said, taking Sarah's arm as though they were bosom friends and leading her from the room, "let us go to my home, where we can talk more privately and become better acquainted. If you like it there, you can stay. All my workers live in."

Sarah got her belongings, paid the landlady, and then walked outside. Mother Augustus was waiting for her in an open coach, and the coachman jumped down to help her up the steps. She sat next to the older woman, feeling somewhat overwhelmed.

"Now, as you only arrived yesterday, I thought that we could go on a short ride around the town, so that you can see your new home. What do you say to that?"

"You're very kind," Sarah replied. "I did go for a short walk last night, and asked about work at some of the big houses."

"But you were not successful," Mother Augustus said, and it was not a question.

"They said I need a character," Sarah replied. "I haven't got one. But I'm a hard worker, and honest, really I am!" she added desperately.

Mother Augustus reached out and patted her hand.

"Hush, child. I can tell by your hands that you're accustomed to hard work, and you were honest about my hairstyle. You don't need a character to work for me, if I'm happy with you. Now, here we are, just turning off Dale Street, and you see these courts, this is where the poorer, more unfortunate people live. There are a great many of them, and the situation is only getting worse, I'm afraid. It's because Liverpool is a shipping area, you see. The town grows richer and attracts people from the countryside – like yourself, who hope to improve their lot."

Sarah looked about with interest at the filthy streets, the smell of which made her feel faintly nauseated. There seemed to be hundreds of people in the narrow alleys, and they were white as ghosts, many of them dressed in filthy rags, the children tiny with bowed legs and no shoes. All of them looked far more sick and emaciated than the poorest people in Alliston had, where fresh air was free and there was always some sort of food available, even if you had to forage for it.

THE WHORE'S TALE: SARAH

Whatever happens to me, even if I end up dying here, at least Lucy will not have had to endure that, she thought.

"Of course, these people are not poor by choice," Mother Augustus continued, breaking into her thoughts. "Most of them would gladly work, but the work available for them is mainly heavy work, and there is not enough of it for everyone to have a job. I speak of the men, of course. The work is far too heavy for women to do. They must depend on their husbands or other male relatives for sustenance. You said that you had been to look for work as a servant."

Sarah turned, to see her companion observing her closely.

"Yes," she said.

"Without a character, you will be unlikely to find work there, though. And if you did, it is poorly paid and the hours are long. Ah, now! We are coming to the docks! You will see a great many ships here, even though it is a quiet time right now. Another problem for the men of course, because the work for them is not constant, and when there is no work, there is no food. And there is the danger of pressing, too. Of course when the ships are in dock then the sailors are paid for all the time they've been at sea, and when they are, they come into town for a little enjoyment, after all the hard months at sea. And they deserve some fun, don't you agree?"

"I suppose they do," Sarah said, having no idea what Mother Augustus was getting at, or what pressing was. Perhaps it was something risky to do with the type of work. She supposed this was normal conversation, small talk, such as the people in the coach she had come from Chester with had engaged in. She must make an effort, she realised, adapt.

"I have seen some ships, in Chester," she said. "I visited my uncle there once, and he showed me the ships. They were very beautiful."

"They are indeed. A lot of them sail to Ireland. Liverpool does a good trade with Ireland, but also with places much further away, where it is very hot. They buy slaves from Africa and sell them to work in the hot British islands, and then bring back sugar. That is why so many people are coming to Liverpool hoping to work, because the slave and sugar trade is bringing a lot of money here."

Sarah had no idea how to respond to this, except with honesty.

"I don't know what a slave is," she said. "A…friend once told me they were as black as tar, though."

"Ah. Well, never mind. They are savages anyway, the slaves, and you probably won't see any here. A few are brought to Liverpool for the rich people to have as servants, but mainly it's the sugar they produce. Do you like sugar?"

"I do!" Sarah said enthusiastically, glad that she could finally join in confidently. "I made some sugar, raisin and cinnamon pastries for the poor people I used to visit in my village. I can remember the recipe, if you would like me to make some for you."

"That's very kind of you, my dear. That would be delightful. Ah, here we are!"

They stopped outside a brick house which reminded her a little of the house her Aunt Patience and Uncle Arthur lived in. It had steps leading up to it like theirs, and was three storeys high, but the door was green rather than cherry-red. It looked very nice, but was not as big as the houses that Sarah had visited the day before.

Mother Augustus opened the door and walked in, leading Sarah down a long hall with stairs to one side. In the hall was a small table on which rested a very beautiful Bible, the gold leaf of the page edges glowing in the light of the candles which were mounted in holders on the wall, small mirrors behind the holders reflecting the light. Mother Augustus did not seem from her appearance to be a devout Christian, Sarah thought, although perhaps city Christians did not dress as soberly as village ones did. Or maybe the Bible belonged to her husband.

Mother Augustus threw open a door at the end of the hall and swept in.

"Here we are, girls!" she announced. "Let me introduce Sarah, who I hope will join our happy family! Make her welcome." She stood to one side to let Sarah see into the room and enter it.

From the announcement Sarah was expecting to see some sort of cosy family tableau, perhaps a husband sitting by the fire and some children. Instead she was confronted by a large but somewhat dark room, being decorated in burgundy and gold, with heavy velvet curtains at the large windows, and thick rugs laid on the polished wood floor. In one corner was a harpsichord and around the room was a series of small tables and chaise longues, on most of which were seated young women, all of them in a state of relative undress.

There was a huge fire burning, and the heat from that, along with that from the candles in the already illuminated crystal chandelier and the dark red decadent feel of the room, gave Sarah the momentary feeling that she was entering Hell. She froze on the threshold, trying to make sense of what she was seeing. Surely all these young women could not be Mother Augustus' daughters? There were six of them, and although they were all very pretty, they looked completely unalike.

"Come in! Don't be shy," Mother Augustus said. "We are all friendly here, are we not, girls?"

"'Course we are. Wouldn't get far if we weren't, would we?" a petite brunette said, dressed only in a thin peignoir which left little to the imagination.

Mother Augustus shot her a disapproving look. "Would you like a drink, my dear? Sit down, make yourself at home."

There was nowhere to sit that didn't have a young half-dressed woman draped on it, so Sarah opted for standing by the wall. She had never felt so out of place and uncomfortable in her life.

"What sort of work is it that you would like me to do?" she asked timorously.

"Oh we can discuss that in a little while!" Mother Augustus replied. "We are very informal here. I think it might be best if you get to know the girls a little. They are really very friendly, when you get to know them. Sarah has an ability for dressing hair, ladies!" she added, causing every eye in the room to go to Sarah's somewhat lopsided braid. Self-consciously she raised her hand to her head.

"I didn't have time to dress properly this morning," she explained. "I had to wash by the pump, and had no mirror."

"Sarah has only been in Liverpool one night," Mother Augustus stated, handing Sarah a large glass of pale yellow wine. "She is from the countryside, in… where exactly?" she asked.

"Near Delamere," Sarah said, not wanting to give the name of the actual village. "I came here yesterday, and the landlady at the tavern said there might be work here for me."

One of the girls, tall, with features that might be called handsome rather than pretty and a riot of dark blonde hair, sat up, smiled, and patted the seat next to her.

"Come and sit here," she said. "I came here from the

countryside myself, two years ago now. It's not easy at first, everything is so different. Come on, I won't bite."

Sarah moved across and sat down on the edge of the chair. She sipped the wine, which was very sweet.

"You've caught us early, before we're ready to meet people," the girl said, which Sarah thought odd, as it was after ten. "We *are* friendly, when we're awake. We mainly work at night, you see," she added.

"I thought perhaps you might like to stay here for a day or two, my dear, and become accustomed to us and the sort of work we do. What do you say? There is a room free at the moment for you," Mother Augustus said.

"Thank you," Sarah replied, feeling a strong urge to run away without knowing exactly why. "But I'll be honest, I don't have any money to pay for a room. That's why I'm looking for work, so I can pay my way."

Mother Augustus waved her hand dismissively.

"Don't worry about money. You can stay here for free. I'll take it out of your wages later if you decide to work here. What do you say?"

Sarah said the only thing she could, because although she wanted nothing more than to leave this strange room and these young women who, although only a couple of years older than her, seemed very worldly, like a different species to her, she had nowhere to go and no likelihood of obtaining work elsewhere.

"Thank you," she said. "That's very kind of you."

"Lily, why don't you show Sarah her room?" the older woman asked. "I need to talk to the others about tonight's… entertainment. You know what to do. Be gentle, mind."

"I'm always gentle," Lily retorted, which made everyone burst into laughter and Sarah feel even more uncomfortable. "Come on," she said, patting Sarah's hand and then standing up, "I'll show you around, and then you'll feel a bit better. Bring the wine with you."

They went upstairs, passing a large middle-aged man coming down, who grunted at them by way of greeting and who Lily introduced as Barney.

"Don't say much, but he's always there when you need him,

give him that," Lily said, turning right at the top of the stairs and opening the door to a bedroom, before standing to one side. "This will be yours if you decide to stay," she said.

At least it was light, not oppressive like the downstairs room. The walls were painted pale turquoise, the mouldings white, and it was dominated by a large bed, which took up most of the room. There was also a dressing table in an alcove formed by the chimney breast, with a mirror and a chest at the foot of the bed. A merry fire burned in the hearth and the room was pleasantly warm.

Sarah put her bag down on the floor and then sat on the bed, feeling the jade green counterpane. It was soft and silky, like the pink one she had loved at her aunt's and uncle's all those years ago. But this room was much nicer than that one in Chester.

"Do you like it?" Lily asked. She had gone to the chest and opened the lid.

"Oh yes!" Sarah said. "It's a beautiful room."

Lily lifted something out of the chest and held it up.

"Might fit you," she said. "You're about the same size as Iris was. What do you think?"

Sarah looked at the dress Lily was holding up, a peach-coloured silk gown with bows decorating the front and a great froth of lace at the sleeves. Her eyes widened.

"Oh, that's beautiful!" she cried. "But won't whoever owns it want it?"

"No. Mother owns it," Lily replied. "She owns everything in this house. Here, try it on. If it fits you, there are another five in here all the same size you can wear. I'll help you put it on. There are stomachers too somewhere. You can't have those stays you've got showing. They've seen better days. We'll get you more. Is that all the clothes you've brought with you?" she asked, looking at Sarah's small bag, which clearly was not bulky enough to contain a spare gown.

Sarah flushed scarlet.

"I...er...I had to leave quickly," she stammered, "just in the clothes I had."

Lily nodded, as though this was perfectly normal.

"I didn't have much when I arrived either," she said. "Just a couple of cheap dresses. But we all wear nice clothes here. Come on, let's see if it fits you."

"Do you work here?" Sarah asked, staying where she was. Something was wrong, and as friendly as this Lily appeared to be, she wasn't about to start undressing and trying on someone else's clothes until she knew what was going on.

"Yes, I do," Lily said. "Don't you want to try this?"

"No," Sarah replied. "I want to know what the work is that Mother Augustus wants me to do. There's no point in me staying here if I can't do whatever the work is."

"Are you a virgin?" Lily asked unexpectedly.

Sarah gaped at her for a moment, too dumbfounded to respond. Lily sighed, put the dress down on the end of the bed and sat down.

"I'm sorry," she said. "I've been here too long, maybe. I didn't mean to offend you. But Mother likes her girls to be…clean. If you're a virgin, then you definitely are, that's all."

Sarah stood up, suddenly decided.

"I think I'd better go," she said. "It was a mistake coming here, I see that now." She put the wine glass down on the floor next to the bed and picked her bag up.

"Wait!" Lily said. "Look, I'm sorry. I shouldn't have put it like that. If it helps, I wasn't a virgin when I came here. Been in service, I had, and the son of the house fu…ruined me. I was thrown out when his ma found out, and came here. Been here ever since."

"Did you have a baby?" Sarah asked.

Lily shook her head.

"But one of the other maids saw him coming out of my room, and told the housekeeper. I didn't want him anyway, but I didn't know how to say no. I was worried I'd lose my job if I did." She laughed somewhat bitterly, then looked at Sarah. "Is that what happened to you?"

"No," Sarah answered, touched by the other girl's obvious candour and responding to it. "No, I thought he loved me, and I did love him. I used to visit his mother because she was very old, and I met him there. He didn't live in the village. He was from…somewhere else."

Lily nodded.

"Get you with child and then run for it, did he?" she said.

Sarah nodded.

"I don't want to talk about it really," she said. "It's over now. I want to make a new start."

"Well, you can do that here," Lily said. "I did, and it's not so bad. Could be a lot worse."

"What do you do?"

"We entertain men. They mostly come here in the evenings and stay into the night, which is why you caught us all undressed, because we sleep late. And the men pay us to entertain them. Mother keeps the house, and lets us wear the nice dresses so the men will like us. Do you think you'd like to do that, wear lovely dresses and entertain men?"

Sarah frowned.

"I don't think I could do that," she said.

"Of course you could. You're very pretty, don't you know that? You'd look lovely in the right clothes."

"Thank you," Sarah said doubtfully. "But I wouldn't know how to entertain a man, especially a city man. I've lived in a small village all my life. I don't know anything to talk about that men would find interesting. And I can't play music," she added, thinking of the musical instrument in the red room. "I don't know any songs or dances. I think men would find me boring."

To her surprise, Lily started laughing, a hearty, infectious laugh that had Sarah smiling even though she didn't know what she'd said that was funny. Then she leaned forward and grabbed Sarah's hands, pulling her onto the bed and hugging her.

"Oh, bless you, child, you remind me of me when I first came here," she said. "I'd forgotten how innocent I was, and how much I've changed. When I say entertain, I mean it in the way you entertained the man who left you."

Sarah's brow furrowed as she tried to comprehend what Lily was talking about. Entertain?

"I don't know what you mean," she said. "I didn't entertain him. If anything, he entertained me. We played games once, at Christmas, and he sung a song for me."

Lily stroked her cheek, very gently.

"Did he buy you little presents? Keep coming to see you?" she asked.

"Yes," Sarah said.

"Why did he do that?"

"He told me…I thought he loved me, but of course I know he didn't now," she said, her voice wavering.

"No," Lily said softly. "So if he didn't love you, why did he keep coming to see you and buying you presents?"

Light dawned, and Sarah's face flushed scarlet.

"You entertain men…you do that, as *work*?" she asked. "Men pay you to do that?"

"They do."

"Oh, God, no! I couldn't do that!" Sarah cried.

"That's what I said when I first came here," Lily said. "Because I was a bit like you. Rodney, that was the son's name, he told me he loved me, that if he could he'd marry me. It was all bull, I know that now. He'd done it before and I'm sure he's done it since, and his mother sorted it out by getting rid of the girls he'd ruined. Happens all the time, it does. You're not the first girl that's been led on by a complete bastard. I was hurt, like you, because I thought he did love me, and when I found out I'd been used I was devastated. But this is different."

"How is it different?" Sarah asked. How could it be?

"It's honest, that's what it is. A man comes here because he wants to swive a woman, without any emotions being involved. He pays her for it. They both know what's happening and why. Yes, you have to pretend you're enjoying it, and that he's the most virile man in the town, because that's what he's paying you for. But you're doing it for the money, and you both know that. So it *is* different. You're not hurt if he doesn't come back or if he asks for another girl next time, because you're not emotionally involved."

Sarah sat and thought about this for a minute, and Lily remained quiet, letting her absorb the new idea.

"But I was only happy doing that with him *because* I thought we were in love with each other," she said after a while. "It just seems wrong to do it otherwise. It's an emotional thing, isn't it, a way of showing you love each other? It's what you do when you're married, you shouldn't really do it at all before that."

"Why shouldn't you? Because some minister tells you that if he says a few words over you both, then it's suddenly alright? Lots of people get married for all sorts of reasons that have nothing to do with love. They do it because their parents want them to, because if they marry Lord Shit then they'll be Lady Shit, or because the man has a good job and they won't starve. It's a business transaction, like what we do, except you have to live with the fool for the rest of your life. And then if you're the woman, you have to do what the man tells you forever and do whatever he wants in bed too, even if you hate him. At least with this, we swive each other, he pays me, and then he's gone. He isn't telling me who I can speak to and what to do. I'm sorry," Lily said, seeing Sarah's shocked expression. "I didn't mean to say all that. But it's what I think. I'm never letting a man tell me what to do again. Outside of working, that is."

"I didn't mean to offend you," Sarah said hurriedly. "I just don't know if I could do that."

"Bless you, sweetheart, I'm not that easily offended," Lily replied. "Look, try the dress on, see what you look like, and then do what Mother said. Stay here for a few days and see what you think. You said you can dress hair?"

"Yes, although I haven't done it for a long time," Sarah admitted.

"Well, then. You try the dress on, just for fun, and I'll go down and tell Mother you're not sure you can work here."

She was very kind, Sarah thought after Lily had left. Her father had called her a whore when he stood her up in front of the church, but she wasn't, not really. She had thought a whore to be a terrible thing, like being a witch or a demon. Lily was a whore though, and so were all the other girls downstairs, but they seemed nice enough.

She picked up the peach dress, tried it against herself. It probably would fit her. It was very lovely. There was no harm in trying it on. She would do that, and then she would take it off again and leave. There was no point in staying here. She couldn't ever imagine doing what she had done with Robert with any other man, let alone one who didn't care for her at all.

She took off the plain dark blue dress, aware of how threadbare and dowdy it looked. And then she started dressing in the peach dress, loving the feel of the soft silk as it settled against her skin, reminding her of her mother's beautiful gown, which had felt the same. The peach dress did fit although it was a little tight at the waist, but that was because her belly was still a bit soft from childbirth. It was getting smaller though. She wouldn't think about that.

It was a lovely dress. It made her feel beautiful, even if she wasn't. She looked at herself in the mirror, and smiled for the first time since she'd entered this strange house. Then she saw the door start to open behind her in the reflection.

"You were right, it does almost fit…" she started, then stopped as she saw Mother Augustus rather than Lily come into the room. "I'm sorry," she said. "I'll take it off."

"No, let me see you," Mother Augustus said. "It looks good on you. The colour brings out your complexion. You have beautiful skin. It's just a little tight in the waist, that's all. Lily told me that you don't think you can do the work we do here."

"No," Sarah said. "I couldn't. It's…it's just not something I could do. I'm sorry."

Mother Augustus nodded.

"What a shame. You are very lovely, you know. What will you do, then?"

"I don't know," Sarah said. "Keep trying to find work as a servant, I suppose. Or…I know someone in another town, she lives by taking in plain sewing. I could try and do that."

"You could. Does your friend live in a nice warm house like this, with plenty of food, and only work for a few hours each day?"

Sarah remembered Maria's red-rimmed eyes, the single pie that she'd shared with her guest, the ramshackle sparse furnishings.

"No," she admitted. "Maybe I could find work dressing hair. That's what I'd really like to do." She started unpinning the stomacher, but Mother Augustus reached up, putting her hand over Sarah's to stop her.

"Keep it on. Why don't you stay here for a few days? The room is empty anyway. You can make yourself useful by dressing the girls' hair, and see what our work is like, and then you can make a better decision." When Sarah hesitated, she continued. "What do you have to lose?"

She had a point. At least she would have a few days to try to look for other work. And she could practice her hairstyling skills.

"I have some hairpieces and clips with me," Sarah said. "It's not much, though."

"Oh, I have lots of hairstyling equipment," Mother Augustus said. "The girls' hair gets very messy at night, so we have to patch it up ourselves as best we can. It will be nice to have someone skilled in the house! So, are we agreed? Can we shake hands on it?"

She spat in her hand then held it out, and after a moment Sarah took it, not wanting to appear rude.

"Excellent!" Mother Augustus said briskly. "Now, unpack your bag, then come downstairs and get acquainted with the girls. And then after we've eaten you can show us what you can do with hair!"

* * *

Mid-November 1739

The two women and one man sat in a tiny back room of the house, which served as an office and private meeting room, and which was at the moment being used for the latter purpose.

"No," Mother Augustus said. "I know you've taken a shine to her, but I've already given her longer than most. It's time to make her decide."

"Oh come on, Jane," Lily said, using her employer's name, as she only did when they were in private. "There ain't no decision for her to make, is there? She just has to accept it, as I did. As we all did, even you, once."

"Of course there's a decision!"

Lily snorted derisively.

"There's a decision," Mother Augustus said firmly, "even if it's between a bad thing and a horrible thing. It's still a decision. I'll talk to her this afternoon. I don't think I'll need you, Barney. She seems docile enough, but be on hand, just in case."

Lily sat for a minute thinking.

"No," she said finally. "You're misjudging her. She's not what she seems."

"Really? In that case, Barney, come in with me," Mother Augustus said.

"I didn't mean that," Lily stated. "You do really want her, don't you?"

"Of course I do!" the older woman said. "She's very attractive, and has an innocence about her. It's a shame she's not virgin, but even so she'll fetch a good price. And she really has a way with hair – it's natural to her. Quite remarkable." It *was* quite remarkable. The girl knew instinctively what would flatter her subject, and could make the hair look thicker and the girls look prettier and more refined, and all in half the time the hair dresser she'd been using until now could. It was obvious she had not been extensively trained in the art, but she had a great deal of natural talent. She was already suggesting changes to the cosmetics the girls wore too, and her suggestions were good.

"Even so," Mother Augustus added, "she cannot pay her board by hair dressing alone. I have the note she signed here. It is time to force her to make the right choice."

Lily looked at the note Mother Augustus pointed to. She had signed one herself over two years previously and at the time had understood what she was signing as well as Sarah did. She leaned across and picked it up, looking at the slightly wobbly signature that Sarah had been so proud to be able to write.

"You won't force her with this, any more than you will with your spit handshake, which she didn't understand the meaning of any more than she did this," she said. "If you try to you'll lose her. She's been broken. I don't know how exactly, because she won't talk much about her past, but she has. And she's fixed herself somehow and found strength. She won't let herself be broken again. She'll die first. And if you try to blackmail her with this, she won't give in. And before you say it ain't blackmail, we both know it is."

"Are you certain of this?"

"No. Nothing is ever certain. But I'd wager fifty on it, if you're interested."

Mother Augustus sat back in her chair and looked at Lily. As this new chit was talented with hair, Lily was talented at assessing people. She was not *always* right, but she was right often enough for her opinions to be worth heeding.

"Very well, then. What do you suggest? Because I can't let her stay here much longer unless she pulls her weight."

"Give me a day with her. Let us go out for a walk, and then give her the night to think about it. And if she hasn't come round then and made her own decision, use your note."

"One day. Do your best for me. And remember, even if you are fond of her, I'm not a charity."

"No danger of me forgetting that, is there?" Lily said. She stood. "Till tomorrow, then."

* * *

The two women stood at the dockside, dressed soberly, with the hoods of their cloaks covering their hair, partly to protect them against the icy November wind blowing in from the sea, and partly to protect them from sailors' advances.

"I do love the ships," Sarah said. "They make me think of freedom, of going to faraway places where no one knows you and you can make a new start."

"Is that what you want to do?" Lily asked.

"Sail away? I don't know. I want to make a new start though, yes."

"That's why you came here."

"It is. But I don't want to make the new start Mother's suggesting. I need to tell her that. It's not fair to stay with her any longer falsely."

"But you want to be a hair dresser. That's your new start?"

Sarah looked out at the forest of masts, all of them bare at present. A lot of the ships would not go anywhere now until the spring, although the ones that operated to Ireland would continue to do so, weather permitting.

"I'd like that. And I'm enjoying the practice of working on your hair. But it's just a dream. I don't have the money to set up, and I don't think I ever will have."

"If you stay with us you can still dress our hair, you know," Lily said. "Mother is really pleased with that part of your work."

"That's good to hear," Sarah said, and smiled. "But if I stay with you I'll have to go with men too, and I don't think I can do that."

To Sarah's surprise Lily didn't try to tell her she was wrong, but just nodded.

"So what will you do then, if you don't stay with us?"

"I don't know," Sarah admitted. "I'll try to get work as a servant, or sewing. There's nothing else I can do."

"And if you can't get work?"

Go back to my daughter, and stay there with her forever.

She couldn't say that, so she just shrugged.

"Let me show you something," Lily said suddenly, reaching out her hand. Sarah, who was now growing used to how tactile the girls were, put her hand in Lily's, who led her away from the dock activity and down a side street.

"Mother told me she showed you these alleys," Lily said, "but you were in a coach, so you don't see it the same. These are the choices you have, as a poor woman. Look at the children you pass, and look at the women standing in the doorways. That's one choice. Get married, be at the complete mercy of the man, and have a child every year, whether you want it or can feed it or not. Because he'll want his rights every night, whether you want to or not. Look at them."

Sarah looked at them as they walked along. Women with young hair and old faces, with dead eyes and sometimes bruises, surrounded by children who, if they were lucky enough to grow up at all, would end up living the same life.

"Or," Lily said, "you can decide not to get married to some brute. In which case you go into service like I did and work fifteen hours a day or more scrubbing floors, making fires, peeling vegetables and doing whatever you're told. You'll earn less for that in a month than I earn in a night. And then if there's a son of the house, which there always is because he's needed to inherit it all, you'll come to his notice as I did, because you're pretty. After that it's only a matter of time before you either sleep with him and then leave, or just leave. And if he wants you he can take you, whether you want it or not, because all his parents' rich friends will make sure he isn't punished for it." They'd reached the end of the street, and she turned to look at Sarah.

"Here we are now, coming up to another choice," she continued, walking down a street that ran parallel to the docks, with a lot of small dingy alleys running through, entered through narrow archways. "This is where the whores work. Not the whores like me, but the less fortunate ones who don't have a nice room to entertain the men in, so do it up against the wall for a penny or two. It's true that Mother takes our money and only gives us a little, but it's a lot more than a penny a fuck. And if a cove cuts up rough with her there's nothing she can do, whereas Barney's there to protect us, and he does.

"In the winter these whores live on the streets, so they spend as much time as they can in the inns, and all the money they earn on gin, to forget how awful their life is. Gin stops you feeling so hungry, and it's also supposed to help you get rid of unwanted babies. Doesn't get rid of the pox though. And these whores can't afford no mercury cure for that."

She stopped talking then and just walked, holding Sarah's hand. Sarah looked at the women and the men, but mainly at the women. It was four o'clock in the afternoon and a lot of them were indeed inebriated, weaving drunkenly down the cobbled street. Some of them had their breasts on show by way of advertising, many of them had dull complexions and pustules, dry cracked lips and lank, lice-ridden hair. Most of them were hideous, and Sarah couldn't imagine why anyone would want to pay to swive them. Even the young ones, the girls like herself fresh from the countryside with clear complexions and glowing eyes, showed signs that they would soon look like their companions.

"I'm sorry," Lily said, eyeing Sarah's pale face and huge shocked eyes with sympathy. "I didn't bring you here to be cruel. But you're right, you do have to make a decision about whether you want to stay at Mother's or not. And before you make that decision you need to know what the alternatives are. I won't lie to you. What we do ain't fun, and it ain't what I'd choose to do, if I could do anything I wanted. But I can't do anything I want, and neither can you. You want to dress hair and you should, because you have a natural talent for it. But if you walk away from us tonight, I can tell you that you'll never do it. Because you'll never be able to save the money to start, and you'll end up like I've just said.

"I like you. I was like you two years ago, thought I couldn't do it. But I changed my mind and I've never regretted that decision, because it was the best I could have, and still is. I have friends, a roof over my head, warmth, good food, nice clothes and protection. And a little money. I spend mine on trinkets. Rose spends hers on the woman who's bringing up her child for her, because we can't have children in a brothel. You could practice your hair dressing on us, save your money, and maybe in a few years move on and start your business. I just want you to make the right decision, and I think you will if you really know what it is you're doing."

They walked down the street for a while, Lily pushing away the imploring hands of begging children or handing certain ones she considered deserving a copper, letting Sarah absorb the mass of information she'd just been given, verbally and visually.

"What made you decide to stay, if you thought you couldn't do it?" Sarah asked softly after a while. "You said you changed your mind. Why?"

Lily thought for a while, and then clearly came to a decision.

"I'm cold," she said. "Let's go in the tavern and get some food. This one is decent, and we won't be pestered here. I'll get us a room to be sure."

"Pestered?"

"We're dressed better than the normal clientele of the inn, so that tells the men we're whores, or likely to be. And we're not with husbands, so even more likely."

She went to the landlord, had a word and after an exchange of coins was shown to a quiet room, small, with chairs around a rectangular table. A brazier in one corner warmed the room nicely.

"I've ordered mutton chops for us," Lily said. "Sit down. This room's usually used by smugglers, but they ain't meeting today so we won't be disturbed."

Smugglers? Lily said the word in the same matter-of-fact tone as her father might have said clergy, or tradesmen.

Sarah removed her cloak and sat down, feeling somewhat overwhelmed.

"Take as much time as you need," Lily said. "Mother's going to ask for your decision tomorrow. I told her I wanted today to talk to you, and she agreed I could. It's your decision, but I want you to have as much information as you can to make it."

"Why are you doing this for me?" Sarah asked. "No one does anything for nothing. Is she paying you to persuade me to say yes?"

"Well, that was honest!" Lily replied, laughing. "And it deserves an honest answer. No, she ain't paying me to talk you into it. I asked her to give me the time, and she wants you, thinks you'll make money for her – and your hair skills are an added incentive. It won't make any difference to me if you say no, except that I like you and so do the other girls, and it's always better when we all get along well together. And as I've said, you remind me of me as I was, and I didn't have anyone to tell me about the reality."

"No. So why did you say yes?"

"If I tell you why, I don't want it to influence your decision."

"Why would it?"

"It might. So you must promise me you won't let it stop you making the right choice."

"All right, I promise," Sarah said, intrigued.

"When I came, Mother offered me a room and a few nights to decide what to do, the same as she did for you. She did the spit handshake with me, which means you've made a binding agreement with each other, like a promise."

"A promise?" Sarah said. "I didn't know it was a promise. I just thought it was some strange Liverpool custom."

Lily laughed.

No, lots of people do it."

"If I'd known it was a promise I wouldn't have shook hands," Sarah said, frowning. "I keep my promises. But if I didn't know it was one, then I don't have to keep it."

"No, I don't suppose you do, because a spit handshake isn't a legal thing," Lily agreed. "And really, for it to be binding you both have to spit on your own hand before you shake. It's like a blood oath, but without cutting yourselves. Anyway, she also asked me to sign a paper agreeing not to tell anyone about the men I saw coming in the house or what happened," Lily said.

"That's right. I signed that as well. I won't say anything about that if I leave. I wouldn't have done anyway."

"You can't read, can you?" Lily said.

"No, not really. My father thought...no. I just know some of the letters, that's all."

Lily nodded.

"The paper didn't say anything about men. What I signed was a note agreeing to pay £5 for the use of the room and the clothes. When I said I didn't think I could stay, Mother asked me how I was going to pay the money I owed her, because if I didn't she would have to inform the authorities. So I stayed, because otherwise I'd have gone to prison."

"What! But that's terrible! Is that what I've signed?" Sarah asked, her temper rising.

"It is. And I knew you'd react like that. I asked her to let me talk to you first, to give you the proper reasons to stay. Because I thought that if she told you that without you having all the information you needed, you'd leave anyway, on a principle. I'm right, ain't I?"

The mutton arrived then, and a jug of ale, which stopped the conversation for a few minutes. When the landlord had gone Sarah looked at the plate of food, which smelt and looked delicious, but her appetite had vanished.

"I don't want to talk about what brought me here," Sarah said. "But part of it was that I swore I'd never let anyone force me or those I loved to do anything we didn't want to do."

"Yes. But sometimes you have to do something you don't want to do for a time, because it's going to give you the best chance to do what you want later, or because it's the best of what's on offer. Especially if you're a woman, because we don't have as many choices as men do. Eat your food. It's really good."

Sarah ate her food, which was really good. And while they were eating Lily changed the subject, talking about the smugglers that usually used the room and some of the tricks they got up to to foil the excisemen.

"Of course the press gangs are the worst," Lily said indistinctly round a mouthful of chop. "Everybody helps the men avoid them."

"Is that what pressing is?" Sarah asked. "Mother mentioned it, but I didn't understand her."

"It is. Being a sailor's a hard life, but it's easier on the merchant ships than in the navy. You can be flogged for nothing in the navy, and can end up being killed or maimed in battle too. It's hard to get men to join. So they get press gangs to go round towns and villages, forcing men to go on the ships."

"Do they shake hands, make them sign notes, and then threaten them with jail if they don't?" Sarah asked, somewhat bitterly.

Lily smiled and swallowed.

"No," she said. "They buy them a beer and drop a shilling in the bottom of the glass, because if the poor bastard touches the shilling to take it out of the glass, then he's accepted the king's shilling and joined up. And that's legal. They have a lot of tricks like that. Or they just beat them and take them anyway. And the life they have on the ships is much worse than we have, I can tell you that. Mother *would* let you leave once you'd earned enough to pay your debt, because if you still didn't want to stay at that point, then she wouldn't force you. She's fair in that way, and she looks after us. Not all the bawds do.

"Press men ain't like that though. A lot of the Liverpool men have got experience on the merchant ships, so the press gangs are really active here and we all hate them. I hid a man in my dress chest once when the press gang came, and offered to swive the officer for free because he was so handsome."

"Was he?"

"No, he looked like a pig, and smelt worse. But I showed him my titties, then licked my finger and put it inside me and told him I was all hot and wet for him, and it made him forget what the hell he was looking for. Jem, that was the boy in the chest, gave me ten shillings for saving him, but I'd have done it for free. Bastards, the press men are."

Sarah laughed. After two weeks of living at Mother Augustus' house she wasn't shocked by Lily's talk, but every day she learnt new things, and realised how little she had known of real life in her fifteen sheltered years in Alliston — even less than a normal country girl would know. There was so much she had to learn if she was to live in a town successfully!

They finished their meal and prepared to head back to the house, Lily saying she had clients that night. But as Sarah went to the door, Lily tapped her on the shoulder and as she turned gave her a quick, fierce embrace.

"Don't let what I've told you about the note make you change your mind," she said. "It forced me to make my decision, but in truth I'm glad it did, because it stopped me ending like one of the women we've seen today. It ain't a perfect life, but it's a lot better than many others."

"I promised you I wouldn't," Sarah said, touched by Lily's obvious concern for her, "and I always keep my promises. The ones I know I've made."

Lily stepped back, and looked at her.

"She's going to talk to you tomorrow," she said. "So think about it tonight."

Sarah nodded.

"I will." She moved to open the door, then turned back. "But whatever I decide, I won't forget what you've done today. It's kind of you."

"Don't tell anyone that," Lily said. "Destroy my reputation, it will, if I get known for kindness."

Sarah laughed, and they made their way back to the house, hurrying, because while they'd been in the tavern it had come on to sleet.

Sarah didn't get much sleep that night, as she did indeed think about it, weighing up her options, which were basically what Lily had shown to her. Or she could return to her father. But she would never do that, no matter what life threw at her.

Or she could go back to the cottage and dig that grave next to Lucy's.

That option would always be open to her, though. But while she had some degree of hope, it was not an option she would take. It was comforting to know she had it though. If life became unbearable, she could opt out.

Suicide was a terrible sin, and a sure path straight to Hell, but so was being a whore. But she was going to Hell anyway. Her father had told her that her whole life.

So before that she would make the best life she could for herself. She could do no more than that. She lay, and thought, trying to be cold and calculating, putting her emotional experiences into one of those boxes she was getting so good at filling and pushing aside.

The next morning she woke up early, or early for the house, although the bustle she could hear in the streets outside told her that the rest of Liverpool would consider her a late riser. She washed, dressed, and styled her hair carefully, by which time the rest of the house's inhabitants were stirring.

She went downstairs, and didn't wait for Mother Augustus to ask to see her, because she knew that if she was presented with the note she had signed in good faith and told that she must make her decision based on that, she would no longer have any choice. She would have to say no.

Instead she went straight through the hell room, as she always thought of the burgundy reception room as being, straight-backed and dignified, looking neither right nor left, not pausing even to answer the other girls' morning greetings, completely intent on what she was about to do. She knocked on the door of the small office room, waited until she heard the response, then walked in, closing the door behind her quietly.

CHAPTER FOURTEEN

October 1740

Sarah stood down by the docks looking at the ships and shivering as the icy wind and rain froze her face and soaked her worn woollen dress. Everyone else, except those who had no choice was under shelter, in a tavern, coffee house or at home. She could have been sitting in front of the fire at home too, if home was what it could be called. But right now she would rather be here. Most of the time she would rather be here, if truth be told.

When she came down to look at the ships she always wore the clothes she'd arrived at Mother Augustus' house in, and was glad that she'd kept them. Of course Mother had wanted to burn them as soon as Sarah had agreed to stay, but Sarah had said no, she wanted to remember what she had come from. At the time she had hoped that one day she would look at the tatty blue dress and compare her horrendous former life with her wonderful current one.

But that day had not come yet, and as she stood here today with the wind whipping her hair, looking like a pauper and therefore attracting no unwanted attention, she doubted that day ever would come. She had been in Liverpool for nearly a year now, and had tried to embrace her new life, had done everything in her power to do that.

But she hated it.

In fairness, she didn't hate all of it. The girls she worked with were very nice and friendly, and although they bickered and argued about silly things, because of the nature of their work they supported each other and stuck together, so it was a little like living in a house with a lot of adult sisters. Or at least Sarah supposed it was, having never experienced such a thing. Certainly the sense of 'us against the world' that she got from them reminded her of the relationship she and Philip had had with regard to their father.

Until he'd betrayed her trust, that was.

She enjoyed her relationship with the other whores, but unlike the others, she never told them anything she didn't want the world to know, didn't reveal anything that they could use against her if they chose to. And because of that, although they were friendly enough towards her, there was a distance between them. She would have liked to open up to them, to really become an intimate part of their group, but she could not do it. She was too afraid.

But even so, the house was warm and cosy, there was plenty of food to eat, and good food at that, which she didn't have to spend hours preparing. And the clothes…ah, the clothes were wonderful. She thought now of how she had dreamed of one day wearing her mother's dress, of when she had in fact worn it, for Robert, and how it had made her feel like a princess.

But now she realised that it was in fact made of a lower quality silk than the ones she now wore, and that although decorated with pretty sparkly beading, the beads had been cheap and the stitching inexpertly done, and the fact that her mother had no doubt treasured it as her finest gown made Sarah's heart ache. For Sarah now wore dresses of heavy silk, gorgeously embroidered, the skirts of which swirled luxuriously around her legs. It was true that the colours were sometimes brighter than she would have chosen for herself, and that they had all belonged to someone else before her, but they were still lovely, and when she wore them she automatically carried herself more regally and felt attractive. Around her wrist, throat and at her ears jewels sparkled, and although they were paste they looked like real gems, and made her feel expensive and classy.

She loved dressing the hair of the other girls too. In fact when she was doing that she was truly confident, truly happy, because this was the one thing in the house that she could do well, better than anyone else there, and better than the hair dressers who Mother Augustus had previously employed. She had a natural eye for what would flatter the person whose hair she was styling, and she could see a hairstyle once and know how to copy it, how to improve on it. Soon she was making suggestions as to how to make the girls' makeup look more flattering too, and after a short while Mother Augustus had paid someone to show Sarah how to mix and apply the carmine rouge and white lead paints that they used. After that, though disdaining to use the cosmetics herself, thinking that in general they made women look hideous and were known to be unhealthy, Sarah spent two hours of each day applying the paints to the girls who did not mind risking their health to look fashionable.

All the prostitutes knew that life was not likely to be long, that even in a warm house with a comfortable bed and Barney to protect them from violent customers, no one could prevent them from contracting the French pox or from getting pregnant and possibly dying of the attempted abortion or childbirth. Many of the men refused to wear the sheepskin condoms that were available, which protected not only against the pox but pregnancy too, stating that it lessened the pleasure. And indeed they were expensive, and Mother Augustus had told the girls that they were welcome to ask the men to wear one, but they must purchase them themselves, and if the man refused to wear it that was no reason to turn him away.

Even if they survived all that, at some point they would age and their looks would fade, at which point, unless they were able to become a bawd like Mother Augustus, death would become a blessing rather than something to be avoided.

But for now the material comforts, camaraderie and hair styling aspects of life at the house were pleasant, and at first Sarah had thought that she would be able to perform her usual trick of focussing on the good when experiencing the bad, and of putting the bad in a box and pushing it away. Or failing that, of indulging in fantasies to get through bad times. After all, these methods had worked very well in her previous life.

But in the cellar at home she had not had a man pounding into her over and over until she was sore, kneading her breasts and sucking her nipples until they were raw, to distract her from her fantasies. She had also not had to pretend she enjoyed being in the cellar, or appear to relish her father's beatings. But she *did* have to pretend that the man who was swiving her at present was the

THE WHORE'S TALE: SARAH

most virile, attractive man she had ever been with, and that she was ecstatic at being asked to suck his hideous stinking cock, to swallow the result as though it was nectar, instead of spitting it out and washing her mouth out with wine as she yearned to do. She had to caress his wrinkled, hairy body as though it was the most exquisite thing she had ever seen. And then when he had finally finished his assault on her body, she had to sincerely express a desire for him to return as soon as possible, and tell him that she would be counting the minutes until she saw him again.

And that she could not do. Over the months she had achieved the transformation from lying like a lump of wood with her eyes closed, to, with a lot of help and advice from Lily and a threat from Mother that she could not be allowed to stay here if she did not pull her weight, managing to appear as though she was not repelled by her clients. But further than that she could not go.

She had watched the others in the red hellroom, had listened to how they flirted with the men and enticed them using all their feminine wiles, from the expert flourishing of fans to the downcast lashes, feigning modesty or outright seduction depending on what the occasion called for. She had learnt to copy them, to play the game by pretending she was in a theatrical play. But once they got upstairs she found it all but impossible to keep the pretence going.

Part of it was that, in spite of vowing to reject everything her father had ever taught her, she still *did* feel that selling your body for money was wrong, that it cheapened you and made a mockery of the sex act, which should be performed, if not as part of marriage, at least as part of an intimate, loving relationship. She had hoped that one day in the future she would be able to have another relationship, but this time a *real* one, based on mutual love and trust.

But her current life had destroyed all hope of that. She had watched them, men with wives and children at home, men of business, even a few men of religion (although she had refused flatly to entertain any of *them*, even when threatened by Mother Augustus), had observed how they looked at her, assessed her as though she was a piece of meat. She knew that they did not see her as a human being at all, just as a thing that would give them pleasure and then could be discarded. If she fell dying in the street in front of them, they would step over her and carry on without a moment's thought. She knew that they were deceiving their wives and sweethearts, and maybe carrying the pox home to them too, which meant they could not love them either, not really, whatever they said. Why would you lie and risk the life of someone you loved? You wouldn't. She wouldn't at any rate. And she wanted nothing to do with a man who would, which seemed to be most, if not all of them.

So she hated them. All of them. And because she hated them with a passion that outstripped everything except her desire to get out of there, to open a shop, and to never have anything to do with a man again, she could not pretend convincingly that she wanted them to fuck her. Because that's what it was, even though the girls were forbidden to use that word in the house.

When she'd agreed to stay, Mother Augustus had told her to choose a different name, which would help her to embrace her new life. She said that all the girls had flower names here, and Sarah had chosen the name Daisy Striby, which was a name she remembered from a gravestone in the churchyard at Alliston. She would forget Sarah completely, she had naively thought, and become Daisy.

She stood now, looking across at the ships, the tears on her face hidden by the rain, and thought that if there was a way she could really forget Sarah Browne and all her experiences, she would do anything, pay anything to do it.

Except for Lucy. She would never want to forget that precious week she had had with her daughter, which she now thought was likely to be the only happy memory she would ever have.

But the past could not be forgotten, so she had to learn to live with it. And she had, to a point. But this life was not for her. She could endure it for now, because Lily had been right; it was the best of the options open to her, and being a whore at Mother Augustus' was far better than being a whore anywhere else, except perhaps at one of the high-class brothels that catered for the aristocracy and the very rich. But even if she was whore to the king, he would still be a man who looked at her as though she was dirt, who pounded at her until he was satisfied then walked away without a thought.

THE WHORE'S TALE: SARAH

She did not earn as many tips as the other, more seemingly enthusiastic girls, but even so she had made some money, and kept it hidden. The *only* expense she indulged in was the purchase of condoms, which she asked every client to wear, although not all did. She did not want to die of the pox just when she had saved enough to escape this life and set up her business.

She would make wigs, or dress hair or both, would own her own little shop maybe, and no man would tell her what to do, ever. She would be free. And that and that alone kept her going. She could keep doing this for now. It was better than life with her father. Anything was better than that.

It was strange how standing by the sea, or by water, helped her to think, to clear her mind so that she could carry on. It had been the same when she had sat by the river in Alliston. There was something about the sound of moving water, of looking at something that was always travelling on, that reminded her she was travelling through life, and that it would not be like this forever. Tomorrow something might happen that would make her life better; all she had to do was get through today, through however many todays there were until that something happened.

She pulled out a handkerchief and wiped her face, then turning her back on the stark, bare-masted ships, the grey sea and the looming dark grey sky, she started to make her way back along the rain-drenched streets to the place she called home.

* * *

On Monday evenings she did not have to entertain men, because she spent the whole day washing and styling the other girls' hair. So that night while the others were with clients, she would sit alone in her room and style her own hair. For the rest of the week their styles would stay in place, but every day Sarah would tidy them up, more or less depending on how boisterous their sexual encounters had been.

She loved Mondays. On this particular one she was sitting in her room wearing her nightdress, her hair freshly washed and hanging down her back, very slowly and painstakingly reading *Don Quixote*. She couldn't make much sense of it, mainly because she was reading too slowly and concentrating too hard on working out individual words to be able to keep the whole convoluted story in mind. But she was determined that she would never sign a paper again unless she could read what was written on it for herself, and so this was a profitable way to spend her precious free evening.

"So then," she read aloud, "his armour be-ing furbi… furbi…" She paused, thought for a minute about the letters Philip had said made different sounds when placed together; s and h together said shh, as though you were hushing someone. "Furbished," she continued, "his morion turned into a helmet."

A knock on the door broke her concentration, and she looked up from the book as the door opened and Mother Augustus came in.

"I have a favour to ask you, Daisy," she said.

"I won't see a gentleman tonight, Mother," Sarah said immediately. "We've spoken about this before, and we have an agreement." She had fought hard to get this concession and treasured it, and had refused to budge on this.

"Yes, yes, I know that, and you know I have not pestered you about it for some time. I know how resolute you are," Mother said. "But hear me out, because this gentleman is different, and if you do not want to see him, then I will turn him away."

"I do not—" Sarah began, but Mother Augustus held up a hand.

"This man said he does not wish to engage in actual copulation with you, which is why I thought you might want to hear what he does want. I thought you might find it easier to pretend enjoyment with him. He'll pay well for your discretion, and the other girls are all occupied. Yours are the nicest anyway, so I thought I'd ask you."

"My what are the nicest?" Sarah asked.

He sat for a few minutes just gazing raptly at her feet, which were indeed the nicest of all the whores in the house, as she had not worn pinching, disabling shoes for years, so had no corns or bunions. She resisted the urge to continue reading *Don Quixote* while he was looking.

"If you wish, you may stroke them," she said finally.

"You are very kind, madam," he replied, and very gently ran his index finger down the front of her foot before inhaling deeply with pleasure. "May I…I would very much like to suck your toes," he said timorously.

You can do what you want with my feet, you fool, she thought. He'd paid enough for it. She reminded herself that one day she would have to tell ugly women that they looked beautiful in her shop, so the practice at falseness would be useful. She abandoned all thought of what 'morion' might mean and focussed on the task at hand.

"You may suck one toe, to start," she said imperiously. Mother had told her he wished her to be firm and commanding. "And then, if you please me, I may allow you to proceed to the others."

While he ecstatically suckled her toes, holding her heel gently in his hand, she observed him. His wig was of the finest quality, as were his clothes. He was a man of some importance in the town, probably. Maybe a sugar merchant or even a ship owner. Whatever he was, if his acquaintances knew that he was paying good money to suck a whore's toes, he would never live it down.

After he had sucked her toes he took off his coat and shirt, and got her to stroke his chest and back with her feet. She circled his nipples with her big toe and periodically insisted that he clean her feet again with his tongue.

He could not be paying much for this, surely? Mother Augustus never told the girls what the clients paid her, but they all knew it was about a sovereign for a good long fuck, more if they wanted to go in the back way, as it were, or for perversions. Lily had told her that a man had once paid ten guineas for a whole night of flagellation, which she specialised in. Ten guineas to be beaten to a pulp. *Father would enjoy working here*, she thought, and almost laughed.

Concentrate, she warned herself.

"You are being very good," she said. "I am pleased with you, and how obedient you are." She was just about to offer him a foot job, thinking that if he was paying well she would at least try to bring him off with her feet, as awkward as that might be, when he suddenly groaned and spasmed, and so instead she wet a cloth and wiped him down using her toes instead, which was considerably easier.

He rewarded her with a crown as a tip. From then on, as Monday was the only night he could come to the house, she took

Tuesday evenings off instead. The following day she spent practising giving a piece of wood a foot job in the privacy of her room, because he was worth keeping as a client. Any client who did not want to swive her or beat her was worth keeping, in her view. And although the other girls asked her what was so amazing about the small, dapper middle-aged man who had made her give up her Monday nights off, she would not tell them. She kept her word. She always kept her word, once given.

* * *

"You were right," Mother Augustus said to Lily a few days later.

Lily, who was sitting at her dressing table in her peach-coloured bedroom combing out her elaborate hairstyle preparatory to Sarah washing it, stopped for a moment and gave her employer a knowing look in the mirror.

"Of course I was. I'm always right," she answered.

Mother snorted, but sat down on the bed.

"I didn't want you to turn her away, either, which is what you were thinking of doing, weren't you?" Lily continued.

"I can't support someone who doesn't pull her weight, you know that. A lot of the girls are like that at first, a bit disgusted and not able to pretend otherwise, but they always come round in time, realise that this life is one of the better choices they have. But she wasn't adapting, and some of the men have told me they don't want the cold fish," Mother said. "Are you soft on her, then?"

Lily put the comb down on the mahogany dresser and turned on her stool.

"No. You know my rules. No relationships with my fellow workers. But I like Daisy, we all do. And we all love the way she looks after our hair. When she washes it she massages our scalps, and it feels wonderful. I asked her where she learnt to do that, and she said she hadn't, but just thought it might be nice. I certainly don't want to lose that. It's very relaxing. I had a headache last week, and it disappeared when she did that."

"Mr Grant was very pleased with her. He's coming back tonight. And she's told nobody what he wanted, not even the other girls. Did you ask her? She's closer to you, so I thought she might tell you."

"I did, told her I wouldn't say anything if she told me what his weird fancy was. She said that you asked her to keep it secret and she'd promised she would. I did pester her a bit, as you asked me to, and she told me I should be pleased she wouldn't tell me, because then I knew that if *I* told her anything in confidence she'd keep it as close. Promises are sacred to her. You need to remember that too, in your dealings with her, if you want to keep her. Don't break a promise you make."

Mother Augustus nodded.

"I have a few other clients I can put her way now I know she's discreet, enough to keep her busy, and profitable."

"Good. As I said, I don't mind teaching her the way with the birch, because she'd be good at it, I think. She doesn't like men. She's not like I am though. She's just had bad experiences with them."

"Yes, but you were right. There isn't enough birch work for two of you at the moment. But it's a relief she can satisfy the others – they pay well, too. I've always worried that the other girls will chat about them, especially the more interesting ones, and that's how word gets out, which would be disastrous, not just for the men but for my reputation. So I'm very happy. Thank you." The older woman placed a few coins on Lily's dressing table. "Has she talked to you about her experiences with men?" she added casually.

Lily turned back to the mirror and picked up her comb.

"I have the same attitude to secrets as Daisy does, Mother. You know that," she said.

Mother laughed, then leaned forward and squeezed Lily's shoulder before leaving the room.

* * *

Sarah's life now got a lot better, if a lot weirder. Within a few weeks she had settled in with her new clients. Most of them were becoming regulars now, which made things easier in one way. And that one way was that once they realised she didn't find them ridiculous in what they wanted, many of them would spend at least half their time with her just talking to her, telling her their sexual problems.

And although Sarah's past had never taught her how to

pleasure men with her feet, or her hair (which one client had raptures about, because it was very thick and long), nor had she learnt how to aim carefully to urinate on one particular part of a man, her past *had* taught her to be a good, and apparently attentive listener.

It was also much easier to pretend to be aroused or fascinated by these men, to be domineering or submissive depending on what the occasion required, because it was possible to an extent to distance herself, or to fantasise, when the man wasn't actually lying on top of her or behind her pumping in and out of her.

She could not get pregnant or contract the pox from a client who sucked her feet, from one who went into ecstasies when she brushed his hair or when she wrapped her hair round his penis to give him a hand job, or from someone who wanted her to urinate in his mouth.

Her favourite client was a Mr Wakes, who came to her room each week to dress in women's clothes; she spent her whole time with him styling his wig and making up his face, teaching him how to walk like a woman, to gesture and use a fan in a feminine way. Next week they were going to go for a short walk up and down the street, about which he was extraordinarily excited. She stored his gowns in her clothes chest, and while she made his face up he chatted happily to her about his life and how he had always wanted to dress as a woman, but had expected the whores to laugh at him, until he met her. She was so kind, he said. She made him feel as though he was not sick and evil at all.

That was easy for her to do. As far as she was concerned, if someone got pleasure from something and they weren't hurting anyone to get it, then there was nothing sick and evil about it that she could see. It was quite an interesting challenge to help a man look like a woman, and was certainly not damaging to her, unlike all the other supposedly acceptable things the men in her past had done to her.

It was acceptable to beat and starve your pregnant daughter, then shame her in front of the village. It was acceptable to seduce a fourteen-year-old girl if you were an older married man, then abandon her when she was having your child.

To her, wearing women's clothes and going out in the street in them was completely acceptable. After all, what harm was it doing? Of course her father would have a different view, but her father was a vicious bastard, a liar and a brute masquerading as a man of God; she knew that now. To hell with honouring your mother and father, even if it was a commandment. It might not even *be* a commandment, for all she knew. Her father had probably made it up. One day she would be able to read the Bible, and would find out for herself.

She had asked Mother Augustus who the Bible on the hall table belonged to, because she wanted to borrow it and try to read it. Mother had told her that it belonged to her, but that she never read it. It needed to stay on the table though, because if any of the authorities came round, it would give them a favourable impression of her home for the rehabilitation of wanton girls. Then she had winked at Sarah and asked her why she wanted to know. So now she had access to Mother's small book selection, although she thought it would probably take her the rest of her life just to read Don Quixote. She was so slow.

The man who loved her hair had told her yesterday that Don Quixote was a fine book and asked her if she was enjoying it. She had admitted that she was learning to read, and that it was a little difficult for her to understand. He had not told her that women should not learn to read, nor that she was stupid because she couldn't understand Don Quixote. Instead he had promised to find a book that was a little easier for her, one that she might enjoy more.

That was another thing about her new clients – some of them were quite kind to her, which was very nice, although she never let her guard down with them. She had done that with Robert, and had sworn never to let a man get under her defences again. The new clients also tipped well. Every tip was a step closer to opening her hair and cosmetic shop, which was what she lived for.

So, as winter turned to spring and then to summer, Sarah started to finally accept her new life, and to realise that it really *was* the best thing she could do with her time for now.

Unlike the other girls she was not terrified of growing older, of getting wrinkles or grey hair. She had no wish to get them, but she was not afraid that if she did she would starve to death on the streets, sodden with gin and swiving men for pennies against a mildewed alley wall.

That would not be her future. Her future would be having her own business in Liverpool, with a cosy room or two to live in. Then she would never let anyone tell her what she could and could not do again. She would never fall in love, and so she would be free.

That was worth fighting for, and it was no longer just a dream. Every coin she added to her little bag hidden under the floorboard in her room brought her a step closer to making it a reality. It would take time to save enough money, but all she had to do now was keep pleasing her clients, accept the few that she had to take who wanted to swive her in traditional ways and try to seem aroused by them, and be patient.

And patience was one skill she had a *lot* of experience of. She was an expert at that.

* * *

June 1741

"So I don't know what to do now, but I have to decide really quick. I've tried everything, but it's clinging on," Violet said low-voiced, her expression worried.

"What have you tried?" Sarah asked.

"So far? Gin, pennyroyal, and savin, which gave me the flux but didn't budge it. Iris told me to sit over a pot of boiling onions."

"What? Really?"

"I know. She said it's supposed to work, but when I asked her who she knew that it'd worked on she said she just *heard* it would. I might try it though."

"You don't want to keep it?" Sarah suggested tentatively. They were walking down Lime Street, but had stopped outside a tavern. "Do you want a drink?" she asked.

"No, too many listeners in an inn. And you don't drink gin," Violet said.

"No, but I thought you might want to try again."

"No. I used to think you were stupid for not drinking, but when you told me to look at the street whores closely, I did, and you're right. I don't want to get like them, and it's easy, because it's really good to escape from it all for a while, and gin does that, but it makes you feel terrible the next day, and then you want more to stop the feeling. So no. I've tried it anyway. For four days I didn't know where I was, just drinking and being sick, passing out, then drinking again, but the little bastard's still there. No, I don't want to keep it. And even if I did, I can't."

"Would she really throw you out? You're one of her most popular girls," Sarah asked.

"No, she wouldn't throw me out, she's not cruel like most of the other bawds. But I'd have to pay her to stay there when I got too big to work, and then afterwards what would I do with the baby? I can't keep it. I need to go and see a midwife that can get rid of it for me, but they cost, more than I have."

They walked along silently together for a while, trying to think of a solution. Sarah was struggling with the conversation, because it reminded her of Lucy, and even though she'd lost her home, her brother, her reputation and finally Lucy herself, she wouldn't change a day of that time, because for one week she had truly known what love was.

She couldn't say that to Violet though. Violet's situation was not like hers anyway, and Violet's personality was different. She was determined to get rid of this unwanted baby as quickly as possible. And it wasn't a sin to get rid of a baby until it quickened, because that was when the soul entered the child and it became a person.

"Have you felt the baby m—" Sarah stopped mid-word, staring up the street wide-eyed. Violet followed her gaze, but could see nothing out of the ordinary. They were in the nicer part of town now, and there were just a few well-to-do couples taking the air as it was a lovely sunny day.

Violet looked at Sarah who had turned suddenly to face her, blocking the way down the street.

"What's wrong, Daisy?" Violet asked. "You look terrible!"

Sarah did indeed look terrible. All the colour had drained from her face, and she was breathing heavily all of a sudden. She cast a hunted look around her, but there was nowhere to hide. She closed her eyes, took three deep breaths and fought for control.

"I'm well," she managed after that. "I just had a bit of a shock. It's nothing. Let's go back."

"But if we carry on to the end we can walk back down the

Manchester road to the docks. You said you wanted to do that," Violet asked.

"I've changed my mind," Sarah said desperately.

"You aren't well, are you? Come on then." Violet linked her arm through Sarah's, and they turned around, began walking back the way they had come. "What were you asking? Have I felt what?" Violet prompted, but Sarah didn't even hear her, was hardly aware she even had a companion any more. Her mind was in turmoil, and she was cursing herself for her stupidity, for not thinking in advance that this might happen and preparing for it. But here she was, and the desire to act was so strong, so compelling, that after a few moments of wrangling with herself she gave into it and stopped, disentangling her arm from Violet's.

"Wait there for me," she said and then walked off immediately, leaving Violet standing confused.

"I thought you didn't want to carry—" Violet began, but Sarah was already gone, striding down the road to catch up with the wealthy couple ahead of her.

She waited until she was just a few feet from them and then stopped, her heart hammering painfully against her ribs.

"Robert!" she called, and in doing so committed herself.

The man turned instinctively on hearing his name called and then stopped dead when he saw who had called him, his face blanching as white as Sarah's had done a few moments before.

"Sarah!" he said. "What—" Then he stopped and looked at her, took in the gaudy low-cut dress which proclaimed what she was. The woman with him, still holding his arm, looked from her husband to Sarah with a confused expression.

"I've got a message for you, from Mother," Sarah called to him, loud enough to cause several other couples to turn and look her way. "She says you can't do what you did to poor Eliza and then not pay for your sick pleasure. You'd better go back and make it right, and that soon. That's all. Begging your pardon, madam," she finished, curtseying prettily to Mrs Grimes. She glanced quickly at him standing frozen, staring at her open-mouthed, and shot him a look of such pure hatred that he actually flinched as though she'd hit him.

Then she turned and strode away without looking back, grabbing Violet's arm as she passed and dragging her with her down the street. They progressed at lightning speed until they turned the corner and were hidden from view, but when Sarah showed no signs of slowing, Violet pulled at her arm until she lessened the pace.

"What the hell was that about?" she asked.

"Nothing," Sarah said. "I don't want to talk about it. Forget it ever happened."

"He was grey," Violet said. "I could see that even from where I was. And who's Eliza?"

Sarah closed her eyes for a moment, forced the lump in her throat and the tears back and then stopped and turned to face her companion.

"How much do they cost?" she asked.

"How much do what cost?" Violet replied.

"The women, the woman, the one who can get rid of your baby?"

"I don't know exactly, but I can find out. I don't think Mother will pay though, you know what she's like about condoms, and—"

"I'll pay for it, if I can," Sarah said desperately. "If you promise on your life not to ask me about what I just did and not to tell anyone else. Can you do that for me?"

Violet thought for a moment.

"Yes," she said. "If it's that important to you, I can do that for you."

Sarah looked at her intently. Violet's brown eyes looked sincere, her expression serious. She had no idea if she could trust her though, and wished that she hadn't given in to her impulse, or that she'd had Lily, stalwart trustworthy Lily with her, who would have understood, even approved of her act of revenge.

"It is," she said.

It was Tuesday, her new evening off, but Gulliver's Travels, the book provided to her by her client and which she was enjoying more than she had Don Quixote, although she was still struggling with it, stayed unread. Sarah sat on the edge of her bed, staring into space and thinking, regretting.

She should not have done that. It was shock, hatred and bitterness that had caused her to accost her ex-lover and his wife, and although the immediate sense of triumph at the expression on his face when she'd told him, his wife and several of his acquaintances that he did something with prostitutes that even they considered sick and sneaked off without paying had been glorious, now she was ashamed of herself.

She was not sorry that she had hurt him, not in the slightest. She could never hurt him as badly as he had hurt her. And when she had seen him walking along in his exquisitely tailored clothes with the woman who was certainly his wife on his arm, dressed equally expensively, the rage had exploded in her, driving out everything except the need to attack, to wound him.

She had certainly wounded him; she had seen that in his face. But she had wounded his wife far more. And his wife was as innocent as she herself was – more innocent in a way, because she was married to Robert, and had not let him seduce her out of wedlock as Sarah had. She might have irrevocably damaged their marriage, which at that moment she had wanted to do. But he had children, and they too would be hurt if their parents argued and grew apart.

"Oh God, I'm sorry," Sarah said to Mrs Grimes, her arms wrapped round herself, rocking backwards and forwards on the bed in a futile effort to console herself.

She sat, and alternated between rocking herself, crying and thinking, but by the end of the evening she had come up with no way to repair this. She could hardly go to wherever he lived, even if she found that out, and tell his wife that she'd lied, that he'd actually had a full-blown relationship with her for months before abandoning her. That was even worse than committing a one-time perverted act with a whore.

She was glad that she'd hurt him, would have happily stabbed him through the heart if she could have done. She should not have hurt his wife. But she could do nothing about that, nothing at all.

The visit to the 'midwife' who could abort Violet's child for her cost nearly half the money that Sarah had saved towards starting her business, but she paid it without flinching, treating it as a sort of penance. She was uncomfortable about paying for someone to get rid of a baby; but Violet had assured her that she had not felt the baby move yet, and if it had not quickened then it had no soul, and so was not murder. And Violet was right – she could not keep the child and stay at Mother Augustus' house, and every other option available would be far worse for both the child and its mother than getting rid of it now.

Sarah worried constantly for a while; worried that Violet would die due to the abortion, worried that she would not be able to resist telling the others about Sarah's strange encounter with the wealthy man, and then worried that Robert would somehow find out where she lived.

But Violet's abortion was successful, and after a week of cramps and bleeding she recovered; she did not break her promise or at least no one mentioned or hinted anything to Sarah, and so after a few weeks she started to relax a little, although she avoided going out of the house as much as possible for a while, and when she had to wore the dullest clothes possible and a cloak with a hood, even though it was summer.

And then, as summer turned to autumn, she put the whole episode to the back of her mind, and focussed once more on building up her business savings.

CHAPTER FIFTEEN

Alliston, July 1741

At first when the knock sounded on his front door Reverend Browne ignored it, thinking that whoever it was, it was sure to be someone he had no wish to engage in conversation with, added to which he was in full flow writing his sermon for Sunday and did not want his train of thought to be disturbed. It was no doubt one of his annoying parishioners with some pathetic problem.

The knock came again, and in frustration the reverend threw his quill down on the table, splattering ink across both it and part of his sermon.

"Damnation!" he cried. The sermon was not going well. Nothing was going well. The knock came a third time, and he jumped to his feet. He would go out and ram the knocker down the visitor's throat!

Halfway to the door however, he rethought. It could well be one of the parish ladies who had taken him under their wings arriving with an excellent cooked meal for him. The actual ladies were tedious and irritating, with their trivial gossip and ridiculous problems, but the meals were usually tasty and always welcome. He slowed down his aggressive stride, smoothed out his frown and opened the door, a smile already forming on his face.

The smile froze. In fact his whole body froze, the blood drained from his face and for one terrible moment he thought he was going to faint. With a supreme effort of will he mastered the threatened swoon and then looked at the woman standing on his step with mingled shock and disgust.

She was of average height, and although no longer in the first flush of youth, was still extremely pretty, with immaculately coiffured blonde hair, blue eyes, and a wide sensuous mouth. She was dressed expensively in a dark green silk gown, heavily embroidered, and emeralds sparkled at her throat and neck. She looked at him coldly, only her eyes betraying her fear.

Reverend Browne's mouth twisted into a rictus.

"What the hell are you doing here?" he said by way of greeting. "You are not welcome."

"Good afternoon to you too, Perseverance," she said, her voice icy, although her breathing was rapid and shallow. "I have no wish to be made welcome by you."

"You have a damn sauce coming here," he growled, "after what you did, you harlot! If you think for even one moment I will have you back, you are in error."

To his surprise she laughed, and her laugh was as silvery as he remembered it.

"In leaving you I made only one error, even though I had no choice at the time," she replied. "I have come to see my children, and that is all. Please tell them I am here."

"You think they would want to see the bitch who abandoned them when they were still babies?" he replied. "They forgot you. They told me they have no wish to see you again. They hate you, as do I for your unnatural heartlessness, abandoning them to pursue a life of wickedness. I hope you are satisfied with your worldly baubles, you Jezebel," he added, waving a hand at her outfit, then at the coach which stood by the gate, a liveried coachman sitting at the front observing the exchange intently.

"I had no choice, as well you know," the woman retorted. "It was stay with you and die, leaving the children to you alone, or leave and find a way to rescue them from your heartlessness. It has taken me a long time, longer than I hoped, but I am here now, and I will see them."

"They will not see you."

"I will hear that from their own lips, not from yours," she said. "You never spoke an honest word in your life, and I'm sure you have not changed in that."

"I am busy, madam," he stated. "You will be about your business. Not that you will find any customers in this clean-living place. Off with you."

He stepped back, clearly intending to close the door in her face, but to his surprise she stepped forward, pushing him with desperate force backwards so that he staggered and the door flew open.

"Damn you, Perseverance," she said. "You will let me see my children or I swear to the God you believe in that you will regret it. I will stay here, and tomorrow I will go to that other church, the one I expect you have driven most of the villagers to, and I will stand up and denounce you."

"You will denounce me?" he cried. "You, clearly a whore, an unnatural mother who abandoned your own children? Why would *anyone* believe a word you said?"

"They will believe me, because I tell the truth. And because although you drove Alice Thomson *and* Jane Miller from this village, and no doubt think yourself safe after all these years, I know where they live, and I have the friends and the influence to protect them now. If I need to I will bring them here and they will tell of what you attempted to do to them. And they will be believed because they speak true, and because they can describe parts of you that no one except myself as your wife should know."

"You are lying," he gasped, his face white as snow. "You evil bitch!"

"All the evil I learnt in this life I learnt from you," she replied. "And your face tells me you know I'm not lying. And I am no longer the young innocent girl you had your abominable perverted way with. That girl is dead."

"Then you have one thing at least in common with your children, dear wife," Perseverance spat. "You have come too late. They are not here. You cannot speak to them."

"Where are they?"

"In Hell I would think, in spite of my attempts to save them from Satan's ways. They are dead. Perhaps if you had come sooner, instead of selling yourself for the money to buy clothes and transport to try to impress me, they might have been able to tell you themselves that they hated you."

He put his hand on her stomach, pushing her out onto the step so forcefully that she would have fallen if she had not gripped the doorpost. The coachman, still watching, jumped down from his position, clearly intending to come to her aid, but the woman raised her arm and he halted, his hand on the gate, waiting to assist her back into the coach.

* * *

Reverend Baxter walked down the aisle of his church, checking to make sure that everything was in place for the service tomorrow. He and Angela had spent a pleasant few hours in the woodland collecting greenery to enhance the roses from the garden they had placed in the church to make it cheerful and welcoming. Every window had a candle in it which would be lit in the morning. The roses were already scenting the church, as was the meadowsweet which Angela had arranged with the roses.

He approached the altar, on which a huge bouquet of flowers and dark green foliage was artfully arranged. Angela really had a touch for such things, and it was lovely to see her smiling face as she walked straight again. Not quite able to ring the bell yet, but hopefully it would not be long now.

"Well, it was Nancy who told me, and I couldn't believe it! I thought she was dead! Everyone did! But there she is, large as life and on his doorstep, arguing with him like a harridan!" Ann Knowles, one of the cleaners informed her companion, who was so shocked by this news that she abandoned her scrubbing of the church floor and sat back on her heels.

"Are you sure?" she asked incredulously. "It must be someone else!"

"No. It's her, and in a carriage no less, dressed like the queen too! That's what I was told."

"I can't believe it. If it is her, where's she been all these years?"

"No idea. But not where he said she was, and that's the truth!"

"Who is this, and where is she supposed to be?" Mr Baxter asked, curious in spite of his former avowal not to get entangled in village gossip.

Nancy put her hand on her heart in shock.

"Oh, Reverend," she cried, "you move like a cat, I swear you do! I never knew you were here. We're nearly done, won't be more than five minutes now."

"Thank you. So who's in a carriage like the queen?" he asked.

"It's Mrs Browne, or might be," Nancy replied, looking at her companion in open disbelief.

"It *is!*" Ann affirmed indignantly. "The other reverend's wife, come back from the dead, it is, large as life, arguing on the step with him! Said she wanted to see her children."

"You won't know her, sir," Nancy said. "She's the—"

Reverend Baxter had not stopped to hear any more, but was running back down the aisle towards the church entrance.

"Well, he's a strange one, and no mistake," Ann said. "Where's he going?"

He ran without thinking things through, out of the church, down the path, out of the gate, and was halfway along the main road when he saw the carriage coming along it at a brisk trot. When it showed no sign of stopping at his frantic arm-waving, he ran out into the road, causing the coachman to rein in the horses so frantically that they shied.

"You fool!" the driver shouted. "I could have killed you!"

Baxter paid no heed to him at all, instead going to the side of the coach and pulling the door open. Sitting inside was a woman, who, though not dressed as richly as the queen would be, was certainly beautifully attired. If the gossips had not told him who she was, he would still have known. Even with her eyes swollen, her skin blotchy from crying, and her expression of shock at his intrusion, the resemblance to her daughter identified her as Sarah's mother.

Colin Baxter held on to the coach door for a moment while he got his breath under control, and then he removed his hat and bowed.

"I'm sorry," he said. "I don't wish to alarm you, but I very much want to ask you a question."

She did not reply but neither did she tell him to go away, so he took that as acquiescence to his request.

"Do you know where Sarah is? Is she well?" he asked. "I would very much like to know."

She stared at him for a moment.

"You are the other minister?" she asked, looking at his clothing.

"Yes."

"Has Perseverance asked you to do this? To make my sorrow even more unbearable?" she said, her voice hoarse with weeping.

"What? No," Colin replied. "No, it is a genuine question. I cared for Sarah. She was a very sweet child, and since she left in such a way, I have worried about her. I would know she is well."

"Then if you speak true, I am sorry to give you the bad news that she is...dead. Both of them are. Now please, let me leave."

He almost did. He actually stepped away, preparing to close the door, when a thought struck him.

"Both of them? The baby died as well?" he asked.

Mrs Browne stared at him, uncomprehending.

"Baby? What are you talking about? Philip was not a baby He was nearly seven when I left!"

No. It was not possible. No one could be that cruel, not even Perseverance Browne.

Yes. He could. He had shown how cruel he could be, and was suffering for it. But not enough. No one could suffer enough for what he'd done.

Colin stepped forward again.

"Mrs Browne, I did your daughter a great wrong, and would make amends for that, if I can. I don't know what your husband has just told you, but...will you give me a few minutes of your time? You will not regret it, I promise you."

She assessed him for a moment then nodded, and he climbed into the coach.

The four people sat in the cosy little cottage which had formerly belonged to Mrs Grimes, but which was now rented by Philip Browne and his wife Mary, who were two of the people sitting in the room, the other two being Philip's mother and the Anglican minister.

Their meeting had been somewhat eccentric, Mary having answered the knock on the door to see a rather deranged-looking aristocrat standing on the step in the company of the Anglican minister. The woman had looked past Mary and then had suddenly and rudely shoved her aside and had run headlong into the arms of her husband Philip, who had returned the fierce embrace, after which they had both burst into tears.

Mary had observed this with a look of complete bewilderment, until the minister had gently taken her arm, causing her to turn to him.

"She is his mother," he said, thereby making perfect sense of the emotional meltdown currently taking place in her house.

Sensibly, Mary had left them to it, leading Colin Baxter out of the house and round the back, so they could enter the kitchen without walking past Philip and Catherine and disturbing the reunion. By the time refreshments were ready to be taken into the sitting room, Mary knew as much as Colin did, and mother and son had calmed themselves enough to be able to sit down.

"He told you what?!" Philip was saying to his mother as the other two returned to the sitting room.

"He told me you were both dead," Catherine Browne said.

"He missed out 'to him', then," Mary commented, setting a tray of scones on the table.

Catherine looked at her, seeing her for the first time.

"God, I'm sorry," Philip said. "Let me introduce you. Mary, this is my mother, Mama, this is my wife, Mary. And this is…er…I'm sure you're welcome, sir, but…"

"Mr Baxter stopped the coach as I was leaving the village," Catherine explained. "He told me that your father lied about you being dead. He brought me here."

Philip smiled.

"Then you are most welcome in my house, Reverend Baxter," he said. "Thank you."

"I wanted to know if she knew how Sarah was," Colin explained. "I have worried about her since she left."

"We all have," Philip agreed.

"He has told me what happened, and what Perseverance did," Catherine said. "I will destroy him for this."

"I think he is managing that quite well himself," Colin commented.

"Mama, I am so very sorry," Philip cried suddenly, tears springing to his eyes again. "I will never forgive myself."

"For what?" his mother said. "You didn't beat her and shame her, did you?"

"No," Philip said. "But I should have stopped him. I told her that when I was as big as Father I would protect her from him, but I did nothing. I did worse than nothing. I betrayed her trust. I'll never forgive myself for that."

"I've told him that there's nothing to forgive," Mary said.

"He's kind and gentle. How could he fight that vicious bastard? Oh, sorry, Father!" she added, blushing.

"I'm not a Catholic priest, Mary," Colin said, smiling. "No need to call me Father. Or apologise. You're right. I think your mother-in-law will concur."

"I will," Catherine agreed. "And Philip, you have done nothing that needs forgiveness. It is I who needs that, from you and Sarah, because I left you to him for all those years. God forgive me for that, because I can't forgive myself."

"He told us you were dead, too," Philip said. "Why did you leave us? Or rather, why did you not come back when you could?"

"This is the first time I could," Catherine said. "I had to leave. I couldn't bear what he was doing to me, or have more children for him to treat as he treated us. He would not leave me alone. I lost two babies between you and Sarah due to his violence, and another one after her. It was terrible. He wouldn't let me leave the house, he beat me all the time, and every night…well, that's not for a son to hear. He would have killed me. I couldn't protect you both from him, and I was so very young. I thought that if I ran away, then at least I would live, and have a chance to get you away from him later. I couldn't take you with me because I had nothing, nowhere to go. I left in my nightdress in the middle of the night!"

"Could you not have left with us when he was on one of his trips to Chester?" Philip asked.

"Chester?" Catherine replied. "He never went to Chester when I was with him. He never left me alone, not for a minute. I was so stupid. I thought I could get work, and then when I had a little place to live, just a room, I could come back and get you.

"But then I found out that the law would never let me have you, because in the eyes of the law, the children, like the wife, belong to the man not the woman. And…and the job I had, the only one I could have, would not allow children. I knew that if I came here and tried to take you he wouldn't let me, and would probably make you suffer for my attempt. So I decided I needed to get rich, rich enough to be able to fight him, or intimidate him."

"And now you are rich enough to fight him?" Philip asked.

Catherine smiled bitterly.

"I am no more rich now than I was the night I left," she said. "But I have a…sponsor, let me say, a very recent sponsor, who clothes me, and who indulges me. He allowed me to use his carriage to come here today, although I did not tell him where I was going, or why. I thought to intimidate Perseverance with my apparent position, and at least beg your forgiveness and see if I could help you, take you away from here and help you to start again, away from him somehow."

"I don't need you to take me away from him," Philip said. "And I give you my forgiveness, completely. How can I not? I am a man, was a man when I let him beat my sister while she was with child. It is I who needs forgiveness, not you."

She opened her mouth to deny that, but he held his hand up in unconscious imitation of his father, and she quietened.

"You should have seen her, Mama," he continued, the tears spilling over his lashes and running down his cheeks unheeded. "She stood there in front of the church, beaten, starved, and anyone looking at her would have said he had broken her, as he had me. I don't know what it was that changed her, but she suddenly straightened up – he'd kicked her, so she was hunched over – and she got this fire in her eyes, like I'd never seen before in her, not ever. And she looked at me…she looked at me as though I was dirt, which I was, and then she walked straight out of the church, like she was the king and we were all of us filth, and she left. It was amazing. And I'll never forget it, and I'll never forgive myself for not standing by her side, for not walking out with her."

"But you left," Colin Baxter said.

"Yes. I sneaked away like a cur when he was away, when I should have walked out like a king, like she did," Philip said.

"But you did it," Mary pointed out. "And you married me. I'm a Catholic," she said to Catherine. "He doesn't like that," she added of her father-in-law with colossal understatement. "And he wanted to stay here, so that that bastard can see him every day and know that his son left and is not afraid of him any more. I think that's admirable," she finished, seizing his hand and squeezing it.

"She's right, I think," Colin said. "You don't make his life easy. I know that, because my parishioners talk about it. And so do his, for more and more of them come to my church every week. And for what it's worth, this minister forgives you."

"And so does your mother," Catherine said. "I'm proud of Sarah for what she did, but what you're doing is brave too. Perseverance is not a man to defy easily. He is a terrible man. I must find Sarah. Have you heard anything of her, anything at all?"

"No," Philip said. "I thought she might have gone to Uncle Arthur, because he was kind to her. So I went to Chester myself a few days after she left and spoke to that old witch of an aunt. She told me he was dead, so I knew then that Sarah would not be there. Then I came back, and I left the next day, came to live with Mary and her family until we could get married. This house belonged to Mrs Grimes."

"I remember her," Catherine said. "She was old when I was a young girl! Or she seemed old."

"It was her son who got Sarah with child," Philip said.

"Robert? But he's as old as me!" she cried. "We used to play together as children!"

"He came to see his mother, and Sarah used to go and visit some of the poor women, and Mrs Grimes was one of them. I had to go with her so she wouldn't do some terrible evil, but we had an arrangement, and I used to come and see Mary while Sarah was with Mrs Grimes. I knew nothing at all about it until he left her and then took his mother away. Then she told me, but she was already a long way on with the baby by then."

"She didn't even know. It was me that told her," Mary said. "She thought he left her because she was fat, but of course he must have known when he saw her. He's married. I knew she was with child as soon as I saw her – my Ma's had sixteen of us."

"She wouldn't tell Father who it was," Philip said. "But she told me, as a secret. We had lots of secrets and she never told him any of mine. But he beat me and beat me, and I thought he was going to kill me. He told me he was, and so I told him about Robert to stop him. I shouldn't have done that."

"I will try to find her," Catherine said. "I will make it my life's work to find her. And if she's alive, I will. And if I do, I'll bring her here and you can ask her forgiveness. And then if you will accept me, I would very much like to be part of your family again."

"You are part of our family, whether you find her or not," Philip said.

"You may not want me to be, when you know what I am," Catherine replied.

"You're my mother, come back from the dead," Philip answered. "That's all I need to know. And you are very welcome here, if Mary has no objections."

"Why would I have objections?" Mary said. "After all, half the village thinks I'm a whore because I kissed other boys before I found Philip, though I've not even looked at another man since," she added hurriedly, "and the other half thinks I dance with Satan at night and am a Jacobite, because I'm a Catholic. Today you've proved that bastard a liar, because he told everyone in the village that you were dead. And now they all know you're not, and what he is. You're always welcome here as far as I'm concerned, and I don't care what you do to live. Whatever it is you must be good at it, to have a carriage and wear clothes like that."

Catherine laughed suddenly.

"Well, we'll see if I get to keep these, once my employer knows what I've done today, and that I intend to find my daughter and grandchild, if I can. But really, I don't care a fig what he thinks."

"Then, Mrs Browne," Colin said, who knew exactly what she did for a living, having experienced enough of the world to recognise her kind, and knowing that a woman of her background and marital status had only one way to come by the wealth she enjoyed, "it's clear where Sarah got her strength and determination from. Which gives me hope that she may after all have survived and be thriving."

"I pray that she is," Catherine said fervently.

"If you wish to do that, I would be honoured to lead you," Colin offered.

And so it was that for the first time ever in Alliston village an Anglican minister led prayers for a Roman Catholic, an ex-Puritan and a Courtesan, all of whom prayed to God with an intensity, sincerity and purity that Reverend Browne would never, if he lived to be a hundred, witness in his rapidly diminishing congregation.

**

Liverpool, September 1741

"No," Sarah said firmly. "I'm not doing that."

"Daisy, he will pay very well. And you have agreed to take such clients," Mother Augustus said.

"I haven't agreed to take that sort, though."

"What *sort?* It's a very common wish. Lily takes men who want to be punished as naughty children by their nannies all the time."

"Let her take him then," Sarah countered. "I won't."

Mother Augustus sighed. She missed the old Daisy, the gentler, shyer one. But this happened to all the girls in this business. You could not survive for more than a few months as a whore, even as a whore in this sort of house, if you showed vulnerability.

"Daisy, do you know how many girls out on the streets, or even in other houses, would kill to live here?" she said.

"If you want to threaten me, do it straight out," Sarah responded. "Are you saying that if I refuse this client you'll throw me out and give my room to another girl?"

"No, I'm not saying that. But I won't let any of my girls just refuse people unless they have a good reason. You know I've already pandered to you."

"No, you haven't really," Sarah said. "What you've done is given me all the clients that either the other girls don't want, or the ones that have desires so strange and secret that you can't trust the others not to talk about them. And those clients pay you well for my silence."

"Damn you, Daisy," Mother Augustus said hotly. Very few of her girls had the courage to speak so bluntly to her, but there was something different about this one, and she was not sure if it was courage that made her do so or a relative indifference to what happened to her. "I will not throw you out for this. But you must tell me why you are being so stubborn. The man does not want to sleep with you. You must tell me why you refuse him."

"You've never asked me to talk about my past," Sarah commented.

"I don't want to know about any of my girls' past lives," Mother responded, "unless it affects their current one and my business. So either take the man, or tell me why you won't."

There was a silence while Sarah thought, and then she sat down on a chair opposite Mother's, a table between them covered with business papers. She pushed a few papers out of the way and leaned forward, her elbows on the table.

"I won't tell you about my life before I came here," Sarah

started, "except to say that it was terrible. Even the things I thought were good became terrible. Except for one thing. You know when I came here I'd not long before had a baby."

The older woman nodded.

"I had one week with her, that's all," Sarah said, her eyes misting. "That was the only good week I've ever had in my life, and I will not let some fat hairy bastard slobber over my breasts pretending to feed from them while I put cream on his arse and a tailclout for him to piss in. It will foul the only good memory I have, and I won't do that, even if you do throw me out. And I can't sing him a lullaby because I don't know any anyway."

Mother Augustus stared at her for a moment, and then nodded.

"I will ask Poppy," she said. "She is newer than you, but she will do it."

"Thank you," Sarah replied, standing again. She wiped impatiently at her eyes, clearly determined not to show weakness.

"You have been honest with me," Mother Augustus said. "I appreciate that. I want to ask you another question, to which I also need an honest answer."

Sarah nodded, and waited.

"Why is a Justice of the Peace trying to find out where you are?"

Sarah's face creased in such a genuine expression of puzzlement that Mother Augustus had her answer before she said anything.

"I see by your face that you don't know," she continued. "He is asking for you not by your current name, but by the name of Sarah Browne. But you told me that you had no acquaintance here when you arrived at my house."

"I didn't. I don't know any Justices of the Peace, anywhere," Sarah said.

"That *is* strange. Because Mr Grimes is asking at every whorehouse in Liverpool, it seems. Not directly, but through an associate of his, who came here yesterday. I told him that no one of that name lives here, which is true, in a fashion. I see you *are* familiar with his name then," she added in response to Sarah's reaction to it. She had paled, sat down again and buried her face in her hands. "What crime have you committed?" Mother asked.

"I will protect you if I can, depending on the nature of the offence, but Grimes is a powerful man in this town. You know that?"

"No," Sarah said in a very small voice, muffled by her hands. "No. I thought he was a haberdasher."

"He is, a wealthy businessman. He is also a highly respected member of the church, and a magistrate. Neither I nor any of the other brothel owners can imagine such a man seeking one of their girls so determinedly unless she has committed a very serious crime. Sarah, look at me, because I must know what you have done, or what he thinks you have done."

This was the penance then, not the loss of half her savings for Violet's abortion. She took her hands away from her face and looked Mother Augustus directly in the eyes.

"I will leave," she said. "I will go tonight. Is there a coach?"

"A coach to where?" Mother asked.

"Anywhere," Sarah replied grimly.

"No, you might not need to do that. What have you done? If you tell me I will tell no one, but I need to know, you must see that. You have lived here for nearly two years, so it must surely be something he thinks you have done whilst here, and that affects me."

"I have committed no crime against him, nothing illegal, and nothing that will reflect badly on your house. I swear that. He doesn't know where I live, and if you say that you don't know anyone of the name of Sarah Browne, then you need not worry. In fact once I've left you can tell him you know me if you want, because it won't make any difference to you."

"It could do if he decides to take out his anger at whatever you've done on my business, if you cannot be found," Mother Augustus said. "He could make life impossible for me, and for my girls."

Sarah sighed. She was right. Damn, damn, damn. Why hadn't she thought it through before she had acted against him? She had truly believed he didn't live in Liverpool, that he'd lied to her about that as he had about everything else, and the shock at seeing him with his *wife*, enjoying a summer walk when he had so completely ruined her, had been too much.

She told the bawd the basics; that Robert was the father of her child, that he had seduced her, lied to her, then abandoned her. She told her that she had come to Liverpool believing that he had lied about that too, sure that this was the one place he would *not* be. Then she told her what she had said to him when she had seen him, and to her surprise, at that Mother Augustus had laughed.

"My God, you have courage, girl," she said. "I admire that. But you shouldn't have done it, you know. You have made a powerful enemy."

"I know. I wasn't thinking straight," Sarah said. "I was so angry with him, and I wanted to hurt him. I've felt bad about it ever since – not because of him, but his wife. It's not her fault that her husband is a worthless shit."

"Let us think," Mother said, "for I would like to help you. Only I and Lily know your real name, yes? And Lily is completely trustworthy. He will grow tired when he cannot find you. He won't come looking himself, not here. And he is not a man who frequents whorehouses. Of course you won't be able to go out in the daytime for a while, but you can go out in the evenings for some air, if you wear a hood. I think we can manage this without you having to leave."

"Someone else knows," Sarah said. "Violet was with me when I met Robert…Mr Grimes. She heard what I said to him, and I think he mentioned my name. But she promised not to say anything. I paid for her to get rid of her baby and she said she'd keep quiet."

"You paid for that?" Mother replied incredulously.

"Yes. She said that she couldn't afford it. I offered to pay if she kept quiet, and she agreed. She hasn't told anyone, I don't think."

"No. But she certainly could have afforded to get rid of her own baby. I let my girls keep all their tips, and I look after the money for them, if they want me to."

"I don't mind," Sarah said. "I thought it worth it, for her silence. And I thought it better for her to abort the baby than for it to be abandoned afterwards. I've seen the street orphans and I wouldn't wish that life on anyone."

"No, you misunderstand me," Mother Augustus said. "Violet will do anything for money. She would take any client I gave her, if he paid enough. The reason I don't give her the men you have, will not give her the man you've refused tonight, is because she wouldn't hesitate to reveal their peccadilloes to anyone who paid her enough to. If she hasn't told your secret yet, it's because no one has offered her any money to. But if she knows your real name is Sarah, and she hears that someone is looking for you, she will find out if they will pay for the information, and if they will she will give you up."

Sarah closed her eyes as a great wave of despair washed over her. She had found a home here, a family of a sort, and had grown used to the work. She was saving, but did not have anywhere near enough yet to open a business, and now because of her recklessness she would have to leave it all, and diminish her savings doing so.

"I will leave, tonight," she said in a tone of infinite sadness.

"No, not tonight," Mother said. "There are coaches tomorrow, to Chester, and then from there to any number of places. Take this evening off, get some sleep, and in the morning before the others are up, you can go. You have to, I think. I am truly sorry for it, though."

Sarah smiled sadly.

"Don't be sorry," she said. "I brought this on myself. I am sorry, because you've been good to me. I know you've made money from me, but you've been kind too, and I know in this business that's rare."

"And you've been courageous, standing up to the man who treated you so badly. I'll be sorry to see you go. I'd like to give you two small gifts before you do, though." She took out a key and opened a drawer, then lifted out a bag. "How much did you give Violet for the abortion?" she asked.

"Seven guineas," Sarah answered, "but as I said, I…" Her voice trailed off as the other woman slapped eight sovereigns down on the table in front of her.

"Take it," she said.

"But that's more than I paid!"

"Take it. Violet owes you that for lying to you. I don't like that. In my house the girls stand together. They don't extort money from each other. She earns more than you in tips because there is no act she won't perform."

"But *you* haven't lied to me! I don't see why you should pay me—"

"I'm not paying you. I told you, I look after some of the girls' tips for them. That's Violet's money, not mine. And when she asks me for it then I'll tell her why it's short, and you will be long gone by then. So take it. And that brings me to my second present to you, which is advice. Keep your courage, because you will need it, but think before you act on it. And be very careful who you trust. You're a lot harder now than you were when you arrived here, but you have a kind nature I think, and you're loyal to those you think deserve it. Loyalty is a precious gift. Don't give it unless you're sure it's deserved."

Sarah picked up the sovereigns, and put them in her pocket.

"Thank you," she said. "I accept both your presents."

Mother waved her hand dismissively.

"You may choose two dresses to take with you when you go," she said. "But don't tell anyone else I said that. I have a reputation for firmness to uphold. In case I'm not here when you leave in the morning, I wish you luck in your future. God knows, you deserve some. Now go, get some sleep."

Sarah went to bed, but was too worried to sleep. So she lay there until the square of window turned from black to pale grey, and then she got up, dressed and packed the two most sober gowns she had, then left the room, closing the door quietly behind her.

She stopped outside Lily's room and raised her hand to knock on the door and then stopped herself, knowing that, as much as she wanted to, saying goodbye to her friend would make it almost impossible for her to leave, because she really did not want to. She had imagined leaving here only to open her business, and then had intended to still come here once a week to dress the girls' hair, remain part of their lives. Even the thought that she would never see them again made her feel sick.

She lowered her hand, turned away and quietly walked downstairs, where Barney was waiting for her, having been briefed by Mother Augustus. He gave her a small package of food wrapped in a cloth, unlocked the front door for her, and bestowed one of his rare smiles on her as she walked down the steps, before closing the door behind her.

She stood for a moment looking up at the house, committing it to memory. And then she turned, and set off to take the coach.

THE WHORE'S TALE: SARAH

She would take the first one that left, because she really didn't care where she went to now, as long as it was far, far away from Robert Grimes.

CHAPTER SIXTEEN

In the end and purely by chance, she went to Manchester. This was because as she was walking to the tavern to enquire about transport to other towns, she was passed by a man with an empty cart who, probably because she was wearing her sober gown and carrying her bag, thought her respectable and offered her a lift. She hopped up gratefully, and in the few minutes it took them to get to the tavern she discovered that most towns were accessed via a coach to Chester, or alternatively she could go to Warrington, from where she could get to any number of places by coach, including Manchester.

He had then added that he was going to Prescot to get coal, and then on to Manchester to visit friends and shop, especially for material for his wife and the five daughters he'd been cursed with, with not a boy child in sight, and that he'd be happy to take her to Warrington with him if she chose to go there, as long as she paid for lunch in a tavern along the way.

As his comment about the curse of daughters had been made good-humouredly and he showed no sign of making advances towards her, Sarah decided that Manchester was as good as anywhere. She preferred not to go to Chester if possible, and a coach to any town would cost a lot more than a meal. Maybe fate was pushing her that way. So she agreed and the two of them travelled together, during which time Sarah learnt everything about the garrulous Mr Cox's life from birth until five minutes before he'd offered her a lift, and he learnt almost nothing about her at all, except that her name was Ivy Smith.

On arrival he dropped her off at the market place, wished her luck in her new life, and then continued on his way. She looked around her new home with interest then, having a little more money than she had on arriving in Liverpool two years previously, she went to the nearest inn and paid for two nights' accommodation in a private room, because she wanted to be alone to think. Having had a hearty meal with Mr Cox in Warrington she decided not to waste money on food, so went straight to her room, where she stretched out on her bed to think. It was already dark outside and it was raining, so she decided to explore tomorrow. Tonight was for thinking and planning.

She had some money that she had saved and the eight sovereigns from Mother Augustus, but it was not enough to set up in business. To do that she would need at least £40, so she did not intend to be profligate with the cash she had. In two years at Mother Augustus' house she had saved just over £20 in tips. She absolutely did not want to remain a prostitute, but she thought that the situation regarding servants here was unlikely to be much different to Liverpool. Even if she was able to obtain employment without a character and avoid the attentions of lusty sons, it would take her many years to save the rest of the money on servant's wages.

If she could find another house like Mother Augustus' it would take her at least two years to save what she needed, depending on the generosity of her clients. She was unlikely to find a bawd as kind as Mother Augustus had been though, so it would probably be two years of hell.

Or she could rent a room and be an independent whore. She knew that Mother had charged around a sovereign to each man who came to the house, more if they wanted 'unusual services'. She lay back for a moment and imagined earning £15 in two weeks, and felt the excitement rise in her. She could endure just about *anything* for two weeks, if it meant she could have her business at the end of it.

No.

Be sensible and realistic, she admonished herself. Mother could charge those prices because she had a beautiful well-furnished house, and a selection of clean, reasonably discreet girls. Whereas if she was on her own in one room, or even two rooms, she could not charge anything like that. But she should still be able to earn around £2 a week. If rent was, say, ten shillings for a reasonable couple of rooms, she would still have saved the money in a little over six months, even allowing for food, coal or wood, and so on.

She sat for a while thinking about it and wondering if the risks of being a solo prostitute outweighed the shorter amount of time she'd have to continue this hated profession before she could say goodbye to it forever. It was worth a try. The fewer men she had sex with, the less chance she had of getting the pox, or pregnant.

The next day she went out and spent the day wandering round the town. It was smaller than Liverpool and not on the coast, so did not have as many foreigners, which made it feel less exotic and a bit more like an enormous village in terms of its atmosphere. Walking about and listening to people talking, it was clear that a lot of the inhabitants knew each other. She discovered that the main manufacture of the town was cloth - cotton, wool and silk weaving, and that the town was very old, had been founded by the Romans many centuries before.

Manchester was dominated by the huge Collegiate Church which sat above the town, as though watching over it. She walked up to it and around the graveyard, not because she was suddenly feeling religious but because from it there was a good view across the whole town. Unlike Chester it had no walls and was surrounded by fields and countryside. She was gratified to discover it had a river, the Irwell, which although wider than the river in Alliston and much dirtier, had a bridge over it, and that the buildings on the other side of the bridge were not part of Manchester, but a place called Salford. It was nice to know there was a source of running water nearby where she could sit and think if she wanted to.

Whilst having lunch in a clean and reputable tavern called John Shaw's Punch House near the market place, she discovered that people here were drinking toasts in the excellent fruity punch to the King over the Water, whoever he was, and wished for him to come over that water to England and take the crown from the usurper, whoever he was.

After lunch she asked the landlord, who seemed friendly enough, if he knew where she could rent a room, or maybe two rooms, in an area that was pleasant but not too expensive, and also who the King over the Water was.

Two hours later she had had a political lecture on the merits of King James III and his young sons Charles and Henry, and had discovered that King George II, far from being the great regal figure depicted on the painting in Mrs Grimes' cottage was in fact a despicable German piece of shit, begging her pardon, whose even more despicable father had accepted the crown when it had been offered to him by some men who had no right to offer it at all and who should have been hung, drawn and quartered as traitors, the bastards, begging her pardon.

She also discovered that the skull hanging on the Market Cross had been there for twenty-five years and belonged to a great hero named Thomas Syddall, who'd tried to get the rightful king James back on the throne. Sarah wasn't told, but presumed he'd failed disastrously in his undertaking. She'd listened politely, but in truth she wasn't that interested in things that had happened long before she was born, and thought that if this James hadn't managed to come back from abroad for over twenty-five years, he mustn't want to be king *that* much.

She had also paid out five shillings and was now the happy tenant of two rooms on the ground floor of a house in the Smithy Door area. It was not a supremely reputable part of town; the house was old, and the street it was on narrow and gloomy. But it was clean and pleasantly furnished, and the sort of place where people minded their own business unless you threatened theirs. It was also close to the market place and a number of taverns, which would provide her with both hot meals and, hopefully, customers.

That evening she washed thoroughly, dressed in the most sober of the dresses she had and went out to tour the taverns. She had no intention of picking up a customer that evening; she just wanted to have a drink in each inn and observe the clientele, get a feel for the places and see if other whores were operating in the same taverns, whores who might be angry about an interloper.

There *were* other whores there, but they were the gin-befuddled, lice-ridden ones who serviced their clients for pennies in the open air. Sarah knew that she was no threat to them, as they were none to her. She would kill herself before she fell that low.

She had just finished her drink in Sinclair's Oyster Bar and was about to call it a day and head home when a man came and sat next to her.

"Good evening to you, madam," he said, politely removing his hat. "I hope you don't mind my asking you if you are waiting for your husband to arrive, or if you are looking for some congenial company?"

Very well put. If she was a respectable woman then she would not be overly offended by his words. As she was not a respectable woman, she knew exactly what he wanted. She turned to look at him. Middle-aged, reasonably well dressed, a good wig and clean. She was not interested in his looks, only in his ability to pay and his general cleanliness and respectability. Although he was quite handsome, it was not that she was observing as she scrutinised his face, but his skin, which was free of pox sores, and of patches which might be hiding a sore.

She debated with herself for an instant as to whether she should reject his offer and start her business the next day as she had intended. But then she realised that if she did, she was just as likely to make another excuse tomorrow, because she was terrified, having had no experience of touting for trade. At Mother Augustus' the men had been introduced to her, and she had no idea how to persuade a client to come with her, how to negotiate a price. She had never had to do it.

She turned to him and smiled.

"Some congenial company would be most pleasant, sir," she said. "I admit I am new to the town and have few friends as yet, but hope to make some."

"I am sure a lady as beautiful as yourself will have no difficulty making friends," he said. "Would you care for another drink, or could you suggest a more…private place for us to become acquainted?"

Damn. How did she bring up payment? Because she wasn't going anywhere with him until she had. Should she ask for it in advance or afterwards?

"I have but recently acquired a comfortable room which would be perfect for us to become more friendly, although the rent for the room is prohibitive," she hinted.

"Ah. Perhaps I could assist you with that? How much is your rent, madam?"

THE WHORE'S TALE: SARAH

"It's ten shillings a night, sir," Sarah replied. This was horrible. It made her feel cheap, mercenary. Although by the look on his face, he didn't think her cheap, at least.

"That *is* a somewhat high rent," he commented. Interesting.

"It is, but the accommodations are very congenial," she said, smiling seductively. "And extremely clean."

"Ah!" he replied, and smiled. "Well, then. I would be most interested in viewing such a delightful sounding place."

They stood and walked from the inn together. Her rooms were just a few streets away and as they walked arm in arm, she fought to control her trembling. If he thought her inexperienced he would not pay ten shillings, unless she was a virgin, but no virgin would go to a tavern at night alone. She would demand to see his money before she did anything, she resolved, sure that Mother Augustus would have, although she'd had Barney there to encourage prompt payment.

The room was still quite warm, and Sarah put some more coal on the fire then lit a candle from the flame, before lighting some others in the room. It looked reasonably nice, but she decided to use his money to buy some glassware, wine, and other such fripperies tomorrow.

In the end she did not have to ask him to pay. When he got into the room he took out his purse and laid two crowns on the mantelpiece, before taking off his coat and placing it on the back of the chair.

"I trust the ten shillings is for the whole night?" he asked. "Although I will have to leave in the very early morning."

"It is, of course," she replied. "I would offer you some wine, but I truly have just arrived and have not had time to shop as yet. Next time you are here, I will be more hospitable in that regard."

"I don't want to waste time drinking wine here," he said. "I want to drink you in instead. Take off your clothes."

She sighed inwardly, realising from the look in his eyes that this man, unlike many of her previous clients, would not want to waste half the night telling her his problems.

Get used to it, she told herself as she started to undress, slowly and seductively. *You will have to work hard to earn your money now. And you need him to be satisfied enough to recommend you to his male acquaintances.*

"Oh!" she said, smiling prettily at him, "I appear to be having difficulties untying my stays. Would you be so kind as to assist me?" She raised her arms to her hair, thereby exposing the pale swell of her perfect breasts, and then pulled out the hairpins, watching his eyes widen with lust as the beautiful waves cascaded around her shoulders.

He moved toward her, and she focussed her whole being on making him very, very happy.

The next day she rose late, partly due to the exhaustion of travelling and partly due to the exhaustion of having entertained an extremely virile man for several hours after which she had douched herself with vinegar and water, because he had told her that if he was going to spend ten shillings he was going to ride her bareback, not wear a coat as it were.

As she went about her business, buying wine, glasses and other fripperies to make her rooms look more cosy and welcoming, she reflected that it hadn't been that bad. The fact that he had paid her before the sex without her asking him to told her that it was something he'd done before, that it was standard practice. He hadn't been rough with her, and she was only sore because she hadn't been aroused at all.

In truth she was never aroused, but in the past she had been prepared for sex and had always smeared some grease inside herself beforehand. She could hardly have done that in front of him though. In future she would attend to that before she went out hunting.

She could do this. Ten shillings for one night. More than a maid earned in a month. That was worth hiding shame and disgust, worth feigning arousal for. All she had to do was keep her eye on the prize and try not to become poxed or pregnant.

The following night she returned to Sinclair's, this time wearing a slightly more provocative dress colour-wise. Last night she had noticed the landlord ejecting some girls who accosted men, so she merely sat in a conspicuous place and smiled at any man who caught her eye. Within two hours she was leaving with another client. Again he paid upfront, although he wanted oral intercourse so her grease preparations were pointless, but at least she couldn't get pregnant from that, nor could she get the pox.

She could do this.

Over the next month her confidence and her ability to attract clients whilst appearing reasonably respectable developed. She did not want to throw herself at men and cling to them as the sixpenny whores did. She wanted to give the impression that she was worth the fee she asked for. She also did not want to be ejected from the taverns she'd selected to frequent, which were the ones that attracted respectable tradesmen, men who could pay ten shillings for a night of pleasure. Such taverns would not tolerate women throwing themselves at men lewdly.

Every night she thanked Mother Augustus for taking her in, and for teaching her how to be a respectable whore. She knew how to behave appropriately and had learnt how to assess people quickly. And now she was learning how to be independent, although she felt very lonely, which surprised her a little. She had always cherished time alone in the past, but now she was alone *all* the time she missed the chatter and support of other women in the same trade. Now every other whore was a rival and therefore a possible enemy.

But she could live with that, and as time went on the initial sense of vulnerability and danger that had terrified her faded. She had been exaggerating the danger in her mind, she thought.

Until she met Nathaniel.

He was soberly dressed, in his mid-twenties, spoke nicely but not with the local flat-vowelled dialect, and had treated her with respect both in the tavern and on the way to her lodgings. He smelled fresh and clean, which was a bonus too. When they got to her rooms he put his money down on the table, then looked around and smiled.

And that was the last pleasant thing he had done in that long, long night.

When he left in the morning he took the ten shillings from the table on his way, doffed his hat to her, thanked her for her company and said he looked forward to furthering their acquaintance very soon.

She waited silently until he had gone and then she limped to the door and locked it before going to the window and watching as he sauntered down the road without a care in the world. Then she lit the fire, thinking that at least some of her shaking must be due to the cold, because it was late October now and the window was rimed with delicate patterns of frost.

The room warmed and the frost melted, but her shaking did not stop.

She douched herself twice, and then washed herself carefully, cleaning the blood from her face and from underneath her left breast where he had cut her with his knife. Her body ached dreadfully from his blows, the toes of her left foot were badly crushed from where he had stamped on them with his booted foot, and one look in the mirror told her that she would not be able to work until her black eye and swollen, cut mouth had healed.

Then she had made a hot drink and had sat by the fire, trying to hold the mug steadily enough to drink it, knowing that she was in shock and that she had to calm herself down. She was safe now. The door was locked and he had gone. She screwed her eyes up against the tears that threatened, telling herself that no man would ever make her cry again, not for any reason.

She sat and looked at the flames, and drank and thought. Last night she had been humiliated in ways that her father, as brutal as he was, would never have contemplated doing. She had done things that she thought she would die before she would agree to do. But she did not want to die, so she had done them, and had lived. She was sure that he would have kept his promise to disembowel her had she not done everything he had told her to do. He had enjoyed her pain and terror, had been aroused by it. And she had been completely helpless.

Because she did not have a protector, and because she could have screamed herself hoarse and no one would have come to her aid, because this was a place where people minded their own business.

Oh God.

Over the next week while her bruises healed, she thought continuously, having little else to do to pass the time, because she could not work. She reasoned that in one month she had saved £5, and had had only one violent client. This was, she thought, because she frequented places where the respectable men went. She had just been very, very unlucky. It would not happen again. If she continued as she was, in another few months she would have enough to turn her back on this life forever. Then she would leave, go to another town and start her new life. She would put the last two years, in fact would put all of her life except her week with Lucy into a box and would bury it so deep in her mind that it would never see the light of day again. And she would reinvent herself.

She could do it. She had to do it, because the only other thing she could do was now unthinkable. She was so close to her dream.

In spite of that, when she had gone back to the tavern some ten days later when her facial bruising was faded enough to be concealed with light makeup, she had been unable to hold her glass steady as she drank, and had struggled to make eye contact and smile at the men, looking all the time for some sign of ruthlessness, of cruelty. But she had seen no sign of that in the soft-spoken Nathaniel, had only seen the cold brutality in his eyes when he had spat in her face in her room, when it was too late to escape him.

When a man had finally come across to her, she had been unable to respond to his polite advances, so overwhelmed with terror that she had finally run from the room and vomited outside, her whole body sheened with icy sweat. After that she had gone home, and had spent the night giving herself a good talking to.

The following night she returned to the tavern and swallowed down her fear, telling herself that she was damned if she would let one violent brute deprive her of her dream. She found a client, took him home, managed to keep the contents of her stomach where they belonged, and also managed to feign arousal. He seemed satisfied, paid her and left without incident. It was a start.

For the next three nights, all went well. On the fourth night she was unsuccessful, but didn't really mind because she was tired anyway. She would get some sleep, and tomorrow would clean her rooms and buy some more wine and dainties. She made her way home, yawning as she opened the door of the house.

She stepped inside, but as she turned to close and lock it, it was pushed violently open. She staggered backwards and before she could recover her balance was seized, her shriek muffled by a rough hand covering her mouth, and then she heard Nathaniel's soft, urgent voice telling her to be silent or she'd be sorry, and she lost control of her bladder.

This time he did not bruise her face, nor did he cut her. In fact he did not hurt her physically at all. Instead he told her to sit down on one of the chairs by the fire, and then sat opposite her, leaning forward and playing with the knife that he had sliced her breast with two weeks before.

In his pleasant, soft voice he told her that he had decided he was going to be her keeper now, that she would still live here, but that he would look out for her, because, as she no doubt understood, she clearly needed protection. He was sure she knew that there was any number of brutal men out there who would not hesitate to beat and rob a woman who was so clearly alone, unless she had someone looking after her, someone who could handle himself and who was not afraid to use force if necessary.

He was sure he had proved his capability to her, and he would be generous. She could keep a full half of her earnings. All he asked was that she paid him five shillings a night, six nights of the week. On the seventh she would satisfy him as she had done on their previous encounter, although of course he would take care not to damage the merchandise, and was sure she would take care not to arouse his temper.

He did not ask her to agree to his proposal, because although he had worded it as a request it was in fact a demand, and refusal was not an option, as they both knew. He celebrated their new partnership by making her grovel on the floor, kiss his feet and beg him to fuck her as she had never been fucked before, after which he graciously acceded to her pleading, before leaving and promising her he would return that evening at six of the clock.

Sarah never found out whether he kept his promise or not, because two hours after he had walked down the street whistling happily, pleased with his new business venture, she left her lodgings forever. Six hours later, having taken a room at a tavern for the night, she had cleaned herself up and was on the other side of Manchester, sitting in a gaudy salon fiercely negotiating with an elderly bawd by the name of Mrs Pelman.

* * *

THE WHORE'S TALE: SARAH

Liverpool, November 1741

The dinner party was well under way and was going excellently. The family had a new cook, who was currently excelling herself and would definitely be considered for a rise in wages after tonight. The wine was flowing, as was the conversation, and some potentially interesting business proposals had been hinted at and would be followed up on later when the ladies retired and the men could get down to serious discussion. All in all it was an extremely successful evening.

During dessert the butler entered and came to whisper in his master's ear.

"I'm sorry to interrupt you at dinner, sir," Johnson said, "but there is a lady here asking to see you."

"A lady?" Robert Grimes replied. "At this hour? That's most irregular."

It was. All the guests he'd invited were here, and normal visiting times were in the afternoon, not the evening.

"I know, sir. I did say that you are entertaining this evening and that she might prefer to visit Mrs Grimes tomorrow morning, but she stated that it was yourself she wished to speak with, and that she had come at this time trusting you would be at home rather than your place of business." Johnson hesitated for a moment, and then decided to venture an opinion. "She is *very* richly attired, sir, and arrived in a fine coach with two liveried footmen, who are waiting outside for her."

Interesting. Perhaps it was some eccentric wealthy woman who wished to put in a large order. It would not do to offend an influential woman, possibly a minor aristocrat.

"Did she give her name?"

"She did not, sir. But she said that you would be wise to see her, if you are at home."

Robert came to a decision. He stood, made his excuses to his guests, and followed the butler to the library, where the visitor was.

"Shall I ask Jenny to bring refreshments?" Johnson asked.

"Yes. I don't want to appear rude, in case it's a potential customer," Robert said. He walked in and closed the door then turned to his visitor, who had been sitting on the chaise longue, but now stood and walked towards him.

"Hello, Robert," she said. "It's been a long time. You've changed."

"I'm sorry, madam," he replied politely. "You have me at a disadvantage. Are we acquainted?"

"Not now, but we were once, as children in Alliston," she said. He looked at her more closely, a puzzled look on his face. And then his expression changed to one of joy.

"Good God!" Robert exclaimed. "Kate Applewhite? It can't be!"

"You're a little out of date, but yes, when you knew me I was Kate Applewhite. You do remember me then. I wasn't sure if you would."

"I can't believe it! The last time I saw you, you were telling me your parents were making you marry an ogre. I remember that. You seem to have done very well for yourself, even so. This is a wonderful surprise!" He moved to her, seizing her hands familiarly, and then remembered himself. "I'm sorry," he said, releasing her, "I'm forgetting my manners. Please, sit down. I've ordered refreshments."

She sat down again, arranging her royal blue skirts around her. They were heavily embroidered with gold thread, and diamonds sparkled in her ears. She had clearly come a long way from playing in the fields around Alliston, as had he. He took a seat opposite her and smiled broadly.

"Your man told me you were entertaining, Robert, so I won't keep you for long. I have a question to ask you."

"Yes, I have some business clients here for dinner, so I can't stay for *too* long, but it is so delightful to see you! Are you in Liverpool for a while? Perhaps we could meet tomorrow, have lunch, maybe? I would love to talk about old times, to find out what you've been doing!"

"Unfortunately I am only passing through, although I will be here tomorrow. But my question is about the past, yes."

"I have such wonderful memories of our carefree friendship, Kate," he said happily. "Ask me anything!"

"Thank you. I will. Why did you think it acceptable to seduce my fourteen-year-old daughter, get her with child and then abandon her without a second thought?"

She watched with interest as his smile froze and the colour drained from his face. He opened his mouth to speak, closed it again, swallowed heavily and closed his eyes for a moment. He really looked as if he was about to faint.

A knock came on the door and a maid entered bearing a tray, which she placed on the table between them. She curtseyed to Kate, and looked at her master with alarm and uncertainty.

"Thank you," Kate said coolly and authoritatively. "We are quite well. You may go now."

By the time the maid was back in the kitchen regaling the other servants with the tale that Mr Grimes looked like he'd seen a ghost, he had recovered himself enough to speak.

"Sarah is your daughter?" he asked shakily.

"Good. You are not denying it then. That's a start. And I assume you are not in the habit of ruining young girls, if you know of whom I speak."

"She told me her mother was dead!" Robert said. "I swear to you Kate, if I had known she was your—"

"Don't swear anything to me, you despicable creature," Kate interrupted hotly. "It should make no difference whose daughter she was. What sort of man have you become, who would utterly ruin a child, because that's what she was, innocent and naive, as you well knew. What did you promise her, Robert, when you took her virginity? Did you tell her you loved her?"

"I did love her," he whispered.

"Damn you for a liar, Robert Grimes," she said. "You never loved anyone in your life except yourself, you heartless bastard!"

"I...I was afraid," he said softly. "I never meant to hurt her."

"You are married with three children," Kate replied icily. "I assume you know how children are conceived. You knew exactly what you were doing, and you didn't give a damn whether she was hurt or not. You made that very clear when you abandoned her to save your own skin. And you have the sauce to tell me you loved her! I thought you could sink no lower in my estimation, but I was wrong."

"I am so sorry, Kate. I...look, I know you have come because she won't want to see me," he said earnestly, "but will you tell her that...when I saw she was having a baby, I panicked. There's no excuse for what I did, and I'm so ashamed, but I'll make it up to her. I'll give her money and a house, and make sure that neither she nor the child ever want for anything. Tell her that after I saw her here I tried to find her to tell her I was sorry. I went to every house I knew of, but—"

"You saw her here?" Kate interrupted. "In Liverpool?"

"Yes," Robert said. "Hasn't she told you?"

"When did you see her?" Kate asked urgently. "How long ago?"

"Last June. Isn't that why you're here, because she's living in Liverpool?"

"No. I'm here because *you* live in Liverpool, and because my son told me what you'd done to her. I came here to tell you that I'm going to make your life a living hell, and that you will regret the day you laid your hands on my daughter."

"You don't know where she is, then?" Robert said.

"No, I don't. I know a few places that she isn't, though, because I've been to them."

"Kate, I've spent months trying to find her, I promise. She walked up to me out of the blue, when I was out with my wife, told me that I had to pay the Mother for the unnatural things I'd done to Eliza the night before, and then walked off. I was so shocked to see her. I couldn't go after her, because I had to…I was with my wife, and she was very upset."

"Where's this Eliza, then? Maybe she'll know her."

"There is no Eliza. I've never been with a prostitute. I knew she was talking about that, because Mother is a title some bawds use."

"Yes, I know," Kate replied, and just managed to stop herself smiling at the obvious courage of her daughter in confronting this man who had ruined her life. She had spirit, then, had not been completely destroyed by him. She did not want this bastard to think she was softening towards him, so kept her expression cold and haughty.

"She said it because I was with my wife, for revenge. I know that. Laura gave me hell, has only just started speaking to me again! I thought about it for a while, and then I asked a friend of mine to make enquiries on my behalf. I couldn't go myself because relations were so strained between me and Laura, and if she'd heard that I was visiting whore houses I think she would have left me. She is a very…er…pious woman," he explained.

"So you think Sarah's a whore now? If she is, it's because you made her one."

Robert flushed scarlet.

"I don't know. She was well dressed, but in a very bright and low-cut gown, and she spoke of this Mother as though she was familiar with her. I didn't know where else to start. But no one has ever heard of her, and I authorised my friend to offer a good sum of money, enough to tempt someone to tell him if they knew her."

"What would you have done if you'd found her?"

"I would have helped her. When I left her, I was terrified. I knew that if Laura found out that I'd had an affair she'd leave me, and her father would make it his life's mission to ruin me."

Kate smiled nastily.

"So you would have 'helped' her only to get her out of your way, in case she caused you more problems, which she could do if she's here. Well, now you're in a very awkward position, aren't you? Because my life's mission is to ruin you, too."

"I wanted to help her," Robert said desperately. "I tried to forget her, but I couldn't. It wasn't just because I felt guilty for leaving her, it was more than that. I missed her, terribly. When she walked up to me and Laura last June, I was so shocked I just froze. But later I realised that in spite of what she'd said and how awkward she made my life for a while afterwards, I was truly happy to see her. I *did* love her, but I didn't really know that until I saw her standing there looking at me with such hatred I felt as though she'd stabbed me straight through the heart."

"Robert, in spite of the fact that I am now both wealthy *and* influential," Kate commented, "I have not lived a sheltered life. And I know bullscutter when I hear it." Robert looked up and the shock on his face was genuine, but whether from hearing such an apparent lady swear or whether he had genuinely convinced himself that he cared for Sarah, Kate didn't know.

"No!" he said. "I really do want to make it right, or as right as I can. I don't think she's in Liverpool any more. If she was I would have heard something by now."

Kate picked up a cake from the plate on the table and took a small bite, and then sat back, hoping he thought she was pondering his words, assessing whether they were genuine. She was not, but she had to get this right. He was clearly impressed by her appearance, as she'd intended him to be. He had not asked her how she had come by her wealth, because he was too shocked to think straight. She needed his help, badly, but could not let him know that, because in spite of his affirmations, she had met enough self-centred men to know one when she saw him. He didn't give a damn about Sarah. She had been a plaything, a romantic dalliance, and he had thought he could walk away from her with no consequences. He no longer thought that.

She had to keep him scared, until she got what she wanted.

Because the truth was that her wealthy keeper had told her that he was not upset she'd travelled to Alliston to reconcile with her children, as she had clearly wanted to for some time, and he was happy to indulge her as she made his life so pleasant. But he had flatly refused to allow her to spend both time and money – his money, he had added – in searching the country for a girl who was most likely dead, if she had wandered out of her village about to have a baby with no way to sustain herself. She had made her peace with her son, and could visit him from time to time if she wished. But she must come to terms with the fact that her daughter had certainly perished, and move on with her life. Because when he came to see her he expected her to be there waiting for him in the expensive apartments he was paying for, not gadding about all over the country searching for a dead child.

Although Kate was still beautiful, and an expert in pleasuring men, she was also over thirty. And there were a lot of younger women snapping at her heels. She was a realist and knew that it was only a matter of time before he discarded her, which would not be too bad if he let her keep the jewels and outfits he'd bought for her, because if she sold those she could live reasonably well. But if she annoyed him too much, he would take them back, and if he did she would be destitute and unable to feed herself, let alone support her daughter.

So she needed to find Sarah without upsetting her wealthy keeper. And sitting in front of her, looking intensely uncomfortable, distressed even, was the man who could help her do it, or rather do it for her.

"I want to make it right too," she said. "Sarah told you I was

THE WHORE'S TALE: SARAH

dead because that's what her father told her after I left him. He was the ogre my parents married me off to. I had good reasons for leaving, but I've never forgiven myself for doing it, even so. It was a long time before I was finally able to go back, with the power and the money to take them away from that monster. I've made my peace with my son, but I need to make it with my daughter. That means a great deal to me. It means even more than being revenged on you for what you did to her.

"So I will make a deal with you. You will do everything, and I mean *everything* in your power to find her. She has relatives in Chester, but she is not there. I've made considerable enquiries elsewhere too, with no success so far. You say she is not in Liverpool. You will have different contacts and associates than I, and between us we have more chance of finding her, I think."

"She could be anywhere by now," Robert said, clearly unwilling to put himself out any more than he already had. If Sarah was not in Liverpool, then she was no threat to him.

"She could. But *I* am here, and even when I'm not, my reach is long. You should remember that." He blanched again, confirming her opinion of him. She smiled icily then continued. "Here is my proposal. Pull yourself together and go back to your dinner. Tell your wife that I am a wealthy customer who is interested in buying a large quantity of silks and Brussels lace, and who may wish to re-outfit all her footmen in a new livery. I have called this evening on my way to the theatre.

"Tomorrow you will visit me to talk about possible uniforms for my servants. You will come to my hotel and we will discuss this further, and come up with a plan to find my daughter. If you find out where she is you will not attempt to meet her, but will tell me you have found her. Only then will I leave you in peace. If you do this, I will ask you for nothing more and will leave you and your precious family alone. If you do not help me, I swear to God I will ruin you, as a haberdasher, a justice of the peace and as a family man. Do not doubt that I can. Make your decision."

"I will help you. You have no need to threaten me. I would have helped you anyway," he said sulkily. He was not a good liar, or maybe her life had just made her an expert at recognising them.

She nodded, and then stood, making her way to the door. Once there, she turned back to look at him. He was also standing, whether from politeness to her gender or in haste to return to his guests, she didn't know.

"One more thing. If I ever find that you have treated another girl as you have my daughter," she added, "I will be extremely angry."

He did not answer, but bit his lip and nodded in acknowledgement, looking very cowed.

Good. She had him. She left quickly before she ruined everything by kicking him in the balls, as she so desperately wanted to do.

CHAPTER SEVENTEEN

Manchester October 1742

When Sarah woke up she lay for a while as had now become her habit, looking at the ceiling directly above the bed and listening to the sounds, both inside and outside the house, which told her roughly what time of day it was.

There was nothing particularly interesting about the piece of ceiling above her. It was painted white but had a very slight crack in the plaster, which was slowly spreading in a diagonal direction. Very slowly. So slowly that she would probably die before it actually reached the wall over the sash window.

The sounds were a little more interesting; the flower seller calling melodiously on the corner of the street, although as it was now autumn she was not finding so many flowers to sell, and could be heard less often. Then there were the people walking along chatting below the window, of which Sarah could hear a few words as they passed, but not enough to know what they were talking about in any detail. Inside the house Millie was walking about sniffing continuously as she always did, unless there were clients around, when she became miraculously cured, Anna was singing somewhere in the house, which was always good to hear as she had a beautiful voice, and Georgiana's shrill tones could be heard complaining about something trivial; her egg was hard-boiled, the water was cold, the bread was not fresh. No one paid any attention to her moans, knowing that she was venting the misery of the previous night on inanimate objects, because she was not allowed to say that her client had been anything less than perfect.

There were lots of rules in this house, far more than there had been at Mother Augustus'. When Sarah had been told all the rules on the day she'd arrived, she had thought Mrs Pelman to be exaggerating, that she was just giving Sarah the official line, and that things would be more relaxed once she actually lived here. But that was not the case.

Some of the rules were easy to obey for Sarah, and made sense.

All the girls had to wash thoroughly daily and bathe once a fortnight.

No one was allowed to drink gin on the premises, and if they chose to get drunk on it outside the house they were not allowed back in until they were sober. This was because gin was so cheap that people became stupidly drunk very quickly on it, and Mrs Pelman would not have her girls vomiting in the house or behaving in unacceptable, indiscreet ways on the premises, ways which might attract the authorities to examine them.

They were not allowed to discuss their clients of the previous night at all. Sarah had thought this would be easy for her to follow, as at Mother Augustus' house her particular clients' peccadillos had been confidential anyway, so she was accustomed to not talking about most of her customers.

But in fact this rule wiped out most of the normal conversation that bound whores together as sisters, and that relieved the stress of a very difficult job. It was normal for girls to warn each other of potentially dangerous men, and to mock or joke about the previous night's occurrences over breakfast. It turned them into a club, made them protective of each other.

But not here. Instead breakfast would be a relatively silent affair. And you could only talk about your past life for so long before everyone knew it all well and it became boring. No one knew about Sarah's past life, or rather Ivy's, which is what she'd told all of them her name was, and they never would. But her flat refusal to talk about her past, and being forbidden to talk about her present made Sarah very taciturn, which the others mistook for snobbery.

Sarah, being Sarah, had asked why they couldn't chat about their clients, and had received the answer that if she didn't like the rules she knew where the door was. Several times she had been tempted to leave, but had remembered her experience with

Nathaniel and the money under the floorboard in her room, and had held back. At least here she was protected from men like Nathaniel by the large and capable Peter, who, though sullen and uncommunicative, was always around to eject any man who wanted to play rough, unless he'd paid for it in advance.

Not much longer now. Maybe a year, two at the most, although she was not sure she could bear to do this for another *two* years. She was very unhappy and missed Mother Augustus and the girls, especially Lily, terribly. If she had known how lucky she had been, she would never have put her life there in jeopardy by attacking Robert as she had. She regretted doing that every day, bitterly.

Not on Robert's account, not at all. If she had met him alone in a back alley she could have stabbed him through the heart and strolled off without a moment's regret. But on his wife's account, for having hurt her badly, and through that possibly his three children too. It was not her fault that her husband was a bastard. She probably hadn't chosen to marry him anyway. And Sarah had made her unhappy, of that she was sure, and was sorry.

And of course she regretted it on her own account, for the momentary triumph of watching him squirm had meant that instead of running her own business, as she would have been by now had she stayed in Liverpool, she was still looking at a year or two before she could start. And she was getting no practice, so when she *did* start she would be rusty.

Mrs Pelman had been completely unimpressed by Sarah's profession of her skills, both with hair and 'unusual' clients. In her house, she had stated flatly, her girls had one job, and that was to give pleasure to men, not to spend hours titillating their hair and faces. She did not encourage clients to always have one particular girl, because then if that girl left the client would leave too, which was not good for business. So she would get what she was given and be grateful.

None of the girls were allowed to have tips, either. If the client wished to tip a particular girl he would give the money to Mrs Pelman and she would keep it safely, along with the five shillings a week wages she paid each girl. Which effectively meant that as well as charging a damn sight more than five shillings per client, Mrs Pelman also kept most of the tips.

Of course the bawd's greed meant that none of the girls worked any harder than they had to with their clients because there was no incentive to, but that didn't bother her. And that was one of the major differences between Mrs Pelman and Mother Augustus.

Mother Augustus had wanted the money of course, and had made a lot of it, but she had also cared about the welfare of her girls. Mrs Pelman cared about money and nothing else. And because of that girls did leave reasonably regularly if they found somewhere better, and there was no sisterly spirit between them.

Sarah sighed, and swung her legs out of bed. It was around eleven, and time she was up. Underneath the edge of the wooden bed she made a little mark with her nail scissors. She made one every Sunday, and had been here for a year. Fifty-two times five shillings was £13. Over the next few days she would start trying to find out the cost of renting premises in the area. There was a small shop nearby that had closed recently, and yesterday someone had put a notice in the window, which might be about how to rent it or the cost of doing so, but she hadn't stopped to read it, partly because she was hurrying and would have had to spend time slowly interpreting the handwritten letters, and partly because she was with one of the other whores, and had never told Mrs Pelman that she could read, because she neither liked nor trusted her and the less the old bawd knew about her the better.

Of course she would need to furnish the place as well, and buy in the materials she needed. But with the money hidden under the floorboard and the £13 in Mrs Pelman's custody, she had enough to start making enquiries now. If she was frugal maybe she would be able to move sooner than she thought. Of course she would need to have enough money to live on for a few months too, until her clients heard about her, and maybe she would need to put an advertisement in the newspaper.

It was all very daunting, but also very exciting, and thinking about it kept her going through the long lonely days and the nightmare evenings and nights.

She was very miserable here. But it was better than being with Nathaniel, and better than being with her father, which had been her other choices. And her life would improve, and soon, which was more than most whores could hope for.

She stood and rubbed her eyes, and started her day.

* * *

It was strange how life was. One minute it was unbearable and the next it was wonderful, and then unbearable again. Nothing could be trusted. Nothing was as it seemed to be.

In the morning she had gone to a local wig maker's, pretending to be interested in buying a new wig for her father. She had worn her least garish gown, but had still not looked particularly respectable. She had professed a complete lack of knowledge about wigs, and had pointedly asked about the most expensive ones and had then seemed a little stupid, needing things to be explained to her more than once.

And during all that time she had looked around the room, taking in the decorations, the furnishings. It was not as friendly and welcoming as her uncle's shop had been, but she knew that initially at least she would not be able to afford a shop as luxurious as his, probably not even as nice as this one. But she would feminise it, make it as welcoming as she could, as she had done to her two little rooms as a whore until Nathaniel had ruined it for her.

She exclaimed about the lovely chairs, stroking their cushioned seats, registering that they were made of oak rather than walnut, were not elaborately carved, and that the material covering the seats was coarse but hard-wearing, which was useful but not as luxurious as the silk brocade of her uncle's shop. But it should be cheaper. She stated excitedly that she had been looking for something very similar for her own salon at home! Where had he purchased it?

By the time she headed back to Mrs Pelman's her brain was full of figures and addresses, and she really wished she could write, because then she would be able to write down the costs of chairs and tables, and the address of a cousin of the wig maker who would certainly be able to make her whatever furniture she wanted, and at a very reasonable price too!

Instead she chanted the information under her breath all the way home, so that she would remember it.

And then she entered the house, trotted up the stairs to

her room to undress and prepare herself for the evening's clients, and stopped, all the data forgotten as she took in the sight of Abigail kneeling on the floor at the side of her bed, of the edge of the raised floorboard, under which were her savings.

Under which had been her savings until now.

At the sound of the door opening Abigail turned towards it, and on seeing Sarah she momentarily wore an expression of horror at being discovered. And then she pulled herself together and stood, the coins in the bag she held jingling slightly, the expression on her face now one of triumph, gloating at her find and the power it gave her. She was the same height as Sarah, but more heavily built, a buxom country girl.

"What the hell are you doing in my room?" Sarah asked, although it was obvious.

"I was going to borrow your hairbrush, but as you wasn't in I couldn't ask, could I?" Abigail retorted. "So I come in for it. Didn't think you'd mind."

"And you thought I kept it under the floor?" Sarah asked coldly. She was trembling, but tried not to show it.

"Tripped over the floorboard, didn't I? It was sticking up. So I thought I'd do you a favour and push it back down, like, so you didn't hurt yourself. And that's what I was doing when I found this!" She held the bag up and grinned.

"You're a liar," Sarah said. "Give me the money and get out."

"Now wait a minute," Abigail replied. "You shouldn't be nasty to me, should you? Mrs P will be ever so angry if she finds out you've been cheating her. We're not allowed to keep tips, you knows that. We all does."

"Not that it's any of your damned business, but that money is nothing to do with this place. I brought it with me. You're not allowed to just walk into my room uninvited either. You 'knows' that, too," Sarah answered, hoping Abi wouldn't hear the tremor in her voice as well as her body.

Abi laughed, revealing that she had in fact noticed both those things, and was about to take advantage of what she perceived as Sarah's fear of her.

"Yeah, well, I don't think Mrs P'll see it like that. She'll believe you about as much as I do. Tell you what, I'll keep this on account and won't say anything, because I don't want you to get thrown out on the street, and you will be if she finds out you've been cheating her. Take that very badly, she will." She made to leave, but Sarah pushed the door closed and stood with her back to it.

"Give that to me," she said, tears of fury filling her eyes.

Abi laughed again.

"No need to cry. I won't tell her," she said, smirking and pushing Sarah out of the way.

Sarah tried to speak again, but couldn't force the words past the lump in her throat. Her vision blurred and then cleared, then the suppressed rage exploded and she turned, gripping Abi's hair from the back and smashing her head into the door with all her might. The other girl moaned and crumpled to the floor, still clutching the bag of money. Sarah's bag of money.

No, not just a bag of money. Her future.

Beyond reason, Sarah kicked her in the side, stamped on her arm, hard, and then bent and grabbed the bag from the girl's now lifeless fingers. She stood over her, breathing heavily, her expression cold, the trembling of rage gone now she had retaliated.

"You're right," she said. "You won't tell her. If you do, you'll never tell anyone anything again, because I'll break your neck. Now get out of my room." She reached down and gripped Abi's injured arm to pull her up, heard her scream in agony through the roaring of the blood in her ears and was too enraged then to realise that such a scream would not go unheeded.

She released the girl, who was now a sickly shade of white but was trying to get up anyway, terrified of this madwoman who had previously seemed to be so meek, so quiet, so harmless.

"What's going on up there?" a voice called from the hall, and both girls froze.

"Oh shit," Abi said softly.

They heard footsteps hurrying up the stairs and then the door opened, revealing Abi crouched on the floor and Sarah standing over her, who had had no more time to do anything than put the bag in her pocket.

Mrs Pelman took one look at this tableau and then spoke, not to the girls but to Peter, who was directly behind her.

"Bring them both to my room," she ordered, then walked away.

Mrs Pelman looked at the two girls standing in front of her, the one angry and arrogant, staring her straight in the face, the other pale and nervous, cradling her injured right arm with her left.

"What has just happened?" she asked.

Silence.

"You both know I will not tolerate such behaviour in my house. If you do not give me an explanation then I will eject both of you from my house immediately, in the clothes you are standing in."

There was another pause, and then Abi spoke.

"I can't say anything, Mrs Pelman," she said. "I daren't." She looked at Sarah with exaggerated fearfulness, which was akin to speaking anyway, as both girls well knew.

"Ivy?"

Sarah sighed.

"I came home and found her in my bedroom," she said. "She—"

"I only wanted to borrow her hairbrush!" Abi interrupted. "She wasn't in, but I thought she wouldn't mind if I used it and put it back."

"I assume from what followed, Ivy, that you have a particular attachment to your hairbrush?" Mrs Pelman asked.

"She wasn't using my hairbrush," Sarah explained. "She was snooping around my room."

"I wasn't! I was—" Abi began, and then caught Sarah's disgusted look and stopped. Silence fell again.

"Girls," Mrs Pelman said, "I have not got where I am today without knowing when people are lying to me. Now, either you both tell me exactly what just happened, in which case we may be able to sort things out, or you both leave right now. But I am telling you, it's very frosty out there and you will have a most unpleasant night, I think. Particularly you Abigail, in your shift and barefoot."

"I'll leave then," Sarah said immediately, still angry. She had defied her father, had defied Nathaniel. She would not let this woman cow her. "Give me what I'm owed and I'll go now."

Mrs Pelman, who had expected her threat to make them speak, looked at her, shocked. The stupid chit was serious.

"I'll decide when or if you leave, Ivy. You've damaged my merchandise. Abi can't work with her face like that. And that arm could be broken."

"Send for the doctor, then," Sarah replied. "I'll pay for him out of my wages. And if her arm's broken, I'll pay for that to be set too. A pound will cover it. So if you give me the £12 you owe me, I'll leave."

"I will not give you anything, either of you, unless you tell me what happened, right now," Mrs Pelman said.

Sarah knew that if she told Mrs Pelman the truth, she would demand the money which was currently in her pocket. If she left right now she would lose her year's wages. If she stayed she would lose her pride, And probably all of her money. She turned to the door and opened it. Peter stood on the other side, barring the way.

"You said she could go?" he asked.

"No," Mrs Pelman replied. He stayed there. Sarah could not fight him, and she knew it.

"She's been taking tips and hiding them," Abigail blurted suddenly. "She's got a bag of money in her pocket. I found it and she hit me and told me she'd kill me if I said anything."

Sarah closed her eyes and felt her anger dissolve, to be replaced by practicality. She turned back towards Mrs Pelman.

"Is this true?" the bawd asked.

"No," Sarah replied. "The money is from my previous work. I hid it so that no one would steal it if they broke your rule and came snooping in my room. Clearly I didn't hide it well enough."

Abigail coloured at that and was about to retort when Mrs P held her hand up, silencing her.

"So why didn't you give your money to me to keep safely for you, as I do your current wages, and the wages of all the girls?"

She could hardly tell the truth and say that she didn't trust the bawd. She thought rapidly.

"I didn't think it mattered, and didn't want to bother you by asking every time I wanted some trifle," she said.

"It's no bother at all," Mrs Pelman replied. "Give me your money now, and I'll keep it safely for you." There was a silence during which Sarah did not produce the bag. "Come now, you really do not want me to call Peter in to take it from you by force, do you? Because he will, if you don't hand it over right now. This is why I make the rule that my girls leave all personal valuables with me, so that there is no temptation for you to steal from each other."

She had no choice. None at all. She took the bag out and put it on the table. Mrs Pelman poured the contents out and quickly counted it, before replacing it in the bag and putting it in her drawer.

"Good," she said. "I'm glad you've seen sense. I will keep it safely for you. Abigail, I am most displeased with you. All the girls have hairbrushes and some of them are in the house now. You had no need to go into Ivy's room if she was out. Clearly you were up to no good, and that is unacceptable. Ivy was understandably angry, and hopefully you've learnt not to enter a room uninvited again. If you do I will throw you out naked, do you understand?"

"Yes, Mrs Pelman," Abigail replied softly.

"I'll send for a doctor to attend you, and I will take his fee and any loss of earnings whilst you recover out of your money, Ivy. Hopefully that will teach you to control your temper in future and bring any grievances to me rather than acting yourself. Now get out, both of you. Ivy, you have a gentleman in half an hour. Get yourself ready to receive him."

Sarah went upstairs, took off her outdoor clothes, put on the dress that was on the top of the small pile in her clothes chest and then sat at her dressing table and picked up her hairbrush. She had been working automatically up to now, but when she saw herself in the mirror she stopped, scrutinising her reflection, which she rarely did any more.

She looked into her own eyes, which had once been called beautiful, but which were now devoid of expression. Her skin was pale, and there were lines forming between her eyebrows. Even her hair, which had been her crowning glory, lustrous and shining, was now flat and dull. She was eighteen years old, but looked much older than that. No one would want to have their hair styled and their faces made beautiful by someone who looked like her.

She put down the hairbrush and thought. She knew full well that she would never see any of the money she had earned either here or at Mother Augustus' again. If Abi's arm was broken, Mrs

THE WHORE'S TALE: SARAH

Pelman would take at least a sovereign a night out of her earnings for weeks. If it was only bruised, she would find another excuse to take it and hide it behind the stone in the chimney where she kept all her money, where the fire was kept burning so that no one could get to it quickly, even if they knew where it was. When the fire was out the door was locked, or Mrs P was in there.

Sarah knew where it was because she'd been unable to sleep one night after a rough session with a client and had gone downstairs, intending to get a drink from the kitchen. She had seen the door to Mrs P's room ajar, had heard the unmistakable clinking of money, and had seen her sitting on the hearth in the candlelight pushing something at the side of the fireplace, and had guessed the rest. Knowing how dangerous such knowledge would be, she had turned round and gone back upstairs immediately.

So she was penniless again, and it would take years for her to earn enough to even think of having her own business, and by that time, if by some miracle she wasn't already dying of the pox, or toothless and ulcerated from the mercury cure for it, she would look so old and ugly that no one would come anywhere near her shop, no matter how nice it looked.

It had been a dream, no more attainable than any of the other futures she had once dreamed of.

To hell with it. She could not have fought Peter, could not get her money back. But she was damned if she would be bullied any more, nor would she earn one more penny for that Pelman bitch. She was better than that. She would not be bullied, and she would not end up as some old ulcerated beggar dying on the streets. She could at least choose one thing, if nothing else.

She locked eyes with herself in the mirror again and smiled, then nodded as if confirming to her reflection that it was time. Then she stood up, crossed the room, walked quickly down the stairs and straight out of the front door, before anyone could stop her and before she could weaken in her resolve.

* * *

Sarah stood on the bridge between Manchester and Salford, her back to the main part of the town, looking over the edge down to the river below. It was deep and fast moving tonight, probably because of all the rain they'd had over the last couple of weeks, which suited the purpose for which she'd come.

She'd left the house full of decision, not even bothering to take her cloak with her and had marched along Smithy Lane to the bridge with the full intention of walking to the middle of the bridge, climbing onto the wall and jumping straight in. But once there she'd paused, looking down into the dark flowing water and had hesitated, because it looked so beautiful with the light from the full moon above shining on it, and the sound of the water rushing through the bridge's arches reminded her of sitting by the smaller stream at Alliston with Philip, back when all the silly dreams they'd had had seemed attainable.

Her latest dream, her long-standing dream, her last dream, had not seemed silly, had seemed attainable. Until now. She realised now how stupid she had been to think that she, a woman, and a whore at that, unable to read well or to write any more than her name could have become a businesswoman, even if she had the money right now. It had been as stupid as her dreams of sitting in a beautiful house waiting for her brother to become a general in the army, or of marrying Robert, or of ever finding anyone who would truly love her.

Damn. She should have jumped immediately. Standing there shivering in her inappropriate dress, her will to kill herself was waning. In truth she didn't want to die, yet she could not live this horrible nightmare of a life any more, but could see no way out of it. She could not bear the thought of continuing to be swived every night by foul-smelling hideous men, of no more relevance to them than as a hole to relieve themselves into, of catching the French pox or becoming too old and then dying slowly and painfully of starvation or disease on the streets.

But that was exactly what was going to happen to her if she didn't summon all her courage right now and jump. It would be cold and terrifying, true, but then it would be peaceful. And over. Unless her father was right about Hell, but she didn't think so. Hell was just an imaginary place made up by evil men like him to make people do as they were told. She was in Hell now, anyway. She climbed onto the wall of the bridge and sat on it, her legs dangling over the edge. Was it worth saying a prayer before she jumped, just in case there *was* a God?

"It's up to you, but I wouldn't," came a male voice, making

her jump. "Bloody awful way to die if you ask me."

She turned her head in the direction the voice had come from, and saw a man standing a short distance away, leaning casually on the wall she was sitting on. His face was shadowed by his hat, but she could tell by his voice and his athletic build that he was relatively young.

"Don't try to stop me," she warned.

He had been looking into the water, but now raised his head.

"Why would I? You can jump if you want to," he said casually. "I'll watch. I've seen lots of people die, but I've never seen someone kill themselves before. I've seen people fished out of the water after a few days though. All bloated you'll be, and your eyes and tongue will pop out. Your skin gets all slimy and soft too, so the poor bastard who drags you out will probably take your flesh off when he does."

"What?" she said, shocked by his casual remarks.

"I'm just saying. You're a woman. Most women I've met care about their appearance. I thought you might want to know what you'll look like afterwards."

"What difference will it make? I'll be dead. I won't care," she said.

He nodded.

"Go on then. Pregnant, are you?"

"No." Why was she even bothering to talk to this strange man? She should just push herself off the edge and have done with it. She placed the palms of her hands behind her on the wall, felt the rough grittiness of the stone against her skin and prepared to push. She closed her eyes, breathed in and out, readying herself. Her companion vanished as she focussed everything on launching herself into oblivion.

"You're a whore, aren't you?" he said, shattering her resolve. She opened her eyes and looked at him again. "Your dress," he added, seeing her expression. He had the advantage of her, as the moon was behind him casting him into silhouette, but was shining full onto her.

She looked down at the low-cut scarlet satin gown she was wearing, and suddenly realised that while she did not mind being bloated and eyeless, she did not want to be remembered as a whore forever. If this man told others what she'd looked like, she might be identified. Her father might find out, and would be overjoyed if he knew that she'd ended her days as a cheap whore, that she'd been so unhappy that she'd killed herself.

She did not want to cause her father even one moment's happiness. She didn't want to give this man the satisfaction of having something exciting to talk about with his friends in the tavern either. She didn't want to give any man any satisfaction of any kind, ever again.

She would go home, change into something more sober and respectable and then come back, by which time this weird stranger would be gone. Then she would just jump immediately into the river and end it all.

She sighed.

"You can go, if you want," she said. "I've changed my mind."

"Oh," he responded, sounding genuinely disappointed. She swung her legs over the wall and hopped back down onto the bridge again. He had not gone, but still stood there, leaning against the wall, looking at her.

"You're very pretty," he commented.

"I'm not for sale tonight," she replied. "Not any night from now on, for that matter. If you want to swive someone, there are plenty of whores outside the taverns."

She walked past him and off the bridge, heading back into Manchester.

"Wait!" he called, but she kept going. After a moment he caught up to her and walked by her side. "You're shivering," he said.

"It's cold," she replied somewhat sarcastically. "Go away. I'm not interested."

"You speak quite nicely, for a whore," he stated. "And you hold yourself erect too."

She ignored him, and just carried on. When she got to Mrs Pelman's she'd go in and shut the door in his face. He might get the message that she wasn't for sale then.

"Why don't you come to John Shaw's with me, have a hot drink and warm up?" he offered.

Now she stopped, and turned to him.

"I. Am. Not. For. Sale," she enunciated slowly.

"I don't fuck whores, not as a rule," he answered. "I don't

want to get the pox, for one thing. You said you're not pregnant. Are you poxed then?"

"No. Not that it makes any difference, because I'm not going to fuck you," she replied.

"I don't want you to, not now anyway. But I might have a proposition for you."

"What sort of proposition?"

"One that means you don't have to be a whore any more. I need to see you properly, in the light though, before I know if you'll suit. And talk to you a bit more. Come on. I'll buy you a hot punch. What have you got to lose?"

It was six o'clock. John Shaw's closed at eight promptly, being a respectable place. By that time all the other girls would have customers, and she could probably go in, get changed and leave again without anyone being any the wiser, except perhaps Mrs P, and maybe not even her. Once her girls were occupied she usually retired to her room. And Peter only made an appearance if someone called for him.

"All right then," she said. "As long as you know that I mean it when I say I'm not for sale."

He nodded, and she half expected him to offer her his arm, but he just walked beside her silently until they reached the warm and convivial punch house, whereupon he walked in, held the door open for her to follow him in, and then took off his hat, heading to a small table in the quietest corner of the room.

She sat down and he raised his arm to gain attention. Once he'd ordered he sat opposite her, and she saw him properly for the first time. He was a few inches taller than her, dressed soberly in a decently tailored olive-green coat and breeches and plain white linen shirt. Not rich then, but with some means. He was handsome in a gypsyish way, with sallow skin and wore his own hair, which was long, dark brown and tied back with a green ribbon. He had a cut and a bruise on his left cheek.

He sat very erect, his cold brown eyes looking her over, but not with lustful appraisal. "So, do you have a name, or do I just call you Mr Proposition for the rest of the evening?" she asked.

He smiled, but with his mouth only, his eyes remaining cold and watchful.

"You are right. Allow me to introduce myself. Richard

Cunningham, at your service, madam."

She nodded and pondered which name to give him. What the hell, she might as well tell the last person she was ever going to have a conversation with her real name. It didn't matter any more. Now she thought about it, a woman drowning herself probably wouldn't be worth more than a line in the newspaper; and even if it was, her father wouldn't find out. He didn't take the Manchester papers. And she was done with stupid flower and leaf appellations.

"Sarah Browne, sir. Pleased to make your acquaintance," she added, although she was no more pleased to make his acquaintance than he intended to be at her service. There was something about him that she really didn't like, but she couldn't identify it. She concluded that she was probably repelled by him because he'd been so genuinely uncaring about whether she killed herself or not, and dismissed her gut instinct, which was to run away.

"So then," she said. "What's this proposition you have for me?"

CHAPTER EIGHTEEN

"I don't have any proposition yet. I said I wanted to see you and talk to you first," he reminded her.

"You did. You can see me now. So what did you want to talk about? I've told you I'm not going to let you sleep with me, and I can't think of anything else a soldier would want from me."

He started a little, surprised. "How do you know I'm a soldier? I'm not in uniform. Have you seen me before?"

"No," she said. "You carry a sword."

"So do a lot of gentlemen. But most of them are not soldiers."

She shrugged and looked past him to the servant who was bringing them a bowl of fruity-smelling punch with two glasses hooked onto the side. When the servant had gone, the man looked at her again.

"I'm serious, and interested," he said. "How do you know I'm a soldier?"

The girl finished filling her glass and then sat back, cupping the hot container between her frozen hands, and looked at him over it.

"Your bearing. You carry yourself very straight. I'd say you've been a soldier for a long time, because it's natural to you to stand and walk completely upright. When we came in you immediately assessed the room as though looking for an enemy. Now this is a respectable place, so it was an habitual action, and even though you know that everyone in here is peaceable you're sitting facing the door, which gives you an advantage, as you'll see if anyone enters with violence in mind. If I was on my own I'd sit where you are."

His thin lips curled up into a smile, but his eyes remained cold.

"But you're not a soldier," he said.

"No. But I *am* a whore, and need to be able to get out quickly if the authorities or anyone else I'd rather not see comes in," she said.

"Good. You see the man over there, dressed in brown woollen breeches? Tall, next to the man in blue."

She glanced and nodded.

"Do you know him?"

"No," she said. "I haven't been in here for nearly a year. I know a couple of the men in here, but not him."

"Tell me about him. Anything that comes to mind."

"Do you know him?" she asked.

"Just tell me what you think about him. I'm not giving you any clues."

She sipped her drink and turned, but naturally, as though she was just contemplating her surroundings rather than focussing on one particular person.

Promising.

After a few moments she turned back and put the glass down.

"He's a manual worker, some sort of heavy work carrying things on his shoulders, but not in the fields. Somewhere around people, where he has to look respectable. Yes. He's very relaxed in here, looks at home – has his own tankard too. He's not expecting any trouble, but not just because this is a respectable place, or because he's a strong man. It's partly because he knows most of the people in here, and is well liked. So he knows they'd likely support him in a fight. He's a local, popular too, a jolly sort, not a fighter by nature. So he's probably a cellarman in a tavern, maybe this one or one nearby. Is that good enough for you?"

It was. Richard did know the man. He worked at an inn on the other side of Manchester, and the whore's assessment of him was pretty accurate. *She'll be perfect,* he thought, but strove not to show that in his face, because he wanted her as cheaply as possible.

"How do you know he carries things on his shoulders and has to be respectable?" he asked.

"He's wearing his working clothes and the shoulders of his coat are much more worn than the rest of it. So he can't work in his shirtsleeves, which he would if he was a farm worker, and must be in some sort of hospitable employment, tavern, hotel, something like that."

Richard raised his glass to her.

"Well done," he said.

"So, do I get to hear the proposition then?" she asked.

"Yes, but not here. There are too many ears. Let's finish our drinks and once you're warmer I'll walk you home and tell you, and if you're interested you can pack your things and come to my house tomorrow. I'm offering you live-in employment."

"But I thought you weren't interested in sex," she said.

"Every man is interested in sex," he replied. "If you're clean I might be. You're pretty enough. But I'm not after a mistress, no. How long have you been a whore?"

"Long enough to know I can't do it any more," she said.

"Is that why you were going to jump off the bridge?"

She hesitated for a minute, assessing him, and he sat back, letting her do it. She was astute, but as he wasn't hiding anything from her, he didn't care if she got the measure of him. It might be better if she did, because then she wouldn't try to cheat him.

"I've got a talent for dressing hair and doing makeup," she said. "My uncle offered me a job, but he died before I was old enough to start. So I became a whore because it's the fastest way to save for what I want."

"What's that?"

"I want to have my own business, as a hair dresser, maybe a wig maker," she said. "I need about £40 to start and to have any chance of making a success."

She wanted to start her own business? A woman?! She was living in some sort of fairy tale. Women weren't capable of running businesses. All women were capable of was fucking and having babies. But he could use her dream to get a hold over her, which he needed to do.

"So why were you going to kill yourself? Someone complain about their hairstyle?"

She looked at him in a way that made him want to slap her, but he realised that he might not find another woman as suitable for what he wanted in a long time. Pretty, presentable if she didn't have a whore's dress on, quite well-spoken, and clever enough for what he wanted. And desperate enough to kill herself, but didn't really want to. If she thought he was giving her the chance to realise her dream, she'd do what he wanted. He needed someone confident and sure of herself, and he could soon teach her that being cocky with him would not be wise. But now was not the moment for that.

"No," she answered. "One of the girls found the money I'd been saving for over two years now, and the bawd took it. I had £20 under the floor, and Mrs P owed me a year's wages, which would have left me with one more year before I'd have enough. But now I'm back to nothing, and I can't do another four years of this. I'd given up."

Richard nodded.

"Have you still given up?"

"It depends on what you want me to do, and if it means I can get away from being a whore and have a chance to start my business before I'm too old. If not, then yes, I've given up. But I'll listen to you, because the bridge and the river aren't going anywhere, are they?"

"Right. Finish your drink then, and let's get out of here."

On the way back to Mrs Pelman's he explained what he wanted her to do.

"Do you think you can do that?" he finished.

Sarah thought for a few moments.

"Yes, I can do it," she replied. "I know how to clean and do kitchen stuff. I've never been a servant, but I used to look after the house for my father. I would think a lot of the work is similar, and I can learn. Why do you want someone to spy on your servants, though? If you don't trust them, why don't you get rid of them and hire some new ones?"

"It's not as easy as that," Richard replied irritably. "Anyway, that's not your concern. Your concern is to be friendly, so that they'll talk in front of you, and then tell me what they say. Especially if it's about me, or anything Jacobite."

"By Jacobite you mean about the King over the Water? James?" she asked.

He stopped in the street and gripped her arm.

"Do you have sympathies that way?" he said. He was hurting her arm, but for some reason she couldn't quite work out, she decided not to let him know that.

"No. I don't give a damn who's king. Doesn't make any

difference to me, does it? I heard someone talking about it a few months ago and asked them who the King over the Water was, and got a lecture for my pains. That's all I know. Is it Charles, the son, and there's another one, Harry?"

"Henry," he corrected, letting go of her arm. "If you hear them talking about anything to do with that, about being Catholic, or anything you think I might want to know. If you're not sure, tell me anyway. And anything at all that my sister discusses with them I want to know."

"And you don't want sex?"

"I might, sometimes. You'll be replacing Martha, who left, and you'll have your own little room. But you can come to mine if I want you. Better one now and then, than ten a night or whatever amount it is you fuck now though, eh?"

It was, but she was still uncertain. She didn't like this Richard, not at all. *But he's not like Nathaniel,* she told herself. *He's a soldier, that's why he seems used to violence, why he seems so hard. It's just a front, but he wears it all the time because he's used to it.*

"All right," she said. "I'll do it. But I want ten shillings a week."

"Ten shillings?!" he answered incredulously. "That's four times a kitchen maid's wages!"

"I know. But I won't be just a kitchen maid, will I? I'll be a spy, and I'll be your whore too. And Mrs Pelman charges a sovereign for every time someone swives me, so you're getting a bargain."

"You won't be my whore," he retorted. "I'll only have you on the odd occasion. I'm not paying you ten shillings. Forget it. Go and jump off the bridge then."

He turned abruptly and walked away. She let him, until she realised he was serious, not just trying to haggle with her. She had no intention of running after him as though she was desperate, so while he was still in earshot, she shouted, "Five."

He stopped.

"Five a week, then. Yes, I know it's double, but I'll be doing two jobs, won't I? Three if you include the sex, so you're getting a bargain. But I want you to do one small thing for me, now. And then I'll spy all you want on your servants and your horrible sister."

* * *

"Where the hell have you been?" the bawd shouted. "I had to send your gentleman away! Don't think you can come back in here as though nothing's happened!"

"I'm really sorry," Sarah said, sounding as contrite as possible. "I needed to go out and get some fresh air, clear my head. I wouldn't have been able to give him a good time, the state I was in. But I'm alright now. And I've got this man here, who wants me. He's a captain in the army, he is, and if I please him he'll recommend all his other officers. He said they're looking for a nice clean house, and good girls to entertain them, isn't that right, sir?"

"Yes," Richard replied curtly.

Within five minutes he'd handed over a sovereign and the two of them were sitting on the bed in Sarah's room.

"What do we do now?" Richard asked.

"We sit and wait. Mrs P will go to bed in an hour or so, once she knows we're settled. Peter sleeps in the room behind her office and will come if anyone shouts for him. He's a light sleeper. But I'm very quiet. I can get my money back, and then we'll leave."

"This is ridiculous," Richard said irritably. "Why don't I just offer to cut the old bitch's throat unless she gives you your money back? That would be a lot quicker."

Sarah looked at him. He was deadly serious. She thought, quickly.

"If you do that, you'd have to kill not only her, but certainly Peter as well, and if one of them calls out before you do the whole street will be out. We'll be lucky to get out alive."

Richard sighed.

"Would you like a glass of wine?" Sarah asked.

"No. If I've got to stay here for a few hours, I might as well sample the goods. I've paid for them, after all," he said.

She'd offered to give him the sovereign back if she retrieved her savings, but what the hell. If he wanted to pay a sovereign for her, he could. Wearily, she started to undress.

As she crept down the stairs two hours later, dressed in her plain dark dress, she was telling herself she'd made the right decision, providing she could get at least the money she'd saved back. She was hoping it would still be in the drawer of Mrs Pelman's desk.

It probably was, because the fire had been burning earlier and even if it was now out, the hearth would still be too hot for her to move the stone and put the bag of coins behind it. She would think it safe in the desk anyway. After all, Peter slept in the room behind with the door open and she would not expect any of her girls to dare to defy her. Sarah had been especially contrite and cowed when she'd returned with Richard, so that Mrs P would believe her completely broken.

The house was in darkness, but she knew it like the back of her hand. Providing none of the other girls or their clients came downstairs to leave in the next few minutes, she'd be alright. She paused outside the study door, and listened to the sounds of the house. Moans of feigned rapture drifted down from upstairs and someone laughed suddenly, a brittle, insincere sound.

There was no light showing under the office door, and no sound from inside. Very slowly she turned the knob and opened it, just enough to slide inside. Just as slowly she closed it again, so that no one passing in the hallway would see it ajar and come to investigate. The room was dark, but the fire was still glowing in the hearth and casting enough light for her to see by. The door to Peter's room was open a few inches, and she could hear him softly snoring.

That was good. If he was disturbed he would stop snoring, and she would probably have time to get out before he woke up enough to catch her. One careful step at a time, she made her way across to the desk and then bent down by the drawer, praying to the God she had rejected that it would not be locked. It seemed He was listening, because the drawer slid open as she pulled it open enough to reach in and feel around inside.

Papers, quills, and right at the back, the soft velvet of the little bag that had been stored under the floorboard in her room for years, first at Mother Augustus' and then here. She closed her eyes for a moment, dizzy with relief, forcing herself to stay focussed, realising that she could not relax now, not until she was out of the house completely.

She gripped the bag as tightly as possible so the coins wouldn't jingle, then lifted it out, closing the drawer very gently, stopping as something in there rolled heavily across the bottom of the drawer. In the other room the snoring stopped.

Sarah froze, realising now in the silence that her thoughts about being able to get out before Peter caught her had been stupid. If he caught her now, then he would either kill her or would alert Mrs Pelman, possibly giving Richard the opportunity to cut throats, which he had so clearly relished the thought of doing. If he did that they'd both hang.

She stayed silent, unmoving, her heart banging so loudly in her chest that she wondered if Peter would hear it, if he had woken completely. While she waited, she wondered if she was doing the right thing in any case. Yes, she wanted to get away from being a whore, desperately, and this Richard was about to pay her the same amount she was earning as a whore to be a kitchen maid and spy. It was a good deal. So why was she wondering whether it would have been wiser to just jump off the bridge and have done with it? She didn't want to die, not really. She just wanted to get away from this life, and she was about to do it.

And yet all her instincts were telling her not to do this, not to go with this strange, cold-eyed brutal man who hadn't waited for her to undress so he could see what he'd paid for, but had just grabbed her, thrown her face down on the bed, twisted her arm up her back until she moaned with the pain and would have cried out except she didn't want to attract any attention, and then had taken her brutally and silently. Even when he'd come he hadn't made any noise other than a grunt, and then he'd immediately withdrawn and let her go, wiping his prick on her dress before sitting on the bed again while she sat up, massaging her twisted arm.

He showed no sign at all that he'd just had an orgasm. His eyes were as cold as before, his breathing normal. She had never had a client who had behaved so icily, and, remembering, she shivered involuntarily now, as she had then.

The snoring started again, and the relief drove Sarah's misgivings about Richard from her mind. She decided not to close the drawer any further and risk whatever it was rolling again and waking Peter up properly this time, so she stood and very carefully made her way out of the room, closing the door silently and tiptoeing back up the stairs.

Richard was waiting impatiently for her.

"Have you got it?" he said as soon as she appeared.

"Yes," she answered. She'd lost her year's wages, but she would not have got those back anyway, so there was no point regretting it.

"Good. Let's go, then," he said, standing up. "Do you have a bag to take?"

"No," she said. "I can put my small things in my pockets. If anyone sees me carrying a bag as I see you off, they'll know I'm leaving. I don't have anything bulky except whore's clothes, and I can't wear those as a kitchen maid anyway, can I?"

He looked her up and down, considering.

"You're about the same size as the slut that left," he said. "Her clothes should fit you. Come on then. The servants'll all be in bed by now, but you can sleep in Martha's room and I'll introduce you tomorrow. Give me the sovereign you owe me now, then, if you've got your money back."

She opened her mouth to protest, saw the look on his face and closed it again. She reached into the bag and took out a sovereign, handing it to him wordlessly.

It will work out, she told herself fiercely.

* * *

When she got back to the house with him he took her straight up to the room she was to sleep in, gave her the candle he was carrying and told her to stay there in the morning until he called for her, after which he'd introduce her to the other servants.

It was a small room, with a plain but solid bed covered with warm serviceable blankets and sheets, a clothes chest, a shelf on which were a few books, and a chair and table under the window. There was nothing ornate or sumptuous about it, but then there didn't need to be. It was a sleeping room, not a room for entertaining gentlemen in. The last time she had had a room of her own just for sleeping in was when she'd lived at her father's. And whatever Richard was, she doubted he would be as brutal to her as her father had been.

She sat down on the bed and bounced up and down a little, then smiled. It would be wonderful to sleep in a bed that would smell only of her, and not of a different man, several different men, every night. At least in here, alone, she could be herself, whatever she had to pretend to be in front of the servants.

After a minute she got up and opened the clothes chest, pulling out the first dress and holding it up against herself. Yes, it would probably fit her, or near enough. There were three dresses in there, all in serviceable dark colours, all clean. There were also stays, aprons, caps and two kerchiefs. Sarah's brow furrowed. Surely Martha, whoever she was, would have taken the clothes with her, or at least some of them? Unless the clothes belonged with the job, as her whore's dresses had.

Down at the bottom of the chest was an item which tinkled as she pulled it out. She looked at it in the candlelight. It was a polished piece of bone with a metal handle. The tinkling noise came from four little bells that were attached to it. It was a baby's comforter, the bone for the teething infant to bite on, the bells to entertain it.

She held it in her hand. Had this Martha who she was replacing had a baby too? Richard's baby? Maybe a baby who had died, like Lucy had? Richard said she'd left. Maybe he'd thrown her out, but why hadn't she taken this comforter with her to remind her of her child?

It would be nice to find out. Maybe she'd ask where Martha had gone, then go and give it back to her. Maybe they could talk about their babies who had died, and comfort each other.

Maybe you can stop dreaming, and accept the fact that friends are for other people, she told herself firmly. If there was one lesson she should have learnt by now, it was that she was better on her own. She put the comforter carefully back in the chest, closed the lid and went to bed.

When Richard knocked on the door in the morning she'd been up for hours. She hadn't been able to wash, as she had no water in the room, and Richard had told her not to leave until he came for her, but she had braided her hair on top of her head and had dressed in one of Martha's gowns, which fitted her very well apart from being a little short and loose in the waist. But her apron hid the looseness at least.

She opened the door and he looked her over briefly, then nodded.

"Come on," he said. "I told Elizabeth that I'd found someone to replace Martha. She's gone out, but you'll meet her later. I'll introduce you to the servants now. Don't forget, you need to report everything back to me." He walked down one lot of stairs, then pointed along the landing to a door at the end. "That's my room," he said. "If I want to fuck you, that's where you'll come. If you have anything to tell me, wait until the others have gone to bed, then come up and knock on the door, four times, softly. I don't want them to know what you're doing. Have you got that?" He looked at her and she nodded. "That's my sister's room," he added, pointing to another one, closer to where they were. "The others are currently empty. There are four attic rooms. Grace and Mary sleep in one of them, John and Ben in the one opposite yours, and Graeme in the one just at the top of the stairs. Thomas and Jane sleep in a room near the kitchen. You'll meet them now."

He carried on down the stairs and straight into the kitchen, where a number of people were sitting around a large wooden table, eating. On seeing him they all stood with varying degrees of alacrity, and every eye focussed immediately on her. Sarah felt the blood rising to her face, and knew she must look like a tomato.

"This is Sarah Browne," Richard announced. "She will replace Martha, and starts today. You will show her her duties."

A plain but pleasant-looking plump woman in her early thirties smiled at her.

"Hello, Sarah," she said. "Welcome. Here, sit down. Have you eaten already?"

"Er, no," Sarah replied, unsure as to whether she was allowed to say she'd been here all night. In fact she was hungry, having not eaten since breakfast yesterday. "Thank you," she added.

"Move up a bit, Ben, and make room," a fair-haired man said to a young boy, who immediately shuffled along the bench. "I'm Thomas, the steward, and this is my wife Jane, who is the cook and helps with housekeeping. Have you got your character with you, Sarah?"

"Are you questioning my ability to choose a servant, Fletcher?" Richard said.

"No, not at all," Thomas replied, somewhat taken aback. "But it's normal practice for me to see a character from—"

"I am all the character she needs. I have chosen her, and that's good enough. Show her her duties," Richard replied, and turning on his heel, walked out.

A short silence reigned, during which Sarah wished she had jumped off the bridge after all, and then an elderly man, who had sat down again the moment Richard had left, patted the seat next to him.

"Take no notice of him, Sarah. Sit down. You're in luck. Jane's just baked some bread rolls, and they're delicious. Help yourself. I'm Graeme. I work in the garden."

She moved across and took the seat next to him.

"So, Thomas and Jane you already know about, they're married, by the way," Graeme continued, looking down at her with astute grey eyes under heavy brows. "John here works in the stables, and helps me at times, little Mary helps Jane in the kitchen, keeping it clean, Ben cleans the shoes and makes himself useful in lots of ways, and Grace – she's not here at the minute, has gone to see her family, is Beth's ladies' maid. We've all got our jobs, as it were, but we all help out wherever we're needed. We're not like most households, all precious about our status as servants. Like a family, we are. If you remember that, you'll do well enough."

Sarah glanced up at him, caught the appraisal in his look, recognised the warning in his last words, and looked down at her hands. Wonderful. She'd been here five minutes and this old man already suspected her.

"Good Lord, Graeme, I think that's the most I've heard you say at one time in years," Thomas said. "What's wrong with you?"

"Well, someone had to introduce themselves, and as you lot were all just standing there looking at the door that Richard just went out of, I thought I'd do it. He's gone. Relax. Help yourself, Sarah." He waved his hand at the table, on which were bread rolls, a big pat of butter, a round of cheese and two jugs of ale.

Everyone sat down. Jane got a pewter cup and a plate out of the cupboard, and put them down in front of her. Graeme reached across to the rolls and put one on her plate.

"Don't be shy, lass, we don't bite. Not unless we have to," he said. She glanced up at him again and he smiled and winked at her, and she knew in that minute that now he'd warned her, he was going to give her a chance and would be friendly to her until she gave him reason not to be.

"So, Sarah, you'll be the housemaid, so will do a lot of different tasks. Have you worked as a servant before?" Thomas asked.

THE WHORE'S TALE: SARAH

"No," Sarah replied, deciding to tell as much of the truth as she could. "But my mother died when I was small, so I kept my father's house for years. I know how to clean, can do plain sewing, and I'm a quick learner." She had thought Richard would furnish the staff with a lie about her background, had not expected to have to do it herself. It sounded plain enough though, unless they asked her a lot of questions. She was good at hiding her feelings, but was not a natural liar. Hopefully she could satisfy them with omission lies.

"Who's looking after your father now?" Thomas asked.

"He died," she said. Well, he was dead to her, so it was only a partial lie. And he might be dead for all she knew. "I had to look after myself, so I came to Manchester looking for work, and Sergeant Cunningham offered me this job. I'm a hard worker," she added, hoping this handsome man would stop assessing her and would instead tell her about the tasks she had to do.

"I'm very sorry," Jane said.

Sarah looked up puzzled, just stopping herself from asking Jane why she was sorry, as she realised that she was talking about her father.

"Thank you," she murmured, looking down, hoping everyone would think she was sad.

"How did you get to know Richard?" Graeme asked. "Sergeant Cunningham," he added, seeing her look of alarm and mistaking it.

"Er...I was in John Shaw's. It's a respectable place, a punch house," she added quickly. "It was cold, he bought me a drink to warm me up, and he asked me some questions, then offered me the job."

"Did he now?" Graeme murmured.

"He showed me Martha's room and said I could sleep there, wear the clothes she left, because the ones I had on weren't fit for servant's work," she blurted, then stopped. *Don't volunteer anything you don't need to,* she told herself. She busied herself buttering the roll, aware that when Richard had burst in on them they'd all been relaxed, chatting. The silence in the room was because she was here, an outsider.

"Well," Jane said after a minute. "I think it best if you start in the kitchen with me for a few days. Mary keeps things clean in here and keeps the fire going for the cooking, but you can peel vegetables, feed the hens, collect eggs and so on. There's enough to keep you busy. Then I'll teach you how to lay fires properly. After that you'll be getting up early in the mornings to light the fires in all the rooms of the house. Except Richard's, that wouldn't be proper. Ben does that one. Then there's cleaning to do, but I'll show you that in a few days, when you're settled in."

"Have you met Beth yet?" John asked through a mouthful of bread. "Sorry," he added, intercepting Jane's disapproving look at him speaking with his mouth full.

"I'm sure you don't use bad language, Sarah," Graeme said. "But you need to know Jane is a stickler for correct manners in the kitchen. It's her kingdom. Don't reach across someone else's plate to get anything. You have to ask someone to pass it. Lose a finger otherwise, you will." She looked up at him, caught the twinkle in his eye and realised he was joking. "Same for speaking while actually eating. I'll write you a list of her rules out later to memorise. I hope you've got a good memory."

"Graeme Elliot, you're a wicked old reprobate," Jane retorted.

"Less of the old, if you don't mind," Graeme said.

"You'll frighten the poor girl half to death before she's even started," Jane said.

"I doubt she's that easily frightened. Are you?" he asked.

"Even so. We should be making her welcome, and if she was brought up properly, rather than being allowed to run round the fields like a savage, she'll know how to behave at table anyway!"

"I was not brought up like a savage!" John protested.

"No, you were brought up by the master. I'm talking about—" Jane stopped as the door opened.

"Talking about me behind my back as usual, are you?" a pleasant voice came from behind Sarah.

"Not this time, you're off the hook. It's me who's the savage today," Graeme said good-naturedly.

"Are you staying to eat?" Jane asked, standing up again to get more crockery.

"I wasn't going to, but it smells so good I will, as you're offering," the young woman said, walking round the table and plopping down opposite Sarah, who looked across to who she presumed must be Grace, the only servant she hadn't yet met. She had intended to say hello and to introduce herself, but the words died in her mouth as she looked into the cornflower-blue eyes of the most beautiful woman she had ever seen.

Her beauty was literally heart-stopping. Small, fragile-looking, with perfect features, flawless rose-petal skin, and the most incredible hair Sarah had ever seen, a heavy mass of glorious silver-blonde, currently trailing over her shoulder in a thick, somewhat wonky braid from which numerous tendrils were sticking out.

The woman looked at her and grinned, then held out a small, perfectly formed hand. Sarah reached hers across, aware for the first time how large and clumsy her hand looked in comparison to this fragile white one. It was gripped and shaken with a strength that was completely unexpected.

"Hello," she said. "Sarah, is it? I'm Beth. Richard told me he'd found someone to replace Martha. I see you're already getting to know the others. Don't let the savage teach you any bad words or you'll offend Jane. It never does to offend the cook, especially one who cooks this well," she added, taking a huge bite of the buttered roll Jane had just put in front of her.

"Every morning someone's character is mercilessly torn to shreds," Graeme said. "I see it's my turn today. Don't worry, Sarah, you won't suffer this unless you get really at home here."

Sarah was confused.

"I thought the other maid was called Grace," she said.

"Oh, sorry. Richard will probably have called me Elizabeth," Beth explained. "He doesn't like the 'servants' calling me by my diminutive. Which is stupid, because they always have and I prefer it. You're probably better calling me Elizabeth all the time, though. Or Miss Elizabeth. You don't want to get on the wrong side of him right at the start."

She said this as though Sarah was bound to get on the wrong side of him at some point, and as though that would not be a bad thing.

"He said he's given you Martha's room. Have you seen it?"

"Yes," Sarah said nervously, thrown by the difference in the servants' attitude towards the master and mistress of the house, and because the sister Richard had described bore no resemblance to the young woman sitting across from her. "It's very nice," she added.

It'll be a bit cold at the moment, because there's been no one in there for a few days. You can make up the fire later if you want, so it's cosy for you," Beth added.

"Thank you," Sarah said.

"Clearly doesn't expect Martha to come back then, does he?" John said. "Seems to me he had something to do with—"

From the corner of her eye Sarah saw Graeme shake his head once, and John shut up immediately.

"I'll show you where the woodshed is, and you can help yourself to wood when you want it," Thomas said. "You don't have to ask for it. We get it for free from one of the farmers, and Jane cooks a meal for him three times a week by way of payment. So there's plenty. Right," he said, standing. "If you've finished, I'll show you round the house and garden properly, and explain a bit more about what we all do. Then you can help Jane prepare the dinner, and have a reasonably easy day of it today, as it's your first day."

Sarah scrambled to her feet immediately.

"Thank you, everyone," she said to the room in general. "I'm sure I'll be happy here."

It was the first proper lie she'd told that day.

* * *

"Right then," Jane said that afternoon, dropping a bag she was carrying on the floor and a pile of wood in a basket at the side of the hearth in Sarah's room, and inviting Sarah to put hers down too. "You can make your fire up any way you want, but I might as well take the chance to show you how it's done in the rest of the house now. I'll show you again when you start actually doing it, but I thought you might want to practice here, so you'll get it right from the start. Sergeant Cunningham is very exacting."

"Is that because he's a soldier?" Sarah asked.

Jane made a soft noise in her throat, very like a snort.

"You might say that," she replied. "So then, in the main rooms of the house you have to sweep out all the ashes from the night before, put them in a bucket and take them down to Graeme. He keeps them and uses them to feed the vegetables. You polish the grates and the fire irons every day by rubbing them with a dry leather, like this." She sat down on the hearth and demonstrated, then invited Sarah to take over, watching her and nodding. "Then you clean the stone hearth with a firestone. It's a bit messy, so be careful with your clothes, and always wear the same apron."

"I used one at Father's," Sarah said, "but not every day. About once a month. I hated it when I was very small, because I had to climb right into the fireplace, and then my clothes got really dirty and it was hard to wash them properly."

"How old were you when your mother died?" Jane asked.

"Four. A woman came to clean for a while after that, but then she left. I was six when I started looking after Father," Sarah said.

"You looked after the whole house at six?" Jane asked.

"Yes," Sarah said. "My brother helped me, though." Damn. She hadn't meant to mention that she had a brother.

"I see. So where's your brother now?"

"I don't know," Sarah said. "He wanted to be a soldier." There, that was true enough. And it seemed to work, because Jane stopped asking about her past now.

"The fire surrounds in the rest of the house are made of marble, and once you've done the polishing you clean the marble with soap and water, and then dry it with a cloth. Then you use the firestone. After that you're ready to lay the fire, which I assume you already know how to do. As I said, you won't do Richard's room. He generally rises late anyway. Be…Elizabeth is an early riser, so the fires in the rest of the house are lit around six in the morning, so it'll be warm for her when she gets up. She banks the fire in her room herself. You said you haven't worked as a servant before, so you won't know that this house is not like most. You must do what Richard tells you, because he's the master here now, and is very exacting, as I'm sure he's made clear to you."

"Yes, he has," Sarah said. Jane watched her as she finished polishing the fireplace, and then proceeded to lay the fire expertly. She nodded and put the cleaning materials back in the bag, before standing and moving to the door. Then she clearly came to a decision, and turned back.

"I'll say this to you," she said. "Elizabeth is very dear to us. If you remember that you'll do well here, and will be welcomed as one of us. We're like a family, as Graeme said, loyal and trustworthy. You couldn't wish for better friends, if that's what you want. But you have to earn it. It's up to you."

Once the fire was lit, Sarah sat looking into the flames and thinking. Not about the tasks she'd done. She didn't need to think about them. The house wasn't enormous, she could remember the layout that Thomas had shown her. She'd fed chickens before and collected eggs, had peeled vegetables. She had learnt nothing that was completely new to her today.

Except for the relationships of the various members of the house to each other, which absolutely nothing Richard had told her had prepared her for. He had told her he was the master of the house, that he ran a tight ship, that his sister was a pretty nonentity of whom Sarah needed to take little notice, except to be polite to her as her rank deserved.

He said that the servants were a sullen lot, who were far more interested in things that were nothing to do with them than they should be, and that was why he wanted her to report back everything they said, and everything Elizabeth said.

She had not been thinking straight last night, or she would have wondered then why he wanted someone to report back to him the things a pretty nonentity would say, and why, if he ran a tight ship, he needed someone to spy on his servants. "It's not that easy," he'd said when she'd asked him why he didn't just dismiss them. At the time she'd thought that perhaps there was a shortage of capable servants, but now she realised that there was a lot more to this than that. He had made her believe that all the servants were thoroughly dislikeable people. She had expected them to be cold, hostile, easy to hate, and therefore easy to betray.

She had been here half a day, and she already knew two things; that she would absolutely love to be a part of this family of servants, of which Beth, regardless of her birth, was clearly an important and treasured member; and that that would never happen if she did what Richard had hired her to do and they found out.

They would find out. She had no doubt about that. The old man, the gardener, already suspected her and had warned her. Jane had just warned her too. It was extremely clear that whatever opinion Richard had of himself, the servants didn't share it. They had stood when he entered the room not from respect as he believed, but because he demanded they do. They had remained seated when Beth walked in because they loved her. Richard was an unwelcome outsider. And he had brought her into the household and inflicted her on them.

But in spite of that they had not been hostile to her, only wary. They were ready to accept her, if she proved herself. And Sarah, so desperate to be part of a loving trustworthy family, recognised that if she gave into that craving she would be thrown out by Richard, and would lose her last chance to be her own boss, to have control over her own life.

She had no choice. Friends, family were not something she could have, not something she deserved. She would do this, had to do this. Because she was alone, had always been alone, would always be alone. And the only person who would look after her was herself. If there was one lesson she had learnt in her life, it was that.

No one deserved her loyalty. No one ever had. Those she had given it to had betrayed her, rejected her. She was done with that.

This was the last time she would have to do something she did not want to do. She would hold on to her dream of having her own business, and would do anything to get that. It was within reach now.

She could do this.

CHAPTER NINETEEN

November 1742

Sarah stood by the hen house, watching the chickens peck at the grain she'd just fed them. It was a pleasant day, the sun shining brightly, but though it looked lovely from inside the house, now she was outside the brisk wind and crispness in the air reminded her that it was winter. Even so, she should be happy. She had a job that paid her the same as she'd earned at Mrs Pelman's, a pleasant and warm room of her own, plenty of beautifully cooked and delicious food, and although the working day was long, it wasn't as long as it had been when she'd lived with her father, and she had no risk of being beaten for nothing as she had at home, or of catching the pox as she had for the last few years.

She wasn't happy, though. She sighed, and started looking for the eggs. The hens weren't laying well now as the season changed, but there were still a good few eggs, enough for Richard to have some for breakfast as he liked, and for Jane to cook and bake with. Jane had said that it would be more difficult soon, as in the past she'd been able to keep all the eggs for cooking or baking cakes in the winter as Miss Elizabeth was flexible about what she had for breakfast, but Sergeant Cunningham was a different matter.

Sarah had commented that perhaps it was because he was an army man, and used to routine, and at that Jane had said no more, although her expression had told Sarah volumes about what she thought of Richard.

But she could not report back facial expressions. And that was why she was not feeling happy. Or, more accurately, Richard was why she was not feeling happy. She had been here for two weeks now, and had heard absolutely nothing that he would find useful.

Even if she had heard useful stuff to report she would not have been happy though, because although the servants were clearly reserved around her, they were still friendly enough and she found herself liking them more and more, even though she tried not to, knowing that betraying people you knew and liked was much harder than betraying strangers.

But it was impossible not to like the kind and motherly Jane, shy and soft-spoken Grace, and the tiny but bubbly Mary. Same with the men, handsome, authoritative but fair-minded Thomas, gruff but kind Graeme, the coltish open-hearted John, and little Ben. Not one of them had done anything to make her dislike them.

The same could not be said of Richard however, who was abrupt, rude, domineering and unkind to everyone, including his beautiful sister, who dismissed his nastiness but was clearly unnerved by it.

But Sarah had to tell him something, and soon, because he was an impatient man, and if she didn't she might well find herself standing on that bridge looking at the river again. And she did not want to die any more. So she would have to try harder.

"Everything all right, lass?" a voice broke into her gloomy thoughts, and she looked around to see Graeme behind her at the entrance to the hen house.

"Yes," she lied. "There are not so many eggs now. Only eight today."

"That's normal in the winter," Graeme said. "No need to be sad about it. Don't forget to close the gate here, though. The foxes get more determined when there's not so much other food about."

"I will," she said. Then he looked over her shoulder into the distance, nodded to her and left. Sarah turned to see what had attracted his attention and saw a barefoot woman dressed in rags coming round the side of the house. He went to meet her and a short conversation took place which Sarah couldn't hear, and then he disappeared into his little shed, returning a few moments later with an armful of winter vegetables, which he gave to her.

For all his gruffness and stern expression, he had a heart of gold, she thought, smiling.

After she'd taken the eggs back to the kitchen she went up to her room to tidy her hair, which had started to come down in the wind. On the way downstairs she stopped on the landing leading to the master's and mistress's bedrooms, picking up a vase of late flowers that were past their best. She would take them down to the kitchen, wash the vase, and put the dead flowers on the compost heap.

It was silent. Richard and Beth were out, and all the servants were about their business on other floors or outside. Looking down the landing Sarah saw Elizabeth's bedroom door was ajar. She put the vase back on the small table and went down the passage.

Later she would tell herself that she had only intended to close the door, but in truth part of her realised that this was her opportunity to maybe find something, anything that she could tell Richard that would convince him she was earning the money he'd agreed to pay her. She hesitated for a moment, her hand on the knob, and then instead of closing the door, she opened it and slipped into the room, closing it behind her.

It was a pleasant room, but not as luxurious as Sarah had expected it to be, although the furniture was of good quality. It was not overtly feminine either, which surprised her. She would have expected such a beautiful woman as Elizabeth to have a bedroom full of lace and fripperies, but everything in the room was purely functional. A painting of a woman who looked remarkably like Elizabeth, but whose old-fashioned costume told Sarah it must be her mother, hung on one wall, but there were no other pictures, no ornaments.

She made her way to the writing desk which was underneath the window, thinking that she might find something there, a letter perhaps, something that would reveal the secret political affiliations of its owner. There was nothing on the desk, but perhaps there would be something in the drawers.

She bent down and opened one of the drawers, remembering the last time she'd done this and reflecting that at least it was daylight and she was safe this time. Then suddenly the door opened and she heard a feminine gasp of shock and realised that she was not safe, not at all.

"What are you doing?" Elizabeth said coldly.

Sarah slammed the drawer shut instinctively, closed her eyes momentarily, pulled herself together with a huge effort and straightening up, turned.

"I was just doing a bit of cleaning, Miss Elizabeth," she replied.

Elizabeth looked at her disbelievingly, which was not really surprising, as she had not yet started her cleaning duties, and even when she did the master's and mistress's rooms would be out of bounds.

"It seems my brother has not explained your duties to you, Sarah," Elizabeth said icily. "Your job is to assist Mrs Fletcher in the kitchen and to wait on table. You have no duties in other rooms in the house."

Sarah hated herself. This was not who she was, someone who sneaked about spying on people, especially on people who had been kind to her. The look of contempt on Elizabeth's face made her shrivel up inside. She had to get out, now. She curtsied quickly and then walked toward the door, her mouth twitching into a nervous smile as she passed the mistress. To her surprise, rather than letting her pass Elizabeth kicked behind her, closing the door.

"Listen to me," she said. "I have no idea where my brother got you from, but if I see you in my room again you will be going straight back there, do you understand?"

"The master told me that only he could dismiss me, Miss," Sarah replied, trying to show the confidence she was far from feeling. Richard had told her that his sister was weak, pathetic, all bluster. If she was, she would capitulate now, and then Sarah could leave and go back to her room for a few minutes, try to compose herself before going back downstairs.

Elizabeth did not capitulate. Instead she too smiled, but her smile was as cold as ice, and the expression in her eyes matched it.

"It is true my brother is the master here," she said, "but believe me, if I wish to, I can make your life a living hell. If I see you anywhere near my room, or if you speak to me in a disrespectful way again, I will do just that, with the greatest pleasure. You will beg my brother to let you leave before I have finished with you. Do you understand?"

This was not bluster. She was deadly serious. Sarah had seen how she was with the servants, and how they were with her; the warmth, the caring. If she told them that Sarah had been snooping around in her room, they would no doubt make her life a living hell anyway. She swallowed, and looked down.

"I'm sorry, Miss Elizabeth," she said, and was. "I won't come in your room again."

She moved forward, and this time Elizabeth let her leave.

Sarah went back up to her room and sat on the bed, her face burning with shame. In her life she had found herself able to do lots of things she thought she would not be able to do, to survive. She had sworn, stolen, fornicated with strangers for money, and had been violent, and all of those things had been easier to do than spying on people she instinctively liked, for a man she instinctively detested.

She had to. Just for a short time. If she found just one useful thing out, maybe Richard would be satisfied, and would then pay her just for being a maid and his whore, which she could do. Then soon she could leave, and would never see any of these people again. And, she swore to herself, after this, once she was free, she would never, never do anything that made her ashamed of herself, ever again.

She calmed herself, bathed her burning face with water from the ewer and basin on the table, then headed off downstairs. It was lunchtime, and as she got to the kitchen she heard the servants chatting together. They never talked that merrily when she was with them. Instead of entering the kitchen she stood outside, enjoying the relaxed happy chatter of the inhabitants, wishing she could go in and join in, rather than be greeted by silence then a change of subject.

"I don't see any reason why he couldn't try a winter campaign," John was saying. "After all, the British army are all in quarters now, so if the king or Prince Charles came now, it'd take them by surprise, surely?"

"No, because it would be almost impossible to prepare a whole fleet of ships and an army to sail to Britain without some spy finding out and betraying us," Graeme reasoned. "And even if they did, and managed to sail here without being damaged by storms, there's another problem. The British army are all in winter quarters, in Britain. So they're here. Much better to wait for summer, when the troops are all off fighting over on the continent to protect Hanover, the land the Elector actually gives a damn about."

"That's true, I suppose. He doesn't give a damn about Britain, that's for sure," John replied.

"Well, I'm just glad we can relax in the winter at least, and not worry about having a war in our own country along with wondering how I'm going to feed us all," Jane said. "I can't understand why you men all want to go off and kill each other. The country's peaceful and prosperous enough right now. If the Pretender comes back and tries to take the throne, our lives will be hell. And if he wins we'll all have to become papists."

"I don't believe that for a second," John said scornfully.

Sarah sneezed unexpectedly outside the door and the conversation died instantly. She sighed and walked in, and Ben moved up to make a place for her.

"Are you coming down with a cold?" Jane asked. "Mary's got one and isn't well at all. I sent her up to bed earlier. I was hoping you could do her tasks today."

"I can," Sarah said. "I think it was just some dust went up my nose. I'm fine. You were all talking. Don't mind me."

"Did you hear what we were talking about?" Thomas asked casually.

"No," Sarah said. "I was just walking down the corridor when I sneezed. I could hear your voices, that's all. It sounded lively though!" She felt her face start to burn again, and hoped they might think she did have a fever after all.

"Yes. We were discussing how much food we'll have to buy to get us through the winter," Graeme said. "Shouldn't be too much though. There was a good crop of vegetables this year, the weather being kind to us."

The conversation continued, lively yes, but not about what they'd actually been discussing before. Sarah sat there quietly, memorising what Graeme and John had said, thinking that this was probably the important thing she could tell Richard, that would make him think it worth keeping her on, worth paying her the money she needed to start her business.

It was eleven o'clock and the whole house was asleep when Sarah knocked softly four times on Richard's door. She heard his voice bid her enter, went in and closed the door quietly, standing with her back against it.

He was sitting on a chair at the side of the bed, wearing only his shirt and breeches, his dark hair loose on his shoulders. He looked at her, no doubt noticing how uneasy she felt being in his bedroom and him in a state of undress. He would know that being a whore, her unease was not due to that but due to the fact that she was afraid of him.

Then he smiled and she knew that was exactly what he was thinking. And he was right. He waved a hand at the bed.

"Sit down," he said. "I assume this isn't a social call, and that you've got something to tell me. If so I'd prefer if you can tell me in a low voice rather than shouting it from the doorway so my bitch of a sister can hear from her room."

Sarah moved forward and sat on the end of the bed, as far away from him as possible. He sat back in his chair, rested one muscular calf on the knee of his other leg and waited. Even sitting there relaxed, smiling, the man radiated barely constrained violence.

Why the hell had she ever agreed to put herself in his power? She must have been insane not to see what he was the moment she met him on the bridge. Nathaniel had been a fluffy kitten in comparison to this man.

And she knew in that moment that she couldn't do it. She could not tell this monster what she had heard the friendly, innocent John and the kind-hearted Graeme talking about. If she did he would act against them, brutally and mercilessly, and she would never forgive herself. But she was here now. She had to tell him something.

"Are you going to tell me whatever it is before sunrise?" he said, interrupting her thoughts. "Because pretty as you are, I'm getting bored. I don't like being bored."

"I…I wanted to tell you something about Graeme," she stammered.

"Graeme. Good." Richard uncrossed his legs and sat forward. "Tell me then. Now," he added when she hesitated again.

"I was in the garden collecting eggs today and a beggar woman came to the side of the house and he gave her some vegetables," she said, the sentence coming out in a rush.

Surely he wouldn't do much to Graeme for giving away a few vegetables? Certainly not what he'd do if he knew the man supported Prince Charles.

"Is that it?" he asked after a moment.

"Yes," she said. "I thought you'd want to know that."

He stood so quickly that she had no time even to blink, let alone run. Then he had her by the throat, squeezing painfully, his face inches from hers. She lifted her hands and gripped his forearm, which was rock-hard with muscle.

"You've been here two weeks. Ten shillings, and all you've given me is that the gardener has given a few parsnips away? What else have you heard?"

"Nothing," she croaked. She tried to pull away from him, and his grip tightened. He smiled, and in that moment she believed he was going to kill her right now, and knew that he would enjoy doing it. She would have to tell him about the kitchen conversation, if she wanted to live.

The words were right on the end of her tongue, and she was praying that she would be able to actually speak around his iron grip so that he would let her go, when he suddenly pushed her back onto the bed, letting go of her neck so he could pull her skirts up roughly, throwing them over her face. Then he shoved her legs apart, pulled her forward so that she was on the edge of the bed, and still standing over her, entered her roughly. He pumped in and out of her, his fingers bruising the soft skin of her inner thighs as he held her in place.

She lay still, her face covered by her skirts, eyes closed tight against the pain, and waited until he pulled himself out of her and she heard the chair creak as he sat down again. Slowly she pushed her skirts down and sat up. He was sitting as he had been before, eyeing her speculatively, his half-erect penis still out of his breeches, resting on his thigh.

"I'm not spending five shillings a week just to fuck you," he said. "I can bring myself off for free, and get as much pleasure. Fucking you is like fucking a dead fish, except you don't smell quite as bad. Come on then, if you haven't got any information, while you're here you can at least show me some of your whore's tricks."

She moved forward off the bed, and kneeling in front of him proceeded to show him her 'whore's tricks', managing finally with her hands and mouth to make him come. She had never been so relieved in her life to bring a client to orgasm. Now he would let her go, surely?

He sat back and watched as she stood up and tidied her dress, then moved toward the door.

I'm giving you two more weeks to find something useful out," he said conversationally as her hand touched the door handle. "And if you don't, I'll make you really wish that you'd jumped off that bridge that night. Am I making myself clear?"

He was making himself very clear indeed.

"Yes," she said hoarsely.

"Get out."

She sat in her room shaking, tears rolling down her face, wondering what she was going to do, and knowing that she was too frightened and upset to make any reasonable decision right now. She washed herself, rinsed her mouth out, and looked at her neck in the small hand mirror she had. It was already darkening, and would be visibly bruised in the morning. But he had gripped her low on her neck and if she tied her kerchief carefully, she could hide it.

She undressed and went to bed. She would sleep, and in the morning, when the shock had passed and she was thinking properly, she would decide what to do.

* * *

Liverpool, November 1742

Kate was just stepping out of her coach at Robert's house when he appeared at the door, looking anxious.

As well he might, she thought. She had heard nothing from him for months and thought he had given up looking for Sarah, believing that Kate had not meant her threat to him. So she had sent him a little letter, one which could be read by anybody in the household, but which Robert would understand well.

And it had clearly had an effect, because just four weeks later she had received a message from him, telling her that he had some information that might relate to Sarah. As she herself had made enquiries in York, Lincoln, Lancaster and Derby and had come up with nothing at all, she was very excited, and on the journey north had had to remind herself forcefully not to get her hopes up too much.

By the time she arrived in Liverpool, having told her lover that she was going to visit her son for two days, as he had expressly forbidden her to keep searching for her daughter, she had managed to calm herself enough that the Kate Applewhite who was shown into the Grimes's drawing-room appeared completely serene.

"So," she said, after the maid had placed a tray of food and wine on the table and had left, "what have you told your wife?"

Robert immediately looked horror-struck, and Kate smiled.

"About the reason for my visit. I may see her, and if I do, I need to know what you have told her." She watched his face relax, just a little. He had got the implied threat then.

"I've told her that you are thinking of outfitting some more servants," he said.

"Good. Then that's what I shall tell her, if we meet. Now, what have you found out?"

Robert sat down on the edge of the chair opposite her.

"It isn't definite," he said, "but it's the first likely information I've had, from Manchester."

Manchester. Kate had already asked there, but of course that was before Sarah had left Liverpool, she realised.

"What is it?"

"A woman by the name of Mrs Pelman, who runs a bawdy house near the market place. She said she'd never heard of Sarah Browne, but when my man described her, she said it sounded like a girl who'd been there, but had now left, who'd called herself Ivy Smith."

"Ivy Smith. So why do you think that could be her, and not just the bawd hoping to get a reward?"

"Because my man asked if there was anything particular she remembered about her, and the woman said she always wore a silver heart-shaped locket." Seeing Kate's blank look, Robert added, somewhat shamefaced, "I gave one to Sarah at Christmas when we were…together. The woman volunteered the information, so she couldn't have known."

"She said Sarah had left. Did she say where she'd gone?"

"No, she said she didn't know, that she sneaked off in the

night. I didn't want to make any more enquiries because you told me you wanted to find her," Robert said.

"And of course you don't want to, do you?" Kate added.

Robert coloured violently.

"Kate, I'm really sorry for what happened," he said. "I would like to know she's safe and well. And I meant it when I said I would contribute financially."

Kate picked up a tiny pastry and popped it into her mouth, then licked her fingers. While she chewed she was thinking, coming to a decision. Then she looked across at him, enjoying how uncomfortable he looked.

"Give me all the details you have," she said. "I will go to Manchester myself and visit this Pelman woman. And if I find Sarah, be sure I will take you up on your offer of financial help. It's the very least she deserves."

* * *

"I already told your man what I know," the old bawd said, looking at the richly dressed woman standing on her step speculatively.

"Yes, I know what you told my man," Kate said. "But I want to hear it myself."

"Don't see why I should say it all again," Mrs Pelman replied.

"Perhaps because I want to hear it? After all, I've already paid for the information, haven't I? And because if you don't, you may well find that I'm not the only visitor you'll have who you'd like to keep on the step. They may be a little more forceful about entering your premises than I am, though."

"Are you threatening me?" Mrs Pelman asked indignantly. In the shadows behind her a man appeared. Kate glanced at him and smiled.

"Of course I am," she replied sweetly. "I'm glad we understand each other. Now, you said that the girl who worked for you might have been the one I'm looking for. Tell me why you think that."

"You're related, aren't you?" Mrs Pelman said. "You look like her. You her mother? Did she run off because you wanted to marry her to some decrepit old lord or something?"

It took every ounce of Kate's experience of hiding feelings not to show her excitement. A locket could be coincidence, but a physical resemblance *and* a locket was something else.

"Well now, it's kind of you to be concerned about Sarah's future, but that's not your business, is it? Tell me what you told my man, and if it's interesting I might reward you a little more."

Mrs Pelman told her what Robert already had. Nothing more, nothing less.

"And when did she leave?" Kate asked.

"Oh, a while ago now…cold it was. I'm not sure. Perhaps…"

Kate flicked a sovereign at her, which she caught deftly, bit, and then nodded before pocketing it.

"I want a damn sight more than the date for that," Kate said. "I want every detail about the day she left."

"It was October, the end of October. And she stole £20 when she went, she did," Mrs Pelman said. "Went off with a soldier, a captain she said he was, dark cove. I haven't seen her since. Probably gone off to the wars with him."

Kate thought for a second.

"Dark? You mean dark hair, dark skin? Did you get his name?"

Mrs Pelman shook her head. "No name, just his rank. Black hair, swarthy, dark heart as well, I'd say. Nasty piece of work. Probably wishes she'd married that old bastard you wanted her to now."

Kate smiled.

"Maybe she does. Did my man leave his contact details?"

"He did, said if I saw her to let him know. So, going to give me the £20 she stole off me?"

Kate laughed.

"How long did she work here?"

"Just over a year. Treated her good, I did."

"I reckon she'll have earned a lot more than £20 for you in a year. A hell of a lot more. No, I'm not going to give you the money you claim she stole from you, because I'm sure you stole a lot more than that from her. But I'm not going to make your life hell either. Yet. Thank you for the information and the warm welcome. Contact my man if you think of anything else. Good day to you."

Kate turned and walked back to the coach, waited for the coachman to lower the steps for her, then climbed in.

Back at the house, Mrs Pelman watched the coach disappear

up the road, spat on the step where her visitor had been standing a few moments before, and then went in, slamming the door behind her.

Kate sat in the coach, staring unseeingly at the scenery on the way to Alliston, thinking. The old bawd seemed to be telling the truth. She'd been indignant about the loss of the money, that was certain, and had no love for Sarah. That had been evident in her face. If Sarah had been able to take £20 without that hulk behind Mrs Pelman interfering, then this dark captain, whoever he was, must be pretty formidable.

"Dark heart as well," the bawd had said.

"Oh Sarah," Kate said out loud. "What have you done?"

If her daughter had become a soldier's wife or woman and gone off with him, she could be anywhere by now, in Britain, Europe or even further away, wherever he was. She would probably think it a better option than being a whore though. At least she'd only have to sleep with one man.

If she'd stolen from the bawd she definitely would never come back to Manchester, even if she survived the disease-ridden battlefields, survived giving birth to the dark captain's babies in primitive army conditions.

I have lost her, Kate thought brokenly. *Unless she goes back to Alliston, and why should she? I will never find her now, will never be able to tell her I'm sorry, never be able to give her the love she clearly so desperately needs.*

She reached up and pulled the leather curtain closed, and then she wept.

* * *

In the morning Sarah realised that Richard had given her two weeks to tell him something relevant. Which meant she had two weeks to make a decision, and really she had only three options to choose from. Either she could tell Richard about the conversation she'd overheard yesterday, or she could leave again, as she had from Liverpool, get on the first coach out of Manchester and go somewhere else, start again. Or she could go back to the bridge and jump off and have done with it.

She didn't have to decide now. She would enjoy two more

weeks of living in this house with good food and friendly people, and then she would decide whether to jump off the bridge or try one more time, in another town.

As soon as she got in the kitchen, she knew that something had changed. The servants did not change the conversation they were having to something neutral as they usually did when she arrived amongst them. Instead they stopped talking altogether, and she was faced with a wall of silence, which continued, punctuated only by necessary comments such as 'pass the butter, please', or 'would you like another slice?' until breakfast was over, and everyone got up and silently went to start their working day.

The only slight hint of concern any of them showed was when Sarah spoke and her voice was barely above a whisper. Grace asked if she had a sore throat and Sarah nodded, after which Jane said she would make double the soothing drink Mary was having, so she could have some.

Then Thomas told her to get a bucket of warm water and a scrubbing brush and clean the whole henhouse, inside and out, and put fresh straw in it, thereby ensuring that she was out of the house for the whole morning. After a silent lunch, Jane told her that Grace had collected the rugs from every room in the house, and as it was a dry day, Sarah could hang them over the washing line one at a time and beat them thoroughly to get all the dirt out.

And then she was told she could go to bed and get some rest, in the hope that her cold would not worsen.

"Make sure you go to your own room, though," Graeme said coldly. "You want me to show you where it is?"

Sarah blushed scarlet, shook her head, and went straight up to her room. It seemed that Elizabeth had decided not to give her another chance after all, but had told the servants straight away that she'd found her in her room.

There was a knock on the door, and when Sarah opened it Grace was standing there with a cup full of steaming liquid.

"Jane sent me with the drink for your throat," she said. "It's liquorice and honey, and should soothe your throat. Hopefully you won't get the cold Mary has. She's really unwell, poor mite."

Sarah thanked her earnestly, and sat on the bed, sipping it and thinking. She could not blame Elizabeth for warning the servants she was not to be trusted, but it seemed she had not told them to make her life a living hell after all, not yet anyway. If she had, they surely wouldn't be bringing her soothing drinks. Instead they were giving her jobs that kept her out of the house, and Graeme, who had warned her gently when she arrived that she would be accepted if she deserved to be, was now warning her less gently that she did not deserve to be, and why.

In fact Elizabeth had kept her word to the letter as she was wont to do, and had not told the servants that Sarah had been in her room at all, hoping that the warning she had given the maid would suffice. That and locking her bedroom door every time she was out of it.

It was Thomas who had told the servants what his wife had seen the night before as she had been coming downstairs from the attic room after tending Mary. As she had neared the landing she had heard the four soft knocks on the door, and Richard's voice. Quickly she had snuffed out the candle she was carrying, and after she had seen Sarah's outline against the lamplight in Richard's room as she'd gone in, she had tiptoed up to the door and listened.

The door was solid, and she could not hear what they were saying, but the voices had been soft enough until suddenly Richard's voice had raised slightly. And then she had heard the rhythmic creaking of the bedsprings, had tiptoed away and back to the room she shared with her husband, and had told him what she had seen and heard.

Judging it too important not to mention, Thomas had sent young Ben on an errand and then had told the adults that Sarah was at the least Richard's whore, and therefore if she was loyal to anyone at all, it was to him, and was almost certainly telling him anything they said or did.

* * *

Later that day, while Sarah was beating the rugs outside, Ben came to tell Graeme that Sergeant Cunningham wanted to see him in the study.

Richard was sitting behind the desk poring over the household accounts when Graeme entered without knocking. He carried on looking at the paperwork for a few moments, and when he finally looked up, the older man was standing looking down at him.

"Beth…Elizabeth used to do all the accounts," he commented casually. "I'm sure if you ask her she'll help you work them out."

A muscle twitched in the side of Richard's face, and he flushed.

"Sit down, Elliot," he said, gesturing to a chair.

"No, I'll stand, if it's all the same to you," Graeme answered. "My hips seize if I sit in a low chair like that. Rheumatism."

Richard was damned if he was going to look up at the old bastard for the whole interview. That would put him at a disadvantage. But if he stood up it would be obvious that he felt he needed to look down at the man to feel superior to him. The expression on the older man's face told Richard that he was fully aware of what he was thinking.

"I insist," he said tightly. Graeme shrugged and sat down on the low chair, then waited.

"I assume you're wondering why I've sent for you, Elliot," Richard began, after it became apparent the gardener wasn't going to ask.

"Not really, no," Graeme answered. "I assume you're going to tell me anyway. Be a bit pointless sending for me otherwise, wouldn't it?"

"It has come to my attention," Richard said authoritatively, "that you have been encouraging beggars, and what's more, have given my property away to them. This is stealing, and I am sure the authorities would take a very dim view of it."

"I've been doing that for years. I doubt the authorities would take a dim view of a servant obeying his mistress's orders. But you can ask them, if you want."

"Elizabeth is no longer the mistress here. I am now the master, and I give all the orders. You will cease giving my things away to filthy beggars immediately, or you will be very sorry. I will not tolerate theft from my own staff!" Richard shouted, cursing inwardly as his voice rose involuntarily on the last syllable, as it always did when he failed to intimidate the person he was threatening.

Graeme looked at him for a moment, his face calm.

"I wasn't referring to Elizabeth, but no matter," he said. "Next time she comes, the beggar that is, I'll tell Thomas to send her to you, if he's still here, that is. Is that all you wanted to talk to me about?"

"I'm quite sure you can tell the woman yourself, Elliot," Richard said. "I have more important things to do with my time than speak to vermin."

"Oh, I could tell her, if I was here," Graeme answered. "But I don't take kindly to being accused of theft, so I'll be leaving now. I daresay Thomas and Jane won't want to stay either, when I tell them."

"Leaving? If you think I will provide a character for you—"

And in any case," Graeme interrupted, to Richard's fury, "I think it only right that you should tell the woman who saved both your life and your mother's that you intend to let her starve to death. It's the very least you can do, I think. Now, if that was all, I'll go and pack. Do you want to supervise me?"

"What the hell are you talking about, man?" Richard said.

"I thought you might want to make sure I don't pack any parsnips or apples in with my belongings," Graeme replied, standing smoothly and obviously painlessly from the chair.

"Not that! About saving my life?"

"Ah. The beggar, Jennet, her name is, she was the midwife who delivered you. Very difficult birth it was, probably why your mother had no more children after you. Your father sent for the doctor, but he was away so Jennet came, and your father was very relieved, because she had a good reputation. Proved it that day, she did, saving you both. Twisted you were, inside your mother, you see. Of course I wasn't here then but your mother told me about her later. She told me that she'd promised always to look after the woman should she be in need, because she'd given her the son she so desperately wanted, and her own life to enjoy watching you grow." Graeme walked to the door. "It was your mother I was referring to when I said the mistress. Jennet's in need now, her mind is going, and she can't work any more. So I give her food when she needs it, as your mother wanted me to. Now, are you coming, or do you trust me to pack just what's mine?"

"She's spying on us," Graeme announced to Thomas and Jane when he walked into the kitchen five minutes later.

He sat down and told them what had just happened in the study, and how he'd thoroughly enjoyed watching Richard splutter and backtrack, telling Graeme he hadn't known that the beggar had been the midwife, and if he had he would have taken a different approach entirely, and of course he didn't want the gardener to leave.

"No, of course he doesn't," Jane said. "No one can grow plants like you can. It's a God-given talent you have."

"That's not why the jumped-up puppy doesn't want me to leave," Graeme said. "It's because he knows that if I do I'll tell everyone what a shit he is – sorry, Jane – and because he wants to keep me here hoping he'll get a better chance to lord it over me. Because all he did today was make himself look stupid, and we both know that."

"Would you really have left?" Thomas asked.

"Not while Beth's here, no. No more than you two will. But the three of us agreed to stand together, so I told him you two would probably leave as well. He won't want his three senior servants leaving together, drop him right in the sh…brown stuff, that would. I won't leave while Beth needs me. But he doesn't know that, and I'm not going to tell him."

"Are you sure Sarah told him?" Jane asked. "He might have seen Jennet from the window. I don't like the girl, and I know she's sleeping with him, but I don't want to accuse her unjustly."

"She must have done. Jennet always comes through from the fields, because she doesn't want anyone to know that she's having to beg for her food. She's losing her mind, but not her pride. No one would have been able to see her from the house. But Sarah was there collecting eggs, and saw me giving her some stuff."

"Well, we can't get rid of her, not if Richard wants her here, so we'll just have to make sure we don't say or do anything in front of her that she can report," Thomas said.

"Don't say anything at all, like we did this morning," Jane suggested. "I'll tell the others, John especially. He's hot-headed enough to slip and get himself into trouble. Maybe she'll leave anyway then, if we make her feel really unwelcome."

* * *

The pattern of silence and tasks which either got Sarah out of the house or ensured she was closely supervised continued for two more days, and she was offered no more soothing drinks. In fact, apart from telling her her chores for the day, no one spoke to her at all, not even a good morning. They didn't even look at her. It was horrible.

So it was something of a surprise when on the third day she was just heading downstairs when Elizabeth came out of her room and told Sarah she wanted to have a word with her.

Expecting to be fired, Sarah was surprised when the mistress asked her how her throat was, in a tone which sounded genuinely caring.

"It's much better, thank you, Miss," Sarah replied gratefully.

Elizabeth smiled.

"Good," she said. "Then I'm sure you'll be well enough to go into town."

"Yes," Sarah said. "What do you want me to do there?"

"Anything you want," Elizabeth replied. "Richard has gone out, but he told me to say you could have the day off, as you've been here for over two weeks now, and he asked me to give you a shilling to spend in Manchester." She held out the silver coin, which Sarah looked at with utter shock.

There was no way that the Richard she had experienced so far would even think about days off after two weeks, not ever in fact, let alone volunteer a shilling for her to spend. This must be Elizabeth's idea.

Sarah looked at her and smiled warmly, genuinely touched by the kind gesture, especially after two days of silent hostility.

"Thank you!" she said. "That's very kind of you…I mean of Richard. When do you want me back?"

"If you come back just before dark, say about four o'clock? Then you'll be home in time to serve us dinner," Beth replied.

Much later Sarah was to realise that Elizabeth had not merely been being kind, but had wanted her out of the way, although it was a very long time before she found out what had actually happened that day.

But at that point she was just happy to get away from this house in which she was so clearly despised. She was used to having no friends, even to being alone, but having to be with people who were making it very clear that they hated her, and with good reason, was much more difficult.

She would go into town and look at that empty shop again, if it was still empty, and see if the notice in the window said how much the rent would be. And she would go to the tavern and find out when the coaches left, where they went to, and how much the fare was. Because she had made her decision now. No matter how cold the servants were to her, she could not give that bastard any more power over them than he already had. Next week she would leave. And she would not do it by jumping off the bridge. She realised now that she had been going to do that not because she wanted to die, but in a fit of despair. Richard was evil, no doubt about that, but at least he had saved her life by talking to her, giving her purpose.

She was eighteen, still young. She would go to another town, be a whore again if necessary, and would try once more to save enough. It was stupid to kill yourself *before* you were poxed or on the streets. There were always bridges, always rivers, if it came to it.

Hopefully it would not come to it. But if it did, it was comforting to know there was a way out, if life truly became unbearable. Just knowing that made it possible to bear much more.

* * *

In the end she had a pleasant day.

The first thing she did was to go and look at the property that was still for rent, because it was on the corner of the street Mrs Pelman lived on, but it was still early so she was unlikely to meet any of the girls as they would still be in bed. She wanted to enjoy her day if possible, and having what would be at least a difficult conversation with any of the girls would spoil that.

She read the notice in the door, slowly. If she'd got it right, then the rent was five shillings a week, unfurnished. It had a nice big window, which would give her plenty of light once it was cleaned, and would save on the cost of candles. She rubbed at one of the small panes to clean it, and peered inside. It had a reasonable-sized room with a counter along one side and a door at the back, which presumably led to another room, probably a store room, but it might be big enough for her to live in. The notice said two rooms, but not the size of them both. Clearly it wasn't meant for her to live in, but that didn't mean she couldn't. If the second room was really tiny, then she could sleep in the shop room on a mattress and put it away in the store room each morning.

It was on a street corner, which was good because more potential customers would pass it. But it was closer to Mrs Pelman's than she would have liked. What could the bawd do, though? She hadn't stolen anything at all. If anything Mrs Pelman had stolen from her, because she owed her a year's wages.

She was not a whore any more, or rather wouldn't be once she'd escaped Richard, so if the old bawd sent Peter round to threaten her she could call the authorities, as she'd be a respectable businesswoman then. She didn't need to waste money paying for a coach to leave Manchester, start all over again. She was sick of that. She liked it here, knew her way around now, knew a lot of the whores too. She could offer them her services cheaply, get some practice in dressing hair and applying cosmetics. She hoped for a more respectable clientele than whores, but she had to start somewhere, and could work up from there.

Even the thought of the words 'respectable businesswoman' applying to her made her smile. So £1 a month rent, and then she'd have to spend a considerable amount buying furniture and equipment, making the place look inviting, which would cut a great hole in her savings. She wouldn't have much time to settle in before she'd have to start earning. But it was possible. What had seemed impossible was now attainable, and in the not too distant future!

She did spend a little of the shilling Beth had given her, buying herself a meal so that when she got home she wouldn't have to suffer sitting through a silent hostile meal with the others. She could serve dinner to Richard and Elizabeth, and then do whatever other solitary chores they found for her.

Whilst eating she thought. She had £20, and if she left at the end of the month, Richard would owe her £1 wages. She didn't think that she could get away with staying another month without telling him anything about the servants; it wasn't worth trying, because he was frightening enough now. She had no desire to experience what he would be like if she really angered him.

On the table that she was sitting at was a business card for a

THE WHORE'S TALE: SARAH

woman who altered clothes to fit. Sarah picked it up and looked at it, then pocketed it. She didn't have any clothes that needed altering, but it made her think. Before she'd gone to Mrs Pelman's she'd rented two nice rooms for just two shillings a week. Maybe she could do that instead of renting a whole shop, could buy some hair and wig dressing equipment, and then could have cards printed, offering her services either in the client's own house or in one of her two rooms. Then she could establish herself, and save some more until she had enough to rent a shop.

Walking back to the house at Didsbury in the afternoon, she actually felt happy for the first time in a long, long time. It was lovely to have a possible future, a bright future even. If she held on to that, she could deal with the next couple of weeks. She had already dealt with so much in her life. She was not about to let a brutal soldier and a bunch of disapproving servants destroy her now.

* * *

She got back just before dark, and ran upstairs to tidy herself up before going down to serve Richard and Elizabeth their dinner. When she walked into the kitchen, Jane told her that Sergeant Cunningham had decided to dine a little earlier than normal, so she had served the first course of broth, but Sarah could take over now.

She walked across to the dining room slowly, carrying a heavy tray with several silver dishes on, wondering why Jane looked so flustered. Maybe the food hadn't been ready when Richard announced he wanted to eat early, and he had told her off.

She knocked on the dining room door and then walked in. There were two places set, but only one person at the table. Sarah laid out the dishes as she'd been taught, and then passed each one to Sergeant Cunningham as he asked for it, and poured him a glass of claret. She wondered whether to ask if Miss Elizabeth was going to join him later, but some instinct told her not to draw any more attention to herself than she had to. He was smiling to himself as he ate, a happy smile. A cruel happy smile.

Standing at the wall, waiting for him to tell her he wanted more of something, she looked at him and realised that she hated him, every bit as much as she hated her father, even though her father had made her life miserable for years, and this man had only done it for a couple of weeks. He raised his hand suddenly, beckoning her, and she schooled her face into neutrality, moving forward.

"I'm ready for dessert now," he said, reaching across and pouring more wine himself. Her heart plummeted as she realised she should have noticed his glass was empty and offered to pour more for him. Should she apologise or would that just draw his attention to her blunder? If she didn't apologise though, he might be angry that she hadn't. Oh God.

"Go!" he said, and she shot from the room, hating herself for being so afraid of him, for giving him power over her, even if only for a short while.

She went down the corridor and into the kitchen.

"The master is ready for dessert," she announced as she walked in, and then stopped, confused.

All the servants were there now, except for John, and all of them were sitting around the table, looking at Elizabeth with worried expressions. Thomas was leaning across the table holding a drink out towards her.

The mistress of the house was sitting on the gardener's knee, half-lying across it, in fact. Her face was white as a sheet, except for a darkening mark across one side of it.

There was a frozen moment, and then everyone except Elizabeth looked at Sarah, who was standing open-mouthed in the doorway. Jane leapt up and shot across to the stove, cutting a large slice from a suet pudding that was steaming there and slopping it carelessly into a bowl. She ladled cream onto it, then turned to Sarah.

"You may take the rest of the evening off and go to your room, Sarah," she said.

"But the master—" she began.

"I will take his dessert to him. Go to your room. I will see you in the morning."

Sarah wanted to ask what was wrong, how the mistress had been injured, but of course she knew that she would receive no answer if she did. She could at least take the pudding to Richard though, and leave Jane to tend to Elizabeth.

"But—" she began.

Thomas stood and turned, his hand raised, his face like thunder.

"Are you offering to disobey my wife, girl?" he roared.

Sarah turned and ran, going straight upstairs to her room, shutting the door and standing with her back to it. There was something seriously wrong, that was clear. It seemed that someone had attacked Elizabeth, and, thinking about Richard's happy expression in the dining room, she would confidently have bet all her savings that he had been the assailant.

Her father had hit her to try to make her be what he wanted her to be, to bring her to God. Nathaniel had hit her because he wanted to live off her earnings.

But Richard hit people because it gave him pleasure. He needed no other reason than that, she realised. He was insane.

She took the little wooden chair and jammed it under the handle of her door, aware that it would not stop him if he wanted to get in her room. He had not come to her room yet, but if he wanted to, he could. He was the master. And if he could hit his sister, who had the support of everyone in the house, what could he do to her, who had the hatred of everyone in the house? If she screamed for help, would they come? Or would they not think it worth risking his wrath to help her?

She had to leave. She could not wait two weeks. It was Thursday today. She would stay until the end of the week, and then would leave on Sunday. No, Monday, because then she would be more likely to find empty rooms to rent immediately, because people usually paid rent weekly and so would leave on Sunday. Otherwise she'd have to take a room in a tavern for a few days, which would eat into her savings. And she was not sure that Richard would pay her for the time she'd worked here, so she might as well eat as much as she could over the next few days.

CHAPTER TWENTY

The next day when Sarah came downstairs for breakfast, everyone behaved as though nothing untoward had happened the night before. They were all completely silent, as they had been for the last few days, and after breakfast Jane said that Miss Elizabeth had gone out early and Sergeant Cunningham had stated he'd have a cold lunch in the library, where he intended to spend the day. This meant that she didn't need to cook until the evening, and as Mary was now back on kitchen duty, albeit still sniffly, Sarah could start her cleaning duties in the rest of the house.

"Come with me, and I'll show you what to do in the drawing room," Jane said.

"I'll go and start in the stable," Graeme commented, before standing up and leaving by the back door.

The two women went across to the drawing room armed with cleaning equipment, and Jane told her what she had to do, watching closely as Sarah laid the fire, dusted, waxed the wooden furniture, swept then scrubbed the floor, and plumped up cushions.

"Good," Jane said finally. "I can tell you're used to cleaning tasks. You don't need to clean out candle holders or replace the candles – that's one of Ben's jobs. Tomorrow you can get up early and start laying the fires in most of the rooms, and then cleaning them after breakfast. Let me make it clear; you do not need to go into any cupboards or drawers. I will check on you every so often, and if I find you doing anything you shouldn't be doing, you'll be sorry."

Sarah flushed scarlet.

"I won't," she said. "I promise I won't."

THE WHORE'S TALE: SARAH

Of course Jane couldn't know how sacred Sarah considered her promises to be, but she felt better just having made it. She was done with spying. Jane nodded.

"Well, I'll leave you to it," she said. "Don't go in the library, but you can do the rest of this floor, and after lunch the unoccupied bedrooms."

It was a relief to be on her own, not to have Jane watching her every move. She carried on, cleaning the windows, wiping down the surfaces, her mind wandering to her future, the one she'd dreamed of for so long, that was coming, soon. Nothing would stop her now, even if she had to start with just the £20 she had at the moment. She was done with whoring and spying, and feeling constantly ashamed of herself.

At dinner she broke the silence by asking if John was ill, and if that was why Graeme was working in the stables. This was greeted by an intensely uncomfortable moment, after which Thomas said, "John left yesterday. Graeme hasn't got as much to do in the garden now, it being winter, so he'll do the stables for now."

His tone made it very clear that that was all she needed to know, and all he was going to say about yesterday, so she decided not to ask if Miss Elizabeth was recovered now. She genuinely cared – Elizabeth had been kind to her - but they would not see it that way. Their opinion of her was set now, and she couldn't blame them for that. It didn't matter, she told herself fiercely. Two more days, and then she never had to see any of them again.

As she went upstairs that night, Richard was waiting for her on the landing. She curtsied then tried to walk past him, but he gripped her arm to stop her.

"What did the servants say today about the situation with John?" he asked.

"He left yesterday," she replied.

"I know that, you idiot," he said. "I dismissed him. What did they say about it?"

"Nothing. I asked where he was and they just said he'd left, and that Graeme would do the stables for now."

"You expect me to believe that's all they said?" Richard growled. His fingers were pressing into her arm painfully, but with an effort she managed not to show that he was hurting her. She didn't want to give him even that much pleasure.

"I can't make you believe it, but it *is* all they said to me," she replied, looking him straight in the eye so he would see she was telling the truth. He locked eyes with her for a few endless moments, and then he looked up the stairs towards her room, as if memorising where it was.

"Go to bed then," he said. "But remember what I said the other day. If you don't come up with something soon, something better than beggars and vegetables, I'll take you back to where I found you and throw you off the bridge myself."

He let her go and turned abruptly, heading to his room.

She carried on upstairs to bed, putting the chair under the door knob again.

Two more days.

* * *

The next night she was exhausted, after working for sixteen hours. In the morning Jane had told her that the laundress who usually came to the house once a week had just had a child, and so she had to help with the washing this week. Of course she'd been given the solitary task of fetching first the wood for the copper boiler fire, and then endless buckets of water from the well, while Jane, Grace and Mary laughed and chatted together as they did the washing, except when she was in the room, when they had all fallen silent.

In the evening Jane had brought a meal outside for Sarah, who was wringing out all the smaller items and leaving them out to dry, and she had eaten it sitting outside near the hen house, shivering, because although the weather was dry it was cold, and her clothes were damp from the combination of sweat and laundry water, so once she stopped working she grew cold very quickly.

She knew why Jane had brought her meal outside. It was because Elizabeth was eating in the kitchen with the other servants and they wanted to talk together, which meant Sarah could not be there.

She had never felt so lonely. It was one thing being tolerated, she was used to that, but being very actively despised by a whole household of people she liked was a completely different thing, especially when she deserved their hatred. *To hell with it,* she thought, *I'll leave tomorrow. It will be worth paying for a room for a night or two not to have to feel like a leper.*

She fell asleep the moment her head hit the pillow that night. At some point in the middle of the night there was an infernal screech which woke her up, heart banging. It sounded as though it had come from inside the house, but she sat listening for a time and heard nothing more, so thought it must have been an owl or something outside after all. She lay down and fell asleep again immediately.

She had no idea how long it was before she was woken again, whether a few minutes or hours. All she knew was that one minute she was having a vivid dream in which she was a mouse cowering in a field while overhead a huge owl shrieked, flying so close that the shadow of its wings passed over her blotting out the sunlight, and then she was awake, still wondering why an owl was hunting in the daylight.

She opened her eyes and realised that the sunlight of her dream was in fact the light of a candle held by Richard, who was standing at the side of her bed looking down at her. Still half in the dream, she was tempted to lie very still, pretend to be asleep, hoping he would fly over her and disappear. But of course that was ridiculous, because he was not an owl, and he would have seen her open her eyes and know she was not asleep.

He had never come to her room before, but the fact that he had now, in the middle of the night wearing just a shirt, could only mean one thing.

She turned her head to look up at him, and he bent down, putting the candle in its holder on the chair at the side of the bed. He straightened up again then, but in that moment when his face had been almost on a level with hers, the light shining directly on it, she had known there was something wrong with him. His face was deathly pale, almost greenish in colour, his dark hair tousled and loose.

Well, whatever had happened there was only one sort of comfort he would want from her, and his prick was almost level with her face as he stood. The quicker she could satisfy him, the quicker he would leave and let her go back to sleep. She was very tired. She pushed back the blankets, freed her arms and reaching across lifted his shirt with one hand and took his balls gently in the other, lifting her head ready to lean across and take him in her mouth.

His reaction to her touching him was completely unexpected. Instead of standing silently while she serviced him as he normally did, he gave an agonised cry and then swung his fist, hitting her so hard in the side of the head that she saw stars. Before she could react at all he leaned down over the bed, grabbed her still bruised throat and raised her into a sitting position before banging her head hard on the wall.

She had no idea why he was so enraged with her, but looking at his face, which was twisted with blind hatred as he lifted her out of bed by her neck, she knew that if she did not defend herself somehow, he would either kill her or do her serious injury.

She reached up, gripping his arm with both of hers, and with the strength of desperation managed to break his grip on her throat, falling out of bed and landing on the floor at his feet. She shook her head trying to clear her dizziness, and then attempted to stand, but as she did he lifted his knee, catching her in the mouth, and then gripping a handful of her hair he pulled her upright before driving his fist into her stomach with all his strength.

Winded, she doubled up and he let her go, so she fell onto the floor again curled up, her mouth opening and closing silently as she forgot everything except the desperate need to get some air into her lungs. She lay there, making gasping sounds as she pulled tiny sips of air in, aware that he was standing over her, watching, and that if he wanted to kill her he could do so easily, because he was far too strong for her to fight, and there was nothing, nothing she could do to stop him.

For a long moment he watched her, standing over her while she gasped, writhed and retched at his feet and then suddenly he turned and walked out of the room, closing the door behind him. Never in her life had she felt such relief.

She lay there until she could finally draw enough breath into her lungs to take shallow gasps, and then very slowly she climbed back into bed, unable to do any more than that. She lay on her side, curled in a ball, vivid waves of pain washing over her, the flame from the candle flickering and casting shadows round the room.

She should have shouted for help right at the start while she was able to, she thought, but then realised that even if she had no one would have come to her aid. They hated her, would have probably laid there thinking that she was only getting what she deserved.

God, she was so unhappy. She had not felt this bereft since she had been locked in the cellar for a week and Philip had not come to her aid, had not even whispered words of comfort through the door.

But it's different now, she told herself. *I'm not locked in. I can leave. I will leave. Tomorrow, in the morning, I will leave. But tonight I must put the chair behind the door so he can't come back and finish what he started.*

She tried to move but the pain when she did was unbearable, and this time when the blackness came she welcomed it.

* * *

She woke to a knocking on the door, but before she could try to answer, it opened and Mary's head popped round.

"Jane sent me up to wake you," she said. "You're late, and it's time for breakfast."

"I'm sorry," Sarah mumbled thickly, without moving. "I'm ill."

"Have you got what I had? Made me feel horrible, it did. Shall I open the shutters? It's very dark in here."

"No," Sarah croaked. She had no idea what she looked like, but it must be terrible. She could not let the little girl see her like this. "Headache," she said desperately. "Terrible headache. Light will kill me. Leave me alone. Please."

Halfway to the window, Mary stopped.

"All right then. You sound awful. I'll tell Jane you're ill. Do you want me to bring something up for you to eat?"

"No," Sarah said. This was the most conversation she'd had with anyone in the household for days, and just when it hurt terribly to speak. "Go away," she said, not wanting to sound rude, but needing to be alone.

After the scullery maid had gone, closing the door quietly behind her, Sarah lay there in the dark, trying to assess the damage. Her throat was hurting badly again, much worse than last time Richard had hurt her. She couldn't open her right eye at all, and when she touched it gently, she could feel that it was very swollen. The side of her face was stuck to the pillow with blood, which was probably from her mouth which was also swollen, and cut. Her nose was unharmed, but when she tried to straighten her legs the pain in her stomach was excruciating, making her gasp, and causing lights to flicker at the side of her vision.

She decided to lie there for a little while longer, and then she would get up very slowly, and open the shutters, after which she'd wash the blood away from her face and see what she looked like. She lay there, realising that she couldn't leave the house today. Just getting out of bed was going to be an enormous undertaking, and even if she was capable of leaving, if her face looked half as bad as it felt no respectable landlord would rent rooms to her, or give her a tavern room if he thought she was some brawling hussy, or had a violent husband or lover who might come looking for her and smash the property up.

Very slowly, inch by inch she straightened her legs, breathing with the pain. In a minute, she decided, she would sit up, very slowly.

The door opened suddenly and someone came in, stopping just inside the room.

"Sarah?" Elizabeth said softly.

Sarah froze, and didn't answer. Maybe if she stayed silent the mistress would think she was asleep, and would go away.

The mistress did not go away. Instead she walked over to the window and started undoing the latch of the shutters.

"Please don't open them, Miss Elizabeth," Sarah croaked desperately. "My head's aching something awful."

The mistress paid no attention at all, and flung open the shutters so that light flooded into the room. Before she could turn round, Sarah pulled the sheet up over her head, thinking only that she could not let Elizabeth see her yet, not until she knew how bad she looked, had cleaned herself up, come up with an excuse, although what that could be she had no idea. She felt the bed sink at the side as the other woman sat down, and then the sheet was gently pulled. Sarah tightened her grip.

She heard a sigh and then the hand moved away, but Elizabeth didn't get up.

"Sarah," she said after a minute. "You know that I did not

approve of your appointment. I'm sure you also know that the rest of the staff do not approve of you either. I know that when my brother employed you he expected you to provide other services for him in addition to the duties expected of a house maid. I have no doubt he also asked you to spy on me and the servants and to report back anything of interest. I do not like you, I will be honest. But I do not blame you for seeking to improve your life, either."

She stopped for a minute, and Sarah lay there, stunned both by Elizabeth's honesty and by the final sentence, the understanding. She had not expected that.

"Last night," Elizabeth continued a moment later, "Richard and I had an argument. When he left me he was extremely angry. I suspect that he's taken that anger out on you. I need to know, and I will not leave this room until I do. I'm not annoyed with you. If you have a headache, I will send Mary up with some willow-bark tea. If you are injured I must know."

Sarah felt the other woman move off the bed, but did not hear her walk across the room. She must be standing, waiting for Sarah to respond. This was not the fragile, passive sister that Richard had described to her. Nothing that she had seen about Elizabeth in the last weeks was fragile apart from her delicate beauty. If anyone could help her break from Richard, help her get out of this house, it was this woman.

Sarah made a decision to trust her, and prayed that she would not be betrayed this time, as she had been so many times in her life. Very slowly she lowered the sheet, exposing her face and shoulders to Elizabeth's gaze, and knew by the expression that crossed the other woman's face and the involuntary gasp, that she must look absolutely dreadful.

"Tell me what happened, Sarah," she said, very softly.

"I didn't do anything, Miss Elizabeth, I swear it," Sarah said fervently, her voice rasping and painful. "I...he...came to my room. You were right, he does want me sometimes but not often. I could see he was angry and I tried to...console him. He just went mad. I don't know what I did wrong. I thought he was going to kill me." She felt a tear slide down her cheek and reached up, brushing it very gently away.

"Do you have any more injuries, Sarah?" the mistress asked.

"He hit me in the belly, Miss, but not very hard," Sarah lied. "It's just a bit sore. I'll be fine in a day or so."

To her utter surprise Elizabeth came round to the side of the bed, sat down and took her hand, very gently. She had gloves on, which was strange. She never wore gloves in the house.

"I will ask Grace to come and tend you. She has a very gentle hand. You cannot stay here. You must leave as soon as you are well again. I'm not dismissing you. You did nothing wrong last night. He was angry with me, not you. But you must know him for what he is, Sarah. He's a bully, and he enjoys hurting people. You cannot still want to stay here, after this."

She didn't. That was the last thing she wanted to do. But she could not leave here yet, could not afford to spend her precious savings lying in a room until she was healed, if she could get a room at all, that was. She had only half of what she thought she'd need to start a business. Every penny was precious.

"He's no worse than many others I've known, Miss," she said desperately, "and better than some. At least I've got a place to sleep at night and plenty of food. I'll be fine. Please don't make him dismiss me."

"Richard will not be here for much longer, Sarah," Elizabeth replied, letting go of Sarah's hand and standing up. "Many things are going to change soon. I have no idea what promises he's made to you, but whatever they are, he's lying. He seeks to move up in the world and will discard you without a thought as soon as it suits him. Be realistic. You have no friends among the servants. Once he's gone, they'll force you to leave. I know them, they're my friends and do not suffer spies gladly."

Sarah was about to tell her the truth, all of it, and that she would only stay for a few days, until she was well enough to leave and then she would never bother her again, but before she could open her mouth Elizabeth carried on.

"I will promise you something, but you must give me something in return," she said. "While I'm here, I'll do my utmost to make sure Richard doesn't hurt you again. I will also ensure that he gives you a reasonable sum of money when you leave, enough for you to leave the area and maybe make a new start. I will be honest with you," she added, "we are not rich, but I will do the best I can for you. In return I ask you not to report back to him anything the servants may say about him. Or anything else, for that matter."

"That won't be hard, Miss," Sarah said, smiling at the kindness of the mistress's words, and wincing as her lip cracked open. "They hardly speak a word when I'm around. I hate being with them, but he told me I have to spend as much time with them as I can. He'll be angry if I don't."

"No he won't," Elizabeth responded. "I will be giving him some very good news when he gets back. You can spend as much time as you want in your room. He's vented his anger on you now, and I don't think he'll be fit enough to require your other services for some days. Now I will go downstairs. I'll send Grace up to you later. Try to rest until then."

After she'd gone, Sarah lay there, thinking. Elizabeth genuinely seemed to care about her, even though she had no reason to. Why? Why would anyone care for someone who'd been employed to spy on them and their friends? She had promised to protect her against that brute of a brother of hers, and had offered her money too. For no reason, no reason at all. Why would she do that? Why not just get Graeme or Thomas to come to her room, pick her up and throw her bodily out into the street?

She was either a truly wonderful human being, or a very good liar. Sarah lay for a while trying to work out which it was, but could not decide. All she knew was that her life experience made her think that the latter was more likely to be the case, so she had better get well as fast as she could.

She managed to get up, and by the time Grace appeared she had washed the blood from her face, bathed her black and swollen eye with cold water, and was sitting on the wooden chair with a blanket wrapped round her, letting her stomach pain subside before she attempted to light the fire.

"Beth...Elizabeth sent me," Grace said, coming into the room and eyeing Sarah's ruined face. She didn't gasp or look horrified, so Sarah guessed that Elizabeth must have described her injuries pretty comprehensively to the staff. "I brought some parsley leaves for you to put on your eye and mouth. It will help to stop the bruising. I think you'll need some for your neck too. It must be very painful. And Jane made some willow-bark tea with honey, for the pain."

Her voice was so gentle and she sounded so genuinely concerned, that to her horror Sarah started crying and couldn't stop herself, even though it hurt her both physically and emotionally.

"Oh now, all will be well, really," Grace said, kneeling by the side of the chair and gently putting her arm round Sarah's shoulders. "Drink the tea while I make up the fire for you, and then I'll make a poultice for your bruising. Come, stop crying now. Beth told us what happened, and we are all sorry about it. She said you can stay here until you're well, and we will take care of you, so you have nothing to cry about."

"I'll leave, as soon as I'm able to," Sarah said.

"Yes," Grace replied. "It's better that way, I think."

With a superhuman effort Sarah swallowed back the tears, and sipped her tea while Grace tended the fire and made the poultice. She tilted her head back to let the warm dressing soothe her eye, and Grace made to leave, saying she'd come back later.

"Grace," Sarah said, as the maid reached the door. "She made me promises. Elizabeth, that is."

Grace stopped and turned back.

"If she made you promises, then she'll keep them," she said. "Beth always keeps her promises. I think maybe you haven't met many people you can trust, but you can trust her."

Was it that obvious? Sarah swallowed hard, wanting to trust Elizabeth, wanting to believe Grace, but finding it impossible to. She couldn't say that, of course, but there was something she could say, something she *had* to say.

"Please, tell the others I'm sorry. I'll tell them myself when I can get downstairs, but I want you all to know I'm sorry for what I've done."

"I will," Grace said simply, and left.

* * *

She stayed in her room for the next two days, and either Grace or Mary came up every few hours to check on her, bringing her food, soothing drinks or herbal poultices. Sarah took the time to plan, deciding that she would definitely take a couple of normal rooms at the start rather than go to the expense of a shop, and would have business cards made, which surely wouldn't be too expensive. She had to try. She was finished with whoring, with doing disgusting things to please disgusting people.

On the Wednesday she could finally stand straight, although it hurt her to do it. Her face was a horror, purple and black and still swollen, although she could now open her eye, the white of which was blood red. She washed and dressed slowly, aware that it must be a nuisance to the others to have to run up and downstairs fetching for her. They must be run off their feet, with John gone and now her not working too. The least she could do, she thought, was to go down to the kitchen and see if she could help in some way. She could peel vegetables if she sat down to do it, or maybe do some sewing.

She had just finished dressing when Elizabeth came up to see her, smiling when she saw Sarah was dressed.

"Are you feeling better, or do you just want to come downstairs for some company?" she asked.

"No, Miss, I'm used to being on my own," Sarah replied, then flushed, realising how self-pitying that sounded. "I thought if I go downstairs I might be able to do something, some light job maybe." Aware that it would be rude to sit down in front of the mistress without being invited to, she gripped the back of the chair against the pain of standing, and Elizabeth noticed instantly.

"Sit down," she said, taking Sarah's elbow and helping her, before sitting on the edge of the table. "I came up to see how you are, but I also brought your character, which Richard has signed. I wrote it though. I haven't sealed it yet, because I thought you might want to read it yourself." She handed over the paper and Sarah took it, glanced at it, then looked up again.

"Thank you, Miss Elizabeth," she said.

"Read it and if there's anything you don't agree with, let me know and I can scratch it out and change it." There was a slight pause, during which Sarah reddened. "I'm sorry, Sarah," Elizabeth added. "All the servants here can read, so I didn't think...my father taught them. Do you want me to read it to you?"

"I can read, Miss," Sarah said. "Or at least I can read printed books, slowly. I've been teaching myself. But handwriting letters look different, and I don't know them as well. I could read it, but it'll take me some time."

Elizabeth took the paper back and read it aloud to her. When she finished, Sarah was silent for a minute, looking at her in amazement. It was glowing. She was honest, hard-working, a quick learner, would be a credit to any establishment.

"Richard signed that?" she asked finally.

"Richard would sign his soul away right now if I asked him to," Elizabeth said enigmatically. "He gave me £21 for you too. A pound is for the wages he owes you, and the rest is an apology for hurting you. You can leave whenever you want to, but don't go until you feel well enough."

Elizabeth was not wearing gloves today, and both her wrists were badly bruised.

"Did John do that?" Sarah asked. "Is that why Richard dismissed him?"

Elizabeth looked down at her wrists.

"No," she said. "John's a sweet, kind boy, always has been. He would never hurt anyone. He left for a different reason."

Sarah's eyes widened.

"Did Richard do—?"

"I'll help you downstairs if you want," Elizabeth interrupted. "Richard is in the library, so you might want to keep away from there. But he won't hurt you again, I'm sure of it. Tomorrow we'll both be out all day, visiting our aristocratic cousins, and if that goes well, then he will forget about you, which I think you want, yes?"

"Yes," Sarah agreed instantly, and Elizabeth laughed, a beautiful silvery laugh. "I can style your hair for you, Miss, if you like," she added, "to say thank you. Unless Grace does it for you?"

"No she doesn't. She can make it neat, but I usually do it myself. I don't normally need anyone to style my hair," Elizabeth said somewhat needlessly, as Sarah had never seen her with it in anything other than an untidy braid. Her beauty was incredible, and yet she didn't seem to care at all about it, not even be aware of how breathtaking she was. "You can style hair?"

"My uncle was a wig maker," Sarah said. "He told me I had a natural ability and was going to give me a job, but he died. You have the most beautiful hair I've ever seen. I would love to dress it for you, if you want me to."

"That's very kind of you," Elizabeth said. "God knows I'm

going to need all the help I can get tomorrow."

She did not elaborate on that comment, instead helping Sarah slowly down the stairs before disappearing.

Sarah sat in the kitchen peeling potatoes and carrots, while Jane and Mary bustled about around her and Grace sat by the fire mending a small tear in the yellow silk dress Miss Elizabeth would be wearing tomorrow, it seemed. Unlike the last time Sarah had been among them, they now talked together, although the conversation was still careful, stilted. Sarah hardly heard it though, being so amazed by the fact that she was going to leave with an extra £21. She had worked here for a month and was leaving with the same amount as it had taken her two years to save at Mother Augustus'. She couldn't believe it.

Later, when Mary said she needed eggs, Sarah offered to go, saying it was about time she got some fresh air. She would walk around the garden a little, try to ascertain how much she could do.

She rounded the side of the house, walking very slowly, and then stopped. Standing at the fence next to the hen house were Elizabeth and Graeme. They were standing very close together, Elizabeth talking animatedly, although Sarah could hear nothing, didn't want to hear what was clearly a private conversation. Then suddenly Graeme reached across and enfolded the mistress in his arms, in a gesture so tender that it brought tears to Sarah's eyes.

She stood, transfixed. In her whole life no one had ever held her with such genuine warmth. Maybe her mother had, but if so she couldn't remember it. Robert had held her in a similar way but it had not been genuine, she knew that now. This clearly was, and showed that regardless of social status the two shared a deep bond.

Elizabeth wrapped her arms round his back and clung to him, and Graeme bent his head, kissed the top of her head and said something before looking up, straight at Sarah.

She turned immediately and went back in.

"I thought you were going for the eggs," Thomas remarked, looking at the empty basket.

"Oh, er...I thought I'd wait a minute," she said. "It's colder than I thought. I'll go and get my shawl and go back out."

Thomas looked at her curiously, then went to the scullery

window and glanced out, before looking back. Then he smiled at her for the first time in a month.

"Don't worry about the eggs," he said. "Jane doesn't need them yet. They'll wait."

She waited, until Thomas and Graeme came in, Grace had served the meal to Richard and Elizabeth in the dining room, and everyone was sitting down. Then she summoned all her courage and took a deep breath before standing up carefully, bracing her arms on the table against the pain in her midriff.

"I have to say something to all of you," she said.

"You don't need to say you're sorry again," Thomas told her. "Grace told us that."

"Good," Sarah replied. "I'm glad of that, and it's true, I am sorry. But I wanted to say some more. I know none of you like me, and I understand that. I don't know if Richard told you that before I worked here I was a whore. I worked at Mrs Pelman's over near the market place in Manchester. But I'd just left. Richard did expect me to…er…" She paused, realising that Mary and Ben were too young to hear what she'd been about to say. "Comfort him," she continued after a minute. "But that's not why he employed me. He told me to spy on you all, and to tell him if any of you said anything about him, or about being Jacobite." She looked at Graeme, who was sitting next to her, his expression neutral. "I wanted to apologise to you, Graeme, because I told Richard about you giving vegetables to the beggar woman. I don't know if he said anything—"

"He did," Graeme answered. "I knew it was you who told him."

"I'm sorry if I got you into trouble," Sarah said. "I hadn't told him anything about you all until then, partly because you didn't say anything important, but partly because I didn't really want to. And then I came downstairs one day and heard you and John talking about Prince Charles."

"And did you tell him that?" Graeme asked, his face and voice hard now.

"No," she replied. "I was desperate to tell him something, because he said he was going to hurt me if I didn't, but when I got to his room I couldn't do it. I had to tell him something though, so I told him about the beggar. I didn't think you'd get in a lot of trouble for that. But I'm really sorry if you did."

"He did send for me. I enjoyed myself. He can't do anything to me. I knew him when he was a snot-nosed little brat, and I'm no more scared of him now than I was then," Graeme said. "Don't worry about that, lass."

"I don't know why John was dismissed," Sarah continued, "but I wanted you to know that I didn't say anything about him, or anything else at all about any of you. And I wasn't going to. I was going to leave, would have done last week if he hadn't hurt me."

"Sit down," Graeme said. "It's hurting you to stand, and there's no need. John didn't leave because of anything you said, and we all know that. It seems I'm the only one you spoke against, and I forgive you."

"Thank you," she said, and really meant it. "I won't ever tell him anything again. I only agreed to spy for him because I was desperate, and as soon as I got here I wished I hadn't, because you're all really nice and he's horrible."

Graeme reached up suddenly and took her arm, gently pulling her down into her seat.

"I believe you. We all do. Think no more about it. Now let's eat before the food goes cold, shall we?"

Sarah looked down at the table, which misted as her eyes filled with tears. Then Graeme squeezed her hand once, and as she looked up at him, he winked.

"We all have to learn," he said. "I think you've learnt a lot these last weeks."

Incapable of speaking due to the lump in her throat, she just nodded.

"Well, then. No more to say. Pass the potatoes."

She passed the potatoes, then wiped her eyes, and then they ate dinner and chatted while they did.

Chatted naturally.

* * *

"Good grief," said Elizabeth, eyeing herself in the mirror. "How did you manage that so quickly? It looks amazing."

Her hair did indeed look amazing. She had specified only that she wanted it to feel comfortable, simple but stylish, and then had allowed Sarah free rein. It was swept elegantly up at the back onto the top of her head and secured with the minimum number of pins Sarah could get away with, and was decorated with some small feathers and a jewelled clip. At her temples Sarah had rolled and pinned a few curls, but had done nothing elaborate, and was amazed that Elizabeth was so impressed.

"In truth, Miss," Sarah said, "you've got the most beautiful hair I've ever seen, and it's so thick and shining, it's wonderful to work with." She carefully tucked in a few tiny strands, and then stood back, smiling. "A lot of ladies don't suit some styles, because it shows that they've got a big nose, or no chin. But you suit everything. I've never seen anyone as beautiful as you are, truly."

Elizabeth frowned at herself in the mirror.

"I know," she said. "And that's one reason why I've got to go and be sociable to people I hate this afternoon. Life would be much easier for me if I was ugly."

There was a silence as Sarah tried to think of a way to reply to this extraordinary statement. She looked across the room at the dress lying on the bed.

"Have you got another dress you could wear, Miss, if you don't mind me saying?" she said.

"Why?"

"That yellow will make you look pasty. It's really not a good colour for you."

Elizabeth glanced at the dress and then smiled.

"Good," she said. "Then the yellow is definitely what I'll wear. I've only got one other good dress anyway, and that needs cleaning from when I fell in the mud last week. This is what you want to do to make your living?" she added.

"Yes, Miss, it is," Sarah said. "I want to be a business woman, make my own money, so I don't ever have to let any man do anything to me, ever again."

She hadn't meant to say that, but later was glad she had, because Elizabeth looked up at her and grinned.

"That is an excellent ambition, Sarah," she said. "I wish I could do that." She reached across and gripped Sarah's hands in hers. "Good luck. Richard told me you were a whore before you came here. You can do much better than that. Don't let anyone ever tell you you can't. And don't let anyone use your past against you, either. I don't know what made you become a whore, but you survived it, and that takes courage. Don't forget that."

"I will," Sarah said. "And you've given me the chance to start again. I won't forget that either."

* * *

Late November 1742

Sarah stood and looked around the room, then nodded, satisfied. It was not perfect, and nowhere near as luxurious as she wanted it to be, but it was clean, comfortable and warm, and that would suffice for now.

In the end she had managed to obtain two rooms for herself at a reasonable rent, and the landlord had raised no objections to her running a small business from them, once he knew what the business was going to be, although he had told her it would cost an extra sixpence a week. She had paid without arguing, because she had already looked at several other empty rooms and this was by far the best. It didn't smell of damp, had no obvious signs of vermin infestation, the walls were painted a pleasant cream colour, the furniture was a bit worn but serviceable and the living room was big enough for what she wanted.

The only drawback was that it was a lot closer to Mrs Pelman's than she wanted to be, just a few houses away in fact, and the old bawd would be sure to hear that she was there. Especially because her first customer, today, was a whore. Not from Mrs P's, but she would certainly talk. Sarah needed her to talk, to tell everyone who commented on her hair that Miss Browne had done it for her, and at a very affordable price, too.

She had bought hair products and cosmetics, but her biggest expenses had been buying two good quality outfits for herself, and the purchase of a mirror. But it was essential both that she look respectable and that her clients could see what she was doing for them. The mirror stood on a table now, leaning against the wall, ready for her first client. She looked at herself in it, dressed today in her green silk gown, her hair neatly styled. She had bought a woollen gown too, and because they would be difficult to clean, had bought several shifts and kerchiefs, all of good quality linen, which would stay white even when washed repeatedly, and so would advertise to all that she was a respectable woman.

She had done it. This was the start of her dream. Now she just had to make it come true.

* * *

By the middle of December she was getting at least one client a day, more often two, and as she charged sixpence to dress hair and threepence to apply lead paint, rouge, a patch and mouse-skin eyebrows, she was almost making enough money to live on. At least she was paying her rent, and had enough to buy coal or wood for the fire, candles and some food. Anything else had to come out of her savings, but as she was used to being extremely Spartan, that was not very much. And word was getting round of how good she was, so she saw no reason why soon she would not earn enough to pay her way without having to dip into her precious savings. It was a good start.

If in her childhood she had dreamed of having middle to upper-class clients as her Uncle Arthur had had, as an adult she accepted what she could get. And what she could get were prostitutes, and the occasional maidservant wanting to impress her beau on an evening out. The prostitutes were growing more numerous, because with her experience in the trade, Sarah knew how to make them look prettier, younger and generally more desirable, which led to them getting more clients. Which was a great incentive to them to return to her.

Overall, she was happy. The girls were friendly and chatted merrily to her about their clients, relaxed because she had been one of them and so would not be shocked or disgusted by their vulgar talk. Their chatter was a reminder of what she had come from, and every day she was grateful that Richard had stopped her jumping off the bridge.

In December she met Grace while at the market buying ribbons. Grace told her that Beth and Richard were now staying with their cousins in a big house at Ardwick Green, and that she was still Beth's ladies' maid there. There were a lot of servants at the house, she said, and they were friendly enough, but she missed the others, who were still at the house in Didsbury. Grace also told Sarah that they would probably go to London soon for the season, and that Richard was very happy about that.

"What does Miss Elizabeth think of it? Is she excited to go to London?" Sarah asked.

"No, not at all. She would much rather stay here. Not with her cousins, but with us in Didsbury. But of course being a woman *and* the cousin of a lord, she must do her duty, and marry someone appropriate."

Poor Elizabeth, Sarah thought later. Even rich women couldn't do what they wanted, they just lived more comfortably than poor women, that was all.

If I can make a success of my business, I will be better off than her, Sarah thought later. *I will never have to marry anyone unless I love them.* And that was unlikely to ever happen. She was better on her own.

* * *

In December Mrs Pelman paid her a visit. In truth Sarah had expected her to come round much earlier and had tensed herself every time there was a knock on the door. She had actually started to relax when the call finally came, and was momentarily thrown, before marshalling herself for battle as quickly as possible.

Mrs Pelman had not knocked, but had just walked in, as though she owned the place. Sarah quickly reminded herself that she didn't, and adopted the cool professionalism she had with all her new customers.

"Ah, Mrs Pelman," she said. "I must admit I didn't expect you to want my services, but you are in luck, as I am free for the next half hour. What can I do for you?"

Mrs Pelman walked across to the shelves on which Sarah stored her cosmetics, running a finger along one and looking at it. She would have to do better than that.

"If you're looking for a cleaning job, I'm afraid I can't help you," Sarah said.

Mrs Pelman rounded on her then, as she expected.

"I assume it didn't work out with your dark captain then. Throw you over, did he?"

"Mrs Pelman," Sarah said. "You might have nothing to do, but I'm busy. If you've come here to ask about my romantic relationships, you're wasting your time."

"You've got a bloody cheek, coming here and offering to do my girls' hair, after what you did to me, you bitch," she spat.

"I'll do anyone's hair if they pay me. I make them look better, and I'm sure you're taking advantage of that by charging the men more," Sarah said, and saw by the bawd's expression that she was right.

"You stole from me," Mrs Pelman replied. "And if you think I'm going to let you get away with that, you're very much mistaken."

"I did nothing to you. I took what was mine, that's all. It's you who stole from me, not paying me the year's wages you owed me, and we both know that," Sarah replied. "You asked about my dark captain, as you call him. No, he didn't throw me over. Quite the opposite, in fact. He helped me to set up in business. So don't you come here threatening me, because if you do he'll not be pleased at all. He wanted to cut your throat that night rather than wait until you'd gone to bed so I could get my money back. I stopped him, but if you give him reason, I'm sure he'll be delighted to come back and do it. And if he does, I won't stop him this time. Now if you've not come to have your hair done, get out."

Mrs Pelman stared at her in shock. It was probably the first time any of her girls had really stood up to her, Sarah realised. *I am not one of her girls any more,* she told herself firmly. *She has no hold over me now.*

"You brazen bitch," the older woman spat. "You'll be sorry you spoke to me like that." She turned and left, banging the door behind her. Sarah heard her storm down the stairs, then the front door bang as well.

She sat down, shaking with reaction. She had done it. She had stood up to her. She had stood up to her father for Lucy's sake, and now she had stood up to Mrs Pelman for her own sake. *I will never, never let anyone treat me like dirt again,* she told herself. *I am my own woman now.*

It was the most wonderful feeling in the world.

* * *

Two doors away, Mrs Pelman was not feeling so wonderful. Peter waited until she had smashed an ugly vase and a china figurine and had swept all the papers off her writing desk, before throwing herself down into a chair, breathing hard from anger and frustration.

"Do you want me to go round and speak to her?" he asked.

Mrs Pelman considered for a moment. They both knew what Peter meant by 'speaking'.

"No," she said finally. "She said that captain she left with helped her set up. He was a nasty piece of work, knew that as soon as I saw him, I did. He's probably got friends just like him too."

"I'm not afraid of no captain," Peter said.

Mrs Pelman looked at him. No, he wasn't, the idiot. But he was faithful to her, loyal, and above all, useful. She didn't want to be burying his mangled body any time soon. Nor did she want a gang of hostile soldiers calling at her house. Sarah might have been lying, but she didn't think so. It wasn't worth taking the chance.

"You could tell that stuck-up woman what came round where she is," Peter suggested. "Then she'd have to marry that old lord."

Mrs Pelman sighed. Loyal, useful, but stupid.

"I don't know if she did want to marry her off to an old man," she pointed out. "I said that, not her. But I'm not going to do anything to help her get rich or better herself."

"But the lady said she'd pay you!" Peter said, knowing the bawd's love of money. "Gave you a sov just for the date!"

"True. But sometimes there are better things than money," she said.

"Like what?"

"Like ruining her," Mrs P said. "Before I've finished that bitch'll be begging me to take her back. And then you can speak to her as much as you want, Peter. For now, leave her to me."

* * *

Over the next week or so, Mrs Pelman's girls stopped coming to the shop, and when Sarah saw them in the street, they turned away or crossed the road to avoid having to speak to her. It was a shame, but she'd known when she stood up to the bawd that there'd be some consequences. And there were a lot of whores in Manchester, plenty to keep her busy. She wasn't worried.

But over the next weeks fewer and fewer street girls came to her, and when she finally managed to corner one of her former customers and ask her why, the girl looked very uncomfortable and just said that she was having a slack time at the moment and couldn't afford to have her hair and face done. But she'd come back once work picked up.

Sarah offered to do her hair for free then, just the once, as a gesture of goodwill. All she had to do was come with her right now, because she had the next hour free but was busy after that. The whore was tempted, Sarah saw that in her face. But then she looked up the street, saw how busy it was, and how many people would see her walk into Sarah's and come out later looking prettier. And then she mumbled an excuse and scuttled away.

Which gave Sarah her answer. No prostitute would turn down the offer of a free hairstyle, not when it was offered in the middle of the day when potential customers were non-existent. Which meant that Mrs Pelman or more likely Peter, were warning all the prostitutes to stay away from her establishment and threatening them with violence if they didn't.

She went home and sat down, and thought about it. She had a few maidservants who came to her periodically, but not enough to keep her afloat. She had some savings still too. Sadly what she did not have was a dark captain who would go round and cut Mrs Pelman's and Peter's throats.

Which left her with two choices; she could either live off her savings for a short time and wait until Mrs Pelman stopped threatening the street girls, or she could move to another town and start again. Either of those options would eat into her dwindling savings, and she couldn't use the cards she'd had printed anywhere else because they had her address on them.

She would stay, she decided, for the next month, for two reasons; she had already paid the rent until the middle of January, and she had two hundred business cards. So she would go to every shop in town and to the taverns and would leave her cards there, and see if she could attract new customers. Mrs Pelman and Peter could blithely threaten whores, but if they threatened respectable women complaints would certainly be made against them to the authorities, and they would not risk that.

EPILOGUE

January 1743

She had just bought a pie from a street seller and was sitting down by the fire to eat it, when there came a knock at the door. She cursed inwardly, but was in no financial position to ignore a customer, even if it did mean her pie would be cold before she got a chance to eat it. She walked through to her bedroom and placed it on the shelf, then wiped the grease from her hands on her handkerchief and opened the door.

Standing there was a handsome well-built man with long-lashed grey eyes, his dark brown hair neatly clubbed. He was dressed in green livery so was clearly a servant, a footman or a coachman maybe. A rich man's servant. A *very* rich man's servant, because only the nobility went to the expense of buying livery for their staff. Most servants wore their own clothes. What was a very rich man's servant doing coming to her house?

The man took his hat off, smiled at her, and bowed.

"Have I the honour of addressing Miss Sarah Browne?" he asked in a soft Scottish accent.

"You have, Mr..."

"Murdo," the man supplied. "Good. My master sent me to ask if ye could attend him now, on a matter of business, if ye'd be so kind."

"Your master?" she said stupidly.

"Sir Anthony Peters. He's in Shaw's Punch House and has asked me to accompany you there. Will ye be able to walk? It's no' far and the weather's fine, if a wee bit cold."

She had never heard of Sir Anthony Peters, but if he could

afford to dress his servants in such high quality livery as this man was wearing and wanted to see her, she would walk to the moon if she had to. Maybe he had seen her card and wanted her to dress his wife's or his mistress's hair, or maybe his own wigs. Whatever, it could be the making of her. And she desperately needed customers, as Mrs Pelman's vengefulness showed no signs of abating.

She got her cloak and they set off.

"Did Sir Anthony say what he wanted of me?" she asked.

"No, he didna. Just asked me to fetch ye. Well, he actually asked his driver to fetch ye, but he was in the middle of his meal, so I offered to come instead," Murdo supplied.

When they arrived at the Punch House Murdo opened the door, gesturing for her to precede him, which made her feel very grand, and then he took her to a corner table at which three people were sitting, before melting away discreetly, his task accomplished.

Sarah's eyes lit up as she saw Miss Elizabeth and Grace sitting there. She bobbed a quick curtsey to Elizabeth before turning to the male of the company, who must be Sir Anthony Peters.

She had read a little about fops, had heard about them from some of the whores at Mother Augustus', but she had never seen one until now. He was extraordinary, a vision in purple velvet and masses of expensive frothy Brussels lace, his face a white mask, with two circles of carmine rouge on his cheeks and a black silk beauty spot at the side of his mouth. He was the most grotesque creature she had ever seen, and her first impulse was to laugh.

She could not laugh. This man might be about to make her business successful. No doubt Elizabeth had recommended her to him. She turned to him.

"You wished to see me, my lord?" she said.

He smiled and waved his arm at her, releasing a cloud of sickly sweet violet scent.

"Oh my dear," he trilled, "you do me too much honour. I am not yet elevated to the peerage, whatever my accoutrements may suggest!"

Having no idea what accoutrements were, Sarah was not sure how to respond appropriately to this, and her confusion must have shown on her face, because Elizabeth leapt in.

"What the gentleman is trying to say," she explained, "is that he is not a lord, only a baronet. Allow me to present Sir Anthony Peters."

"Enchanted, my dear girl," he said, reaching out and taking her hand in his lilac suede gloved one, pressing his lips to it ardently. When he released her she managed to restrain herself from wiping her hand on her dress and was about to ask him what he wanted with her, when he turned to Grace and smiled.

"Miss Miller, would you do me the honour of giving me your assistance in choosing a present for my goddaughter?" he asked. "It is her birthday soon, and I have no idea what would be suitable for a four-year-old."

Overriding Grace's reluctance to leave her mistress in a tavern alone, he soon dragged her away. Sarah watched them go. My God, just the lace the man was wearing would keep her in luxury for a year, probably longer.

"Sit down," Elizabeth said, beckoning to the chair Grace had just vacated.

Sarah sat, and was about to ask her former mistress if this was the man she was going to marry, when Elizabeth spoke.

"We don't have much time," she said, "so I'll be brief. You have used the money Richard gave you to set up as a hair dresser, am I right?"

"Yes Miss, although I have only used a little of it as yet." This was true, although she had used most of her earlier savings, and if business didn't pick up soon she would have to use the rest of it to move and set up again.

"How good are you at dressing hair? Not as you dressed mine, but more elaborately."

"Very good, Miss," Sarah replied, desperate to promote herself and attain whatever business Elizabeth was about to put her way. "And I can apply makeup as well, and—"

"You will have problems though, in obtaining a respectable clientele, won't you, being known in the area as a prostitute?" Elizabeth interrupted. "Graeme and Thomas tell me your main customers at the moment are Mrs Pelman's whores?"

Sarah blushed furiously. Elizabeth had been so kind to her. Why was she trying to hurt her now?

"I'm not trying to insult you," Elizabeth continued, clearly reading her thoughts, "but I don't have time to dress my words up. I am going to London on the nineteenth with my cousins. I need a ladies' maid. Would you like the job?"

Whatever she had expected, it had not been this. Sarah looked at the other woman, dumbstruck.

"You're not serious," she said after a moment. "You don't even like me!"

"Graeme has decided he was wrong about you, and that's good enough for me. If you accept I will expect you to behave impeccably, be absolutely loyal to me and no one else, and to be utterly discreet. If you are not, you will be dismissed. No second chances, although I will pay your coach fare back to Manchester. If you are as good as you claim, it could be the making of you. Not only will your past be completely unknown in London, but I will recommend you to every lady of distinction I meet. And it seems I am going to meet a great many. When I marry, or return to Manchester, you will be able to remain in London if you wish and set up a business there, which will have a far higher chance of success, especially as your abilities will already be known to the aristocracy, and your past will not. Do you need time to think about it?"

Sarah thought rapidly. Her business was failing here, and she had already decided she would have to get away from Mrs Pelman's obnoxious influence. But to go to London, the capital city, and to have such a chance! This was too good to be true. Was it some sort of malicious joke?

"Why me rather than Grace?" she asked warily.

"Grace belongs here. Her family and friends are here and she is not a city person. You are. Your former life means that you must be adaptable, and capable of keeping confidences if necessary. I do not want my cousin or my brother to employ someone for me who will report back on everything I do. I think you now know Richard for what he is, and if Graeme is right, your loyalty is to me rather than him. Am I right?"

"Yes," Sarah said emphatically. "But if your brother is going to London too, won't he tell your family what I am?"

"What you *were*. No, he won't, because the moment I get home I am going to announce to the whole family that I have engaged someone who he employed as a house maid, but who is eminently more suited for a better position, and that I am merely trusting in his superior judgement of character in engaging somebody he thought so highly of. And if you're worried about his violence, don't be. He's desperate to impress my noble family and is doing his utmost to behave like a gentleman. Just don't let him get you alone, where no one could hear if you screamed."

This was not a joke. She was serious. Sarah laughed out loud, from pure joy.

"My God, he got you wrong, didn't he?" she said admiringly. "He told me you were pathetic and weak, and would do whatever he said."

"I am, and I will." Beth smiled. "That is why I am employing you, because my dear brother thought so well of you. When can you give me your answer?"

"Now," she replied, as Sir Anthony and Grace walked back through the door. Sarah resisted the urge to fervently embrace this woman who was about to give her the chance of a future that she had never in her wildest dreams envisioned, and instead spat on her hand to show she promised to be loyal and trustworthy, then held it out. "You've got a deal," she said.

Elizabeth smiled, copied Sarah's gesture, gripped the proffered hand and shook it.

"Excellent," she said. "You'll have to call me Elizabeth when Richard or my cousins are around, but when they're not, please call me Beth. I absolutely hate Elizabeth. My father only called me that when he was very angry with me, and my mother *never* called me anything but Beth. How soon can you start? Next week? Will that give you enough time to sort out your things? You can store any furniture you've bought at my house if you want."

When Sarah got home she sat down on the little wooden chair next to the fire. There was only the mirror to take to Didsbury. That was the only substantial item she'd bought. Everything else she could take with her, and the two dresses would not be too fine for a ladies' maid to an aristocrat to wear. Her stomach rumbled and she remembered that she hadn't eaten since this morning. She stood up and went into her bedroom to get the pie, then sat back down with it in her hand. She blushed as she remembered she'd actually spat in her hand and then expected an aristocrat to know what she meant by it and shake it! But Elizabeth *had* known, and hadn't hesitated to respond appropriately and accept the bond.

It was unbelievable. Elizabeth knew she'd been a whore, and yet she was giving her the opportunity to live in the same house as a lord, to move to London, and would recommend her to the nobility. She could end up styling the hair of the most blue-blooded people in the land!

An enormous wave of exhilaration washed through her and she squealed with sheer ecstasy, loud enough for the people living above her to bang on the floor, which made her laugh.

She lifted the pie to her mouth, then looked at it. It was cold, the meat pale and cheap, the fat in it congealed. She screwed her face up in disgust, then threw the pie on the fire.

To hell with the expense. Tonight she would go out and eat a proper meal, and drink claret, and celebrate the most wonderful day of her life, excepting only the day that Lucy had been born, of course.

This was the greatest opportunity she had ever had, and she intended to make the very best of it. And she would never, never forget what Elizabeth Cunningham had done for her today.

Finally she had found someone who she truly believed deserved her loyalty. And in that moment she gave it, wholeheartedly, swearing that if she ever had the opportunity to repay Beth for this wonderful chance, she would do it, regardless of the cost.

And then she went out to celebrate, alone.

* * *

I hope you've enjoyed this book. If so, you'll be pleased to know that Sarah's story, and that of Elizabeth and Richard Cunningham, continue in the Jacobite Chronicles. Book One, Mask of Duplicity is free to download on Amazon and at other ebook retailers.

Amazon: http://mybook.to/MaskofDuplicity

Follow me on:

Website:
www.juliabrannan.com

Facebook:
www.facebook.com/pages/Julia-Brannan/727743920650760

Twitter:
https://twitter.com/BrannanJulia

Pinterest:
http://www.pinterest.com/juliabrann

HISTORICAL NOTE

It's become expected now that I'll write a historical note about some of the events in my books, and to be honest I enjoy writing it, so here goes!

Firstly referring to Reverend Browne. I have purposely not stated which branch of Christianity he belongs to, merely that he is a dissenter, and there are a couple of reasons for this. In 17th and 18th century England a dissenter was anyone who did not conform to the established faith i.e. was not an Anglican. As many of the dissenting branches of Christianity still exist, although in much amended forms, I did not want members of any particular group to think that I was trying to attack their beliefs or their faith base, and this is one reason.

The other reason is that Perseverance Browne is quite clearly not representative of any particular Christian sect, but is an extremist, twisting the words of the Bible and theological doctrines to suit himself rather than any particular denomination of Christianity to which he might claim to belong.

I have mentioned on more than one occasion, however, the words 'elect' and 'reprobate', when referring to Sarah, so thought these might need a little clarification. These two words are linked to the doctrine of predestination, that is the theory that human beings are incapable of saving themselves, being too sunk in evil. In fact, we are incapable of even choosing to accept God's offer of salvation. Only God can save us, by enabling us to accept his offer, and if he does that, we cannot refuse it.

The problem with this theory is, that if we are incapable of saving ourselves, then our salvation is God's choice alone, and if God chooses to save some of us, he must then also choose to condemn others. This indicates that it doesn't matter how good we try to be, we will only be saved if God chooses to save us, and if he chooses not to, then there's nothing we can do to change that decision. So whether we go to heaven or hell is predestined, and not based on any good or bad deeds we as humans do.

This doctrine is mostly associated with Calvinism, but in fact originated with St Augustine, and was also believed in by Luther, although many Protestant reformers found its assumptions morally offensive for obvious reasons.

Reverend Browne has taken that doctrine on board too, but as with many extremists, has decided that the will of God mirrors his own will exactly, and therefore women in general will go to hell (are reprobate) because Eve paid heed to the serpent in Eden, and that men have a much better chance of being chosen to go to heaven, (to be elect) with himself being obviously guaranteed a place. This total belief that he has puts him in a very secure spiritual position, with every action he makes being grounded in the belief that he is one of God's chosen, and with his attempts to make Sarah pure being grounded in the unlikely hope that God might choose to save her and will enable her to accept his offer.

Aunt Patience and Uncle Arthur live in Chester, and I spent a pleasant day there this summer with a friend, wandering around the walls of the city with an 18th century map for guidance. It really is a beautiful place, and I would highly recommend you visit it if you ever get a chance. Everything Uncle Arthur shows or explains to Sarah on their tours of the city is true. I wanted to talk a little about the Rows, in one of which is Arthur's wig shop, because they really seem to be unique.

Chester is an extremely old city - the Romans lived there in the first century, although most of the ruins we now know of, including the amphitheatre, had not been discovered in the 18th century. As with most ancient cities, existing buildings have been adapted and changed over the centuries, and it isn't possible to say exactly how old the Rows are, but they certainly date back to mediaeval times.

In the Middle Ages it was normal for people to live above their place of business, so the shop or business would be on the ground floor, and the accommodation above it. Underneath the business a cellar would be dug for storage, but in Chester the bedrock of the city is close to the surface, with the result that many of the cellars were partly above ground level. To be able to work with this, balconies were built, with steps leading up from the street to the door of the shop. The accommodation above overhung the shop building, acting as a sort of roof and effectively giving the row of shops a covered walkway, by the 14th century. Obviously it wasn't essential that they be built this way, and while there are lots of theories abounding for the reasons that they were built in this unique manner, we don't really know for sure.

During the 17th century siege (when Charles I was on his tower watching the conflict) some of the buildings were damaged, and in later times others were amended or even demolished to build private homes, so many of the Rows that are still in existence today are not exactly as they would have been originally, but there are a few that are still as they would have been in the 14th century. And many other buildings in Chester today would still be recognised by Sarah and Arthur, were they to walk about the walls today!

When writing this book I also had to do some research on wig making, and all the information in the book is taken from 18th century practice. The wearing of wigs as a fashion statement probably originates from King Louis XIV's time. It's said that when he started to go bald, he chose to wear a wig, which then became a fashion amongst his court, and soon spread to other royal courts. In the 18th century the long mass of hair was replaced by the smaller formal wigs for men, usually white and powdered. Initially wigs were worn only by men, with women's hairstyles tending to use their own hair, with lots of additional hairpieces and pads when necessary.

Wig makers would not only make wigs, but would dress them, powder them and repair and clean them – including cleaning them of vermin! I have to say though, that around 80% of the population did not wear wigs, but instead wore their own hair, the men often wearing it long and tied back. Wigs were expensive and therefore a status symbol, and, as I indicate in the book, the type of hair from which it was made was one of the indicators of how wealthy the wearer was.

In Chapter Eleven Sarah has her baby in a ruined cottage, and is alone when she does so. This might seem an impossible thing for her to be able to do on her own at the age of fifteen, but in fact poorer women would often rely on the help of female friends and relatives, being unable to afford a midwife, and girls who were giving birth to illegitimate children might well do it secretly and then abandon the baby, as their lives would be quite literally ruined if it was known that they had had a child out of wedlock. There are numerous court cases of unfortunate girls who have been accused of murdering their secretly born children, where there were no witnesses to the event, as the girl had given birth alone and privately. With the clothing of the day it was far easier to hide an advanced pregnancy than it would be now!

In the book Mary, who has helped deliver several siblings, has given Sarah the benefit of her practical advice. There were a lot of superstitions about childbirth at this time, and the blue cords that Mary gives to Sarah, which she wears round her neck as she's giving birth, was one of them. They were believed to prevent fevers while lactating, and the older the cords, the greater their powers.

In general women were given little practical advice on how to prepare for birth at this time. Advice given was usually a mixture of old wives' tales and previous experiences, both of which could cause great alarm in the pregnant woman. Midwives would be reluctant to reveal their secrets, as this might mean they would put themselves out of work! Midwives, especially rural midwives, were unqualified and usually conducted their services by trial and error, and of course could unknowingly cause terrible infections by probing the woman with filthy hands or attempting disastrous manoeuvres to assist childbirth.

Sarah is at least spared these risks, and the bulk of the information Mary has given her is based on personal experience, with no desire to keep information secret, as midwives would do. So although alone at the birth, Sarah is actually not much worse off in practical if not emotional terms, and possibly better off than she would have been with a rural 'grannie' midwife.

Still on the subject of childbirth, in a later chapter when Sarah is pondering paying for Violet to have an abortion, she's consoled by the fact that the baby has not yet moved in the womb, and therefore has no soul. The creationist views of St Augustine and Thomas Aquinas were widely held by Christians until the 19th century. Their view was taken from Aristotle and held that the foetus developed in stages from vegetative, sensitive, locomotive to intellectual, and that the soul was not present until the foetus was fully formed. In the Gospel of Luke it is stated that the Virgin Mary's barren cousin Elizabeth became pregnant in later years and was in her sixth month when the baby leapt in her womb, and Elizabeth became filled with the Holy Ghost.

It was therefore held by many Christians that the soul did not enter the foetus until it moved in the womb. Certainly the law took this view, stating that abortion was acceptable and not murder until quickening, when the soul entered the foetus.

On to prostitution, which is a huge subject and on which I'll only touch here as it's relevant to Sarah's story.

Firstly, it was common for innkeepers to look out for girls arriving fresh from the countryside looking for work, as they were more likely to be innocent of the ways of the town, and therefore more likely to be duped. They would notify the local bawd or brothel keeper, and would receive money for this. Sarah, and Lily before her, are entrapped by being invited to stay for a few days at the house and to sign a paper, which is then revealed to be an agreement to pay a sum of money, which obviously the girls don't have. This was a common trick, and effectively forced the girls into a life of prostitution, as they would be threatened with arrest and told of the terrors of life in a debtors' prison, which could be horrendous for the friendless, as prisoners had to pay for all amenities, including food, beds and blankets.

In the popular view of the people, bawds were truly evil, although in actual fact, once a prostitute had lost her looks and appeal it was one of the few ways that she could continue to make a living. Nevertheless, bawds were demonised, and sometimes understandably so. In reality some of them were reasonably kind, as we see with Mother Augustus, and some were not, as is Mrs Pelman. Although both of them seem like saints compared to descriptions of some of the real-life bawds I have read about whilst researching for this book. One particularly nasty bawd in London, Mother Needham, widely known as a corrupter of young girls, was sentenced to stand in the pillory for an offence and was stoned so badly by an outraged mob that she died a few days later.

It was the custom for a man to live at the house too, who could act to both protect the prostitutes or intimidate them as required.

In the 18th century the options open to women were few – Mother Augustus and Lily outline them when showing Sarah round the town. Obviously the information they give her is designed to encourage her to become a prostitute, but there's still some truth in them. Women in general were expected to marry and have children, and when they did marry, they were ruled completely by their husbands. If a woman chose not to marry, then she could either act as an unpaid servant for members of her family, go into paid service, where she would work up to seventeen hours a day, or become a laundress, needlewoman etc, all very poorly paid jobs.

A 'ruined' woman had even fewer options, as few men would want to marry one, and she would be less likely to be taken on as a servant in a decent household. A large number of girls became prostitutes because they had been seduced and abandoned by their lovers, or raped by sons of the houses they were servants in.

Prostitution was not illegal in the 18th century, but that didn't mean the authorities didn't take an interest in them. Bawdy houses were well known as places of rowdiness and illegal activity, and street prostitutes were associated with pickpocketing and robbery. But in the early 18th century the real threat to brothels and prostitutes came not from the law, but from moral reformers. As the law was not helpful to them, in the early days the reformers would use *agent provocateurs* turned informants who would then make a complaint about an alleged offence to get the house raided. Constables belonging to the reformers society would then arrest the prostitutes, who might be sent to the local Bridewell for a month or so. This was not strictly legal though!

It also wasn't always easy to do. Soldiers and sailors regularly visited brothels and could become extremely violent if the house they used was raided, which resulted in some constables being murdered.

The Bible on the hall table in Mother Augustus' house was a common trick used to hopefully fool any inspectors into believing it was a respectable house.

And finally, the words I've chosen to describe the act of sex, which may have offended some people. The word 'swive' which may be new to some of you, was a relatively common vulgar word for sexual intercourse, derived from Old English *swifan* - the modern vulgar use of the word 'swivel' comes from the same root! I've used it along with the word 'fuck' which modern readers may find more offensive as it is still widely used, but in much earlier times whilst being vulgar, it was not considered quite as extreme a word as it now is. As both words really indicate the action of having sexual intercourse without any emotion whatsoever being involved, I made the choice to use them here.

If you would like to know any more about any of the historical aspects of this book or of the Jacobite Chronicles, don't hesitate to contact me via Facebook or Twitter, and I'll be happy to answer your questions if I can! My social media links are at the back of this book.

Sign up for my newsletter
(no spam, just book releases and important information)

http://eepurl.com/bSNLHD

Printed in Great Britain
by Amazon